VOLUME 1

THE BOND OF BROTHERS

A WOLF TALE

PAUL T. BARNHILL

authorHOUSE®

AuthorHouse™
1663 Liberty Drive
Bloomington, IN 47403
www.authorhouse.com
Phone: 1 (800) 839-8640

Published by AuthorHouse 07/10/2019

ISBN: 978-1-7283-1881-3 (sc)
ISBN: 978-1-7283-1880-6 (hc)
ISBN: 978-1-7283-1879-0 (e)

Library of Congress Control Number: 2019909351

ALL LEGENDS HAVE TO START AT A point in history; the story about brothers, caught up in a war that lasted for over a hundred years, but theirs stretched across time, as one's love for father and country became his curse. In the beginning both served justice, until the love for a woman drove them apart. Immortality is the price they paid. One brother holds his beast in, and one lets it run free. Will faith and love win out or will evil prevail? Go back to a time where fables are born and a price is paid to be a thing of great legend.

Chapter One

LEGENDS ARE BORN

IT IS THE YEAR OF OUR LORD 1455 A.D. Two noble families arose to lay claim to the throne of England. The Lancaster's, whose flag bore a red rose, and the York family whose flag bore a white rose. The hundred years wars had raged on and neither side could gain an advantage over the other. The York family turned to black magic and a sorcerer Tyrolean.

"Father we are defeated at every turn and the men grow weary of battle," Edward York proclaims adding, "we need to find a way to gain an advantage over the Lancaster's hold on the land, or we shall not have enough men to hold the throne once we gain it!" David York looks over to his son sitting at his right hand saying, "I do not know what else we can do. Our soldiers fight the best fight they can. We are going to have to rely on faith to show us that it is our side that will stand in the end." Tyrolean stands in front of the fire listening to his rulers speak. "Tyrolean, is there no way to defeat the army that stands in our way?" "My lords there are ways to defeat any army. One simply has to be willing to pay the price." Edward, seeing a way for victory, raises his head asking, "What price would have to be paid?" Tyrolean waves his hand over the fire as the flames move in rhythm of his motion. "There is a spell. It is of the darkest magic. The price would be immortality and an everlasting hunger." "How could we attain this power you speak of?" Edward eagerly asks. "I must first have a wolf brought before me and it is to be alive, for the life force inside the beast is the power you will need." "Son, stop with this path of thought. The power is of the devil and my soul will already weigh much when I leave this world." David York states, the age shows in his face for the many years has taken its toll upon his body, "But father I," Edward, trying to reason, says before his father cuts off his words. "I will hear no more of this!" his father stress. "As you wish my Lord," Tyrolean says. David York gets up from the throne and leaves for bed. "Tyrolean if I get you what you need can it be done?" Edward asks. "Edward, I will not disobey your father, for he has in his keep that which holds my life's force." "My father grows weak. When we gain the throne, to whom do you think will run this country and in my keep your life force will be!" Tyrolean looks over his shoulder at Edward knowing within him lies a power craved man and answers, "Yes if you bring me what I ask, I can make you into the greatest hunter, warrior, the world could see and give you the power to make your enemies your footstool." Edward rises from the table, holds on to the handle of his sword, grins with turning and walks out of the room to gather his two closest soldiers, Contour and Damien. When he finds them, they leave the castle riding out into the wilderness to retrieve what they are after. Riding along with night engulfing them, "My lord what do we seek out here in the middle of the night?" Contour asks. "I have been assured by Tyrolean that if we retrieve a wolf and bring it to him, he will grant us the power to lay our hands on the throne," Edward answers. Damien rides up from the forest saying, "My lord there are fresh wolf tracks in the valley to the right." They turn their horses and begin to track the wolf. Their journey is short before they have the wolf trapped with its back to a cliff to keep him from flight. "Get the rope around his neck!" Edward commands with the wolf in front of them. The wolf lashes out snapping and biting at the rope with his mighty jaws with clawing at the earth, standing his ground. "Get it in the net!" Edward yells. The wolf lashes out at Damien, and bites his arm ripping at the flesh its mighty jaws have found. "Get it off me now!" Feeling the teeth sunk in, Damien yells. They rush in and pull him from the jaws of the beast. Damien draws his sword from its sheath raising it in anger to strike at the very heart of it. "No Damien we must bring it to him alive," Edward reminds. "Damn it," Damien kicks dust from the ground sheaths his sword and grasps his arm. They bind the wolf and place it in the cage drawn by horses pulled by soldiers of less meaning. "Sorry brother I know your wrath must have no limit but when we reach the castle it will be worth the pain," Edward tells him as he puts his hand on his shoulder then turns his horse to follow behind the caged beast. Edward and his loyal soldiers make their way back to the castle.

"Father we are victorious again," William Lancaster boasts as they raise their glasses toasting their deeds. "Father I grow weary of this never-ending battle. Is there no end to this conflict for the throne?" Alexander, William's younger brother asks. "Son, I know sometimes the battles we have do seem to be endless, but you must keep in mind that if the York's win out, the people of this land will suffer at great ends for they only care for the power but never the people. It is a noble man's Christian duty to protect the people from evil." William wedges between them, "Come brother drink with the men, I am in need of your company!" William puts his arm around his brother and pulls him close. "Alex my brother we have seen the torments laid on our brothers in battle due to the evil sorcerer, Tyrolean. We cannot fail at the task God has placed before us. The York family is known for its hard treatment of the people of this great land." William states. "I know brother I just cannot help but to think of the men that lay dead on the battlefield from my sword. What of the families that wait for their fathers that will never return?" William downs his drink then pats him on the back, and joins his soldiers in a victory song they are singing in their drunken state. Alex sits his drink down and heads for the church to pray for the fallen. He goes through the doors, and the priest is there lighting the candles. "Father," Alex says in a greeting to the priest. "What troubles you this night young noble?" the priest asks lighting one of the candles. "Are we to be judged for the people we kill even if we think it for a noble cause?" The priest lights another candle as Alex sits down on a bench. "Does the bible not teach us to destroy evil where we find it?" The priest asks of him. Alex looks distant for a moment then says, "But the men I kill in battle are not evil. They are just sent by evil people to die on land they could never call their own." "War is troubling at times young Alex and it takes a great leader to have companion on his enemies." "No, not for me, my brother will be King and I will serve him as best I can. This is the way it has been done since the beginning of time, the oldest rules," Alex remarks. The priest walks over and places his hand on his shoulder, knowing them from the time of their births saying, "I think you would make a much wiser King than your brother." Alex confesses his sins, prays then takes his troubled mind for rest leaving the priest to his duties.

Edward and his men return to the castle passing Tyrolean, Edward informs, "Tyrolean I brought what you requested and now I require you to perform the task." "Bring the beast to my stay and by tomorrow night when the moon is at its fullest, you shall have what you desire," Tyrolean says. "Don't play with me sorcerer you will find me a great enemy if you cross me," Edward stresses. Tyrolean looks at him and bows his head saying, "I live to serve the house of York. You will have what you wish my Lord." Contour takes the beast to Tyrolean's cave in the base of the castle. With the beast secured they turn in for the night; resting from their night's conquest.

The Morning After, with the day breaking, Alex dresses and heads down to join his family over their morning meal. "Good morning to you brother," William says as Alex enters the room. "Morning father, brother," Alex says as he sits down at the table. "Today is a great day," their father says, "We are to welcome your brother's new bride to be to the house of Lancaster. It is time for the future of this noble house to be set." "Who have you chosen for me father," William asks with lack of excitement. "From the house of Sand, with their house and this one joined, it will strengthen the house of Lancaster ten-fold." He pauses before informing, "I know what you are thinking son. How can you take someone as your own that you have never seen? Just trust me you will be pleased with the one I have chosen for you!" They dine and talk of war strategy, and make plans for her to arrive planning the feast for the night. The castle begins to come alive around them.

"Tyrolean, where are you?" Edward asks entering the cave. "I am here my young lord," Tyrolean says coming from out of an opening door, with the beast growling to its capture. "Where is this new power you have promised me? I grow impatient, "Edward informs. "The spell shall be cast by the fall of the sun." "I hope so, for your sake," Edward boasts. "Have you chosen who will join you," Tyrolean inquires. "Yes, Contour, Damien and Jayland shall share in this power." "Choice wisely my young Lord, for whoever possesses this power will be unstoppable to mortal man," Tyrolean warns. "I trust them with my life each time on the field of battle I see no reason to doubt them now." Edward assures. "As you wish my lord, bring them into my stay before the sun has fallen and I will bring you the victory you seek," Tyrolean says with confidence. The day moves forward dusk slowly begins to take over the day.

The Sand family arrives at the castle after their long journey, and the great hall is dressed for the affair. Elizabeth keeps her face covered as she walks into the room moving through the gathered crowd, her gown flows with her movements. Her handmaids follow in her footsteps lifting the dress from the floor as she walks. They form a line as she walks towards a noble man's throne. Everyone turns their attention to the throne and rise to give respect for her in her new home. "Welcome to the home of Lancaster and a home for you as well," Lord Lancaster says as he takes her hand. She bows her head and removes her covering. The beauty of her steals the room. Woman of the castle cannot help but to feel envy for the beauty before them. The men gathered also, feel the pull of her to their heart's desires. Edward's eyes spring open for his new wife to be. "For once father your rumors are true," William says as he bows his head to his father. Elizabeth's eyes catch Alex standing in the background finding his face more pleasing then his brothers. The flame of her heart burns bright as if she has found a piece of her that was once lost. Her body longs to feel his touch. "My lord," Elizabeth says, as she bows her head to him. Their father places a ribbon around their wrists as a symbol of the joining before their wedding will occur. He kisses her forehead to give her his blessing. Alex looks upon her and his heart is taken. Within his very soul, he fights off the sensations that grip him. He too feels as if a piece of his soul stands before him. "Come everyone let us drink to celebrate the night," Lord Lancaster requests to the crowd before him. They drink and dine. William and Elizabeth walk among the room. The people of the castle show their respects to the future lady of the house.

Edward brings his faithful to the stay of Tyrolean with his entry he asks, "Tyrolean are you prepared for us?" "Yes, my lord, everything is prepared." Tyrolean brings out a cup one with age upon its sides, then places it on the table in front of them saying, "Come sit!" Tyrolean draws a symbol on the table and begins to make his chants. His cursed witches bring forth the wolf. They chain him so he hangs from the ceiling as he chants. Tyrolean opens his eyes and they glow of red. As the spell is cast, the symbol on the table begins to glow, circling the men seated keeping them pinned where they sit. "Ola, omgon, wolfen el tor," Tyrolean chants. The symbol leaps from the table burning the image into the forehead of the men. "This is the cup of the betrayer of the holy one," Tyrolean informs as he draws out his dagger, "I give you the power of the wolf and all his strengths and desires! You will become immortals only finding death by silver, blessed by a holy man or if your head should be bitten off by the same breed you shall become." Tyrolean proclaims, as he stabs the beast in the heart. The blood begins to drain out of its body he fills the cup, he turns, and offers it to them saying, "Drink and find what you desire!" He hands the cup to Edward so he would be the first, the strongest of the men gathered with him. Edward looks into the cup stares down at the blood filling its volume then takes a deep breath and gulps down the crimson color into his body. The first taste is bitter to his tongue, a taste he cannot put a word too but as it slides down it becomes sweet to his senses. He passes it around the table, and all partake of the offering inside the cup. Minutes pass before Edward states, "I feel nothing of this power you proclaimed do you think of me a fool!" Edward grabs Tyrolean by the neck and pulls out his sword. "What is going on here?" David York asks as he enters the room. "My lord," Tyrolean says bowing as he walks into the room. "I told you to let go of this nonsense," Lord York says to Tyrolean adding, "I will see to what you have done," turns to his son and the men saying, "Edward, you and the men, up the stairs now!" Lord York shakes his head to Tyrolean then follows behind them leaving the room, moving up the stairs and out into the courtyard. Edward's father scorns them as they walk into the moonlight. "Father I am not a child." Edward's voice becomes broken, as he braces his self against the fountain in the center of the courtyard as the transformation begins to take hold. His father stands in disbelief, as his eyes behold them changing before his very eyes. Their bodies pop, as the bones rearrange and the fur begins to grow over their skin. Their jaws stretch as their new teeth come out, and as a mindless beast they take to the night. Three of them run into the village. Edward being in his new form pounces on his father, and tastes his flesh. "God in heaven help me!" David York cries out as Edward bites ripping and savoring the taste of blood and human meat. Tyrolean watches from his doorway as he lets the body hit the ground letting a new howl which screams into the night. The first of many that mankind shall hear before taking flight into the wilderness. The peasants for the first time hear their cries from the blackness of night and fear takes hold.

"Elizabeth this is my brother Alexander," William says as they stand before him. "It is a pleasure to meet you," Alex says as he kisses her hand. Her blonde hair flows. The blueness of her eyes takes Alex to the ocean at first light but he hides the passion he feels. "William, there is rumors of an attack planned by our rivals. One of our spies has brought back news of some form of black magic weapon," One of Lancaster's finest tells William, breaking the conversion between the three of them. "Alex, I leave her in your care. I need to bring this to Father's attention." William says before walking off and every fiber of Alex's body is glad to have her to his self but the love for a brother makes him wish he had never seen her. His eyes sneakily flowing over her body. "Alex, my lord, is there no special someone promised to you?" Elizabeth asks as they begin to walk. "No. my lady, my brother is to be named noble of the house of Lancaster and to who I marry is no importance to my Father," Alex informs. "I hear the gardens for this castle are breathtaking," Elizabeth states fighting her own desires she holds inside. She too lets her eyes flow over his body but keeps her lady standard. "They are something to see," Alex informs before adding, "but they cannot hold a candle to the beauty that is walking with me now." Elizabeth blushes, her heart knows she is trapped with the wrong brother, and it cries for the one who walks with her now. "I am sorry my lady. I should not have spoken to you in that manner," Alex says to hide his desires. "It is okay, I took no offense in the words you spoke," Elizabeth informs with a sparkle showing in her eyes. Alex looks upon her and, in her eyes, he can see the feelings she has for him. They walk through the castle enjoying each other's company, just like they have always been with one another. "My lord your father requires you," a servant comes up and tells Alex breaking the easy conversation between them. "My lady he will take you on the rest of the tour of the castle, I must take my leave," Alex bows his head to her and walks to the battle room of the castle.

Edward and his minions rip through the night as their newly wolf forms have control. They hunt in a pack coming upon a farm in the night. They can smell the scent of live meat that their hunger craves. They hide in the darkness slipping slowly, for their meal, lurking in the cover of night. Walking out of the barn come two young maidens, who have just finished taking care of the last chores of a day, one of the sisters' screams as Edward leaps from the place that has kept him hidden from their eyes, swinging with his claw he rips open the first as the blood spatters her sister's face. "No!" she screams in terror rushing for the door of her home with the beast pursuing her. Edward catches her just before the door and his mighty jaws bite her neck, and brings death to her in a moment of time. Hearing his daughter's screams, their father rushes out the door, his eyes fly open when he sees the horror that stands before him. In an instance, he grabs a spear keep by the door. He throws it and pierces Edward in the chest. Damien, perched on the roof, jumps down ripping and biting him sending him the way of his daughters. Their mother hides inside. Contour enters the house looking for the meal of the night driven by animal hunger. He runs his claws down the walls of the home, listening to the beat of her heart race from the piercing sound. The thumping of her heart leads him to where she hides. "No, God please!" she cries to her maker before a howl sounds out into the night. He swings his mighty claws tearing her to pieces. The pack eats of the kill filling the hunger within.

The morning shines upon another day. Edward and his brothers in arms awaken naked and covered in blood. The event plays out in their heads as if they were there in a third-party sense with no control over the beast. A flash of their deed comes fresh to their minds. "Come on let's get out of here before someone makes notice of us," Edward suggests. They walk back into the forest to make their way back to the York castle trying to find some landscape to let them know where they are. Their journey home is longer than their flight into the night. They trample over the earth naked as the day they were born. Finding their way back to familiar scenes they take clothing hung to cover themselves. With their journey complete Edward reaches the door of Tyrolean. His fist beats on the door with his screams, "Tyrolean come to the door!" Tyrolean opens the door bowing saying, "My lord." "What is this you have placed upon me?" Edward demands of him, grabbing him by the neck. "My lord, please," Tyrolean asks adding, I've only done what you requested." "To be a mindless beast with no control of the power I now have?" Edward proclaims. "My lord, your father interrupted before I could give you what you need to control the beast," Tyrolean informs. Edward takes off the rags covering his body and covers himself with a coat hanging in the doorway. He sits down at the table. Tyrolean places twelve silver medallions upon the table in front of him. "These were forged from the silver Judas received for betraying their Christ. If you keep these on your body, you will have the power to control the wolf, and use its power to serve you. You will be able to change at will. Only during the full moon will you have no control over changing," Tyrolean explains. "How can I change at will?" Edward requests. "Like anything you do in life you will have to learn." Edward looks distant for a moment then says, "I killed my father as the wolf. I had no control over what I did. I keep getting flashes and images of the event." "I know my lord," Tyrolean says adding, "and you are now the noble to run the estate of York." Edward leaves and takes the pieces of silver with him going through the castle until he finds his minions. "Contour, Damien, Jayland Tyrolean has given us what we need to control the gift we now have, just place it next to your skin," Edward informs handing the amulets to them, then lays out the rules they have to follow then sends them out to gather the other's that will share in the gift given to him by Tyrolean. Rexstin, the warlord, Kirkland, a man with no compassion upon an enemy, Duncan, the mighty for his strength no one could match. Devilian, his name matched the souls he had taken at the edge of his sword with no quilt of any deed done by him. Enos, for his loyalty was unmatched, and the twin brothers from his most regarded soldiers Eric and Derik. Edward made his last choice, Titus for his size matched Duncan the mighty. As they leave, a servant comes in informing, "My lord, your father has been found dead in the gardens attacked by some wild beast!" "What?" Edward says to act surprised before following him through the castle and out to the gardens.

"My lord," A peasant from the land of Lancaster comes into the throne room imploring before guards block his path to the noble. "It is okay. I will hear what he would say, "Lord Lancaster informs. The man parts the soldiers and steps up to the throne informing, "My brother and his family, it is horrifying to the eyes," a tear streaks down his face," I have found them torn to pieces by some kind of wild animal. I fear for the safety of the people and the house of Lancaster." The look of horror written on the man's face sets Sir Lancaster into motion. He turns and requests, "William, Alex go and find out what you can." He turns back to the man requesting, "Take them to your brothers stay," then turns back to his sons informing, "We must protect the people of our lands. Find this beast and kill it." "As you wish father," they say bowing their heads then leave for the stables. The dishearten man goes with them. They gather their horses and their most trusted to accompany them alone their journey. With the men assembled William turns to the man and says, "Lead the way to the house of your brother." He kicks his horse into motion and the others follow in his steps. They travel towards his brother's farm talking along the journey. "What do you think of my bride to be brother?" William asks with a smile on his lips. "She has the beauty of the star's brother. She will no doubt make you a devoted wife." Alex answers hoping and praying his brother cannot see the fire that burnt in his heart for her. How he would have given the world to have her as his own. He longs for his brother to see what he keeps hidden wishing he would tell him he could have her for the love he feels for him "I was wondering if you had noticed her beauty." William suggests. "You would have to be blind or dead not to brother." Alex answers with a small grin. William pats him on the back and gives out a hardy laugh. "My lord, come look at these tracks and tell me what you make of them." James, one of their most trusted says. Alex rides over, looks down at the tracks saying, "They look like wolf tracks but they appear to be as big as a man or bigger." William rides up and Alex asks of him, "What do you make of them brother? I have never seen the likes!" "They are strange to the eyes," William replies. They journey to the farm as they follow the tracks left by the beasts. Jayel, one of the soldiers with them being ahead of the pack, waves them over and as they look at the bodies ripped to pieces, he speaks, "This is no way for anyone to die." Alex looks away not wanting to see the carnage of the young maidens cut down in their youth. "I agree but the task at hand is to find out what done this and kill it before it kills again," Alex states. "Jonas, take Jayel, Lushan, Darius and Kronus, go that way and see what you find. The rest of us will go this way and see what we can find," Williams orders. The men go their separate ways in searching for answers. Time moves forward as they follow the strange prints left in the earth. "Alex there is something strange the tracks, look like they came from the York land." "Brother let's return and make preparations for patrol parties. It will take more men than we have to kill this beast," Alex suggests. They ride off back towards their castle. The land is trampled beneath the hooves of their horse. Time passes, arriving at the bridge Elizabeth stands waiting for them to return with their father and once again, Alex loses his breath. Taken by her beauty, he dares not look upon her for too long. The fire inside him burns hotter with every glance. "Father we found strange tracks and things the devil himself must have done," Alex states making it to him suggesting, "We need to send out patrols to hunt this beast." "I would agree father the work of this beast is savage in nature", William adds. Together they walk inside as the servants see to their horses and things. "Father it appears the tracks came from the York's land. We could not follow to their origins," William informs. Elizabeth walks along side of William and Alex lags behind, but in her heart, she knows her place is to walk with him knowing in her heart of hearts her worries were with him and not to the man beside her. "My lady you must take your leave we need to discuss plans to hunt this beast," their father informs. The men bow their heads as she takes her leave and they walk into the great hall to where many times before, battles have been planned. "Father I think they have raised some kind of a breed of wolf to attack us during the night," Alex says. "No one could train something that is meant to be wild," William explains. "Brother whatever this beast could be, it cannot be something of nature," Alex quickly replies. "No matter. We need to find whatever it is to protect the people in the area," Their father informs before their discussion lingers on for many disagreements between them have been placed at his table in the times before. "My lord," a servant urgently walks in saying. William the father turns and takes the parchment from his hands. He reads the words on the paper then hands it to William. "What does it say Father?" asks Alex as his brother reads the writing. "Sir Richard, the lion heart has entered his name to the claim of the throne of this great land, and I would say he would make a fine leader to the people." Their father says looking up towards the heavens. "Then you would suggest we withdraw our claim and support him?" William asks. "I am beginning to think like you young Alex. I grow tired of this endless war, but that is a matter to be discussed at a different time this is the matter at hand," Lord Lancaster replies then turns to his youngest, "Alex make ready for patrols. William you will begin to gather the army and prepare them for battle in case we have to ride out to face Sir Richard in combat." The brothers do as their father requests seeing to everything, he desired of them.

"You must learn to focus my lord it is the only way to bring out the beast," Tyrolean states adding, "the power is in you, all you need is call upon it." Edward stands inside of his room trying to change to the wolf but his efforts go unrewarded. "Then what will the power do for you when the Lancaster's leave you to lick your wounds again like many times before leaving you yet again with your ass kicked? They laugh at the claim of the York name! "Tyrolean says to strike at the anger in him. The anger begins to swell inside of Edward and the rage and hatred for the very name of them surfaces, bringing out the wolf that lay silent. His eyes turn a different color like the emerald fire of the earth as the ears begin to grow. Tyrolean stands watching as the hair begins to cover his flesh and his fingers begin to gain length as the claws form, listening to the bones pop, as he is transformed before him. The wolf walks towards Tyrolean grabbing him by the neck showing him his teeth, as his mighty jaws open slowly, "My lord, my lord!" Tyrolean cries out staring into the eyes of the beast. The wolf gives a slight laugh mixed with a growl and sets him back down on the ground. Then slowly, he begins to change back to his former self. Edward kneels on his knees weakened by the change looking towards him he informs, "Don't worry Tyrolean it worked, I can control the beast now." Edward wraps himself in a cloak relaying, "I just wanted you to see what will happen to you, my sorceress friend, if you ever cross me!" "My lord I live to serve the house of York," Tyrolean reminds bowing his head. Edward turns, pauses, smiles over his shoulder then walks out of the room into the castle. His soldiers return from their duties he sends those chosen to share in this power to Tyrolean for his pack to be set.

Alex walks into the church to pray, enters, but finds no priest. He sits down on the bench and bows his head praying for the days ahead. "My son," the priest walks up saying. Alex opens his eyes knowing the face before him. "What troubles you this day?" the priest asks. "Father I have sinned, Alex looks down at the floor saying, "I covet my brother's future wife. From the first time I saw her she took my heart! How am I to deal with these feelings? I know it is wrong for me to want her." "Love is the greatest gift God gave us. But I fear it can be troublesome at times." The priest looks up at the statue of Christ hanging on the cross as the words seep from his lips, "I find myself hoping not to return from the future battle that lay ahead I fear it would be the only way to rid me of this eternal fire that is burning in me," Alex truthfully replies. "Dear Alex, some things are written and cannot be changed. You may live just till tomorrow or die a thousand years from now." Alex looks over to him asking, "How could a man live a thousand years?" "There are ways long forgotten by the men of these times," the priest informs with a kind smile then adds, "I will pray on the matter and when you return, I will discuss it with you in greater detail." Alex finishes his prayer as the priest sits beside him, stands and begins to walk out of the church. "Alex my son, you will have tough choices in the days ahead," he informs. Alex turns back towards him inquiring, "What do you mean father?" The father says nothing just lets his words rest upon his ears. Alex walks down the hall, opens the door, and walks back towards the gardens lost in his thoughts. "My lord," a voice says. He turns and sees her leaning against a statue in the garden. "I see I am not the only one who comes here to rest their mind," she suggests. "Elizabeth, what troubles you this night?" Alex asks of her taking in her beauty, following the curves of her dress sneakily as it forms to her body. "I should not speak of it," she informs turning to look in the other direction. "Is it something I could offer my help with?" Alex softly inquires. "Oh Alex," she says turning back to him adding, "I am troubled by you. It is improper for the feelings I have for you." "For me?" Alex's asks with his heart, his very essences wanting to reach out and hold her, to taste her lips, feel her skin as his hands would caress and hold her, but his noble blood holds strong. "Yes, for you! From the moment I laid my eyes upon you my heart was yours, and I sat here trying to come up with the courage to tell you this. I know it is wrong for I am promised by my father to your brother," Elizabeth replies with tears running down her face. She turns to look up into his eyes imploring, "Please tell me you feel the same! For my soul could not last it if you do not!" Alex looks to the heavens he knows what he should reply, a scorn to her would be the easy road taken, but with the love inside he replies, "My lady from the moment my eyes met yours you took the very heart from my chest and I found a love to last a life time! My insides cry out for you, to kiss the lips on your face could be maddening to me." Elizabeth moves close wraps her arms around him as she moves in to taste his lips. "No, my lady! My heart will always be yours, and while there is breath in me, I shall love no other, but fate has set you and me on a different course and my brothers you are to be," Alex explains brushing softly down her cheek. Elizabeth's eyes fill with tears of pain looking at him replying, "I should have known it would be this way or you would not be who you are." She turns and runs back to her room crying into the night, her heart once whole breaks into pieces with every strike of her foot upon the ground. "What is wrong with the future woman of the house of Lancaster?" William, their father asks. Alex, surprised by his presence there turns to look at his father hoping he has missed the words spoken between them answering, "Nothing that was not handled father." He walks toward his son but before he can speak, "Father it is late if you would excuse me," Alex says turning to leave his father.

Edward and his minions meet in the great hall of his castle. "My brothers, not only in battle but also in the blood of the wolf," Edward announces walking around the table where they are gathered adding, "we have always longed for an advantage over the nobles of this land and a York to sit on the throne of England but this war has raged on through the years!" War cries are given as he speaks, "But now with the help of Tyrolean we have the power to make the other nobles of this land our footstools! Show me brothers; show me the power of the wolf that rests in you!" Edward stands as they transform into wolves. His pack now before him with a devilish smile on his face, he transforms as well and they howl together crying out from the hall striking fear into the people of their lands. Tyrolean bows his head as Edward in wolf form looks at him. The fur covering his flesh is as black as night, his claws like razors, and teeth white as the new fallen snow on a mountain top, fiercer than any beast with the man inside to control its everlasting hunger driven to rule over men now feeble to him.

A new day dawns with Alex walking into the room where his family eats their first meal of the day. "Good morning Father, brother, my lady," Alex remarks before sitting down at the table. The servants place his meal in front of him. "My lord, I do not feel well this morning. I would like to take my leave now," Elizabeth says with her heart heavy from the man before her. "As you wish my lady," Lord Lancaster informs. They stand as gentlemen as she walks from the table then out of the room her scent feels Alex's senses striking down into his heart. The feeling of her heart opened to a man not bound to her, and to see him in the same room so close but a life time away is too much for her to bear her tears fill her eyes with her silent walk through the castle. "What do you think that was about brother," William asks regaining his seat. "I could not say but if I were you I might follow her to see," Alex answers with the feeling inside buried deep as if his soul was a door chained and locked. The love he feels batters the door wishing to run for her. He does his best to cover his feelings but inside his heart cries like a child for his mother. "She was fine until you came in. Have you said or done something to upset her?" William smugly asks. "My brother, I would not do anything to upset your bride to be, she is to be my future lady of this house," Alex replies looking up from the meal before him. "I think you have or why else then would she leave in that manner?" William suggests. Alex looks up again from his plate their father knowing them from their birth sees where this will lead recalling all the times, he had to break them up over the years. Curing, he slams his fist on the table exclaiming, "I will not have my house divided in this time of war so whatever this is put to rest." Alex stands to his feet requesting, "Forgive me father for I have offended your table." Alex bows his head to his father. "Brother, I have offended you and I ask your forgiveness as well." William throws down his napkin on the table stands and walks out of the room. "Do you have nothing to say to your brother?" Lord Lancaster asks looking at the backside of his son. William lets his father's question fall on deaf ears walking out of the room through the castle and into his room. Alex lets silence fill the room as he sits back down, finishes his meal then stands to walk out. "Son is there something you wish to tell me? Are you troubled by something?" "No father I have nothing to say," Alex answers before walking out of the room. His father watches him walk out, the pleasant table before him sits barren and silent. Alex walks through the castle wishing he had the courage to tell his father the love he feels for her, the fortitude to have fallen to his knees to beg his father for her but his footsteps just echo the castle.

Edward sits on his horse with the break of day well pasted, the flag with his family symbol waves on the poles beside him. His minions and his army stand on a field of battle as a different noble family with claims to the throne wait before him with their castle resting behind them. Three riders ride out to meet Edward along with his most trusted slowly they approach each other in the center of what is to be a battlefield. "York! Take your army from my land," the noble of the castle demands. "I cannot do as you wish," Edward answers with a smile adding, "besides I like your land the vast trees with the open valley to the west it would be a great asset to me." Edward suggests cockily riding around them looking over the landscape, "I tell you what if you renounce your families claim to the throne and stand with my army then there will be no need of a battle today. "The noble does not answer. "If you swear allegiance to the flag of York then you will live and the land, we stand on today will be yours for all time as long as the flag of York flies above yours or you can face my army and die this day!" Edward proclaims stopping in front of the noble. "Idle treats coming from an army we have defeated before does not quit bring the response you would desire," The noble answers. "As you wish," Edward cockily remarks the beast inside shows in his eyes the noble before him catches the glimmer of his eyes. The riders take their leave and rejoin the ranks of their army. "Little bastard thinks I tremble at his army! Men stand ready and defend the land of our flag! Archers prepare," The noble proclaims making it back to his ranks. "My lord what do you command," a ranking officer asks. Edward pauses for a moment as he watches his rival army, begin to march out to the field of battle then turns back to his army, "Soldiers of York ship! Stand your ground for we ride out to face them and no matter what you see stand your ground!" Edward turns back to his chosen waiting by his side "Come let us strike fear into the hearts of men from this day forward." Edward begins to move his horse his brothers of the wolf follow in his tracks the army behind him stands ready. Their horses begin to gain speed as they ride for their rivals. "What is he doing? This man wishes to die," the noble proclaims adding, "and we will give him that which he desires." Turning toward the army behind him, "archers fire at will!" The archers let their arrows fly like birds of many they swore towards their target finding their marks. Edward and his minions fall from their horses like dead men. The soldiers strike out into the field running up to them. "How stupid is that," a soldier asks poking Edward with a spear "Are you really going to die for someone so stupid," another soldier yells towards the York army then rolls Contour over to see what lies before him. "What kind a devil is these," the soldier asks trying to make his feet move. Standing frozen his mind tries to grip what he and the others see. Edward stands as his body cracks and transforms to the wolf. "Run they have the devil in them, "a once frozen soldier blurts out. The soldiers turn to retreat but like sheep before a feast they retreat to late. The wolf's run them down tearing through them like a strong wind would remove a fog. "What madness is this," the noble horridly asks watching the pack get ever closer. The York army with seeing the pack charging for their rival army begins to charge the field the rumors whispered now has come to full light. "Retreat, back to the castle," the noble orders turning his horse to flee. Edward knocks him from his rest ripping out the throat of the horse then pounces on top of the noble. His claws grip him by his shoulders raising him from the ground and as he hangs there in horror his body locked with fear the jaws of the beast stretch for the kill. Edward toys with him for a moment then in an instant dismembers his body. Contour and his other minions rejoice in the kill as they tear the army to pieces brave men become short work to the beasts before them. Edward transforms back to his human form with his breath regain, "Hear me men of a fallen noble there is no honor in dying today." The men on the battlefield begin to stop their fighting. Contour and the rest of the pack still in wolf form surround what soldiers are left. Edward walks through the beast requesting, "Join me and honor the flag of York or join your noble on this field of battle in his useless death." The soldiers bow down to their knees giving the loyalties to their new noble. The pack transform back to their human form. The York ship soldiers stand in amazement of what they have seen and their own fears take hold. Edward looks over the soldiers seeing their fear he remarks, "My brothers in arms fear us not for we are the same as before! We just have the power now to bring an end to these hundred years of war the same war that has taken many loved ones to the grave, stand with us now and together we will bring this destructive conflict to its end." The soldiers lose their fears and begin to shout their victory sounds. "York, York, York," the soldiers chant as their voices ring out over the land. Edward lets the lust for the throne take hold from the victory cries ringing out over the land. "Damien, take a small portion of the army and blend some of theirs in with you then inform their house that they now serve the flag of York, leave a few to make sure they truly serve us," Edward orders coving his body with a garment. Damien bows his head before turning away to take care of the duty before him.

"Why? Oh why lord, have I been placed into this moment in life. I am promised to another but my heart longs for Alex. Perhaps I am a bad and impure woman," Elizabeth thinks sitting in her room locked away from what her hearts desires, locked in her duty being promised to William from her father as a sign of loyalty to the house of Lancaster. She weeps for her heart as her servants comfort her tears. Alex finds himself in the church praying for the strength to overcome the love for his brother's bride to be. "Alex what troubles you in this hour of day," the father asks taking a seat beside him. "The same thing that has plagued me ever since I have seen her," Alex answers adding, I cannot help these feelings I have for her from the moment she looked upon me my heart was hers. Tell me father what must I do?" "You must find the way to keep it locked inside you must find a way to love her without wanting her, I will pray for you on this," the father assures. The doors of the church come open suddenly and a servant in the house of Lancaster comes in informing, "My lord, your father has need of you! A rider from a fellow noble has come here with wild stories of the day!"

Alex pats the father on the shoulder then takes his leave heading for his father's battle room and as he walks into the room. He can just catch a few words being spoken. "I tell you Sir Lancaster it is as I say! Edward York has a demon inside of him! He and his closest have made a pack with the devil himself!" William the father motions for someone to take him his body is bloody from the battle of the day. "Take him and tend his wounds, give him drink and food see if you can quite his mind for a bit." The servants take him from the room. "Father the man's mind is lost. He speaks of unbelievable things," William states. "Perhaps but father it would explain the bodies we found and the tracks leading to the York's land," Alex suggests. "Regardless if the story is true or not his noble has fallen to Edward and his army now grows," their father informs. "We must send a spy to keep an eye on them," William suggests. "I think we should let the ones who support our flag know what has happened and gather our numbers father attack upon this castle will be imminent," Alex stresses. "Alex you take charge of warning our fellow nobles and William select someone to go to their castle, and find out what he can." The two brothers bow their heads and speak not a word to one another as they walk from the room. The love of a woman has now wedged between them. "Eden, go and tell young Elizabeth I wish to speak with her," Sir Lancaster requests. "Yes, my lord right away." The servant heads out of the room to retrieve her. William the father speaks with his generals about the plans ahead. The servant goes to Elizabeth's room knocks on the door and waits. "Yes," she asks opening the door slightly. "The Lord of the house wishes to speak with you my lady," Eden informs. "Tell my lord I will speak with him before the day is gone," Elizabeth answers.

Damien arrives at the castle of the fallen noble. The flag of York rides high beside him. "Riders are coming," the lookout screams from his perch on the wall. The general remaining at the castle by his noble's request rides out to meet them clasping the flag resting just inside the gates proudly he raises it to the men before him, his older hand holds tightly to the pole flashes of former battles come fresh to his mind the days of youth resurface. "Lower that flag, Damien orders adding, "your house has fallen in battle and this land and castle have now fallen under the flag of York." "I have severed this house longer than you have been alive. I will not surrender this house to you," the old general replies. "General please, they have a power no mortal man can stand against," a soldier riding with them pleads. The general puts on his helmet everything about him has grown old except a pride a man carries with him with the helmet fully on he proclaims, "Then I will join my noble in hell!" The general draws his sword charging with his horse knocking Damien to the ground. He thrusts back his sword and drives it into his heart. "You soldiers have become weak to join this York ship army so fast they are but mortal men I have driven the York army from these lands before most of you wore born," the general states moving his horse around his fallen foe. As he speaks to the men Damien changes while his back is turned, the horse sensing the beast begins to act wild. Damien pulls him from off the back of the horse. The general stares into the jaws of the beast as he prepares to taste flesh once again. Damien stretches out his jaws to let the horror set into the old man's mind then bites, tasting the blood as it flows from his once life filled body. With the taste savored Damien drops him to hit the ground dead at his feet. He turns and looks back towards the castle as he transforms back to his human form. The people of the castle cross their chests as they kneel to him. "Join the noble house of York, or join him," Damien commands standing naked before them.

Edward sits on what was once his father's throne centered in the great room as the people of the house celebrate the great victory of the day. "My lord who should we conquer tomorrow," Kirkland a brother of the wolf asks. "No one my brother I think we can find ways to motivate other nobles to our cause without destroying their armies. The rumors and tales of what the world has seen today will precede us from this day forward. Drink and enjoy the ladies of the house I shall retire," Edward boasts before getting up from his seat. The music and festivities stop until he walks from the room. He goes to his room with devilish things looming in his heart he has a taste for blood in his mouth, enters his room closes the door behind him, removes all his clothing, takes off the metal to control the beast from against his skin, covers himself with a robe and slips out into the night. He rides his horse, leaves it tied in the forest, walks and wonders as the night goes on then slips up to a peasant's home watching from the tree line looking at the meal to come. His eyes begin to turn the color of the wolves as he lets his body change, his legs grow and bones pop as the beast's chains are removed. Driven by the animal lust he breaks into the door of their home. The family sits around the fireplace as their father reads them a story. The loud noise swiftly gets the father's attention, "My god in heaven what are you," a father's panicked voice screams out. He rushes out to protect his family but the claws of the beast are to strong striking him dead. The little girl flees from her home as Edward rips and tares at her mother, his first feast of the night. Her heart beats from out of her chest, running until her little feet can go no more, like a nightmare brought from her dreams she stands in the silence of the forest with Edward lurking for his finale meal. She can hear the ground move; fear strikes inside her tiny heart her mind screams for flight but her little frame cannot respond. The wolf enjoys her fears waiting for the right time to strike. Then with no pity for someone so small he leaps from the forest striking her down and savoring on her flesh. The animal lust devours her body Edward howls into the night drunk from the hunt of human flesh

"My lord you wish to see me," Elizabeth asks entering the room. "Yes, my lady I did. Please have a seat," Lord Lancaster requests. She sits down at the table where he was seated before her entry then he retakes his seat. "Elizabeth is there something that is troubling you? Has someone in this house offended you?" "No my lord, everyone here has made me welcomed," she answers looking down at the table. "Well then tell me what troubles you my child I cannot help if I know not what the problem could be." "My lord if I speak to you will you still think well of me," Elizabeth inquires slowly looking up. "Yes, my lady you are to be my daughter in the coming days," Lord Lancaster kindly replies. "I have been promised to your son to marry but the one you give me to my heart does not desire", she looks back to the table her blonde hair spills out over her shoulders, "I feel I have brought shame to your house and that of my father's." William the father leans back in his chair then says, "I see now, so that is why you stay so distant from Alexander," her eyes spring open by the name flowing into her ears and in her heart, she knows her buried feelings have shown. "How does he feel about you?" "Though he has not spoken to me of it out of respect for this house and you I know in my heart of hearts he loves me the same," Elizabeth answers with surety. "Love is a powerful thing. I know now by what you tell me it would be only a matter of time before my son would leave this house or the two of you would find yourselves in each other's arms," Lord Lancaster states with his hand resting under his chin. The long gray hair of his head spills out over his shoulders his time of the long days of ruling shows in his eyes. "I beg of you my lord please will you find another to marry William and send me home to my father before I cause pain in this house," Elizabeth spills from her chair grasping his hand looking up pleads. Lancaster stands up from his chair pats her hand ever so softly then answers, "Fear not my lady there is always a solution to matters of the heart. Now go and rest easy, I will figure out what I must do you have brought no shame to this house or your fathers." Elizabeth regains her feet wipes the soft tears from her cheek leaves with her heart lightened.

The sun shines, the rays of sun splash over the forest creatures who call it home begin to peek out from the night. Edward wakes from the stalk of the night his face and body covered in blood the beast relished in. He stands naked and starts back toward the castle steals a cloak from a peasant's line, gathers his horse still resting in the forest. The earth moves under his feet like the ticking of the clock. He arrives back to his castle slips back into his room keeping his nightly feeding to himself washes the blood from his body then rings the bell for his servant. She enters and he requests, "Go to Tyrolean and tell him I wish to see him this morning." "As you command my lord," the servant answers, turns to leave her eyes catch a glimpse of the blood covered rags used to clean his body. The horrors of him keep silent in her mind with the closing of the door behind her. Edward places back on the metal that gives him control for the beast.

William the noble, Elizabeth and William din on the morning feast. "My son will not be joining us this morning," Lord Lancaster asks a servant placing the meal before them. "No, my lord, he rode out early this morning to go to the other nobles and tell them what has happened. He said he would return before night fall," the servant informs. Elizabeth looks down out the table. Her heart has been let down, knowing she will not see him today. "Father I do not know why my brother dishonors your table by not being here," William trying to gain favor in his father's eyes remarks. "Tend to your meal and I will tend to your brother," Lord Lancaster quickly suggests. "How is the food this morning my lady," William asks Elizabeth trying to gain her favor as well. "The food is good," Elizabeth answers. "I was wondering if you would go for a walk with me this morning. The gardens are lovely to see with the sun just coming up," William says with a smile. "As you wish my lord," Elizabeth says holding her duty to heart but her mind holds with Alex and where he would be at the very same moment. She glances upward to him knowing his face would be pleasing to most but her desires for Alex closes her heart to the man before her the conflict between duty and love burn like a fire within.

"Do you think the stories could be true Alex," Darius a faithful soldier asks but, in their youth, and now Alex would consider a brother. "I cannot say truly but something is amiss," Alex says in a withdrawn way. "What troubles you Alex? You have not been yourself these last few days," Darius inquires. "I would say nothing but you know me too well old friend," Alex looks down the road then back at him asking, "Do you believe in true love? I mean the moment you see it or smell it you know it was meant for you?" "Yes, I do, but I have never encountered it. I usually just love the one for the night," Darius states with a small laugh resting with his words. They ride on a little farther with silence setting the mood. "Well do not keep me in the dark! Who is this love that has got you so tied up in knots," Darius readily requests? Alex smiles but does not give a reply with kicking his horse to gain more speed. Darius shakes his head and follows in his tracks. They approach the castle of a fellow noble hearing from the walls of the castle, "Halt who goes there," The guard yells inquiring in his duty. "It is I Alexander Lancaster. I wish to speak with the lord of this castle," Alex yells from atop of his horse. "Sir Lancaster, I did not know it was you," the guard informs then orders the bridge to be lowered. They wait as the gate creaks and lowers with the dust raising, they ride into the castle. "I will take you to the master of the castle," a servant says rushing out to meet them. They climb from their horse and follow him inside. "My lord we have guests this morning, Sir Lancaster is here," the servant accounted as they enter into the great hall. "Alex come in and welcome to my home," the Lord of the castle says then claps his hands and servants come in and take their swords, cloaks, and helmets. "Come join me in this morning feast," the castle's Lord requested. The servants place food in front of them as they sit down at his table. Women surround the room their faces covered mostly with veils but the blue eyes of one of the maidens bring the look of Elizabeth fresh to his memory but his duty overwhelms him. "My lord I bring news of the York flag. There are some wild stories coming out about their house," Alex states. "Yes, I have heard them too and I find them most unbelievable wicked lies set out to strike fear into the men they wish to engage," the Lord informs. "I find the stories unbelievable as well but regardless my father feels they will be gathering against us and everyone who stands with the house of

Lancaster. We will need you to be ready for war and our army will be ready to stand beside you to defend this house as well." "Yes, as always, the lord informs then with a slight prideful smile adds, I will stand on the field of battle with your father this is the way of it since as long as I can remember," with the words fully released he stands and toasts to their names. They talk of battles past and those yet to come enjoying each other's company. They share in the meal and they depart heading for the next noble's castle. Along their journey Darius requests, "So Alex are you going to tell me or what?" "My brother in arms," Alex says with pride looks up from the road informing, "it is my brother's bride to be that has taken my heart and I am tied up in knots knowing she will be bound to my brother forever, but at the same time I am also glad for my brother. She will make him a fine wife and one day maybe a queen to this land." "Now I see why you have not been around her and your brother," Darius relays. "I know you must think badly of me now," Alex stresses. Darius pulls back on the reins of his horse stopping it in its tracks and with a proud tone answers, "My lord you have always been my friend from the time of our childhood. You have never looked down upon me. I serve the house of Lancaster but I serve you most of all I would dishonor my family name and stand with you." Alex looks at him sets a smile on his face then kicks his horse they start to move again. The land rolls in front of them as the sun rays come and go upon the earth. The vast hills and clear streams set out over their eyes making their journey a pleasant one. Darius talks of his women of the night but in Alex's mind only one rests. "I tell you Alex, what she did with her mouth last night. I had never had a woman do. Maybe I'll send her to you tonight that should clear your mind." Alex shakes head and Darius laughs and pats his shoulder. With the day gaining length they arrive at another castle of a noble.

"Tyrolean glad to see you could join me this morning," Edward informs as Tyrolean enters the room. "I always come when I am asked my lord," slightly bowing his head Tyrolean relays. "This power you have given me is great I will now have the strength to take the throne of this country and hold it," Edward boasts pulling something from under a cloak adding, "I believe good service should be rewarded. Take it you have earned it." Tyrolean reaches out and takes the thing his father kept hidden. His life force placed inside a small crystal from a spell cast against him. With a smile Tyrolean takes it saying, "Thank you my lord." "I free you from your word to my father go in peace if you wish," Edwards grants. "I would stay and serve you my lord," Tyrolean informs. "I am glad to hear you say that, because I have a task for you." "Whatever you wish my lord." "Take my brothers of the wolf and go to the other noble's castle make them to understand that they will serve the house of York," Edward states. "What if they do not wish to serve you my lord?" "Then show them what would await them," Edward suggests with a devilish grin. "As you command," Tyrolean responses before quickly leaving to gather the pack. With the York flag flying and other men joining them they leave the castle in search of their task.

"Do you find the garden lovely this morning," William asks. "Yes, the flowers are pretty under the new form of day," Elizabeth answers cupping one of the flowers in her hand walking through the gardens. Butterflies and small birds enjoy the flowers savoring the pollen as the sun warms them. William does his best to win her heart but all she can hear inside is her cries for Alex nothing he would do or say could ever change what her heart desires. "My lord I have enjoyed our walk this morning but I think I will take my leave now," Elizabeth requests bowing her head to him. "As you wish my lady," William bows feeling the disappointment inside knowing her distant behavior she turns and takes her leave. Day slowly begins to give way to the shadow of night. Alex returns to the castle with his tasks complete, walks inside going to tell his father of who they can depend on and to what they have heard. "Father I bring news from the other nobles," Alex informs walking up to the throne. His father bends an ear listening for who will stand to fight and to who that will remain uninvolved. "You have done well my son," Lord Lancaster informs before pausing in his speech. Alex sensing his next question speaks out, "Father if that is all I will take my leave to rest from an early morning." Alex does not wait for a response turns to walk away but his father's words to him stops him in his steps, "Before you go son. I will ask you one more time, is there something that is bothering you?" His father waits for his heart to tell him the feelings buried inside. "No father all is well." "Are you sure? You know you can tell me anything I will love you the same," Lord Lancaster informs with a father's tone. Alex almost tells him of what is troubling him but he keeps silent answering, "No father all is well." He turns and leaves heading for the church to speak with God. He enters the church and the father lights the candles placed on an alter seeing him Alex says, "Evening father." "Alex, good to see you today sit and talk with me," the father requests. Alex sits down silence sets the room before Alex asks, "Father, do you believe demons walk the earth?" "Why yes I do. Why do you ask?" "I heard things today about the noble family York. Things that are unbelievable, things only the devil could do," Alex confused informs. "What things?" "There has been strange howling in the night. The people fear of the moon, other nobles have also found their people butchered, as if an animal have ravished them." "My son you speak of dark magic and of evil things," the father warns. "Yes. I know father, but something has gotten the people stirred up." "How are your feelings for the young maiden?" Alex does not answer at first then informs, "I have not seen her today for I fear the longer I see her the more I desire her. Why must I love something I cannot have?" Alex expects no answer to the question as if he asked the lord above why I am here. The father and he talk of things with no answers found he leaves, trolling through the castle doing his best to avoid what his heart longs for.

"Who goes there," an archer asks perched atop of the walls surrounding a castle. "It is I, Tyrolean of the noble family York," Tyrolean answers the rest of the men join his side. "What do you desire this time of night," the guard asks with Tyrolean replying. "I wish to speak to the lord of the house." "For what purpose," the guard swiftly requests. "I bring a piece offering from Edward York himself." The lead guard makes a motion with his hand archers quickly line the walls then he informs, "Stand there make no more steps toward the gate or we will fire upon you!" "Enough of this foolish man," Kirkland says he begins to let the wolf come out. "Stop Lord Edward has plans for them I will tell you when to strike," Tyrolean reminds. Kirkland stops his change and bows his head to Tyrolean. Moments pass with the guard's return, "Our noble lord will hear you now." The gates begin to part soldiers form a line to protect the castle as they slowly ride inside. "Dismount and stand by your horses," a captain of the guard tells them with soldiers surrounding them. "We have no weapons of any kind we ride under a flag of peace," Tyrolean smoothly informs. Despite the words of Tyrolean, the guards search them and bring them into the great hall of the castle. The noble sits on his throne. Tyrolean and the others bow their heads to pay respect to him with his head raised Tyrolean informs, "My noble lord we bring an offering of peace from noble Edward himself." "What is this offering of peace," the noble Lord requests. "Edward offers you all the land you now have and the land north of you," Tyrolean generously informs. "The land you speak of already belongs to another noble." "Their house has fallen on the battlefield. They now serve the flag of York," Kirkland boasts. "York has sacked the noble's home," the noble leans forward in his throne asking then states, "That house and mine has shared the battlefield together on many occasions the noble you speak so poorly of has saved my life on more than one occasion. If your noble wants this house, he will have to take it by force!" The noble claps his hands and the guards rush in and surround them and he stands to his feet informing, "I will leave one of you alive to tell your noble my answer." "Wrong choice my lord," Titus informs with a grin finding his face. The soldiers drive their swords into their bodies and the men fall. "Wrong choice did you hear him speak with such arrogance," the noble of the house relays then turns back to the bodies informing. "He does not look so cocky lying dead on the floor." The pack lay dead and Tyrolean stands alone. "Tyrolean. I leave you alive. Now go and tell your noble I will be at his gates by the rise of the sun," the noble proudly announces. With a spell cast causing a mist to form Tyrolean informs, "No my lord by morning you and your men will be dead." The men who rode with Tyrolean start to transform on the floor the mist fills the room the mighty growls of the beast soon begin to echo the room. The soldiers back off as their bodies begin to pulse and change fur where skin once was, taking full form of the wolf; they stand and howl together, a thundering scream to fill the ears of brave men. With his eyes filled with the outline of the beast engulfed in the mist the noble cries out, "My god in heaven what witchery is this!" The noble falls onto his throne. Connor growls, stretches his claws walking up the steps leading to the throne. The noble sits frozen gripped with fear into his very soul. The first strike rips open his face but the mighty jaws remove his head from his body. The cries of the brave soldiers' echo into the castle as the pack feasts upon their bodies. Tyrolean walks among their feeding finding Duncan filling his hunger upon a soldier. "When you are filled bring me his son alive, so I can find where his loyalties lay," Tyrolean requests with a hardy grin. Duncan howls into the night runs off through the castle climbing the walls until he goes out of sight. Tyrolean walks back into the great room. The noble body lay motionless in the throne itself he walks up and rolls his body to the floor. "I told you by the dawn you would be dead," the coldness seeps from Tyrolean's lips with a kicking of his crown, it makes its clanking sound down the steps, with its sound echoing the room Tyrolean sits upon the throne of a conquered noble. "Oh, I see you are still alive," Tyrolean says to the captain of the guard. Connor drags him across the throne room floor throws him at the feet of Tyrolean sitting in the throne. The captain lies quite at his feet when Duncan returns with the noble's son clasped by his garments in his jaws. The young man looks around at the bodies their blood sips onto the floor he reaches his hand towards his father but the sentimental motion is broken by the words of Tyrolean. "By now you should know you cannot defeat this army of York. I offer you a peace offering," Tyrolean informs before leaning forward in the throne adding, "Join your father or join Edward York!" The young noble looks at his dead father lying lifeless on the floor gathers himself, sits fully on his knees, bows his head and requests, "What does Edward York wish my lord?" A smile comes across Tyrolean's face. A parchment is unrolled before his face the young noble places his mark on the paper. The soldiers who laid in wait enter the castle to ensure the castle remains under the control of York. The captain of the soldiers comes into the room even before the ink can dry. "Captain you shall remain here with Contour to bring this house into the order of the York name," Tyrolean orders. "As you command," the captain replies. Tyrolean and the other minions of Edward leave the castle with another noble soon to fall before the night's end.

The sun shows its face upon the land within the night many nobles have sworn allegiance to the house of York the face of a beast used to turn many. Lord Lancaster along with William and Elizabeth sit at a table dinning on the morning's meal. William sits with Elizabeth by his side their father sits at the head of the table. Alex walks in, and for a brief moment, he gets a look into her eyes and his very soul cries out for her. Like a spear colored blue her eyes pierces his soul. "Good morning to you father, brother, my lady." He sits and the servants place the meal in front of him. "Is there any kind of news on the York family brother," Alex inquires. "No, our spy has not returned from their land," William informs. "I have heard disturbing news it seems that another house has pledged their loyalty to the house of York," Alex informs then looks to his father. "Father we must strike against their house before we appear weak in the eyes of the nobles that support this house," William suggests. Elizabeth reaches for the salt resting on the table and Alex looking at his father reaches for it too their hands touch like lighting striking their bodies responds to their interaction. She smiles from the joy of his touch. Alex feels the joy in his soul as her blue eyes burn through him. William feels his first jealousy towards his brother. "Do the two of you need to be alone," William rudely inquires. "What are you implying my brother?" William looks at her saying, "I expect better conduct out of a future wife of mine!" She looks down at the table. William pulls her face up and towards him inquiring, "Do I make myself clear?" Alex stands up with a passion fire burning, "Brother I have never had cross words with you only normal family issues, but if you put your hands on her like that again." William drawn back by the words of his brother begins to gain his feet. "Stop this foolishness now," Their father demands pounding his fist on the table. "Forgive me father I have dishonored your table," Alex says. "I also ask your forgiveness brother." William says nothing. Alex throws down his hand cloth on the table turns and walks out of the room. "My lord may I take my leave as well," Elizabeth asks with her eyes down to the table. "As you wish my lady," Their father says with William standing from his seat as she begins to walk from the room he informs, "You will be my wife Elizabeth as promised by your father, so get used to it." "William you will conduct yourself like you are a ruler of men," Lord Lancaster requests looking at him with disappointment on his face. "I will not have my brother lusting after my future wife," William responds. His father shakes his head informing, "Wife huh, did you not have two chamber maids in your room last night?" "It is my right as a noble," William boasts. "That may be the case, but I choose a wife for you for love she is not something to possess." William turns and walks out of hall and out the door. William their father sits back down in his chair at an empty table. Alex walks in the doors of the church. He kneels in front of the alter praying to God. "Are we troubled this morning Alex," the father asks touching him kindly on the shoulder. "Yes father, I cannot overcome these feelings for my brother's bride. I so long to have her it is taking me places I should not need to go. Our rivals' grow their numbers and a woman divides this house but by no fault of hers. What do you think I should do," Alex rambles with his thoughts being so scattered. "Men can lose themselves when it comes to matters of the heart," the father relays." What would you know of love father I thought holy men were not bothered by such things," Alex implies. The father smiles with a reply, "I was not always a father of a church young Alex. What did you hear of your rivals?" "The same as before stories so tall I cannot find the way to believing them but whether the stories are true or not there will be a battle to come where men will die because a man should think himself noble," Alex response with a heavy heart. "My lord, have I not always led you in the right direction," the father inquires. "Yes, I find you a man of faith and God fearing." "Then keep the faith in me and hear me out," the father requests before standing up mumbling a spell. His face changes to show his real face to Alex from a baby to boy even as a young man this face is unknown to him. "What is this? The devil rests in you," Alex says standing and draws his sword. "My lord, my lord, hear me out please I am still the man you have come to see since you were a child!" Alex grabs the lantern off the stand and holds it to see his face better with his face clearly lit he says, "Tyrolean it is you!" Alex raises his sword to strike Overlain falls to his knees saying, "No my lord I am not he just please hear me out!" Alex finds companion and sheaths his sword, "Get from your knees and have a seat. I will listen to what you have to say." The father sits on the bench then relays, "My true name is Overlain and it is true I bare the face of my brother for we are twins but only by birth. When we were very young a holy man blessed us with the power we both hold in us. At first, we both used the magic to heal the sick and we were thought of as miracle men, just and right before God. I still hold my truth in the knowledge I was given, but my brother became drunk with the power and he went on a different path. We once faced off and I lost against him." Overlain recalls the battle in his mind the clanging of the swords the spells cast against one another run like a movie before him. "What happened," Alex asks. "I was not willing to kill my brother when I had him down. I should have finished it but I could not find the strength to kill him. I showed him mercy and when I turned to walk away, he struck me through the back with his staff the blade at the bottom of it found its mark. The blow knocked me over a cliff and I found myself hanging on by a limb my brother could not find it in his heart to help me he just stood over me while the branch slowly gave way but before I could fall, I placed a sans curse upon him." "What would that be," Alex inquires for the words where unknown to him. "I placed his life force inside of an object. A large crystal he liked to keep with him with hopes that someone would have the courage to finish what I could not. You see he thinks me dead," Overlain informs." "Well that is a good tale one for the round tables of old but where does it leave us?" "I told you this and showed you my true face because you needed to know what stories you are hearing could bear much truth. Tyrolean used a spell from one of the oldest books of magic ever written down and he has brought upon the earth the curse of the wolf," Overlain stresses. Alex shakes off the tale as if it were a bed time story, "You tell me the wildest stories how am I too believe such things?" Overlain casts a spell and the flames from a candle engulf him surrounding the outline of his flesh, "Alex my young friend it is possible!" Alex sits down on the bench the flames reseed from Overlain saying, "What am I to tell my father? He will have you put to death just for being what you are." "Alex magic is like anything else it is only evil if the one casting the spells is evil," Overlain implores. Alex looks at the cross and stands for a moment revealing, "None of it matters to me anyways I am going to leave this place." "My young Lord you cannot leave us the people of this land need good man like you," Overlain states" "What choice do I have? I will not stand in my brother's rule and I cannot help but feel the way I do. I love her with every fiber of my being I cannot change that nor keep them buried forever." Overlain places his hand on his shoulder requesting, "Why don't you let her decided who she will love the people that serve this house need you and so does this land." "No. I hold no lust for the throne and I grow tired of this endless battle for something I do not desire," Alex states. Overlain slides his hand from his shoulder saying, "I can see you have made up your mind and for what it is worth I meant no harm in the form I took." Alex turns and looks him in the face informing, "I hold no ill will against you. From the time I was a child you have comforted me a many of nights and I still believe you are a man of God." Alex turns and walks out of the church. He walks through the castle and into his room. He gathers his things and slips out to the stables; he puts his saddle on his horse.

Chapter Two

A Love Divids

"My lord, are you going to leave?" A voice from the darkness asks. Alex's heart knows who is speaking to him like a favorite song to his ears her voice finds his soul. He turns and looks at the beauty that stands before him. "You shouldn't be here," Alex responds. "Yes, I know my duty tells me this, but I cannot bear to live without you, even if it is just for a glance a day it would be better than a lifetime without you." Alex closes his eyes the very words are like a sweet taste to his senses. She moves closer requesting, "Please take me with you. Alex we were meant to be together I know it in my heart this is the way it should be." "My lady, you have my heart and all that I am from the very moment I saw you I have loved you every day and I will for all the days to come, but you belong to my brother and I cannot let my feelings stand in the way of this house." Alex turns to climb on his horse. She walks up behind him and places her hand on his shoulder. "I love you Alex please do not leave me behind I need not all of this, all I will ever need out of life is you." Alex turns the doors to his heart opens the chains bust firmly and with her face in his he grasps her; all the passion built up inside over flows and he kisses her lips. Their passion begins to burn hot, the pinned-up feelings fill them, no honor or duty enters their minds, driven by the passions of the heart. He pulls down her top and places her nipple in his mouth. Her body burns like fire with every touch of his hand. They fall to the stable floor and begin to feel each other's body; her innocence kept she will now give to him. At this moment everything that had kept them apart is gone. He kisses and caresses her like a delicate flower, loving the way her body feels beneath him. He eases himself into her; holding off his desires, until her pain has passed; then as their passion flows, he begins to move himself into her over and over. Her passionate moans feel the stables. They are too involved in their passion for each other to see William walk into the stable. He looks at them making love to each other and his eyes burn with fire. He turns and walks back to the castle. Elizabeth's wonders kept to her most delicate places find their answers in the night, with it her love grows deeper with every wave of passion from the man bringing pleasure to her.

The Lancaster's spy walks through the castle, sneakily gathering what information he can. He doesn't realize one of Edward's faithful has spelt the scent of Lancaster upon him. "You there, where do you think you are going," Enos asks of him. "Sir, I am new to the castle I was just trying to find a place to rest," Paul the spy replies. "Rest I could have sworn you would be a spy against this house," Enos relays. "No, my lord. I am but a traveler roaming from place to place," Paul ready informs with more guards arriving. "We shall see. Seize him," Enos orders. The guards grab him and bring him before Edward into his great hall. "Sir Edward I believe this man to be a spy sent here by the house of Lancaster," Enos informs. "No, no my lord I am but a traveler come to find shelter in the castle," Paul pleads kneeling at Edwards feet. Edward leans forward and lets the scent of him flow into his nostrils then states, "You are a spy sent here to deceive us," Enos reveals starting to let the wolf come out. "No! My brother I have better plans for this one," Edward says with pleasure into his ear keeping his words from the others then turns to the guards ordering, "Take him to the dungeon." The guards come over and take him to the dungeon in the lower part of the castle. "My lord. Why do you keep him alive? It would be better to kill him now. He will tell us nothing." Enos suggests. "That is why I sit on the throne. You see, my brother. What would be better than to give him a gift and send him home," Edward relays. Enos bows his head and walks out of the great room. Edward leaves and goes into his room. His taste for blood fills his senses and rushes out of the castle from his room, leaving the medallion behind, letting the wolf come out, with every step towards the vast land, he gets closer to taking the form of a beast, letting out a powerful cry into the night. Alex holds his new love as they lay inside of the stables. He can hear the faint cry as Edward howls into the night, going in search of fresh meat.

"Alex, I love you, I knew it was so, from the first moment I laid my eyes upon you," she tells him with his hands caressing her body. Alex kisses her lips fully. Then looks deeply into her eyes saying, "My lady from the moment I saw you I knew my heart was gone. I will love you all the years of my life, until I find my death." They hold each other in the hay covered ground making love in the night falling asleep in the love they have for each other.

The sun rises and in the peak of the new morning with Elizabeth and Alex slipping back into the castle. "My love I will see you in the great hall," Alex says standing in front of her door. "Alex what of your brother," Elizabeth inquires. "We will tell my father and I will ask for the blessing of my brother." "What if he does not approve?" Alex looks into her eyes gently brushes the hair from her face answering, "You are all I will ever need in this life and I will take you and go." "What of your right to be a noble man and the name of Lancaster?" "My lady what is it to be noble without love?" Alex turns and walks down the hall and into his room. The servants wash her then dress her for the morning.

Edward creeps back into his castle leaving another family butchered at the hands of the beast he lets himself become. He rings the bell and the servants enter his room. "Tell Titus I wish to see him this morning." The servant goes out of the room tending to the task that is placed in his hands. "Have another night to feed" Tyrolean asks. Startled by his voice Edward blurts, "Tyrolean, you sneak around like a mouse in this castle!" "No, my lord. I came to bring news to you, but you were not here, so I waited." "What news do you bring me," Edwards inquires. "The Lancaster's have placed a spy in our mists." "You tell me things I already know, we have him in the dungeons as we speak," Edward informs. "Why not just kill him and be done with it?" Edward looks away asking, "What will happen if he were to be bitten and he lived?" "My lord, he would become a savage beast when the moon is at its fullest with no way to control the beast inside but only during the full moon he will be different from you." Edward smiles as he turns to walk out of the room. He walks down the hall and into the great room where his throne sits. "My lord you called for me," Titus asks walking up to the throne. "Yes. I need you to go into the dungeon and speak with the spy, but do not let him know you think him a spy. Question him this morning and again today then release him by night. Place him on his horse and allow him to leave," Edward requests, "Leave my lord," Titus not fully understanding asks. "Why yes, but on the road, he will meet a beast that will place his mark upon him. Then they will have a wolf in their mists." Titus with the plan revealed smiles and says, "As you command my lord." Titus leaves and heads down to the dungeons. He walks into the place of doomed men. "Where is the prisoner accused of being a spy," he asks a guard. "This way," the guard walks down the hall of the dungeon; screams come from cells as the people inside pay for what they are accused of. The dungeon guards give little thought to guilty or innocent they perform their task with the greatest of pleasure. "Stand to your feet," the guard demands as they enter the cell. "What is your name prisoner," Titus asks. "My name is Paul," he answers his lips trembling with fear. "Do you know the penalty for spying against this house is death?" Paul falls from his feet onto his knees "No my lord no! I am but a traveler upon this land. I was just looking for a place to hide from the weather." Titus takes the whip from the guard's belt. He strikes it upon his back. "You are a spy," Titus relays laying the whip upon him. "Crack, Crack," the whip finds its mark. "No, my lord, no I am no spy," Paul moans out as he tries to cover his body. "Are you sure?" "Yes! Yes, I am sure! Please," Paul pleads. "I tell you what. I will bring this to the master of this house. I will return, and let you know what he says," Titus playing his role informs. "Thank you, kind sir and please assure him I am no spy." "If I find you are lying to me you will find me the most unpleasant of a person." Titus walks out of the cell the door clanks closed behind him. "Make sure no harm comes to him. Lord Edward has plans for him," Titus orders to the guard then leaves the dungeon and reports to Edward.

Alex walks into the room his brother and father sit at the table eating the first meal of the day. "Good morning father, brother." "Good morning to you my son." William does not speak to his brother. They turn their heads as Elizabeth walks into the room. "Morning my lady," They say as they stand from their seats. She takes her seat beside William and they retake their seats. "I came to your room last night my lady, but I could not find you," William relays. Alex looks up from his plate. "I took a walk in the gardens last night my lord my mind was restless." Elizabeth replies." "A walk indeed, William states with sarcasm blurting, you are a liar and a whore!" The words barley escapes from his lips before Alex leaps from his seat and knocks him to the floor. "Call her a whore again, and we are not brothers! I will forgive you once," Alex informs with rage. "What else do you call a woman who sleeps with my brother," William inquires wiping the blood from his lip. Alex lets him stand. Elizabeth sits looking down at the table her tears drip down her face. "Tell our father Alex! Tell him how you and my future wife were in the stables pleasuring each other last night!" Alex looks down at the floor. His brother turns to walk out of the room pausing with his hand on the door, "Do not worry my brother I have no need of her anymore and I charge her as impure in the eyes of the lord!" William shoves the door open and slams it behind him. Their father takes his seat on the throne. Alex steps before him. "I am sorry father. I have dishonored your home and dishonored my brother, but I love her with every fiber of my being," Alex implores. "My son, I asked you many times if there were something that you needed to speak to me about. You gave me no reply," Lord Lancaster remarks. "Matters of the heart can close a man's tongue father." "My lord I cannot let him take all the blame, for I too love him with all my heart!" She moves from the table and takes her place by his side. "I cannot over look what has happened. Are we not to be governed by the same laws the people of this great land live by? It is unlawful for a man to take another's woman into his bed," Lord Lancaster reminds. "Yes. I know this father." His father looks up toward the heavens. Then he looks back at him stating, "I strip you of all noble right to this house. The name of Alex Lancaster will be stripped from the record books, and you my lady you will suffer for your fate! You will wear the mark of the scarlet letter for the rest of your days as a sign to those around you for your adulteries act." His father stands from the throne the crown resting on his brow weighs heavy this day and walks out of the room. Alex holds her as the door closes behind him. "I am so sorry my love I brought this upon your head." Alex brushes the hair from her face. "You cannot help but what your heart wants. Take your leave from here sweet Elizabeth, go and gather your things. I will be by to get you before the sun goes down. I will take you and find a place to call home." "And if they should try to stop us," Elizabeth asks in fear. "Then this house will find me a mightier foe then the ones wishing to over throw this house." She leaves the room knowing in her heart that she will have dishonored her father and her heart is heavy but the knowledge of her being with Alex the rest of her days brings warm thoughts into her soul. Alex goes to see Overlain. He walks into the church asking, "Overlain are you here?" He walks from the back room answering, "Yes. What can I do for you this day?" "I have come to say farewell. You have been a good listener down these long years and have guided me down the right path a many of days." "Where are you going and why," Overlain requests. "I let my heart take control of my life and my father has taken my noble name," Alex relays with a pride lost. "Young Alex it is not a name that makes a man noble but his heart." Alex smiles at him for his kind words. "I will take Elizabeth and leave this house and leave these wars behind me, I no longer have the stomach for it!" "I can see you have made up your mind" Overlain remarks taking something from his pocket requesting, "Take this my young lord, it will lead me too you in the time to come or summon you if I have need of you." Alex takes a small jade crystal from his hand and leaves the church. He goes to gather his things not letting anyone else know he is leaving. William brews in his room; letting his anger eat at him. "I trusted him, protected him, while we were kids and he betrayed me at the first chance he had," his mind screams. The day moves forward as each person moves toward their lives ahead.

Titus returns to the dungeon as the day grows long with his entry into the cell Paul asks, "My lord what did the master of the house say?" Titus does not speak at first; he derives pleasure from watching him wait. Letting the horrors build in his mind breaking a silence he informs, "He says you are to be released and taken out of this castle. You shall be free by dusk." "Thank you, sir, and tell the master of the house, I am grateful," Paul requests with his sprits lifted. Time passes as the sun finds its way behind the curtain of the world. Titus comes back to the cell and gathers him. They walk through the castle and out into the courtyard. Titus hands him over his bag suggesting, "Here is your horse, and if I were you, I would make it known to the guards of the next castle you come upon as too what you are doing there." "Sounds like good advice sir," Paul relays then kicks his horse and rides from the castle. His heart beats fast knowing he has been freed thinking he has pulled it off. He rides awhile then slows the pace of his horse. Titus in wolf form keeps pace with him slipping, hiding in the forest that surrounds him, lurking, waiting for the right moment to strike. "Well old boy I think we pulled it off. Just remind me the next time someone wants us to spy on someone we turn it down," Paul says to his horse suddenly the horse begins to become restless, sensing the presence of the wolf. Paul pats his horse on the neck trying to settle him down asking, "What is it boy? Do you hear something?" As the words come from his mouth, Titus strikes, and knocks him from his horse. His mighty jaws bite down on his shoulder, sinking his teeth down into his flesh. The pain of the bite enters his body. Titus runs off into the night leaving him bleeding on the ground. Paul tries to gather what has happened. He stands to his feet; placing his hand on his shoulder as he tries to slow down the flow of blood. "Come here boy," he calls staggering around then he whistles for his horse doing his best to fight off the pain. He takes a few steps down the path he was traveling his horse returns and with all the strength he can gather pulls himself up on his horse and rides for home. His horse gallops and runs as he holds onto the saddle. Blood flows from his body, finding it hard to remain concuss. He ties himself to the horse as it runs.

Alex and Elizabeth, begin to slip from the castle hiding their faces as they walk for the stables. They make it out to the stables when Alex hears his name. "Alex where do you think you are going," Darius asks. "Darius what are you doing here," Alex inquires. Darius walks towards him and Alex places his hand on his sword. "Your father sent me to watch the stables incase the two of you tried to leave," Darius informs then walks up to put his hand on top of his placed on his sword saying, "Relax brother I just wanted to say good bye. You should know by now I am loyal to you not this house." Alex smiles at him. "You need to go out the back of the way. James stands guard and he feels the same as I, you will have no problem getting out of the castle going that way." Darius turns and looks at her saying, "May love and happiness follow the two of you all of your days." "Thank you, brother, you are a true friend," Alex saying then puts her on a horse. "You will have to answer to my father if he figures out you let us go." "It will not be the first time I have had to answer to him," Darius reminds with a smile. He looks back at Elizabeth, "My lady I can see how you stole my brothers' heart." Alex shakes his hand and they leave out the back way. Paul shows up at the front of the castle. He is passed out, and sitting on his horse, the guards come out and take him into the castle. "My lord Paul returns," a captain informs as the men lay him on a table. Lord Lancaster looks down at him bleeding and bitten ordering, "Bring in the healer!" They wrap his shoulder to try to stop the bleeding, "My lord," Paul says using all he strength to speak. He reaches up and puts his hand on his shoulder. "Just you rest now to save your strength," Lord Lancaster requests gripping his hand. William comes in the room and stands over him inquiring, "Father what has happened to him?" "I know not he was brought into the castle as you see him." The healer comes in and they back away letting him look him over. "Help me by holding the light, if we do not stop the bleeding, he will not make it much longer," the healer requests as a servant girl who finds favor with Paul comes in and holds his hand. The healer heats the needle over the flame. Paul's breath goes short as they stitch up his wounds. "Father it looks like he was bitten by an animal." "It appears that way but unless he makes it we will never know truly what happened," Lord Lancaster reminds. The good father comes in to say blessed words over Paul as he lies on the table. He glances down upon the wounds knowing what beast has placed its mark upon him. "My lords I beg of you do not save this one's life he has been marked by the beast and he will destroy us," Overlain still playing the role of a priest backs up informing. "I am surprised by you, holy man! Is it not a Christian's deed to help someone in his state," Lord Lancaster implies. "Yes, my lord but to let him die will be more of a noble thing then to leave this man cursed." Lord Lancaster lets his words fall upon closed ears. Seeing that his words had no weight. Overlain closes his eyes, says a few words over him and makes the sign of the cross. Then takes his leave from the room. "Healer do you think he will live," William asks. "I cannot say my lord his wounds are deep but there is something strange his wounds show signs of healing a wound that bad should have killed him," the healer relays. "I have seen men in battle survive wounds of that nature it is his will to survive that guides him now," Lord Lancaster implies with the men looking closely at the mark upon his shoulder. They take him from the room and place him in another the servant girl clings to his hand. A guard comes into the room to report, "My lord I went to check on Miss Elizabeth but she was not in the room and Alex is missing as well." "They could not bear to live with their descent of me," William implies turning to walk off. "Is that all you can say for your brother? He has gone missing and you will not see him again," Lord Lancaster says stopping William in his steps. "They made their choice father," William reminds looking back over his shoulder. "You would lose your brother forever over a woman you cared little for?" "It does not matter he took her in his bed knowing she was promised to me after all did you not take his name and lay down the charge of the scarlet letter upon her," William relays "What I did was as the ruler of this house not as the father to a son. You will learn that to be a ruler means you have to make decisions that will not be easy, Lord Lancaster states with a father's voice requesting of a son, "William you could give your brother's name back to him and release her from the charge. Can you not be happy for them? They have a love most men would search a life time for." "What and have them mock me with the very sight of them," William prideful implies. "William son I fear you will not make a good ruler of this house," Lord Lancaster implies turning to look upon the throne informing, "To sit in that seat you will have to give up many things you do not wish too! Now I implore you to go and retrieve your brother and bless what your brother has found." Lancaster walks over to face his son places his hand upon his son's shoulder. William looks at him and shrugs off his hand saying, "I will not father she is his whore now!" William walks out of the room leaving his father standing inside of the room that has long since become his prison.

"My lady your eyes shine lovely in the moonlight," Alex tells her leaning over in the saddle. Elizabeth blushes then asks with a smile, "So tell me my love where do you lead me?" "I know not my lady," Alex shrugged his shoulder saying lost in the beauty before him. "It really does not matter your arms will be around me tonight and that is all I care about!" Alex kisses her hand as they ride down a road well-traveled riding under the moon and stars; their hearts full of the love that swells inside of them. The night grows long being traveled far into the forest passing the bounds of the land the noble's battle for. They come upon a wooden house long abandoned by its builder the well held structure looks to them as if a castle was before them. "This looks good enough to stay for a while," Elizabeth states not caring about the where just the company that will hold her. Alex helps her from her horse. They gather wood for the fire. Alex builds the fire and as the flames grow, they snuggle under the stars in heaven. She runs her hands up his muscular arms getting drunk off the feel of his skin loving how his chest muscles feel firm chiseled by a sweat of a brow. Elizabeth looks to his face resting upon his chest with love in her voice she says, "My noble man. I love you more with each passing moment of time; I hope and pray the lord in heaven grants us an eternity of time!" "It matters not for if I had you for an eternity it would not be enough to fill my soul." He leans in and kisses her fully upon her lips. Her breath becomes short as her body longs to have him inside of her. She gets drunk with passion as his hands roam across her body. The firelight reflects the skin that is now exposed to the night. She stares deep into his eyes as he moves inside of her body. Bringing the waves of passion over and over, with each thrust, their love grows stronger. Their bodies intertwine into the night.

Morning arrives. Bringing the hopes and promises of a new day. The morning birds sing, as the new day dawns. Alex lays awake looking at Elizabeth curled up beside him. He is content in the world he has chosen. No more a noble man by name but in the eyes of the one who lies beside him, he is of the noblest a person could be.

William walks into the throne room his father dines on the morning meal a once well gathered table he now sits alone. "Father Paul is awake if you wish to speak with him." "I will speak to him when I finish." William turns to walk out of the room his father asks before he can depart, "William can you find it in your heart this morning to bless what your brother has and bring him home?" "No father and I care not to discuss this again they chose the bed they share." "As you wish but the day will come when you will regret the loss of a brother." The cold bitter truth lays upon William with the weight of a feather the jealousy inside binds his heart. His father looks back at his meal and William takes his leave. Finished with his meal Lord Lancaster goes to where Paul is resting. "Paul how good it is too see you again, we thought for a moment we might have lost you," Lancaster informs looking down at him resting. Paul picks his head up and places his hand on his shoulder with the strength to say, "Morning Lord Lancaster." "Easy Paul just rest now and save your strength." Paul lowers his head back to the bed. "Can you remember what happened to you," Lancaster inquires. "Something attacked me from the darkness it was wolfing like but much bigger than a man," Paul relays. "Did you find out anything while you were behind their walls," Lancaster asks. "Yes! They planned to attack this castle in force they are rounding up their numbers now." With his words bringing alarm to his ears Lancaster stands to leave. The healer comes in to look over his wounds. He peels back the bandage and the wounds have healed as fast as if a week has gone by. Lancaster looks upon the bite and says, "You rest now Paul we may have need of you in the days to come." Lord Lancaster steps into the hall and Overlain waits. "My lord how is he this morning?" "He is healing well." "As if the wounds are weeks old," Overlain asks with the face the castle has come to know. "He appears to be healing very quickly if that is what you are asking." "My lord. I implore you take him from this castle or he will be the death of us all! He has been marked by a beast that hides inside of a man." Overlain pleads. "I don't have time to hear of fairytales. I have a battle to plan for," Lord Lancaster walks way to gather his minions with a battle plan beginning to fill his head. Overlain bows his head in respect as he walks off.

"Did you achieve what you set out to do," Edward eagerly asks. "Yes, my lord. I tasted his flesh. He will be a beast at the first full moon," Titus answers. "Good we will attack the house of Lancaster the morning after the beast has taken its toll upon them, they should be rattled by the night's adventure," Edward informs letting a smile run over his face, knowing a former foe will fall quickly before him. Edward sends his minions to gather forces conquered by the house of York. Shields, swords, horses and men begin to gather to take the castle of Lancaster.

"Darius, "Yes, my Lord, he answers with Lord Lancaster speaking his name. "Take Lucas, James and go to find which house still support our cause." "The ones Alex spoke of," Darius asks. "I will remind everyone here that his name has been stricken from the words of this house," Lord Lancaster reminds. Darius holds his true tongue and answers, "As you command my lord." He takes his leave going to take care of the task placed in his hands. A brother's memory still holds proud with in his heart. "Lucien," "Yes my lord." "Take Jayel and Jonas and go to the house of the nobles who have not supported us in the past. You must plead the case that York has over run the other nobles and has doubled his army. Make sure you fly the flag of peace and let them know it is in our mutual benefit to band together to beat back a common enemy," Lancaster implores. "As you command," Lucien answers then takes his departure riding out with the others to gather nobles for the battle ahead. Men of battle hearts begin to swell, knowing in the days ahead, their steel will be tested. "William," Lord Lancaster turns and says preparing to give him a task, "Yes father?" "Gather our troops then take the previsions in from the fields. Round up all the old and young to shelter them inside the walls of the castle." "As you command father," William answers then walks out of the room into the halls of the castle calling, "Knights, squires, archers, prepare for battle!" The castle comes alive. The men begin together swords, shields and spears. Overlain comes into the throne room. "My lord my I speak to you?" "Speak priest. I have much to plan for," Lord Lancaster relays. "My lord. I know you do not take me at my word but the man who rests and gathers strength will kill us all by the light of the full moon. He has the mark of a beast upon him," Overlain pleads once again. "Father, I have other things to worry about this day other than a man healing from battle wounds and things that only live in nightmares." "What of Alex?" "He has made his choice and I will warn you this time that name has been stripped from the house of Lancaster." Overlain knowing he cannot change his mind turns to walk out. "Father did Alex come to see you before he left?" "I thought you said the name was stripped from these walls." "I did as ruler of this house, but a father's heart would know. "The crown must weigh heavy in times like these, Lancaster nodes his head, yes my lord he did." "Do you know where to find my son?" "No, my lord, he did not say where he was going." Overlain turns to walk away, he pauses for a moment and looks back saying, "My lord your son loves the woman he took. Is it so wrong to love?" Lancaster gives no reply to his question but a father's breath speaks, "I fear I will never hold my son again." Overlain leaves, a father, a ruler of men to the choices a man has made. Then heads back for the church. He enters the church and heads for his room tolling inside looking for what he seeks. Finding what he is after, takes a chunk of silver in its birthed form and places it in a pot to melt it while blessing it for a weapon in the days ahead

Elizabeth stands looking out at the horizon watching the clouds move across the blue sky. Alex walks up behind her wrapping his arms around her waist, taking in the scent of her hair as he softly places a kiss upon her neck. "How long will we stay here Alex," Closing her eyes to his touch filling his breath flowing over her skin she asks. "Just long enough to gather food from the forest for our journey," Alex answers. "Where do you want to call home?" He turns her around so he can look into her eyes saying, "Where do I want to live?" She looks deeply into his eyes the blueness of them burns their way into his heart gently twirling her golden hair in his fingers he informs, "Just beside you for the rest of my days. The place doesn't matter!" He leans down and fully kisses her lips, as their tongues entangle. The feelings of love fill their souls. Breaking their kissing, she reminds, "You can kiss me like this every day for the rest of my life!" They spend their day enjoying the time they have together. Taking a bath in the river that flows through the forest. Making love on the bank, gently explore all their bodies have to offer. The world around them moves on.

"My lord," Titus says as he enters the throne room. "What of the other nobles," Edward inquires. "Three will gather and two will not stand against the house of Lancaster." "Which two," Edward asks with an arrogant tongue towards men who would defy him. "Barns and Lump my lord," Titus informs. Edward stands from his throne proclaiming, "Then let them suffer for their loyal actions. Gather the soldiers! We will go and teach others not to make the same mistake as them!" Titus leaves the throne room, gathers Edwards' brothers of the wolf and the best soldiers that fight in Lord Edwards's army. Edward and his faithful leave the castle and head for another slaughter of men. The taste for flesh begins to build in the mouth of the men that turn into the beast men fear. The army marches on and the sun begins to fade to the dusk as they approach the castle of the noble Barns. The battle flag of York waves proudly on the stick that is held in the hand of a loyal soldier. They form a line in front of the gate. Archers gather on the wall of the castle. Edward looks up as he can hear the sound of the strings pulling back. A line of men forms just behind the gate of the castle. Waiting for orders from their noble to attack. The smoke from their horse's noses float into the air as they get ready for the charge. "York! Take your men and leave my castle," the noble Barns yelled from the wall. Edward turns to the men in line beside him. "No one leaves this castle alive!" The gates of the castle begin to open, "Noble Barnes you will lay dead at my feet before the dawn," Edward proclaims. The sound of the wolf begins to take the place of his voice as the words come out of his mouth. The horn of the captain of the guard gives out its sound and the soldiers inside the gate begin to make their charge. The pack begins to change in front of their foes. The soldiers take their place behind them waiting for the attack to begin. The disbelief of what they see, takes hold of the men charging out to face them. The pack howls into the night before charging the horses, slashing, ripping into the flesh of men. The archers shoot their arrows into them with little affect. The pack enters the castle devouring everything that stands in their way. They bite and rip woman and children along with the soldiers of the noble. The soldiers in the York army finish off the ones not quite dead as the pack becomes drunk on the taste of blood and the taste of meat as their mighty jaws feast upon flesh. The screams of the people echo into the night, as the demons of men's nightmares walk the earth. The city inside the castle burns into the night. The pack full of the hunt transforms back to their human forms as the soldiers celebrate the victory of the night. "To my faithfully minions, no army will ever stand before us! Let this night serve as a reminder to all who do not follow this flag," Edward covering his body with a cloak proclaims. "Wolf, wolf," the soldiers begin to chant to honor their noble, who would be a king. Contour stands beside Edward and waves the flag high for all to see. The victory is glorified into the night.

Another day begins as the sun rises. The ashes still burn in the morning light. The York army rests inside their castle. Alex and Elizabeth go farther into the forest leaving their old life behind. William the father sits at his table eating the meal of the morning. "Father," William says walking in with Paul by his side, "He is not to full strength, but better as time passes." "My lord," Paul says in his greeting. "Come and sit and join us in this meal," Lord Lancaster requests. Paul with William sits down at the table. The servants place food in front of them. "Any news of the York army son," Lord Lancaster asks. "Nothing new, but all the scouting parties have not returned as of yet." "My lord, while I was among them, they had grown their numbers by two. I could not find out what would possess the other nobles who had stood against them in the past to now support their flag. There were wild stories of Edward among the people." "Well it seems we will face this army soon father, to claim the throne out right he will have to defeat this house," William reminds. The doors swing open and those sent out to take care of their tasks return. "My lords," Darius says bowing his head entering the room with them adding, "Three other nobles will rally to this cause." "Come, sit, and eat your journey was long," Lord Lancaster requests standing to make room at the table as everyone returns. The men eat and tell him of the wild stories across the land. Lancaster listens to the stories reaching the ears of men. Lucien comes in announcing, "My lord the house of Barns burns in ashes! York has destroyed his castle and its entire people!" Lord Lancaster looks on with disbelief written on his face. "My lord their army now goes way beyond the numbers of this house," Lucien states. "If he had the men to sack Barnes the battle ahead will be hard, "Lord Lancaster says walking to his throne and sits with the weight of the conflict to come, upon his brow. "It is good to see you up and about Paul," Darius says grabbing the bread for his feast. "Yeah my shoulder feels better with every hour it seems. My sword hand should be ready when the battle comes," Paul boasts. "What little use it was when you were at full strength,"

William says with humor. The men joke inside their circle. They pat him on the back as they laugh with him. "Paul can you remember anything more now," Lord Lancaster asks sitting upon his throne. "No, my lord. After a short time of finding out what I could they placed me in the dungeon. Then released me. I took my leave and rode for home when something jumped from the forest and attacked me. I don't know if the thing I saw was real or the vision from the loss of blood. Whatever knocked me from my horse left as fast as it came! I gathered myself and told the horse home. The next thing I remember was waking up on the table and hearing your voice," Paul informs to him and those gathered for the meal. "Go and take your rest Paul for we will need every man able in the days to come," Lord Lancaster requests.

Edward and the pack feast at the table, "Kirkland." "Yes, my lord," he responds. "Take Devilian, and go back to the other houses who have turned us down and let them know if they cannot join this house, they will suffer the noble Barn's fate," Edward commands with the feast finished. "As you command my lord," Kirkland says before taking his leave.

Alex and his love ride down the stream, the thoughts of home, duty, and father, weigh little with him. The beauty before him fills his life's essence. "How do you feel today my love," Alex asks. "Great my noble man! I find time with you the best of all things," she reveals with a smile. They approach a waterfall with a cave on the side. "This looks like a good place to stop my lady," Alex suggests pulling the reins of the horse to stop. Alex climbs from his horse and walks into the cave. He looks it over; making sure it will be safe for his love. The hard stammer of him catches her eyes, his hand rests upon his sword ready to face his death in protecting her. With her love growing, she asks. "Alex will it serve what we need?" "Yes, my lady. I think it will serve for a night," he yells down from the mouth of the cave. She slides down and walks up to where he stands. "Wait here my lady," Alex requests before running down removing the blanket from his saddle making haste back into the cave and places it on the ground for her to rest. Taking her hand until she is seated. Alex goes back and unpacks their things. Gathers wood from the forest for the fire; he approaches the cave; he can see Elizabeth naked inside of the waterfall as she baths for the morning. Her nipples stand firm as the water pours over her body; her sexy legs shine as the sun does it's best to warm her. Taken in by her beauty.

Alex walks over to the water and he removes his clothing, joins her under the fall. They press their naked bodies against one another with nothing in the world but the two of them. She leans back against the stone wall as he enters her, moaning in her delight pulling at his hips, keeping the rhythm she wants, her cries of passion echo off the fall and into the forest. Their passions reach its climax and they hold and fondle each other still building the foundations of their love.

"Father all the previsions are within the walls and the soldiers return from the field," William informs before his father upon his throne. "Good we will need every hand in the days ahead." The world moves on. Paul and the other men of the castle rest to regain their strength. The nobles rally for the days to come. Edward and his minions rally houses to his ranks. The battle day lay ahead.

"Alex what is glowing in your saddle," Elizabeth asks with the light of it filling the cave. "A man who I knew as a priest for most of my life gave that to me before we left." Alex retrieves it from his saddle bag and holds it in his hand and it glows brighter. "Why does it glow like that my love," Elizabeth asks looking over his shoulder. "I know not." The light grows hot and it falls from his hand and as it lands on the earth then Overlain appears before them. "Alex, I implore you too come home I cannot get your father to listen too reason, the dark days that lay ahead will bring down this house and leave a dark mark upon your family!" Alex looks away not wanting to hear what he has to say then just as fast as the crystal glowed, the light with Overlain fades. "What did he mean dark days ahead," Elizabeth inquires with his back turned to her. "I knew the man as a priest inside the church of the castle. Many troubles were laid at his feet when I was a child but he revealed his true-self to me before he gave me the crystal." Alex walks over to her, brushes her hair back over her shoulder continuing the story, "He said he was Tyrolean's brother and he spoke of dark magic. Of how a beast had been let lose upon the earth." "Alex you cannot leave your people to this you must return," Elizabeth suggests turning to face him. "No, my lady. We left that all behind. I am dead to my father and you will bear the mark he laid upon you." "My love. I care not but I know you as the man I love just cannot leave them to this. I would not let the love you have for me to change your heart," Elizabeth places her hand on his face adding, "I would live out the rest of my days named a whore on the lips of men before I would have you change the man before me. You must return my love." Alex kisses her hand and walks out into the forest with the weight of a man's desire and a noble man's duty.

"My lord a rider brings news!" William announces walking into the throne room. A man catching his breath quickly walks in behind him informing, "Lord Lancaster the York army marches for this castle!" Lancaster quickly turns to his son ordering, "William send riders to hurry the troops that should be arriving from the other houses." William leaves the room taking care of the task at hand. "How many days travel," Lord Lancaster asks of the man. "They should be here within a day!" Lord Lancaster sits upon his throne the day's events begin to weigh heavy upon his mind. The day moves on the men gather for a feast to enjoy the company of each other and to build up the confidence in one another. "Tomorrow we will be victories like many days before," Lord Lancaster proclaims with his glass raised high. The moon grows full as the night goes on. "Paul, you have eaten enough for five soldiers," James proclaims. "Yes. I know brother. I just cannot get my fill this night." "Too eating all you can stand! May the woman stay in our beds and this house to be victorious," William proclaims. They all stand and raise their cups. Paul stands then bends over in pain with the moon beginning to take its toll. "What's wrong brother the amount of food you have eaten catching up," William slaps him on the back asking laughing with the men. "No! I don't know what it is...Oh urrrr," Paul answers falling to the floor in pain, his painful cries echo the great hall. The music and celebration stopped as they turn their attention to him. His body pops as the wolf begins to come out. "What devil is in him," James fearfully asks watching the event. The soldiers stand back as the wolf stands, his jaws drip of juices as the hunger burns in his mouth. A soldier rushes in with his sword and with one mighty trust, drives it into him. The wolf spins around and his mighty claws tare into his flesh; spilling his blood on the floor. "Men attack, kill the beast," William exclaims drawing his sword as the men begin to attack. "Protect our nobles," Lucien driving back the beast with a torch commanded. The wolf runs through them killing at will. Overlain rushes in the doors, his true form known upon his face. He draws back his bow and fires his arrow into the back of the beast. The silver tipped blow takes its toll and the beast falls to the floor. Overlain moves for the finale blow, raises the sword blessed by a spell and with one mighty blow, cuts off his head. The room regains itself as the soldiers gather their minds. "Lord William," Darien screams seeing William lying out on the floor. Lord Lancaster looks down on his son as the beast's bite mark shows on his body. "William," Lord Lancaster says with a father's concern moving over him then checks how much damage has been done requesting, "Take him to his room and call the healer." Servants move in and take him to his room. "I know your face Tyrolean," Lord Lancaster proclaims in a ruler's tone turning towards Overlain. "No Sire! I am Overlain his twin brother and I severe this house," Overlain informs bowing his head with respect. James and Lucien move around him. "Do not trust him my lord he has been sent here to deceive us! Look what sorcery he placed upon Paul," Lucien remarks seeing Paul body return to its human form. "No, my lord. I tried to tell you what he would become," Overlain reminds. "Enough of this, Lord Lancaster announces then orders, "Put him into the dungeon. I will decide his faith in the days to come!" "No, my lord, please! Let me warn you of what you will face," Overlain pleads. His loyal soldiers take him from the room and place him inside of the dungeon. "My lord the army arrives," A servant informs. Lord Lancaster goes out and stands on the walls of the castle looking out at the torches as they begin to grow in numbers. "Open the gates and welcome our brothers," He commands. They open the gate, lower the bridge and the soldiers pour in. "Welcome this night has been busy," Lord Lancaster informs greeting their commanders. "What time will his army be here," a new arriving commander asks. "They should be here by the break of day," Lord Lancaster relays. The night moves on and the newly gathered army prepares to meet its foes. Lord Lancaster leaves the task of preparing to his most trusted. Looking in on his son, Lancaster sees the mark made by the newly found beast. The wound is swallow but enough to let the magic enter his veins. "Father," William regaining his senses says. "How do you feel son," Lord Lancaster softly asks. "Well, I will be ready for the battle ahead, what did you do with the good father," William inquires moving to sit on the edge of the bed. "I placed him in the dungeon until we can sort through the things that lay ahead," Lord Lancaster informs. Overlain sits inside a cell requesting, "Guard please send for the master of this house I need to tell him things he would need to know before the battle is waged!" "Quite down back there you will be dealt with in time," the guard yells. The night grows short and at the first light of a new fallen day a horse appears on the horizon the rider holds in his hand the battle flag of York. The breeze of a new day waves the flag as it dances upon the pole and the numbers appear behind him. Lord Lancaster stands on the wall of the castle, holding his emotions inside, not letting his soldiers know he has the fear of a common man. The sun peers from behind the mornings cover. The birds gather for the feast that lay ahead and out of the silence that seems to be in the world a cry rings out from Lancaster lips, "Soldiers of the house of Lancaster and of noble men prepare for battle!" James, Lucas, Darius, Kronus, Lucien, Jayel, and Jonas take their places inside the lines formed at the gate. William the master and William the son stands on the walls to protect their castle and their noble virtue. "My lord a rider approaches," James yells from where he stands. William and his son walk down from the wall step to the ground still muddy from the night's dew then climb upon their horses. The horses become unsteady as the gates part and the bridge slowly lowers. With pride for their names and in their noble house they ride out to meet a well-known foe, his most trusted ride among him. The rider sits out away from the castle too far for an archer to reach. "My lord Sir Edward wishes to speak with you," the rider requests as the horse stop in front of him. They form a line to ride out to where Edward waits with his finest. Kronus, Lucien, James and Lucas, ride along his side with other trusted soldiers. Reaching their destination. The horses stand nose to nose. "York, take your army from off my land," Lord Lancaster demands. "I cannot do that! I need your house to be with me when I lay claim to the throne, "Edward informs with a stern tone. "I will not renounce my houses claim on the throne, "Lord Lancaster proudly answers back. "Perhaps I didn't phrase that right, what I meant to say was, Edward pauses lets a smirk fill his lips before proclaiming his words, "I need this house to stand with me or exist no more." William lets his feelings be known saying, "You expect this army to fear you?" He turns and looks down the line speaking with an arrogant tone, "Look how we tremble, our air comes in labored gasp!" The men with the house of Lancaster laugh to the words spoken. Edward full of lust for the throne relays to the brave men before him, "We will burn this castle into but a memory in time and the noble name of Lancaster will be no more." The men break from their gathering with their pride swelling each go to their own places. "His ass thinks he has nothing to fear," Edward tells his minions angered by the events. Turning to the soldiers behind him he orders, "Prepare for battle!" Kirkland takes his place in front of the army holding up a flag to signal the infantry to form its line. "I guess he wasn't use to such delicate speaking sir William," Lucas suggests with a smirk tone. James putting on his helmet gives out a hardy laugh. Lord Lancaster rides his horse out in front of the men prepared to meet their ends saying, "Men of this noble house and brothers from other house, but all men of this country, stand now and fight against a man who would end this country if he ruled! Let them feel the sting of our swords and the strength of our backs!" "Whoosh, whoosh,' the soldiers chant to build up their courage. Lord Lancaster after a well-made speech with William takes their places back inside of the castle to watch the battle from above where men of a higher right do stand. "Archers be ready," William calls out from the silence. The line of men from the York army starts to walk onto the field of battle. "Infantry, form the line," Darius commands. "I wish Alex was here, we could use the swing of his sword this day," Jonas tells James starting to walk the path leading to the death of men. The armies stand yards from each other; then give their battle cries towards each other. Then a silence fills the air, as each man standing; flashes to his own horrors but like many times before they find their strength to fight. Their chests rapidly move as the adrenaline builds inside of each and at the cry of a crow the battle begins. The pawns let their swords clang, as the shields men carry splitter and bust. The cries of dying men ring out over the country side. Kronus kicks his horse into motion, letting his voice ring out to his horsemen, "Ride to protect this land and the noble name of Lancaster." The mighty roar of the horse's hooves pounds the ground as the men ride towards the battle ahead. "On your left," Darius yells as he slings his sword and it finds its mark killing a soldier that Jonas had not seen. James jumps from his horse landing upon the ground and drawing his sword with his strength being unmatched; many find their death upon it. The York soldiers lay dead on the battlefield. "Is that all you have," Lucas cockily yells towards the York army. As the sound echoes over the land it is replaced with the sound of soldier's feet pounding the ground as the soldiers that were hidden show themselves. "Ba ck, back to the castle," James commands seeing the numbers before him. The soldiers of Lancaster ride fast and quick with their foes following in their footsteps. the dust from under the horses fills the air and as they reach the walls. William gives a command, "Archers, release!" The twang sound of the bow strings sounding off with the unity of arrows flying through the air, and for a moment the sunlight is hidden. The sound of their flight whistles in the air. The arrows fall and striking at them, some in the horse's; others in the men. The ones that lag behind pull up on their reins and retreat. "Lucien," Lord Lancaster calls out. "Yes, my lord," Lucien answers from the ranks. "Slip outside of the city and rally more troops for their numbers are many!" "But my Lord I can stay and fight!" "Do as you are told or we won't last the night!" "As you command my lord," Lucien dreadfully answers. The thoughts of leaving brothers in arms in the time of battle weigh heavy on him. He bows his head and takes a few soldiers with him heading off to perform the task. "Free me so I can help defend the castle," Overlain screams at the guard. The guard lets the sound fall on deaf ears. Overlain casts a spell; his eyes begin to glow as he calls on the power within heating the bars until they spill to the floor like water, slips down the hall and into the castle, through the courtyard and into the church. Overlain finds what he needs then slips out of the city. "My lord, why do we play with this army? When as men we are equal but with the power we are given, they are no match," Kirkland asks. "Because on this day we are lies and things of legend, and I do not wish for our forms to be known, we only need to play this out till dark." "We will loss many soldiers today Lord Edward," Kirkland reminds. With a coldest tone Edward informs, "Well we will be able to rebuild are ranks. The dead cost nothing." Edward sips his drink as the castle is put to the test. Replacing his cup upon a table he relays, "You see my brother of the wolf. Richard the lion heart still lays ahead, we need to be things of rumor." A conquered noble walking up informs, "My lord I am losing many of my soldiers! We must pull back from the city." "We will not pull back," Edward proclaims with a cold expression written in his face adding, "I suggest you figure the way to birch their gates or all of you will die." The noble bows his head and walks away; back to where the soldiers are keeping out of range from the arrows. "Do we give the retreat order sir," a soldier asks. "No. We will stand our ground as too his orders," the noble dreadfully replies. "My lord we will all be killed," the soldier remarks. "What do you have me do? You have seen the power they possess! If we do not do what he says, they will devour us where we stand." The noble looks around the battlefield then sees what they will need. Ordering to those closest to him, "Bring to me all the line shields you can gather." The big shields placed on the ground are removed from their resting places then carried over to the noble. "Take half the men and give reinforcement to the soldiers laying siege at the back gate," the noble orders with the shields in front of him "We will not be able to enter through there my lord!" "We need not enter, just keep them busy until we can get this done," the noble relays. The soldier takes his leave taking half the soldiers with him. "My lord they are increasing the numbers at the back gate," Jayland rides up on a horse informing. "Archers cover the front gate, you men come with me," Lord Lancaster commands as Jayland turns his horse to ride back for the back gate. William takes his stand at the front gate as the men leave making sure to keep the back gate secured. The soldiers arrive fighting off the ropes and ladder placed against the walls for their enemies to breech the city. Lord Lancaster sees a young soldier engaged with two leaps from his horse as the men watch the courage in his veins. He draws his sword just as one tries to strike the young soldier and as he closes his eyes for the blow to come, he hears the clank of the swords. Lord Lancaster cuts through him and kills the other. With the men fallen, he turns and asks with a hardy laugh, "Are you going to lie there all day?" The young soldier finds courage in his veins and grabs his sword to engage another. "That old dog still has it," Kronus proclaims to a fellow soldier before his sword meets a charging man. They fight off the attack and the men retreat from the back gate. "My lord your son sends a message they need you at the front gate," A soldier rides up informing with the men behind him giving a victory shout. The men make the trip back to the front. William stands on the wall and his father walks up to look at what he is seeing, with his eyes beholding he informs, "He was always a cunning warrior!" They stand looking out to the field, seeing the shields joined and placed inside of wagons drawn by horses; they peer as their archers enter into the wagons along with foot soldiers. "Father how are the archers supposed to shoot at them now," William asks looking at the horses moving towards the castle. "We cannot! We will have to engage them hand to hand." "With their numbers we will not last long," William relays. "Perhaps, but engage them we will. Men to the horses," Lord Lancaster proclaims. The other men climb on the backs of their horses' as Lord Lancaster sits high in his saddle. They wait for the gate to swing open and they ride out with speed on their side. The dust rises from the ground and the men give out their battle cries. "Take the left flank," Lord Lancaster commands. Darien and

William his son follow his command and they part so they can attack from every side. The soldiers run out from under the covering of the shields to engage them. Their swords clash. "On your right father," William screams over the cries of men, and the steel clanging together. Lord Lancaster turns and blocks the sword. The battle is short and the soldier lies dead at his feet and in the distance, they hear the horn blow and Edward's army pulls back. "Back to the castle," Lord Lancaster commands. "Father we should go after them and take this fight to them," William suggests. "No. The light is fading and he has too many numbers to engage them at night. We will go back to the city and hold up for reinforcements!" The men move back into the city. The mighty gates close behind them. "My Lord do you think Lucien has found anyone to help," James asks standing by his side watching from the great wall. "If not, then God be with us," he answers in a prayer like manner. The night covers the land fast and the moon gives her light, the men stand guard on the walls for the men who will attack in the night. The flames of the torches sway with the breeze. "Lord William what do you think they are doing," Lucas asks as he points out into the night. William climbs to the top of the wall. "Why do you think they hold torches in a line like that," Lucas inquires. "I cannot say," William answers then turns to the men on the ground ordering, "Men prepare for battle!" The soldiers stand ready for the next wave of attacks. "Kirkland, bring out the special soldiers," Edward commands. "As you wish my Lord," Kirkland replies with a grin upon his face. The soldiers take their place in a line by the torches Kirkland and all Edward's brothers of the wolf take their place on a field of battle. In the silence that is night a chant begins to echo across the land. "Wolf, wolf, wolf," the army of Edward cries out. "What do they cry out Lord William," James asks. "It sounds like wolf." "What do you think it could mean." James inquires next. "I do not know, but it cannot be good." Edward faces his men as the full moon shines. "To my brothers of the wolf and to my pack, no one leaves this castle alive! Let the slaughter begin!" Edward turns back toward the castle as the wolf begins to come out all the soldiers that were marked begin to transform by the moon holding its sway; with Edward leading their charge. Tyrolean casts a spell keeping the mindless beast moving to the castle. The soldiers of Lancaster cannot see what is hidden by night but the cries of the wolves begin to scream through the blackness. The pack moves closer to the castle with the scent of the men in their nostrils and the thirst of blood in their mouths. Their forms become clear drawing closer to the gates. "What from out of the pit of hell is that," James shaken by the sight asks. "God be with us as we fight demons that walk the earth," Lord Lancaster declares. The wolves travel fast and scale the castle walls. The archer's fire their arrows but the effect has none. The beast attack swinging their claws ripping and tare into the soldiers. "Sir we must flee! We cannot stand up against demons from hell," Jayland says as the horror fills his eyes. "No! We must defend the castle," Lord Lancaster declares swinging atop his saddle rides in on his horse. He strikes one of the wolves and his arm hit's the ground. The wolf howls in pain. Lancaster is taken back as he sees the arm take back to human form, distracted by the sight, Kirkland knocks him from his horse. Lord Lancaster lay on the ground at the feet of the wolf; it slowly drags him from the ground, his feet dangle as Kirkland in wolf form stares into his face, his mighty jaws open, the scent of human flesh fills his nostrils. Lancaster sees the saliva drip from his teeth, with one mighty bite his jaws remove his head from his body, a noble man gone; heading on a journey to the river of sticks. The men seeing their fallen noble pull back as the horror of the blood squirting from his neck fills their eyes. Kirkland drops his body and howls to the moon. "Father," a son rings out. Kronus and James rush in and begin to pull him from the battle saying, "Come on my lord we must retreat and save ourselves!" The soldiers who can, retreat, as William, and the best soldiers his father had begins to leave the castle. Edward in wolf form with a child in his claws, her lifeless body drags by his side, releases her then begins to transform back to his human form; stands naked as his brothers of the wolf come closer. The mindless beast run into the night having served Edward's purpose. Those who remain are put to death as mindless beasts. "Burn this castle to the ground victory is ours," Edward proclaims. The pack give out a unified howl and it screams into the night. "What in the devil are those things," a soldier asks hiding with Jonas inside the castle. "I know not, just keep moving let's get as far from this place as we can," Jonas answers. The men of a fallen castle roam into the night; running from the fear that demons walk the earth.

Chapter Three

A Noble Returns

The sun shines in the birth of a new day. Alex and Elizabeth ride over the horizon to see the smoke rising from the earth. Horrors fill his mind for his family and friends. They ride by a cave he used to play in as a child and he requests, "Elizabeth, stay hidden in here until I return." "I will not my love my place is by your side," she replies in return. "Please my lady I cannot face what lay ahead and protect you too," Alex pleads with a love filled heart. Elizabeth reaches inside of his cloak draped over the back of his horse her hand finds a sword. "You ride out and I will follow you." Alex loves the beauty before him but the doubts of the strength of her arm guides him. She can see it written on his face twirling the sword around her body she inquires with the blade resting against his neck, "Do you doubt me my love?" "You are full of surprises my lady," Alex replies with a well-placed smile kicks his horse and they ride for the unknown. The bodies lay on the ground as they approach the castle. The flames still reach in to the air that men breathe. The crows feast upon the departed. Elizabeth turns her head at the horrors she sees as a raven forcefully removes an eye from his feast. They ride through the place where the gates once stood proud and mighty, but now lay, the sight of his people are in full view; women, children ripped to shreds, and soldiers he once shared the battlefield with, then he sees what he knew in his heart. "Father," he screams with a son's tone jumping from his horse grabbing at his father's feet, his body blows in the wind hanging from the pole that once held his flag so proudly, his head placed on a stone for all to see. "Father no," Alex cries out again swinging his sword to cut down his father's body. He takes his cloak and covers his father's head then stands looking out at the castle's remains, and a proud man lets the tears stream from his eyes. Elizabeth walks up behind him sharing his sorrow and her tears begin to fall. "My love, my lord. I am so sorry for you. I know I brought this guilt upon you!" She wraps her arms around his stomach her head presses against his back she sobs for him. Alex just stands frozen in the world around him. Slowly he turns around he wipes the tears from his face picks her head up and looks in her face, "My love you didn't bring this fate to him our enemies did. I love you today more than I did yesterday, my love for you surpasses all things." They embrace and hold each other for a moment. Alex takes his shovel from his saddle and begins to dig a grave for his father. He places him down in his eternal resting place, takes a moment to remember the man, places his sword beside him. The rose handle sparkles from the sun's light. Alex covers him, places a cross to mark the grave. Elizabeth and he hold each other as they pray for the fallen. Overlain returning to the castle sees them his heart fills with gladness then walks up from behind implying, "My lord you heard my call and came." Alex turns and sees who is talking seeing him he demands, "Overlain who done this!" "Edward and his minions. I tried to warn your father of what he would face, but he would not listen. He placed me in the dungeon thinking I was my brother. My lord I am sorry for the loss you have found." "Overlain I am not your lord anymore. I am no longer a noble man he took that from me," Alex reminds. Overlain bows his head does not argue the point, walks over to say a finale prayer over his father. With his return to where they stand Alex asks, "Overlain did anyone else survive?" "Yes, Alex they fled into the woods," Overlain informs pointing to the forest that lay towards the south. "Did my brother make it out?" "I cannot say, but I have not found him among the dead," Overlain replies. "Do you have a horse," Alex requests. "No, my, he pauses then finishes, "Alex and there are none in the remains of the castle." Alex helps her back on her horse then turns and gathers the reins of his requesting, "Come on and ride mine." "What about you," Overlain inquires. "Just get on the horse old man," Alex requests with a smile. "Wait I have something's I need to gather." Overlain leaves, retrieves what he is after then climbs in the saddle. Alex takes the reins on the horse and walks towards the forest.

The army of York makes it back to the castle full of the night's victory and boasting as they enter their refuge. "Titus what a great victory now there is no one to stand in the way of the throne," Duncan boasts. Edward rides up beside him reminding, "We have not defeated them all Richard still lays ahead," but requests, "but for this day celebrate make love to the women enjoy yourselves!" The town's people give to them glasses of rum and beef from freshly butchered animals. The music plays as they are given a victorious welcome. They hold in their hearts that he will be the next King to rule. The army indulges in the festival of the day giving praise to the ones who made it from battle and to the ones no longer with them.

"Do you see which way they went," Overlain asks as Alex follows a horse's tracks. "No there are so many they ran in so many different ways." Alex hears something in the forest he draws his sword. Jayel steps from the forest saying, "Alex I never thought to see you again." Alex shakes his hand with his rushing over to him. "Nice to see you made it out of the castle," Alex with a smile says. "Alex your father," Jayel looks towards the ground. "Yes, I know I buried him before we came." Jayel looks up at the horses and he sees Overlain's face he pulls his sword screaming, "My lord that is the one who deceived us!" "Put down your sword! He is not who you think him to be," Alex requests placing his hand on top Jayel's hand grasping his sword. Jayel sheaths his informing, "Everyone is gathered at the river. We have set up camp." They follow him down into the forest until they can see the fires and the men gathered. "Alex," James screams out then runs up and picks him up with a hug. "Alright big man you can put me down," Alex requests. He turns and sees Overlain on the horse. "My lord you have brought a deceiver to this camp," James states making a move towards Overlain. "James, stand your place! He is not who you think he is," Alex orders. James steps back from his approach. Alex turns and helps Elizabeth from her horse, they begin to walk from the horses. "My lady," they all say as she walks with Alex with their motions, he turns his head back to James asking, "Oh James please help Overlain down from my horse." James walks up to do what Alex requested. "Thank you, big man I am glad you are on my side," Overlain relays with his feet on the ground. "You know if it was not for Alex. I would have snapped your neck," James informs without the smallest of guilt. Overlain turns and walks down to catch up with Alex. "Do you know where my brother is," he asks a peasant man but before he can answer he hears, "Yes my lord. He is down by the river coming up with a battle plan," Darius says with a smile. Alex welcomes his warm favor and grips his hand saying, "Darius my faithful friend. I wonder if you would take my lady to a place for rest and stay with her. Let no harm come to her and see to it Overlain is made welcome here, these things I leave in your care." "No harm will come to her my life I will give to see to this," Darius confidential replies. Alex pats him on the back he kisses her hand. Darius takes them to a place for rest. "Your brother will not be glad to see you my lord," James says walking with him on the path that leads to the river. "I am not your lord James it's just Alex and I care not of his opinion but the safety of the people still left." "I will be here by your side my lord." James replies. Alex knows there is no changing his tongue for he has been James's favorite since birth. They walk up to the river and the talking slowly stops. "Well my brother does have a spine," William rudely relays." "William this is not about the two of us but what we should do for the people here." William replies with a smirk, "You talk in this circle like you have a say you have no noble name anymore no one here hears you." "I think we should hear him speak," James steps into the circle saying. The men take their sides the ones loyal to the noble name and the others stand with Alex. "You men stand with the lover of a whore in the eyes of God!" Alex can hear no more he lashes for his brother and they face off in circle of the men. "Come get your ass whipped like the days of old," William boasts. "Those days are gone brother today is today," Alex proudly informs. The brothers strike each other punching with all their might, kicking and tearing at one another. Alex punches him hard and knocks him to the ground, like a loin he springs on his prey grabbing him by the throat reminding, "I told you not to never call her a whore, you do all this for someone who meant nothing to you except the fact she didn't want you, woman have always been things of play to you!" Alex pulls a dagger from his chest holds it over his brother's throat. "You better kill me brother or you will suffer my wrath," William informs with the blade resting against his skin. Alex weighs the life of his brother knowing you never let an enemy up but the thoughts of better days cloud his mind. Overlain busts in exploding the flame from his torch announcing, "Enough of this, the enemy is out there not here!" "You speak to us about enemies after you deceive everyone," James states moving to challenge him. Overlain casts a spell taking the strength from the big man's legs. He falls like a mighty oak in the forest. Alex releases his brother. "Does no one still find pride in my name," William asks with a wounded pride regaining his feet. With no answer given he leaves taking his wounded pride with him. "Overlain release him from your spell," Alex turns and requests. Overlain does as he wishes. "We will listen to what he has to say," Alex tells everyone still gathered in the circle. They settle down and begin to listen. "Good men of Lancaster. I am Overlain. I do share my brothers face but not his views, he has unleashed a dark curse over the land. He has turned men into beasts!" A man blurts out within the circle, "What we faced are the hounds of hell, not men of this world!" "I know it seemed that way but I tell you magic was used to achieve this, Overlain relays." "Magic is against the church we will not hear of this witchery," another relays. "You did not find it witchery when your lone daughter was dying and you brought her to me in the church," Overlain waves his hand in front of his face and for an instant they all see the good father saying, "Magic is evil if it is used for evil things as everything that was given to us." "Overlain, how can we defeat what we face? I think the people would like to know," Alex suggests. "We must use arrows with silver tips blessed with holy water or a sword dipped in silver with a blessing upon it," Overlain informs. "Where are we to get silver," a soldier asks. "There is silver in the castle remains," James reminds. "Not enough to wage a war against the numbers we face," Alex says. "We talk of madness! The castle no longer stands. We must flee there is nothing left for us to lay claim for. The Lancaster noble name will mean nothing. We were defeated under the eyes of God this is the way of it," a member of the crowd says. Alex looks around at the men, takes his place at the center of the gathering. With everyone looking he speaks, "You are right sir. My name means nothing to the ones who would sit on the throne, but this is not about a noble man but about free men who will suffer greatly if the York house sits on the throne. My father never wanted to rule this nation but he was willing to give his life to stand against the people who would lust for the throne with evil inside of their hearts." "We are but a few and no match for his army. I still say we flee and take our chances," a captain of the guard suggests. "We are a few that is why I say we join with Richard against the York army. He is the last of the nobles that could stand against a common foe," Alex suggests. The people talk among themselves. Overlain walks away from the circle heading back to where Elizabeth waits for Alex. "Lord

William," Darius says seeing him coming. William walks up towards the tent. Darius stands guard at the entrance. "Is she inside the tent," he asks. "Yes, my lord she is." He goes to walk by him but he stands in his way. With his path blocked William demands, "Move aside!" "Sorry I cannot your brother gave me a task and I will see it through," Darius informs. "I am the rightful ruler to this house not my brother," William states. "That may be true to a noble man's eye but I stand with your brother not with a house or a noble name," Darius moving closer to him informs. Overlain walks up, they stand in a face off, he walks up beside Darius to stand with him. William places his hand atop his sword. Darius stands ready. Overlain moves between them requesting, "My lord do not take this action there has been enough blood shed in this camp tonight." Alex walks up the trail he can see them standing in front of the tent his pace quickens when he sees his brother. James and the others lay their hands on them keeping them from getting to one another. "I told you to stay away from her," Alex screams out lunging towards his brother. James's mighty hand keeps him at bay. "You stole her from me you took my father's love and now you return from running after this house needed you and stand in my way of my right to this house," William screams. "You cared nothing for her and I never tried to take your right to rule. I care nothing for it. Edward York took your noble name and father took mine this isn't about our name but about keeping a truly evil man from getting his hands on the throne of this country!" William replies with a hate filled tone "Follow a whore lover if you wish you men betray my father's name." Alex doing his best to speak through his rage informs, "From this day forward we are not as brothers." "So be it," William proclaims. Elizabeth sits inside of the tent her eyes fill with tears for the wedge she has placed between the brothers, her heart is saddened and heavy. The want and need of the man she loves makes it all worth her heavy heart. The men release their grip. William's shirt moves and Overlain catches a glimpse of his wound. William walks off and Alex enters the tent. He walks in and she weeps. He sits down beside her and pulls her close holding her tight as she lets her tears fall. "Alex, I wish sometimes, I had not seen you, for all the pain I have caused you my love," whimpering she states. Alex softly turns her face to his, he looks into her eyes he places a small kiss upon her cheek saying, "My lady you did not cause this to be, if we stood in different parts. I would have blessed what my brother had found for the love that would be with him." He wipes away her tears informing, "I love you and I will always and forever, my brother is lost to me, but I have to look at what I have found." She kisses him passionately having her love restored. "Go now down to the river and clean yourself up and wash away these feelings of guilt" Alex suggests. Alex takes her outside of the tent. Darius stands still guarding the entrance. Alex walks up with her on his arm saying, "Darius thank you for what you did. I am indebted to you." "You owe my nothing my lord," Darius proudly states with a small bow of his head. "Now I ask you to take her down to the river so she may bath," Alex requests. Darius gets a grin on his face. Alex sees no humor in his reaction. With a slap on the back Darius laughs and replies, "Relax brother. I just wanted to see what you would do." "I have so many great friends," Alex informs with a humorous way. An uplifting tone lifts into the air between them. Darius with her walk off towards the river. He walks beside her like he guards his sister. "Am I to worry about you Darius," Elizabeth inquires. Darius looks at her with the serious of faces answering, "My lady you are Alex's love and I would give my life so he could have you for all the days to come." She finds her answer in the words spoken by him and the truth in his eyes. They walk on until the reach the water's edge; three men sit around a fire. "You men take yourselves somewhere else the lady would like to bath now," Darius orders with Elizabeth behind him. "What and miss the show," a soldier says. James walks up and stands with them. "We were just kidding," a soldier replies before leaving with the others. Elizabeth finds a darken place removes her clothing wraps herself in a thin robe announcing, "I am ready to come out and get in the water." Her blonde hair spills over her shoulders the blueness of her eyes is captured by the light of the fire, her firm breasts show through the thin material before a lustful glance can set, they turn their backs as she enters the water. Her naked body shines in the light of the now rising moon for her beauty is unmatched. William rests on his horse having watched her walk into the water hiding in the denseness of the forest. He gazes on her and he feels the lust in his heart for what his brother has. The hate grows in his heart for his brother and he rides off into the world ahead. Like two statues they stand as she cleans herself true and loyal for the one, they call lord or a brother.

Overlain walks up to Alex as he discusses things with the men of the camp pleading, "Alex I must speak with you" "Speak no one has secrets here," Alex relays. "Alone please my lord," Overlain implores. Alex turns to those gathered saying, "We can discuss this in greater detail in the morning." The men walk off and they enter the tent. "My lord I bring you news that will not be easy to hear," Overlain reluctantly informs, "Speak this seems to be a night for things I wish not to hear." "Your brother has been marked and the curse now flows in his blood," Overlain informs. Alex walks to a table. Seated he inquires, "What do you mean marked?" "He has been bitten by the beast and now he will become the thing that God fearing men fear!" "How do you know this?" "I have seen the wound upon him my lord." "How do you know he will become this thing you speak of," Alex asks after standing and walking to the front of the tent peering out the mouth. "Just like Paul was marked and I warned your father, the beast is in him and he will have no control over what he will do come the light of the next full moon." "What do you have me do, is there any way to save him from this curse?" Overlain walks up beside him placing something in his hands, "There is young Alex, I can use the book of spells to save him in the mean time you can place this upon his skin." Alex looks down at the thing in his hand a half dollar sized metal medallion. "What would such a small thing do," Alex asks. "This was forged from the nails that held the Christ to his cross. The blood split upon this will keep the wildness in the beast at bay it will only let the attitude of the one who wears it peeks out." "You mean whatever the demeanor of the ones is it will still be," Alex inquires. "Yes, my lord." "That doesn't give me much comfort he is angry with the events that life has transpired." "Yes, my lord I would agree, but if we leave him at the mercy of the beast then he will do unspeakable things to the people of this land." "Then we must find him before the next full moon maybe he will listen to reason and you can rid him of the beast." "It is the only way to save your brother for the beast is wild at heart." Alex looks out at the fire as it dances in the breeze of the night. "One more thing my lord it will take the power of the wolf to bring everything back into the balance of nature," Overlain warns. "Meaning," Alex turns to him asking. "We can forge weapons sure but the strength of the beast is mighty and its speed is unmatched. We will need the wolf to be on our side." "How would we achieve this?" "With the book of spells, it was written long before this age of men," Overlain steps around him adding, "I could transform you and those you chose into the form of the wolf." "No. The power is too great for anyone to have. Like you said the beast is wild at heart. We have already seen what it can do, its mark flows over the country now. We would just add more lives to be ruin by this curse upon men." "Yes. I agree my lord, but it matters not. Tyrolean has already unbalanced things everything could be set back in balance. We could end the war then we would just have to remove the spell and everyone would be as they should," Overlain informs. "It might come to what you speak of in the days to come but not today this day we must fight as God created us as men," Alex says before starting to walk away but in his steps he pauses and requests, "Where would we find this book of spells?" "It will be in the care of my brother we hide it long ago." "That means in the heart of the York army." "Yes, my lord, but it is the only thing to set it right and to save your brother from the fate that is placed upon him." "Then how could you transform us into the wolf without this book." "The holy man who blessed us in our youth gave three books to us. Two held the spells to cast, it is written in the book I keep in my care. The third holds the way to remove a curse from the world. I dare not perform the spell without the one to remove it. The master book was told to us to always keep it hidden so we buried it in a place that we only knew. Years after my battle with my brother. I went to retrieve the book but I found the place barren. He must have it or at least knows where it is." "How would a mortal man know this book," Alex asks. "It would appear as an ordinary book but the crystal I gave you to call you home will let you know you have found it." Alex knows in his heart his brother will never hear the words that would come out of his mouth. "Thank you Overlain. I will take what you have said into my rest tonight and talk with you in the morning." Overlain looks down the path he can see Elizabeth coming up the trail he passes by them as they approach Alex. The loyalist soldier any man could have returns her to his care. "My lord I bring her too you," Darius says. "Thank you, brother," Alex says holding unto her hand. "My lady," Darius says taking her hand and kissing the back of it adding, "Your beauty is breathtaking there will never be another to match." Elizabeth blushes from his comments. Darius's charm and his good-looking stature do not go unnoticed but her heart belongs to the man holding her hand. James and Darius turn and walk back down the path. "I see you could not wash the beauty from you," Alex tells her. "Alex you know what a woman loves to hear," she pulls in and kisses his cheek. "Not a woman but a lady." They turn and walk into the tent. Alex closes the flap as they enter inside. He sits down in front of the pole in the center of the tent, placing his back against it. Elizabeth sits beside him and places her head upon his chest, holding each other silence fills the tent. "What troubles you Alex?" "What do I do? Overlain says my brother is marked from the beast, he will not listen to what I have to say," Alex implies brushing back her hair. "I cannot tell you what you must do my lord. I will love you the same no matter what you chose," she relays with compassion upon her breath. "I cannot let him run across this land without telling him what he will become and cure him of this curse." "I ask you my lord what will happen if he likes what he is and doesn't want to control the beast. What will you do then," she asks staring up into his eyes. The color of them reminds her of water clashing with the sands of the earth his black hair flows upon his shoulders. Alex searches his soul but he cannot find any answer. She looks in the lost look of his eyes she kisses his lips, softly runs her hands down his chest, she gathers herself; sits upon his legs facing him, she slowly releases the top of her dress her breasts slowly come into view. She looks at him with love in her eyes requesting, "Rest your mind my love, things will be brighter in the morning." Alex places his hand on her breast feeling the softness of her skin, lightly rolling her nipple in his fingers. The firmness her nipples take lets him know her fire goes hot. They kiss with passion loving the feel of one another. He rolls her over, pulling off her dress. He sits up and removes his clothing. Elizabeth lays on her back with him naked before her kneeling between her legs, her eyes take in the build of her man, her wetness becomes strong and her body longs to have him in her. Alex lowers himself and she gets drunk off the feel of his body pressed on hers. He pushes inside and her passion calls out. She pulls at his hips keeping the pace she desires and with every push she flows deeper into her passion. Alex feels the warm and wetness of her loving, the look she holds in her eyes for him. He has never loved anything else like the woman who lies beneath him. "My lord I love the feel of you in me," her breath comes quick talking through her moans, "the feel of your skin upon mine the way my skin reacts with the touch of your hand, you can do this to me for all of my days." "You are so wet to the feel of me, the beauty of you is enough to drive a man insane, the softness of your skin is intoxicating. I love you my lady!" Their breathing becomes short and they release the passion buried inside, holding onto one another in the night.

William rides through the forest with nothing but the hate and the jealousy he holds inside. The nakedness of her body as the light of the moon shined on it plays in his mind. He rides with his lust for a place to rest.

The sun of a new day shines over the land. The rays wake up the forest as the birds begin to sing. William wakes from his sleep resting inside the place of a fallen noble, only a shell of the castle remains. He scratches at the mark left on his shoulder as it heals faster than normal. An outcast of his people with no noble name or family to call his own and by his hand this has found is head. "I must find men who will follow me and take back the house I was promised," he plots in his mind. "He even got to bury my father," the anger swells driving his sword into the earth screaming with anger, "and I do not even know where he laid him!" He sits with his thoughts as they lead him to rage.

Alex lays awake with the tasks he must do heavy on his mind, but for the moment he enjoys the feel of her resting on his chest. The warmth of her body against his. The softness of her skin gives him the sensation as if he had a wool blanket to comfort his soul. The flap on the tent moves. "My lord, the men need to speak with you," James dunks his head inside to say. Alex places a finger to his mouth whispering, "She still sleeps. I will be with you in a minute." Alex slides out from under her slowly and gently not to disturb her rest. He takes a moment to enjoy her body before he places the covers on her. Alex puts on his cloths and walks outside to hear the men. "You wish to speak with me," Alex asks making it to where they are gathered. "Yes, Alex. We have discussed this thing among ourselves and we cannot follow you. We feel it will be safer to leave these lands. We hold no disrespect for the Lancaster name it's just a hopeless battle that lay ahead," a soldier explains. "All you men feel the same as he," Alex turning towards his most trusted asks. "Not I my lord," James quickly informs. Alex's faithful follow his lead. Darius, Lucas, Darien, walk to his side then with Lucien steps his brother Lushien then Jayel, Jonas finale Kronus each with the same loyalty inside of their hearts. "Thank you, my brothers." The men turn to walk off Alex speaks out, "What will you do if you leave here now?" One soldier turns around saying, "We will live far from these wars." "How much time will it be before the beasts you fear conquer more lands? Sooner or later, they will find you and your families. Edward York lusts for power. Do you really think with this new found power he possesses he will stop at the throne?" The men look to one another with Alex adding, "If we do not stand together, he will go out to conquer the world." The men keep walking letting his words fall upon deaf ears but some find the courage inside their hearts. "Come on he speaks the truth," a soldier says. Of the men leaving only twenty find the courage stay with him. "I will go after them," James suggests. "No. My brave friend, they must have it in their hearts to stay besides I have another task for you," Alex informs. "What do you need of me," James asks. "The task I hand to you will not be easy, I need you to track my brother and bring him back." "What if he does not wish to come?" "You need to bring him here for his own good," Overlain comes up to the crowd seeing him Alex requests. "Overlain go with them and see to it he is brought here." "You want me to travel with him," James asks. "Why yes my big friend it will give the two of you something to find common ground. Who knows you may even like one another," Alex says patting him on the back with a smile. Overlain and James look at one another. "My lord before we go on the task you send us to there is one thing, I need to tell you," Overlain informs. "What is it?" "Your father's sword you must retrieve it. I blessed it, and bathed it in holy water before he went out for battle; its core is silver and will give you a weapon against our enemies." "So that's why it cut the wolf," Kronus says. Overlain points to one of the servants setting him into motion. He brings out arrows with silver tips and weapons against the foes that stand against them. "I took the time last night to fashion weapons for us," Overlain relays. "What do you think Lucien," James asks picking up a big battle axe. "It fits brother," Lucien suggests with a smile. "I and a few others will go to retrieve this book of spells we will meet in the hidden caverns that rest in the foothills before the next full moon," Alex orders. Overlain, James and Lucien with his brother Lushien leave tracking William. They take the weapons needed to defeat those who oppose them. "My lord why didn't you wake me," Elizabeth asks coming from the tent. "You were resting and you looked so peaceful. I saw no cause to wake you love," Alex says before kissing her cheek adding, "You look lovely this morning." Elizabeth and Alex walk down the trail. The sun shines on her face bringing out the beauty of her eyes. "So, what decision did you make my love," she asks him. Alex stops bends down and picks a flower. He places it behind her ear informing, "I see no choice but to retrieve my brother and I have sent men to take care of this task." "What are you going to do?" "I will take some men and go to retrieve this book of spells so Overlain can remove this curse upon man. For to win this war we must set everything as it should be." They walk a little farther their arms locked as are their hearts. "What of me," she asks. "I will leave Darius here with you and loyal guards. They will take you to the hidden caverns and there you will wait for me to return," Alex requests. "No Alex I want to go with you." Alex stops and looks at her informing, "My lady I think it best if you stay here it will be safer for you." Elizabeth kisses his lips and looks at his face. "You may be the one I love and you may have my soul, but I go where I please." Alex knows in her eyes she means what she has said, for the sake of argument he replies, "Yes my lady then we must eat and rest for the day. We will ride out early in the morning." They spend the day by each other's side enjoying a time well spent.

"My lord here is the information brought here by the spies," Devilian says as he hands him a piece of parchment. "I see his numbers match our own. Richard will not be as easy as the others," Edward suggests. "They cannot stand against the beast we become. We will run through them like all others," Devilian confidently says. "We must not get to over confident getting the throne will be easy but we must have a standing army to keep it, if not we will have civil wars for the many years to come." "Tyrolean is there something you could pull out of the book of spells maybe something to give us the finale edge," Edward turns to him asking. "I will see that something is found my lord." "Tell the men to enjoy themselves within one week we will have but one more house to conquer then we will bring the fight to Sir Richard himself and we will see if the lion heart can stand against a wolfs howl," Edward proclaims. The men gathered in the room raise their glass and drink to boast of the day to come.

"Overlain I do not see why my lord finds favor in you," James says rudely as they follow the trail. "Perhaps our young lord is not as closed minded as you my big friend." Overlain's remarks do not fall on the favor of him. "You know it will pain my heart to know how Alex will be down, when he hears the tragic news of your passing," James boasts. Lucien and Lushien ride silent shaking their heads. "My very big friend did you know there are spells that can make a man think of himself as a chicken. Would you care to see?" Lucien bursts into laughing when he hears what is said. With a smile Lushien says, "I can see this journey will be adventurous." The men carry on following the tracks made by William. They follow as if hounds waiting to find where the trail will end. "He stopped here to camp," Lucien informs. They get off their horses and search around. "The hand of York reaches across this land," Overlain says looking at the burnt remains of a once proud house. The men walk through the remains of a noble's home just a shadow of what it once was. "He was not worried about anyone following him he left this behind," Lucien says holding in his hand a piece of clothing. "Bring that to me," Overlain requests. He hands it to him asking, "What are you going to do with this?" "I plan to make our search easier." Overlain wraps the top of his staff with it closes his eyes mumbling a spell then removes the cloth. "What is that going to do Overlain," James smugly inquires. Overlain points his staff in different directions and the crystal at the end of it begins to show the way. "He went that way." James is taken in with the magic in his eyes. "He headed off towards the York owned land. What would he be thinking," Lucien asks. "That I cannot answer but we must be swift before we are discovered," Overlain suggests. They mount their horses and begin to follow the path in front of them.

"My lady I never intended to return or even get caught up in this war. I was happy just being with you," Alex says. They lay on a blanket on the side of the river with no one around but the two of them. "Alex my love, in your heart of hearts you knew you had to return. Brave men needs someone of faith to lead them through the darkness that is this world," she relays with pride for her love. "They need a political man not someone as I." Elizabeth leans in and kisses him suggesting, "Any great leader of men would have said the same." The day moves forward. Alex is content spending it with her what lays ahead weighs nothing on his mind. The men sent out continue to track William and Edward lays out his plans of battle. "My lady Darius will stand in my place to watch over you, I must retrieve something before I lose the light. I will only be gone a short while," Alex assures her. "Yes, my love. I will miss you until you return." Alex kisses her hand then turns requesting, "Jonas come with me please." Jonas and he mount their horses to ride for a fallen home. "What do we seek my lord," Jonas asks along the way. "Jonas, for the thousandth time I am no longer your lord just Alex," Alex relays but his word finds no favor with him. He smiles and adds, "we go to retrieve my father's sword. I buried it with him and I will need it for the days ahead." They ride a short while with the sun beginning to hide its face in the horizon. The day begins to take on the feeling of fall in the air as night begins to move in. "Where did you bury him my lord?" "Under the oak that use to be in the gardens," Alex informs. "I cannot believe they burned this place to ash," Jonas says looking at the remains of the castle. "Yeah it seems what it takes a life time to reach can be laid to waste in hours," Alex dishearten says. They get off their horses and Alex gets his shovel and begins to unearth his father. He digs for a while then pulls the sword from out of the dust saying, "Father if you would please forgive me for disturbing your finale place of rest, but I will need this to carry out what you started." They cover his father once again. Alex lays the sword down on the ground and removes its wrapping. The seal of the red rose carved into the handle shows it beauty. The blade sharpened and glimmers to the eye. "You know Jonas I never wanted to have to wield this sword. I took my place behind my brother this should be in his hands." Jonas walks up and places his hand on his shoulder saying, "My lord I am glad you have returned and in my eyes the sword found its proper place." Alex places the sword in his sheath he watches as the last light of the day fades into darkness. They climb onto their horse and ride for the camp "My lady Alex returns," Darius says. Elizabeth comes from the tent and meets him as he rides into the camp. She waits for him to place his feet upon the ground she wraps her arms and him then kisses his lips. "You were only gone for a few hours," Jonas comments. All the men surrounding them give out a chuckle and Alex shakes his head. "We will see you after dinner," Darius says. "Come love your food is waiting in the tent," Elizabeth requests. Elizabeth grabs his arm and leads him off to the tent. The men gather around a fire waiting to hear what plan is to come. "Did I embarrass you my lord," Elizabeth inquires watching him eat a well-earned meal. "What? A kiss from you could never embarrass me. I longed to have your lips upon mine for every moment of my life," Alex proud says. "Well I wouldn't want you to loss the roughness in the eyes of your men," Elizabeth informs with a smile. They talk and finish their meals. Alex leaves her as the servants bring in the water from the river she washes as he talks with the men. "Darius I will leave you to guard Elizabeth, it will not be an easy task her anger will be great when she sees I have gone. You must take her and the remaining men and hide in the foothills until we return," Alex orders. "Where do you go my lord," Darius asks. "I will take Jayel, Kronus and Jonas with me. I will go and retrieve the book that Overlain needs so that the nature of this world will be as it should." "You will need the speed of my sword," Darius suggests. "My brother I need you to protect the thing that means the most to me, against anything that would harm her," Alex looks him in the eyes and he finds the importance in his task. "Then as you command my lord," Darius states. "Alex, Darius please, it's just Alex, there is no more my lord," Alex pleads with no avail then shakes his head adding, "Lucas will stay with you to help move the people to the foothills." With the men given their tasks Alex returns to the tent. She sits naked washing her body from the day. He sits behind her taking the cloth from her hand, washes her back down to the top of her ass. His hands find her breasts as he kisses her neck. She leans her head upon his shoulder. His hands roam her body. He places them between her legs as he brings her passion with his touch. "Your hands are like a burning flame upon my skin. You bring the pleasure in me," she pants. Her pleasure is reached and she turns towards him. She pulls at his clothes, undresses him to return the favor. She takes the cloth from his hand. Her hands wash his body flowing over every place there is to touch. He lays back and she climbs upon him sliding him inside of her. She digs her nails into his chest nothing to hurt but for a spark to his skin, picks up her pace as her passions builds getting drunk off the feeling of him inside of her. Alex raises and rolls her to her back driving into her as her passionate moans echo in the night. His pace is fast taking all the energy she has to give. She falls into slumber resting in his arms. The night grows long and he takes a moment to look upon her knowing he goes to face the evil in men. Alex slips out of the tent with Elizabeth sleeping resting with the sweetest dreams playing inside her head. "Are you sure you have the strength to ride my lord," Jayel asks him with a smile upon his face. "My brothers in arms, we have a smart ass in our mists," Alex replies bringing a hardy laugh from the men. Alex sets his horse in motion. The others follow in his steps. Alex passing Darius pauses for a minute saying, "I leave her in your care my brother I." "Do not worry my lord I will give the last breathe in my body so that she will be here when you return." Alex pats him on his shoulder and rides out to catch up with the rest of the men. They ride fast and hard putting much distance from the camp for Alex knows she will try to follow.

James sits around the fire with his companions. "Overlain tell me how you came to be," James asks as he puts an edge on his axe. "We were just like any other children of this world, until a Wiseman blessed us with the power we hold inside, but with everything that is power it can be corrupting and it did to my brother. He thought we should rule people with the magic. I felt it should be used to heal and guide men along and if I would have had the strength in me. We would not find ourselves in this world as it is, but I couldn't kill my brother," Overlain relays. "You can leave that to me," James says with a smile then pulls his shirt down revealing a scar adding, "I owe him one." "It is a hard thing to realize that the world would be better without someone you have loved in a past time," Overlain states making marks in the sand with the end of his staff. The men talk until they find their slumber and bonds start to build.

The sun warms the earth and Elizabeth wakes she reaches for him but her arms find nothing. She reaches for her cloths, dresses and goes outside of the tent. "My lady mite you be hungry this morning," Darius asks stirring a pot over a flame. "Where is Alex," she asks of him with a worried tongue. "He left in the night. He placed me to watch over you." She rushes going for her horse and begins to saddle it. Darius walks up taking the reins of the horse informing, "My lady they have the whole night in front of you. There is no way you will catch them." She looks out over the land her heart longs to be with him and her tears fall from her eyes. "My lady he will return with time," Darius assures her. "What if he dies and I could never see him again? My heart could not bear this burden," the horror of her words fills her essences. "My lady. Alex is wise and fierce in battle. He will return I promise you," Darius states placing a hand on her shoulder. She runs from her horse and back inside the tent, sits holding a shirt with his scent in her nose. Darius walks over to the men gathered ordering, "Gather what you can. We leave for the hills as soon as we can."

"Alex how do you think we will be able to get inside the castle without being noticed," Kronus asks along their journey. "I cannot say but I am sure there will be something to present itself." "What of your brother do you think they will be able to fetch him back," Jonas inquires. "You are all full of questions this morning, are you not," Alex says smugly before riding out a little farther from them. "Did I over step my place," Jonas asks to Kronus. "No, he is just down about leaving her behind, and his brother will make his fate his own." They ride on as the day grows long.

William rides into a town along his way. He looks around at the people in the town his face is not known to them. "Is there a place I could stay for the night," he asks a town person as he passes him. "Down at the end of this path. There is a place that will keep you," he answers. He kicks his horse and rides to the end. He climbs off and walks inside, with his entry, the people inside drink and talk among each other. "The man down the road says you might have a room," William relays to the end keep. "We have a hut behind this place." He tells him the price. "That is a little much," William suggests. "Well tell it Lord York his taxes are heavy," the end keep informs. The man looks at him inquiring, "Do you want the hut or not?" William places the money on the table. A servant takes him to the place out back. The servant does not speak until they reach the hut. "My daughter will be here by sunset with food." He walks from the place, and back to the tasks his has to perform. William puts his things on the table and washes his face with the water inside the bowl on the counter.

"Overlain are you sure what we follow is correct," asks Lucien along the path adding, "This path he takes leads to the land of the noble Letin. He and York have been long since in league with one another," "I trust in the crystal we are on the right path," Overlain assures. "The sun grows long and we will not pass water tomorrow. We will camp here tonight," Lucien says staring down at the stream. They climb from their horses and begin to make the camp for the night.

"My lady I know your heart is heavy, but we must go," Darius says from outside the tent. Elizabeth comes from the tent her eyes red from crying saying, "You are right. I behave like a school girl over this. I will trust in the lord for the return of him." She walks over to her horse. Darius helps her and he climbs upon his. The personal soldiers of her ride out with them. The servants stay to pack up the last of the things in the camp. Darien with Lucas remains like a watchful eye making sure no harm would come to them. "My lady he will return to us," Darius assures riding beside her. "I know. I was more upset that he would leave me behind," Elizabeth says with pride in her womanhood. "My lady the battlefield is no place for such a delicate thing," Darius relays with a little cockiness. "So, what you are trying to tell me is woman cannot be a warrior too," Elizabeth asks with a smug tone. Darius doesn't answer. Elizabeth pulls up on her reins her horse comes to a stop. His disbelieve stirs her anger once more. "Get off that animal soldier," Elizabeth demands. "Is this going to turn into some kind of argument," Darius inquires adding, "I mean no disrespect to your womanhood it's just the strength of your arm I would question." His words strike at her and with his arrogance before her she asks, "Do you shoot a bow soldier of Lancaster?" "My bow has no match" Darius proudly informs. "Climb from that horse and I will make you eat those words." The soldiers around them taking all this in begin to wager among themselves. "My lady, please do not take what I say personally," Darius implores with a smile. Elizabeth takes a ribbon from her hair she walks out forty paces and ties it to a tree making it into an x on its base. She turns and walks back to where they stand. "The closet to the x," she informs before walking back to one of her handmaids. She gathers her bow from her maiden's horse. "My lady I see no point of this. We should be moving not proving my point." "The point is I will make you eat those words," Elizabeth informs. He feels pride swell inside. Elizabeth stands her ground waiting for him. "Okay my lady if you wish." He places an arrow upon his string a breeze blows lightly across the landscape, the clouds wash over the face of the sun. Darius picks the target out in his eyes, relaxes and lets his arrow fly. "You cannot top that," his arrogance riles her again with the arrow placed dead in the center of the x. The men boast of the flight of the arrow. "Carissa do you care to wager a beat," she asks her handmaid. Carissa smiles looks at the men saying, "Which one of you brave men care to put your money wear your mouth is?" The men gather their money letting their pride talk. "My lady, are you sure the strength of your bow can reach such lengths," Darius asks in a humored manner. Elizabeth raises her bow takes the arrow in her eyes, she relaxes and fires, the arrow flies true and split's the arrow he fired. "Can you top that," she asks him. The men sit back in their saddles her maid collects their money and Elizabeth mounts her horse saying with a well-deserved smile, "Are we going to stay here and look at it or move on?" She rides out front and her personal guards ride off with her. Darius stands looking out at the arrow. The captain of the guards stops by his side. "I guess she showed me," Darius relays. The captain gives a hardy laugh before Darius climbs on his horse with his pride not so full. "It happens sometimes," the captain says. Darius shakes his head and they ride off to catch them. With the speed of their horses Darius takes his place at her side informing, "My lady your eyes are not only beautiful but sharp as well!" Elizabeth smiles towards his words. "Who taught you to shoot like that?" "My grandfather, Elizabeth says proudly adding, "I think he wanted a grandson but he got me instead. He also taught me how to use a sword. Would you care to give that a try?" "No, my lady. I think you have embarrassed me enough this day." She laughs and they ride towards the foothills.

Alex looks out over the land they can see riders crossing the plain. "Who do you think those men are my lord," Jayel asks as they sit on their horses looking down. "I do not know but I think we may have just found a way to get into the York castle if my guess is right, they are reinforcements to the York army," Alex suggests. "How do you want to play this," Kronus asks. "Let's ride up and ask them if we can join," Alex says with boldness. On their way Kronus suggests, "My lord cover your face the rest of us can blend in but there may be someone there who would know you as a Lancaster." Alex pulls a scarf over his face before making it to where the soldiers are gathered arrived Jayel asks, "My good men where are you off too." "We go to the army of York our noble sends what he requests," a soldier answers staring over to Alex with his face well hidden. "Do you think he can use some more good men we are strangers to this place and soldiers for hirer," Kronus relays. "Come with us we will see. We ride for the lake in the base of the hills we will meet the others there." "You haven't been seen by the men you meet," Jayel inquires. "No York has called numbers from all who follow." "Jonas, did you hear, they haven't seen them yet." "Why would that matter," the soldier asks. "Nothing I was just wondering." Alex moves with speed drives the dagger into his neck. The others with him are over taken by his loyal men. They pull the shirts from their bodies baring the mark of their noble. "This should get us into the castle," Alex assures. "My lord this noble's house knows your face," Kronus relays. "I believe you may be correct. I will figure something out." "You better find something pretty quickly more riders' approach." They look out ahead riders come from across the land. Alex wraps his face again. "We will tell them I was wounded in battle and my face is scared this scarf hides the grueling sight of it." "We should have thought of this long ago my stomach is easier already," Kronus informs bringing a laugh to the men. "You know with friends like you I wonder why I stay," Alex states securing his wrap. The soldiers riding over the landscape wave them over Alex and his men ride over to them falling in with their ranks time slips forward. "The soldiers from the house of Keller are here," a soldier informs Titus seeing them coming over the horizon. "Good then every house is here, Lord Edward will be pleased," Titus says. Alex and the men stay in the back to stay hidden among the other soldiers.

William sits inside of the hut and a knock comes on his door. "Yes enter." "Sir here is your meal for the night," a peasant girl says before placing the food on the table. "Girl why is the towns' people so uneasy?" "Lord Edward has seized this land and strange things are seen in the night," she informs before remembering the light fades fast. She hurries from the hut making sure she is inside when the curtain of night takes hold. Everyone finds their places in the world.

The sun rises upon another day. Alex and his faithful ride towards the castle. "Why does he cover his face," a soldier asks Kronus riding with them in their formation. Jonas speaks up informing, "He is my brother. He was wounded in battle by a sword, it cut off the base of his nose and his lips knocking out his teeth, he has a hell of a time keeping out the maggots and bugs. Would you like to see?" The soldier gets a grime look on his face and rides off. "Well played Jonas," Alex relays. "Well I really didn't lie you are my brother in arms and ugly to boot," Jonas says with a smile. Alex shakes his head they ride on. "So, tell me my lord how does someone like you end up with such a woman of beauty," Jonas asks in a picking way. "It must be my charm and well manners," Alex resorts. The men laugh and keep moving with the others.

William walks out of the hut smelling the aroma of cooking from inside. He goes for his morning meal. He steps in and soldiers of York are there eating what they desire. "Who are you? I have not seen your face here before," a soldier requests seeing him enter the inn. "I am but a traveler along this path. I just came in for the meal then I will be one my way," William replies. "There is a tax to travel these roads," the soldier relays with a smirk. "How much will it cost me to travel," William inquires. "Let's say four tavels," the soldier relays. William places the coins on the table; he quickly snatches it up saying, "You may carry on." William sits down at a table and begins his meal. The soldiers in the stable discover the Lancaster flag rolled in his pack. "Look here it is the flag of the house of Lancaster," one announces. "Go and find out who would carry this," a Sargent in the York army orders. The soldiers go and search the town. They toll up and down the streets. "I have a better idea," one of the soldiers says adding, "Come on we will wait in the stables to see who this belongs too." William eats, finished,

he walks outside then gathers his things from his place of rest. He walks to
the stables and up to his horse, places the saddle upon its back, and reaches
for his saddle bags. The top lays open and he looks for the flag. "Are you
missing something," he hears a voice ask. He turns to go for his sword but
the men over run him. One punches him on the side of his head knocking
him to the ground. The others kick him for good measure. They pull him
to his feet the blood drips from his face to the ground. "William Lancaster,
the last time in saw you we were burning down your castle," the Sargent
reminds. William struggles to get free but his efforts gain him nothing, they
bind him in the cage pulled by horses. "We will take him to Lord Edward,"
the Sargent states. William looks out of his cage as he passes the girl who
brought him dinner. Her eyes quickly turn away with the others in the town
quickly making it off the street.

Overlain and the men find their way to the town. "I will go and check in
the stables to see if his horse is still here," Lucien says with Lushien following
behind him. Overlain and James make their way to a tavern walking inside
they feel the eyes upon them as they take their seats. Moments pass before
Lucien and Lushien join them. Seated Lushien informs, "His horse is not
in the stables." "You bar keep did a stranger come through here," James
inquires. "We have people pass through here all the time. I cannot keep
up with everyone who comes in here," the bar keep quickly informs. "Well
then how about a bottle then," Lucien requests. He walks over and places
a bottle on their table. James pours the glasses full toasting, "To Alex." "To
Alex," the group says before gulping down their drinks. "Come let's see if
we can find which way he went," Overlain suggests. They walk through the
doors and into the street. The girl who brought his dinner stands by a pole
when they pass, she informs, "The man you are looking for was taken by
soldiers and they dropped this." She hands them the flag stained with his
blood before quickly turning to walk away. "Do you know where they are
to take him," Overlain asks with her walking away. She turns her head in
her steps answering, "They said to the castle of York." James flips the girl a
coin, she catches it, then quickly moves on with James saying, "Thank you
for your help." They get on their horses and follow the road that leads into
the heart of their foes land.

"Darius do you think you could have the soldiers bring up some water
I would like to bath from this day," Elizabeth asks knocking the dust from

her. She stands in front the mouth of a cave her home for now. She leans on the stone and her mind drifts to Alex her heart longs to hold him. The men bring the water and place it inside. Darius stands like a stone in the caves entrance, guarding against anyone who might view her naked. "My lady Alex is okay. I know it in my heart he will be here to hold you again," Darius assures as his back is turned to the beauty of her. "Alex should be proud to have a faithful friend as you. Am I that transparent," Elizabeth asks running the cloth over her body. "No, my lady. I worry for his return too for I have seen the beast that men fear," Darius states.

"What are we to do? We cannot rescue him from the castle of our enemies," Lucien says as they follow the path of William. "We will find away too do what Alex requested of us," James relays with a stern voice. "There is always away to do what we must," Overlain says with assuredness. The men follow the path before them.

Elizabeth baths then dresses. "Darius, I think I will sleep now if there is something you need to take care of," she says walking up from behind him. "No, my lady. I have but one task until the return of my lord," Darius states in his sworn duties. She places the blanket on the floor, covers herself, her thoughts lay with Alex to where ever he may be, her heart feels the sadness and her skin is cold against the night's air missing the warm of his body, tears fall from her eyes as she slips into slumber.

The dawn breaks and the men saddle their horses. "You men form a line so that when we arrive at the castle, we appear uniformed in front of our lord York," a rider rides through announcing to all. "Come let's get somewhere in the middle so we are not easily seen," Alex suggests with the rider moving on. They fall in and keep themselves hide and the unit rides together slowly for the York castle.

"Why don't the three of you wait on the outskirts of the castle, wait then hide in the township. I will see if I can find him and then we can make a plan of rescue," Overlain suggests. They look upon the castle placed on high hill; people move about the township getting ready for the soldiers to arrive. "They will see you and think of you as your brother," James says. Overlain waves his hand in front of his face his appearance changes before them informing, "Not likely my big friend." They split. James, Lucien and Lushien ride for the out skirts of town. Overlain pulls up his hood and rides for the castle. Overlain makes his way to the gate passes by guards standing their posts with one ordering, "Halt what is your business here?" "I am but an old traveler along this land. I come to celebrate our new king's victory," Overlain swiftly informs. "Come down from that horse." Overlain slowly comes down from his horse. The guards check everywhere they can. "What are you men doing," Duncan rides up and asks. "We are checking to make sure he has no weapons," the guard relays. "I think this army can handle a simple old man now get back to your posts before Lord Edward sees you," Duncan orders, the men hurry back to the gate he turns to Overlain saying, "On your way old man." "Thank you, my lord," Overlain bows his head saying then pulls his horse by the reins and walks to the stables. The castle is dressed for the big affair. Soldiers move inside the castle's perimeter they walk with loose woman celebrating the day. "My lord the noble's troops are arriving," Damien relays. Edward walks out onto the balcony watching as the soldiers come from over the hill. "They are about the numbers we expected," Damien informs. "You see we didn't have to destroy all the nobles just enough to let what we can do be known," Edward informs with a devilish smile, standing like a grand statue perched on the balcony as the soldier enter the gates of the castle. They form the lines for him to see and they sound off with a mighty salute. "Welcome men of fallen nobles, though we may have been enemies on the field of battle. I now welcome you to the house of York as brothers of my flag," Edward announces. The men give another salute as their voices carry, he announces again, "Our differences laid aside we all go out to put a king upon the throne and bring order back to this great land! Make love to the woman of the castle, eat be merry, for in two days this force will set out to conquer one more noble and then Richard the lion heart!" A might shout is given to praise this would be king, he turns and walks back inside the castle. The men wait for him to leave then they break the formation. Alex and his men blend into the city they walk until they find a quiet corner. "Jonas, Kronus, Jayel make your way into their mists. I will try to figure out where Tyrolean would keep this book, if you are asked you share no allegiance to me." "My lord I should stay by your side," Kronus implores. "It's Alex remember, he shakes his head to their blank stares adding, "We will be better served to be part now do as I asked," Alex relays again. They break from the corner each going their own way. "Lord Edward. I think I may have someone you will wish to see," the Sargent relays standing before him upon the throne. The soldiers bring William in with his feet and hands bearing chains. "Lord Edward, see who we brought to your feet," the Sargent announces." Edward stands up from his throne saying, "William Lancaster I see you survived." "Yes, sir York. I did, I have no more family and no noble name I can do nothing against you I am but a humble man," William implores. "What should we do with him my lord," Damien eager to place his hands on him asks. Edward walks up to him looks at the mark upon him then flashes of the battle reenter his mind. Edward remembers the mark he himself placed upon him turning away he orders, "Take him to the dungeon I will see to him later!" The men pull him from the room and take him into the dungeons. Overlain in his hidden form watches from the back of the room. He turns to walk out and bumps into someone. "Watch where you are going old man," Tyrolean says. "Sorry please forgive an old man," Overlain replies back trying to hurry away. "Do I know you, old man," Tyrolean inquires with a feeling from long ago. "No, my lord, I am but a simple beggar trying to get warm please forgive an old man's ignorance," Overlain bows his head and goes his way. Tyrolean walks into the throne room. "My lord," Tyrolean bows his head before him. "Have you found something to give use a better edge," Edward of him. "Yes, my lord I have. We will use this potion I have been working on to strengthen the shields and to sharpen the swords we wield. If that is not enough. I have found the spell we need to raise an army from the mostly dead." "Explain that to me," Edward asks with great wanting. "Long ago legend has it a fierce band of men rode out into the sun conquering anyone and everything in their path, they were tricked by a sorcerer like me and their life force was taken from them but they did not die as mortal men. They lay trapped between this world and the next," Tyrolean explains "An army of the mostly dead," Edward says letting a smile come over his face adding, "You have done well my old friend now join us for the feast!" "We must find a certain cross before I could release them from the place they rest," Tyrolean reveals. "I will send out soldiers on a quest to retrieve this cross," Edward informs stepping from the throne. "Send them to me and I will inform them where to find it," Tyrolean suggests as they walk to the table in the great room to eat and talk of the days to come. William sits with his hatred of the place he finds himself. A once proud noble man, now in the keep of an enemy. Alex wonders about the castle listening to what he can catch. A soldier stops a young maiden inside of the hall with Alex a hidden witness. "My pretty young lady, why not stop and celebrate the day with me," The soldier requests lusting for her. She can see the look in his eyes quickly she informs, "Lord Tyrolean demands this to be brought to his stay and I cannot let this leave my hand or I will suffer his wrath," she implores. "You could let it rest for a few moments we could watch over it together," resorts the soldier. "If you do not let me pass, I will have no choice in telling him what delayed me," she coldly replies. The soldier releases her arm she walks on her way. Alex waits then follows her path. He watches her until she goes into Tyrolean's place of stay. Alex hides and waits until she leaves then enters the room. "Tyrolean, I was wondering what would happen if someone were to drink my blood from the cup," Edward asks while they dine. "You were the first and it would give them the power in your veins," Tyrolean informs. "So, they will not be as the others? Mindless beast at the sight of the full moon?" "No, my lord. They will have the ability as you to change at will with the power of the medallion to keep the beast's heart at bay as long as they drink from the cup that is what makes the difference." "Go and bring me the cup." "As you command my lord," Tyrolean says then leaves the room going to retrieve the cup as Edward requested. Alex searches around the room with no idea of what it will look like, pulls books from off a table and resting on a shelf, passing by a chest resting on the floor with the lid closed its contents become a mystery with his hands resting on each side of the lid, the crystal he wears on his neck, a gift from Overlain begins to burn his skin. He pulls it from his skin and backs up rubbing his chest the light grows dim and as he approaches the chest it begins to burn bright again. Alex opens the lid and what he seeks is inside. He grabs the book and the burning light goes away. He slips the book under the cloak he wears, slips back out of the castle into the small city inside. Overlain sees him from afar even with his face covered he knows his walk. Moving towards him soldiers pass by ready to stop Alex in his tracks. Overlain intervenes saying, "Would you happen to have spare change that an old man might eat this war has taken much from me," Overlain mumbles a spell causing a great stench to rise from him. "Good God old man you stink," the soldiers back off saying "Please just a tavel or two so an old man might wash himself," Overlain begs. The soldiers push him away knocking him to the ground they smell their hands in doing they forget about Alex and he pass on. Alex reaches into his cloak for change and hands it to him, then helps him from the ground standing before him he sees a familiar face. "Overlain what you doing here at the castle," Alex strongly inquires. "Your brother is here in the dungeons." "Do they know who they have?" "Yes, my lord," Overlain answers. "Then I must go to rescue him." "My lord would he do the same for you," Overlain reminds. "I cannot answer what is in a man's heart only mine, Alex relays adding, "Here take this and leave the city go back to the foothills." Alex pulls the book from his cloak and hands it too him, "The others wait at the outskirts of town take James and the others with you. I will find my way back with Lucien and the others." "The men will not want to return without you my lord," Overlain states. "Getting this book away from here so that you might have the time to take this madness from the world is the first priority! Tell the men I ordered them to flee with you, they must guard the book," Alex says before trying to move away. Overlain grabs his arm imploring, "Lord Alex please rethink what you are doing your brother would leave you to the mercy of your enemies! He is as drunk with power as Edward himself." "Careful old man, we have had a difference in life but he is still my brother. I will not leave him to this fate now take the book and set everything right, if I we do not return and the war seems lost, use the spell to make things even. The men who call me lord would be worthy of this task. Tell Elizabeth I love her if I do not return and I will be sorry I can never hold her again but if I do not free him then I would not be the man she loves." Overlain does as he is asked taking the book from out of the city. Alex slips through the streets going for the dungeon. Tyrolean walks into his room unknown to him the master book has been taken. He removes the cup from where it is kept and walks back out of the room. He passes through the castle, soldiers stand their guard, he walks until he reaches the throne room. Entering he informs, "My lord here is what you request." Edward takes it from his hand turns saying, "Damien go and be among the soldiers build up their confidence for the battle ahead." "Where do you go my lord," Tyrolean requests seeing him rise from the throne. "I go to make an old foe a friend," Edward relays with a grin leaves the room walks down through the castle, men snap to attention as he passes them by. Alex slips and watches through the opening above he almost speaks to his brother below but Edward walks into the cell with him. "Sir Lancaster," Edward says entering the cell. "Stand to your feet," a guard instructs him. "What is your name soldier?" He snaps to attention and tells him. Edward back hands him and knocks him to the floor ordering, "Now stand up and leave him too me!" The soldier walks out of the room with his pride handed to him. "Sir William, I am sorry for your treatment," Edward states. "There is no sir. I have no noble home, your army took care of that," William sadly relays. "William, we have been at ends all of these years your family and I had the same claim to the throne what I did was just in the eyes of war." William looks at him with the truth setting in his heart, for the wars had gone on for years. "I gave your father a chance to join me with his noble name in place. He left me no choice. If you had the advantage of me would you have not done the same? You were there did I not ride out under a flag of peace you and your family are fierce warriors and your father died with honor," Edward proudly claims. "Why do you tell me this I am but a fallen foe," William looks up to him saying then adds, "Now I implore you to give me a noble man's death and send me to join my father." "I come to offer you a deal," Lord York informs. "What kind of a deal?" Alex heart breaks for his brother seeing them as they talk. "I will restore your noble name and give you the land that goes with it. I will need battle lords such as you with a respected name to hold the throne when I achieve it. You support me in the laws I lay down and perhaps one day your child my lay a claim to the throne after all I will not live forever even as I am." William's greed for the throne and the power of a noble's name set in. Edward seeing him leaning to the deal adds, "Please do not make the same mistake as your father." "What must I do to be granted this deal?" "Just a small token of faith," Edward suggests before slicing his hand then lets the blood flow into the cup and the cut closes by itself before William's eyes. "Just drink and we can be brothers let my blood flow in you and take back your noble name." "Brothers huh? The last man that called me that took the woman I was promised into his bed and stole what army I had left." Edward sits down beside him on the bench. "Do not do this my brother he is evil at heart," Alex's soul screams. "So be it," William declares then drinks the fill of the cup. "Come my new found brother let us feast and prepare for the days ahead," Edward proclaims embracing him. Alex rolls over and looks towards the heavens in disbelief of what his ears have heard and his eyes have seen. He stands and walks back into the darkness his heart heavy from the last minutes he has lived. "I cannot believe he would side with him this is my fault. I took her from him I should have left before I let my feeling take hold." Alex thinks as he wonders through the city. His soul hurts from the choice of his brother. He walks on but begins to find comfort recalling her skin against his with the warmth of her eyes. Edward treats his new brother with the finer things of the world a noble man's clothing would be place on his back. "Come William take a bath and let the servant girls wash you their services are most enlightening," Edward boasts with a well written grin. William smiles looking at their beauty. Edward leaves him to the care of his maids. "My lord why would you keep him around he was an enemy now you make him part of us," Duncan asks when Edward makes it to a hallway in the castle. "Who runs this castle you or I," Edward asks in a displeased manner. Duncan bows his head assuring, "You my lord!" "Then bare that in mind before you question me again," A growl slips out from under his breath with the beast trying to get out. "Sorry my lord I beg your forgiveness," Duncan requests. Edward leaves from him. William indulges in the pleasure of the woman, turned on by the power in his veins, he takes them, bring pleasure to each. The other servants come in and dry his body. He dresses and goes into the great hall. "William, come in take a seat at the table of York," Edward requests. The others gathered at the table stand in respect to his given name. "I see you are in a better state than the last time I saw you," Edward laughs and pats him on the back saying. "I don't know what it is maybe it is my name restored or the feel of a good woman but I feel great like I could do anything," William states. "Eat fill yourself you must be hungry from a good night's work!" The men of York keep mostly with each other noticing it Edward inquires "Is there a reason to exclude my guest from this table?" The men keep silent. Edward rises from the table slams his fist upon the table like a hammer drives upon a nail informing, "He is a brother in this house and he will be treated so he has the same right as you in the house of York!" With his words resting in their ears he requests, "Come, William, Jayland and walk with me for a while." The men gathered at the table rise and bow their heads as they leave the room. Edward speaks with them as they roam through the castle.

With the men who shared in the journey with him making their way back with the book in hand. "I still don't think we should have left him we need to go back," James states with a worried tone stopping his horse in its tracks looks over his shoulder back towards the way they came seeing his motion to return Overlain reminds, "No, Alex commanded us to bring the book back to the foothills without it there will be no way to win this war!"

Overlain can see the look of his eye. The worrying grips hold of his emotions he moves back towards the way to the castle. Snapping him back Overlain says, "James." "What," James angered turns and replies. "We must do as he commanded. I worry for him too! Now come, we need to keep moving it is what he wished," Overlain stresses. James does as a loyal soldier should letting go of his worries and fears. He turns back they ride for home as fast as the horses will carry them.

Alex walks in the night to find those who were with him, asking those he passes if they had seen the ones he seeks. Finding where they have been waiting, he enters the door, seeing who is there he asks, "Jonas, Jayel, where is Kronus?" "He should be returning shortly." They leave the room gathering their horses Lucas says as he points in his direction, "There he is my lord." Alex turns and sees him coming when he reaches them, he informs, "Come, we leave for home." "Where is the book we came for," Jonas inquires." "I gave it too Overlain. They ride for the hills and we must do the same." "Then William is here," Kronus asks. Alex does not answer just pulls himself into his saddle. "Alex if he is here, we should rescue him," Jayel suggests. Alex looks back at the castle and says, "My brother is a lost cause he has made a deal with the devil." Alex kicks his horse into motion. The others look at each other and follow his lead. They stop just short of the gate seeing no guards Alex suggests, "Okay go for the gate I cannot see any guards." They slip through the gate but Kirkland follows slipping in the form of the wolf his jaws drip of the taste that will come. "What did you mean my lord when you said he had made a deal with the devil," Jonas asks as they ride across the landscape with the castle growing smaller behind them. "I slipped to the cell which held my brother. Edward came in and gave him back the noble house of my father if he would side with him." "He may have only taken the deal to get out of the situation he was in," Jonas suggests. Alex looks at him informing, "He drank the blood that flows in his veins. My brother's lust for power brought him to this. The only way to save him from what he will become is for Overlain to use the book we now have and release this curse from the face of the world." The horses become uneasy with their speech and begin to stomp their feet and buck. "Easy now what is it boy, "Alex says petting his horse's neck as they sense the wolf close, hearing the heartbeat of the beast that waits. Kirkland stands watching and waiting his eyes lust for the meal ahead his claws stand ready to tear the flesh from their bones. "Something has them uneasy my lord," Kronus states drawing his weapon. They wait and listen to the sounds around them. Their hearts beat for what may lay ahead. Their hands stand ready to pull their swords from their sheaths. Alex sees a flash and falls to the ground his horse runs from its fears, the wolf pounces and strikes at Kronus spilling his blood across the earth. The wolf spins as Alex regains his feet. "Watch out my lord," Jonas screams. Alex pulls his father's sword from its sheath. The wolf lunges forward the dust from the ground stirs into the air with his mighty legs pushing off the ground. His mouth hangs open his teeth shine bright. Kirkland works his claws to stir fear in their hearts. Alex's heart pounds his eyes amazed at the look of the beast that stands before him. He now beholds clearly the beast men fear. Kirkland gives out a devilish growl. Jayel shoots an arrow from his string striking the beast in the back and for the first time the animal feels fear with the sting of the silver piercing its skin. The wolf spins and lunges at him. He falls to the ground and the beast savors the fear as his eyes standing ready for the next world. Alex runs and with a mighty swing cuts off its arm and the wolf howls with pain. The next strike removes his head from its body and the beast lays died. Alex rushes getting him to his feet backing from it. Jonas yells in amazement, "My lord look!" Kirkland takes back his human form his body lay naked with his head apart. "Kronus," Alex yells with running over to kneel at his side. "My lord the wound is deep," Kronus suggests trying to hold his blood back. "Just rest easy," Alex says to keep his mind steady. "Bring me some bandages and some water and the whiskey!" Jonas brings it too him. "Hold still my old friend this is going to hurt," Alex states washing the dirt from the wound pouring the whiskey upon it. Kronus shifts and moves his body but he holds in the pain. In his weaken state he requests, "My lord leave me. I will only slow you down. The beast has taken me." "I will do no such a thing," Alex informs before calling his horse. With its return they build a rack for the horse to pull; placing him upon it with Alex relaying, "Come we need to get moving or our brother will not stand a chance!" They climb up on their horses and start the journey for the foothills.

A Brother is Born

Chapter Four

A Brother is Born

EDWARD, WILLIAM AND JAYLAND WALK THROUGH THE city within the castle's territory. "My lord is there something you wish to show me out here," William asks. "Yes. Now that you bring it up," Edward relays with a slow drawn smile. "What do you wish to show me," William asks with the servants bringing out their horses. "Come ride and I will show you." William unsure of what lay ahead gets upon his horse. "No need in fear William. You are my brother from this day forward," Edward says. They ride out into the darkness and across the stretch of the land. The moon burns bright in the curtain of night they move over the earth until they reach a farmhouse. "What are we doing here my lord," curious William asks. "Come and I will show you." They climb off the horses and slip up to the outskirts and stand in the woods to watch. "Tell me William has the hunger stayed with you," Edward asks from out of the darkness. "Yes, it has I cannot get my fill," William feeling the pull of the wolf states. They stalk as the family stands around the fire. The children play like normal with their parents' enjoying the warmth of the flames relaxing in the peace of night. "Just look out at them! Does the hunger grow? Listen to the sound of their hearts beating and the blood that flows in their veins," Edward suggests taunting the wolf within. William listens and the lust begins to build, his eyes burn and he can see the warmth of their bodies and the blood flowing within them. The fire inside begins to burn and he turns to see them in wolf form as he begins to change himself. His body pops, not use to the change,

86

he cries in pain as the wolf begins to take form. "What was that," his wife faintly hearing the cry asks. "Shoosh," he tells his children. They become quite the night echoes its silence as he leans an ear to the night. He stands and walks a small distance away from the fire. The wolves in full form slip upon them in the night, like sheep in the pasture. "I don't hear anything now," he says turning back to his wife her screams echo as she sees the horror before her eyes. Edward strikes and rips at his throat. Jayland leaps in and pulls away his wife as she kicks and screams into the night. The sounds of her body ripping and breaking fall upon the children's ears. William leaps out in front of the children savoring the meal to fill his soul. The children's screams fall upon the ears of the forest as he strikes feeding upon their bodies and is baptized unto the pack. They howl together the strange howl echoes over the land. Alex and the rest can hear their cries scream into the night. They pull up on their reins and pull their swords as the wolf howl travels into the deadness of night. They wait with the fear of the unknown. Jonas looks down at Kronus lying in the rack. "My lord, do you think he will make it?" "Not if we do not make to the foothills in time, his will is keeping him with us now," Alex sheaths his sword then kicks the horse back into motion. Their pace quickens and they ride through the night.

Dawn comes upon another day. William wakes in the forest. He can remember the night with the beast controlling him, his brothers' wake with him. "Here cover up with this," Edward requests throwing a cloak to him. "What was that last night," clouded William inquires. "That was the gift I gave to you. Do you remember the power the fear in their eyes the knowing that nothing can stop you," Edward asks with pleasure? William relives the night and he finds lust in the power. "Come on my brother we will return to the castle." "Lord Edward how mite. I control this power," William asks. Edward reaches in and pulls out a medallion hands it to him informing, "Place this next to your skin and it will give you the power over the beast. It was forged from the silver paid to the one who betrayed he who was sent here for us." William places it around his neck, content in the thing he can become.

"My lady riders are coming," Darius walks in saying. She rushes from the cave her heart hoping he will be there. "Overlain, James, Lucien, Lushien it is great to see you," Darius informs as they ride up and stop. Elizabeth looks and her heart is heavy. "Do you have word from Alex," she asks with hope in her voice. "Yes, my lady. I seen him inside of the castle he gave me this," Overlain places the book into Darius hands. "I told him his brother was prisoner inside the castle and he went to free him," Overlain adds climbing from his horse. "You left him there," Elizabeth says with anger upon her lips. "Not by the choice of ours. He gave us orders to make sure the book was brought here," James readily informs. Elizabeth holds her anger inside knowing they did what they had to do, she turns and leaves them to themselves. "She is not pleased," Darius says as the men begin to unpack their gear. Elizabeth walks inside of the cave she changes and puts on a pair of pants, digs out her sword and places her bow on her back grabs the arrows with the tips of silver puts them along with the others inside of her quiver. With a warrior's gear resting over her skin, her maiden asks, "My lady what do you plan to do? "Go and have the servants saddle my horse," she orders. "But my lady," the maiden says before Elizabeth cuts her off saying again, "go and do as I have requested!" "As you wish my lady," the maiden says before going to have the servants saddle her horse.

Alex sits in the saddle. The new day wakes him as he sits on the horse, having pressed on in the night. He turns to look at Kronus and then reaches for Jonas. "Wake up," he says as he lightly touches his arm. The sounds wake up Jayel dragging a little behind. "Jayel are you still alive back there?" Jayel blinks his eyes waking from his slumber. "My lord we have pushed these animals far if we do not stop and give them rest, we are going to kill them," Jonas says. Alex looks down at his horse and the others the sweat pours from their bodies though inside he wants to keep moving he knows what he says to be true. "We will stop by the creek and rest the animals." They pull up on the reins. Stopped they unpack the horses and pull Kronus under the shade. "Look my lord his wounds heal fast," Jonas says as he peels back the bandage. Alex says nothing for he knows what is inside. He walks down to the creek splashes water on his face begins to wash the night from his arms. The cool breeze and the sound of the water takes him back to when he held her in the water of the fall, and his heart longs for her.

Edward and his pack walk into the castle. William being born into them finds his place inside with the other members of Edward's minions. "My lord we cannot find Kirkland! He was not at his post when the men gathered this morning," a soldier comes in to inform. "It is unlike Kirkland not to inspect the men in their morning formations go and search for him,"

Edward orders. "Did we have another long night my lord," Tyrolean asks with a smirk. Edward just looks his way but does not speak a word. "My lord where will you find a use for me," William asks feasting on a meal. "You have been friends with the last noble to still hold a claim to the throne. I need you to work with my battle team and find the best way to defeat him with the least amount of the army lost," Edward requests. "As you command my lord," William replies, finished with the meal he departs to carry out a task given to him.

A servant brings Elizabeth her horse. Darius walks up with seeing her new attire he asks, "Are you going somewhere my lady?" "Yes, I go to find the man I love," Elizabeth proudly informs. "My lady he gave me orders for you to stay here," Darius reminds. "No, he gave you orders to protect me and if you are going to do that you better mount your horse," Elizabeth suggests mounting her horse then pulls the reins and the horse begins to move. James rides out in front of her with his horse blocking her path he inquires with a bowing of his head, "Does the lady of Lancaster need help in her task?" She smiles to give her answer. He turns his horse and they begin to move together. "Overlain guard the book and if we should not return put your efforts with Richard as ordered by Alex," Darius instructs before quickly mounting his horse then rides out taking a few soldiers with him. They ride fast and hard until they catch up with her. With James and Elizabeth seeing their pursuit slow down the stride of their horses with Darius reaching them he says, "My lady I come to keep my oath." Elizabeth with a delightful smirk asks, "You say you are sworn to give your life to protect me?" "That is my vowel to him and I will keep my word," he relays with the pride of a faithful man. "Then we shall put that to the test," she informs kicking her horse. The men gather speed with her. She rides proudly in the saddle with her heart longing for the feel of his touch and her soul is burden with the unknown of the man she holds dear.

"We will give the horses a little longer and then we will press on, we need to get him to Overlain," Alex says with worry in his eyes as he looks out towards him lying in the rack. With time moved forward and the horses rested. Alex and the men ride for home again. Elizabeth and the men ride to find him pushing the animals that carry them. Edward and the war lords make their plans for the throne. With Kirkland still missing Edward sends more soldiers to find him; everyone finds their place in the world.

The day is all but gone. Alex and his faithful move slowly across the land. "My lord riders' approach," Jonas rides back informing. Not knowing who they are and a wounded friend. They hide themselves in the lay of the land. "How much longer my lady? These horses will need rest," Darius yells over the thundering of the horse's footsteps. Elizabeth caring little drives the animals on being led by her heart. Jayel Jonas and Alex spring from their cover. Darius pulls his sword not recognizing their faces. "Alex," she screams then leaps down from her horse rushing into his arms with her lips finding his. "My lady your kiss is like a fine wine to a drunkard," Alex states with his heart. The moment lasts and then the world returns. Darius rides over to them, "I thought I told you to keep her from harm," Alex relays to Darius. "My lord I," Darius stumbles to say, "Do not blame him he has done what you requested, I came for you and he had no choice but to follow," Elizabeth quickly tells him letting her anger rise to the surface adding, "by the way do not think I have forgotten that you left me!" She lets her displeasure be known to him. The men surrounding them keep quite as she rambles her feelings with a finale note of, "You may be the love I hold dear, but you are not my lord and husband yet! Do not lie to me again Alex Lancaster!" She turns and walks away from the men leaving Alex with a wounded pride. "Darius take Kronus back with speed I will gather the men and bring the lady back," Alex requests. Darius gathers Alex's horse with the rack and heads back for the camp. Elizabeth stands by a giant tree her tears find her face. The feeling of happiness and anger flow out of her body. Alex walks up from behind saying, "Forgive me my lady, I should have not tricked you like that, I just found it better to leave you in safe hands." She turns and looks at him her eyes still red from her tears. "Alex, I know you thought it best for me to stay behind, but my place is with you, and if you should find your death. I would find mine as well." He reaches for her hand she has played mad long enough, she embraces him holding on to what her heart has longed to have. Alex looks down at her attire and the bow on her back suggesting, "You were prepared to save me." "Alex my love, I would come back from the pits of hell to save you from harm," Elizabeth proudly boasts. Alex looks deeply into her eyes and he finds the truth of her words. "My lord I do not mean to interrupted, but the horses are rested if you wish to return," James walks over saying. "Give the order lets head for the foothills." Alex walks beside her to her horse helps her onto the saddle. He takes the reins of Darius's horse, climbs up into the saddle and they make their way to the place they now call home.

Time turns and the morning has found the land. A patrol party finds the body of Kirkland. The animals of the forest have had their meal of him. "Sir it is Kirkland," a soldier tells his superior. The commander gazes upon his body informing, "Gather the head and his body we will take it before Lord Edward." The men gather his remains wrapping it and place it on the back of a horse, then make their way back to the castle.

Elizabeth sits outside of the cave looking out at the people roaming the camp, she sees Overlain approaching. "He is still resting?" "Yes, he still slumbers." "Will you tell him I wish to speak with him it is of the highest importance," Overlain asks. "As soon as he wakes. I will let him know." "Thank you, my lady." Overlain turns and walks his way. "Miss Elizabeth," Darius walks up saying she looks at the bow in his hand with Darius adding, "Since the master of the house sleeps. I would like to give the arrow shooting another round." "Are you sure you want to make a fool of yourself again," giving a well-placed smile she asks. "No, my lady. I under estimated you the last time," Darius boasts. Elizabeth looks back in the cave. Alex sleeps and is lost in his dreams. She reaches for her bow and walks away with him. The soldiers watch and begin to gather. They face the targets placed for the archers to practice. Some hang from the tree's others placed on the ground. With everyone gathered Darius informs, "The field is yours my lady." She takes her aim and fires her bow the arrow strikes centered in the target. "That is a nice shot," Darius informs before taking his aim then fires his bow and the resting arrow is split. "Good shoot," she says bringing a smile to his face then ads to shrink his pride, "but not good enough!" The shooting goes on as the men are amazed. Each impresses the other with the skill in their eyes. Alex wakes and stands in the entrance of the cave; he blinks his eyes trying to be sure what he sees. He slips out of the cave, walking down to the gathering. "Try this shot Miss Elizabeth," Darius suggests taking aim with the placing of two arrows upon his bow. He releases and they find their mark boasting with arrogance sipping from his lips, "Not just anyone can do that!" She takes her stance, placing the arrows on the bow. She relaxes her breathe, taking her aim, focusing the targets in her eye. Alex slips up and the men keep silent he places his hands on her sides at the time of the release her arrows fly wildly. She turns to see who would touch her in such away, Alex smiles informing, "I was just trying to save my brother from embarrassment!" She smacks him on the arm in a playful manner then he kisses her lips saying, "I didn't know you could shoot in such a way." "There are many things about me you do not know," Elizabeth suggests. Alex walks with her their arms entangled. "My lord, Overlain came to see you this morning, he says he wishes to speak with you," Elizabeth relays with their steps. "I will go and see what troubles him." He kisses her hand and then turns to walk off. "I will have you something to eat when you return," Elizabeth says. Alex walks down the path until he reaches the cave of Overlain. Entering he asks, "You wished to see me this morning?" "Yes, Kronus heals fast and you know in your heart why." Alex looks down at him resting in the cave. "Yes, I do, he has the wolf's blood flowing in his veins. Is there any way to heal him" Alex asks with a worried voice? "Yes, my lord, if I had the original source of the spell." "I though you told me you could rid men of this curse your brother brought upon this land." "I can cure him with a new spell but after finding the spell that was cast. I must have the cup they drank from which the spell requires." "You said nothing of a cup," Alex informs. "There are many spells that have the same purpose my brother chooses wisely, with this one. Knowing without the original source of what they drank from there was no way to remove it, Overlain explains but adds, "there is another way," "Do not speak to me in riddles," Alex requests adding, "just tell me what we can do." "If I cast the spell using a different cup, one I hold in my possession, he would still have a beast inside but I could then cast the spell to remove it with him drinking the blood of a virgin lamb mixed with blessed water using the same cup." "Will any cup work," Alex looks over his shoulder from the entrance asking. "It has to have a power within it first for it to hold the spell," Overlain relays explaining, "Say a cup held by a prophet or blessed by a divine stature of a man." "Do you have such a cup?" "Yes, my lord. I do." "What do you wait for cure him," Alex suggests. "My lord I cannot grant you what you wish if I were to give him this power. He could corrupt it with he being the first of a new bloodline to be created. He would be the strongest and could turn on us all," Overlain relays. "What do you suggest we do, Alex asks adding, "we cannot leave him as he is. The moon will be full soon, this month has grown long." "I would grant you this power you being the first will mean you are stronger than the rest." "What do I need this power for?" "My lord you may not agree yet but we cannot win this war as men. We need the wolf to stand with our side," Overlain implores. Alex looks out over the landscape not wanting to admit what he has said informing, "Let me think on this. I cannot answer you at this time." Alex walks away and heads back to his place of stay.

Edward sits in his throne room his most respected sit with him. The soldiers come in with the body of a fallen brother. "My lord, we found him this way!" Edward uncovers his body then covers him up. "Take him and get his body prepared to be buried," he turns and looks at the room, "everyone who is not a soldier, leave this room now!" The servants and others hurry from the room and the last closes the door behind him. "Tyrolean, I thought you said no one would know how to defeat us," Edward angered reminds. "My lord, I am the only one who would know the spell, I cannot understand how he could be killed" Tyrolean implores. "We cannot attack without knowing if the secret is out," Devilian says. "My lord I may know how they could have found out," William speaks up saying. "How would that be Lord William," Tyrolean asks. "Your brother has lived among us for years, I did not think it important before this time he showed his true form when Alex returned," William relays. "My brother, there is no way it could be him! He died long ago and by my hand," Tyrolean boasts recalling the memory in his mind watching his brother fall from the cliff. The curse flashes in his eyes placed there by his brother. "He bares the face of you," William relays. "Could they achieve the power we have," Edward eagerly asks. "If he had the spell and the things he needed, but he would not without the master book and I hold it in my belongings. It is the only one of its kind it has the spell to remove the beast within," Tyrolean states. "What do you mean a master book of spells?" "There are many magical books in the world this happens to be the book with every spell cast since the beginning of time and the way to remove them," Tyrolean informs. "You spoke nothing of this master book perhaps you keep it from me for your own lusts," Edward suggests with a displeased look on his brow. "No, my lord, besides it would do me no good unless you wanted the power to be taken from you. The subject has to be willing to be released." Edward does not let this fall on deaf ears demanding, "Go and bring me this book!" "As you command my lord," Tyrolean informs before leaving to retrieve the book. "You did not find it in you to tell me of this brother of Tyrolean," Edward asks of William. "No, my lord, I did not think it important until now." "Do you know any plans they may have," Edward asks. "No, my lord, my men found the favor of Alex and not with me. I left an outcast in their mists." Edward sees the hate in his eyes then asks, "Can I depend on you to stand against them?" "Yes, my lord I will stand with you. I have regained my name by our hand I serve this house," William stands and says. "Well spoken, William Lancaster." William finds favor in Lord Edward's eyes.

"What troubles my lord in this early hour," Elizabeth asks noticing a distance about him. "What must I do? Overlain says he can balance the world with casting a spell but the price would be high." "What spell would this be," she asks of him placing a hand on his shoulder. "He could turn us into the beasts that walk this world the thing that men fear." "What would be the cost of this," she asks. Alex looks out towards the land replying, "What if something went wrong and the beasts, we have become went wild. I could not live with the thought of what I would do in its animal state." "What of Kronus, what will his fate be," Elizabeth asks wrapping he arms around him. "If Overlain should cast his spell it would turn him from the beast of his brother but he would still be a beast just of a different kind." Elizabeth runs her fingers through his hair suggesting, "If it is to save him then why not?" "He will not cast the spell without making me the first, so that I would be the strongest of us." "He sees the good in your heart and the greatness you have in you," proudly she informs. "I just don't know what I should do." She kisses his face and puts her arm around his neck requesting, "Eat my love. The choice will come to you in time."

"Did you find what I wanted," Edward asks of Tyrolean as he enters the room. "No, my lord. The book has been stolen!" "This would explain why our brother was killed your brother must be alive the two of you are forged from the same coin," he informs Tyrolean. "William! I put your loyalties to the test tell me where they would have gone." The room grows silent, William lets the sight of seeing them naked in each other's arm control his feelings informing, "They would hold up in the foothills of my land. I will show you where to find them." "Titus, Devilian, Connor go with William, take what men you will need and bring back his book and make sure no one survives," Edward rises and orders. "We will leave at once," William pledges. "No. We bury our brother. Everyone can leave at the suns first peek," Edward reminds, then sits restless with the thought that someone could rise up against him.

Alex sits in the circle of men. "My lord what are we going to do? Edward and his army will march for the one noble house left we must bring support to them," James suggests. "Overlain how much longer will it take for Kronus to heal," Alex asks. "With the way the wound looks now. He should be up and around with-in a few days but I must stress to you the moon will not be in our favor with him." Then we will start to pack tomorrow and make are way the next day. We will bring support to the noble Burns." The men leave the circle and go their way. "My lord, are you sure you want to travel with him," Overlain asks with the men departed. Alex does not reply he walks back towards the creek. "Where is Alex," Elizabeth asks passing by Darius with him replying, "I saw him walk towards the creek his mind is burden my lady." She leaves and walks towards the sound of the water. She sees him sitting upon a stump throwing pebbles into the water walking up she asks, "Does my lord wish to be left alone?" Alex gives a smile replying, "No, I am glad you are here." He takes her hand guiding her to his lap. "Your beauty is enough to empty a man's mind." He kisses her lips. They sit listening to the sound of the water fill the forest. The birds sing as the shadows of day begin to fade. She can see his mind is still heavy. "Come Alex let me take your mind off the things that trouble you." She leads him by his hand they walk towards the camp through it she leads him inside of the cave. He sits down on the bed made of skins she lets her cloths fall to the floor. He gazes upon her body, her skin a glow of white, her hair flows around her shoulders, her breast firm. He stares in her eyes as she lays down on him. They kiss with his hands roaming her body. She slowly undresses him running her hands down his chest loving the feel of his skin. She presses on his chest as her pace begins, his hands run up and down her sides causing the goose bumps to form, she holds on to his hands as she places them above his head taking what she longed for all day. The sweat begins to cover their bodies as the love they make takes its toll, her breath quickens and her cries of passion fill his ears, their passions over flows, their love is released, she falls upon his chest they hold on to one another as they watch the last bit of sun leave the cave.

The soldiers stand in a single line on each side of a path leading up to the place where the ashes of men lay. They place his body on top and Edward takes the medallion from his neck, sets fire to the base of the wood gathered.

The fire grows big as the faithful soldiers watch his body burn. They give their salutes into the night giving respect to a brother now laid to rest.

The dawn breaks and they ride from the castle. The horses gallop with a thunderous sound, they push their hoses to ride through the day. William leads the men to conqueror someone he once called brother.

"You are as lovely in the morning as you are in the night," Alex says to her brushing her hair from her face. "Can we just stay here and you can hold me today," Elizabeth asks with a loving tone. "We left that life behind us when I returned to this place. The men will be waiting for my orders today." She kisses his face then admires his ass as he stands up and begins to dress. "Will you need my help in packing anything," Alex placing the sword on his side asks. "No, the servants can handle what I have, you tend to what needs to be done. I will have everything ready to go." Alex blows her a kiss then walks out of the cave. The people busy themselves gathering things to pack. "Darius old friend see that nothing is left I return to the castle of my father there is something I need to find." "Alex there is nothing left there," Darius suggests. Alex just smiles and mounts his horse saying, "Tell the lady of the house I will return before night fall." Darius stands there watching him ride away. He turns and walks through the camp helping everyone in need to gather their things. Like the waves of the ocean removing the sands of the beach time passes quickly. Alex rides into his old home plundering through the rumble in the part that was once his father's room. He pushes over a dresser it reveals a hidden place in the floor. He opens it and reaches for the box inside, opens it, looks at what it holds, he places it in a bag he carries, his mind drifts to better days of his home, a time before he could fight in this war, a time when a mother's arms could hold him. He walks out of the castle mounts his horse and heads back for the camp.

"Where is Alex," Elizabeth asks finding Darius. "He said he needed to get something from the castle he will return before night fall." "Darius we should be ready to move by dawn tomorrow," James comes up informing. "Job well done old friend," he relays in return. "How is Kronus today Overlain," Jonas steps in and asks. "See for yourself he is up and awake." Jonas walks over to where he is resting. "Kronus I am glad you are still here among us," he informs sitting down beside him adding, "at the rate you are going you will be out of this cave in no time." "I will be ready to fight with you, God has smiled on me again," Kronus suggests. "Well rest for now. I just came by to check on you." Jonas gets up and begins to walk out of the cave with Overlain asking, "Has our lord returned?" "No but he should be here soon." Jonas walks his way leaving the cave.

William and his new brothers walk their horses only giving enough time for a short rest. They travel across the land fast. "I know what you told Lord Edward but can you really kill your own brother," Titus asks of him walking among him. "A brother does not take your future wife in his bed, then take her with the shame of it and leave his family to the slaughter of an enemy. He will get what he deserves from me," William boasts to those around him. "Your brother took your woman into his bed now that is betrayal of the worst kind," Devilian remarks. "I think we have let them rest enough," William says in a harsh tone as he climbs back on his horse. The men riding with him follow his lead.

Alex returns to the camp. "I was just about to go and look for you my lord," Jonas says. "Where is Elizabeth?" "She waits for you at the cave." "Is everything in order?" "Yes, my lord. We will be ready to move come first light," Jonas answers with Alex walking away heading for the cave. "It is nice you can tell someone you will be leaving," she says as he comes walking up sitting down by a fire burning in front of the cave, her maids and others gather with her. Alex does not say a word walks up to her and kneels before her, he reaches out and takes her hand saying, "My lady I am sorry for not telling you where I would be going, but I realized in all this time I have not done the thing that matters most." He reaches in his bag and pulls out the box sits it on her lap. "What is this," she readily asks. "Open it." She opens the lid and the tears fill her eyes. "I was so overwhelmed by your beauty that I forgot to ask for your hand in marriage." He pulls the ring from out of the box and gently slides it on her finger vowing, "To whatever this life holds for me noble or common would you be my wife? I know in my heart I could not stand to be without you!" She looks down at the ring and she smiles at him. "Well come on my lady do not leave me hanging." "Oh, Alex yes, yes and its beautiful!" They kiss for the moment and others gather round. "My lord what is going on here," James asks with a glorious smile. Elizabeth rushes out to show him. "A beauty for a beauty," James tells her looking at the ring on her hand. "Wait what am I saying bring out the wine," James proclaims. The music begins to fill the night air, as they celebrate a union to be. "Where did you get this," Elizabeth asks still bedazzled by its beauty.

"It belonged to my mother. My father kept it in a safe place and I could find no other I would want to have this." She kisses his lips and Darius pulls her away taking her to dance with the others by the fire. Alex watches as she smiles loving the fire sparkling in her eyes. "You have chosen well my lord," Overlain walks over saying as he places his hand upon his shoulder. "You see I told you everything works out as it should in this world. Elizabeth was always meant for you." Alex raises his glass and drinks to what he has said. "You placed the book in safe keeping," Alex asks with his duty still holding. "Yes, young Alex it is safe." They celebrate into the night not knowing what will lie ahead.

The sun's rays shine over the land and the people are ready to leave the foothills to journey to another place. Alex helps his wife to be on her horses her bow rests on her back. Alex mounts his horse when the thunder reaches their ears. "What is that sound Alex?" "The sound of horses my lady," Alex informs. James pulls his axe from its sheath. The men prepare for what is to come, their eyes lay hold of the numbers they face. Elizabeth screams as her eyes behold the wolf that has slipped in among them. "Elizabeth," Alex yells in fear for his love dashing in as the wolf leaps knocking it from its target. "Get her into the cave," Alex commands as the men ride in from the hills. Darius and Alex's faithful engage with the soldiers rushing in to destroy them. James jumps from his horse his size best suited for the ground. "Archer's fire," Elizabeth orders from the cave. The arrows fly into the air striking at the men. "James, look out," Jonas yells seeing a wolf sneaking up from behind him. Darius fires an arrow the silver tip strikes it in the shoulder it howls in pain and moves back from the battle. William in wolf form sees her peering from the cave and he sets out to take her from his brother. Overlain using his magic drives back the wolves with the burning light of his crystal. "Overlain protect the book," Alex commands before looking over his shoulder seeing the beast creeping for the cave, he turns his reins and rides hard for the cave. Elizabeth does her part firing at the men as they ride. She lets her marksmanship be known. She does not see the beast but her ears hear the sound of the forest moving beneath its might paws. She turns and leaps for her. "Elizabeth," Alex screams as he rides with his heart pounding for the horrors he envisions. She backs into the cave she pulls her sword from its sheath. The wolf draws near she can see the glimmer of his teeth, he scratches his claws on the wall of the cave savoring the taste of her soon to be in his jaws. "Nooo," Alex screams leaping from his horse knocking the wolf from its path his sword falls from his hand. The beast turns and even in the form of the wolf Alex knows who it is. William turns with speed, and leaps at him he grips him in his claws his feet dangle from the ground. His brother opens his mouth for the kill. Elizabeth fires a silver tipped arrow from her quiver it finds it mark in his neck. William slings him from his claws howling as the silver burns his skin. William in pain leaps from the cave. The men have fought well but no match for the wolves in the mist of the army. They surround them in a circle and a commander rides in. "Overlain I know you are here come out with the book or the wolves will rip them to pieces!" Overlain comes out from the cave holding the book in his hand informing, "I have what you seek I will give it to you if you and your men will leave." "We came for the book, that is all we need. I will spare you and the others now bring it here!" Overlain walks down to the circle. He places the book in his hands. He smiles when he hands it too him ordering, "Kill them all!" "I was afraid you were going to say that," Overlain relays slinging tiny blades of silver then throwing down a crystal to the ground creating an explosion with a light as bright as the burning of the sun. The silver finds their marks and the wolves pull back the light drives the sight from their eyes and he drops the book to the ground. The men retreat towards the mouth of the cave the archer's fire arrows into the pack. The silver does its job and they howl in pain retreating. Overlain runs for the cave but a wolf leaps knocking him down and takes the book from his hands then retreats into the wilderness. "Lord William," a soldier says as he walks back naked. The arrow having driven the wolf inside. The soldier pulls the arrow from his neck. Connor comes up and begins to take his human form he holds the book in his hand saying, "Give the order to retreat they can do no more we have what we came for." The soldier blows on his horn and the men begin to pull back and gather with them. The pack returns and the soldier remove the arrows from their bodies. "William will you be okay," Titus asks to him holding his neck where the arrow struck. "Yes, I believe I will be fine!" William assures. Lord Edward told us to leave no one alive. William looks at the book saying, "We have the book. I have given a fatal blow to my brother he is the driving force behind this clan of men. They will lose hope and the will to rise up against this house." "What of Overlain," Titus asks. William looks out at the men who cannot see and his brothers of the wolf pulling silver from their bodies saying, "You are welcome to go and kill him if you desire." William and the others cloth themselves and they ride for the York ship castle. The victory of the day is theirs.

Chapter Five

A New Pack is Born

ELIZABETH SITS WITH ALEX'S HEAD IN HER lap. His father's sword runs deep into his body being driven there by throw of his brother. Her tears pour over his face. "You will be fine my love just hold on," she sobs clutching his hand. Darius rushes inside the cave seeing Alex with the sword driven in him screams, "Alex my lord." Elizabeth holds onto him her tears flow from her body. "What has happened, Overlain hearing Darius scream, runs in asking. "My lady you must release him," Darius softly informs. They drag him from her arms and she watches as they pull the sword from him. Her body aches watching him turn in the pain. Seeing her sprit tormented James yells, "No, no, get her out of here!" The soldiers pull her from the cave sobbing and weeping she staggers from the pain filling in her heart. Overlain walks from the cave his hands covered in blood seeing her he kindly says, "My lady." "Will he live," she asks through her sorrow. "I fear not the wound is too deep," Overlain replies with a heavy heart. Elizabeth turns her head to the ground. The tears flow freely, in her state, she looks up at him saying, "He spoke of a spell." "My lady the price will be high." "I do not care about the price. I will pay the fairy-man with my own life, if you can pull him from the jaws of death, then let it be done!" Darius walks up as they speak. "Darius you will go and get what he needs and do it with all swiftness," she demands through the tears in her eyes. "My lady we should," before the sentence is finished, she blurts, "Are you going to go or do I have to do it myself?" "As you wish, what do you need?" "Go to the foothills across the plain in the cave you will find a gray wolf capture it alive and bring it before me." "How will we know which cave," Darius inquires. Overlain quickly pulls a crystal from his cloak hands it to Darius instructing, "This will show the way." "James, Jonas you are with me," he calls out. They gather their horses and ride out for what they seek. "My lady you need to come with me to make sure he makes it until they return," Overlain requests. She follows him into the cave. She kneels down in the blood-soaked animal skins, that is their bed. She holds on to his hand. "Overlain rings out a spell holding a green crystal in his hand it begins to glow of its color. Finished he instructs, "Take this and hold it in your hand! Keep his in the other it will give you some of the pain and strength from your body to his." Overlain hands her the crystal. She holds on to his hand and the crystal does its magic. The pain enters her body she aches from the pain of him. She cries out with the pain his body is feeling, but her love holds on never daring to release his hand. The men ride swift and come upon the cave. "Hurry Darius or we will be too late," James informs. They poke at the beast and he lets his wrath be known they trick it into their nets and subdue it. They place it onto the back of the horse its mouth tied shut, and its mighty legs bound. "Come on let's get this back to the cave." The horse's feet pound the ground returning to the cave, running with all the speed the men can muster from them. Elizabeth holds onto his hand even as the blood begins to flow from her body sipping from her lips. The pain drives her mad, crying and screaming fighting to hold on. Her love just keeps him a float in the river of death. Alex in his mind sees the fairy-man doing his best to pull him across but he is held tight in this world bound down with the weight of a woman and the might of her love. "No! You will not have this one!" Alex hears her scream as the fairy-man pulls at him. "Overlain they return," Lucien bursts into the cave informing. "Bring the beast to my cave," Overlain quickly stresses. James and Jonas take the beast and place it in the cave. Darius walks over to her imploring, "My lady you must release him or you will die!" He tries to pull her from him. "No let me be," she demands with the pain that roams her body. "My lady I will hold on to him and give him the strength from my body," Darius assures. Her tears flow, her body hurts with the strength she can muster she replies, "Life without him no! If he is to die. I will die with him!" Darius seeing her in pain and Alex near death rushes from the cave to see how much longer the spell will take. Overlain draws the marking on the floor he casts his spell his eyes glow of the magic, the symbol burns into the cup, he takes the knife in his hands and spills the blood of the beast filling the cup within his hands. "Take this cup to him and return with his faithful," Overlain commands. Darius runs the cup to the cave. He walks up to them and he pulls her from him her body is limp the pain has been too much but her hand never leaves his. Darius pours the blood unto his tongue he swallows it down. He pours a little more the symbol drawn on the cave floor burns bright in his forehead then vanishes before his eyes he covers him up. "Take her from here put her in a place she can rest there is nothing more she can do for him now." The servants take her and put her in a tent her faithful servants wipe her brow and wash her body covered from her sweat. The wound on her side retreats and she begins to regain her strength. "Overlain I return with what you asked," James, Jonas, Jayel, Lucien, Lushien, Lucas, Darien all loyal to Alex." "You men know what is in the cup it will give you the power to stand against the darkness of this land. You will not die unless a wolf bites off your head or a fatal cut from silver with a blessing upon it. Do you accept the gift I give you," Overlain asks? Each in turn nods their heads in agreement. Darius walks to the cup he looks at what it holds. The taste is bitter to his tongue but with each taste its flavor turns to sweetness in his body, with it fully resting within him. The symbol lights upon his forehead then fades away. "It tastes better than it looks brothers," Darius informs passing the cup. James sips from the cup the others follow in his step. "Take what is left to Kronus the wolf lives in him already but the gray will rule over the black," Overlain instructs." Darius takes the cup to him and he tastes of what the cup holds. "Take these and wear them upon your skin always, it will keep the wildness of the beast in you from rising to the surface," Overlain relays with his return. They place them next to their skin. James takes one to Kronus healing from the mark placed upon him. Darius takes the last to his young noble. Alex grows stronger by the pass of the clock he bends down and places it around his neck saying, "Rest now my lord. In the morning you will be better." He goes and looks in on her. "How is she," he asks her maiden. "Resting my lord, she will regain her strength rest is what she will need"

William and his brothers ride back for the castle their speed much slower than their ride to conquer a fallen brother. "William you have proven yourself to me. I will doubt you no more," Titus tells him riding by his side.

"Thank you my new found brother. I hope you are more loyal than the last!" Titus pats him on the back they ride on.

The clouds cover the earth and they weep upon the land. "Kronus you are up and moving," Darius seeing him standing says. "Yes. I feel as strong as ten horses and ready to face our enemies. Where is Alex," he asks. "He is recovering from his wounds it is only by the grace of Overlain he is still with us." Elizabeth wakes in the tent she looks franticly around not seeing Alex, she uses what strength she can usher and walks from the tent the rain beads off her head as she does her best to make her way to him. Darius looks out and sees her he leaves his dry place and runs to her saying, "My lady you must rest!" "No take me where I can see him," she requests falling and he catches her then takes her up the hill and into the cave, then places her beside him. She looks at his face struggling to put her arm around his waist then passes out beside him. "How does the wound look," Overlain walks in asking. "It heals fast." "Good then we got it to him in time." They walk from the cave leaving them holding on to one another. "Overlain with the book gone do you have a way to release this beast from us," Darius asks. "Yes. I took what we need from the book. I have the pages of the spell with me," Overlain explains. "What is the metal inside of these medallions?" "They were forged from the nails that pierced his skin, take care of them for they are the only of their kind." "How do you use this power you gave us when will the wolf come out?" "You can change at will only the full moon will hold her sway over you." "But how can I gain control over this," Darius questions as they walk among the camp. "When our lord has regained his strength, we will come together can figure it out." The rain pours harder and they go inside the cave with the men.

"My lord they return," a servant in the house informs. Edward walks out to the balcony and watches as they come over the hill and into the walls of the castle. "Tyrolean. I found something you lost!" Titus places the book in his hands with Tyrolean waiting just inside the gates. They ride to the stables and then they go into the castle. "My brothers you have returned and victorious," Edward rises from his throne greeting says. "Tyrolean is the book as you left it?" "Yes, my lord it appears to be." "My lord they know how to hurt us. I have seen his brother in their mists," Titus states. "I hope you destroyed them before you left." "We did our best. His brother I know to be dead. William Lancaster is the last to hold his mane." Edward slips a grin over his lips to praise what he has heard. "Go and rest we will attack the last noble in the days ahead. I will need all of you at full strength." "As you command my lord," Titus says in bowing his head. The men take their leave and go their way the sound of the rain falls upon the castle as the days grows long.

Alex begins to cough as new air flows into his lungs. The sound of it wakes her from her rest she raises as he opens his eyes rejoicing in his movement she says, "Alex my love!" He blinks his eyes as the sickness leaves his body. "My lady I have had strange dreams. I thought you dead." "I am here Alex just rest here for now, I will stay by your side the hands of time cannot steal you from me." Alex closes his eyes and slips back to slumber. "My lady," Jonas says to wake her from her sleep requesting, "Eat and regain your strength." He hands her the plate and stands silent before her. "Jonas do you need to speak with me," she inquires. "My lady I just wanted to say thanks for the strength in your veins and the love it took to save him." "I would have given everything I have so that he could live." Jonas turns and walks out of the cave. "She is a stubborn woman is she not," Darius asks of him as he comes from the cave. "She is something! I could think of no better woman for him." "Yes Jonas, Alex found a love that comes but once in a life time," Darius proudly says.

Edward and his minions gather for their meal in the great hall of his castle. "My lord news comes from afar Richard moves across the land." "We will destroy the noble and then we will ride out to meet him." "My lord I have a way to gain more numbers against their army," William relays. "How would that be? The nobles in the south are with me and the conquered nobles of the north follow him." "Yes, but what if we send word to Elizabeth's father telling him that Richard caused her death. We would truly find favor with him." Edward sips his drink as a smile finds his face. "William you are a cunning general in this house. I am glad you found favor in me!" "To Edward soon king of this land," William toasts. They raise their glasses in praise to him. Bonds are built while they dine with each other. The rain leaves the land but the clouds stay covering the world they know with a look of dusk. Alex sits up she lays by his side. He is careful not to wake her. He finds his feet still weak from his wound. He walks for the mouth of the cave. "Alex," James says in his delight. He comes up and hugs him strongly. "Easy my very large friend," Alex requests filling his strength wrap around him. He releases him and helps him walk out a little farther. "My lord you should be resting," Lucien says. "Where is our lady," Jayel asks. "She rests," Alex answers then asks, "What happened?" "You do not remember my lord? "No, I remember the wolf attacking me in the cave but after that I cannot recall just a dream I had." "What dream my lord" He turns and looks back towards the cave answering, "I was at the river of sticks and the fairy-man was trying to take me but a hand kept me here." "That would be our lady in waiting she almost died to save you," Darius informs. Alex looks down and sees the medallion around his neck. "What is this?" Alex loses his strength. "Come my lord all will be answered you need your rest," Jonas suggests. They take him back to the cave and place him beside her. She wakes as they come inside of the cave. "My lord you are up and about you should be resting," she implores. They lay him back in the skins with her informing him, "Do not leave my side again until you have the strength to stand alone." The men look at her. Alex sees the look upon her face saying, "As you wish my lady." She covers him with a skin and he closes his eyes. "Bring some water and a cloth so I can wash the last few days from him." They leave the cave for what she asks. She kneels beside him and takes the medallion in her fingers knowing what it took to save him. She runs her hand through his hair gently places a kiss upon his cheek. "My lady the water you asked for." "Thank you." They put it down in front of her she takes the cloth and dips it in the bucket they turn and leave as she begins to wash his body. Her soft hands gently wash the blood from around the wound she can see how the magic heals him. Her hands flow over his body as she washes the dirt and sweat from his skin. She replaces the covers to keep him warm and the night sets in. She warms him with her body falling asleep upon his chest.

The sun burns away the clouds and shines its face upon the earth. "Devilian round up the provisions and the men. We set out to conquer the last house of this land," Edward readily orders. "William you will fight alongside of me in the days ahead." Devilian walks out of the room and begins to prepare for the battle ahead, gathers the ranks water and food making sure all the weapons are ready and loaded for the trip. "My lord. Why do you need me to stand with you? I would be served on the field of battle," William eager for battle stresses. "No, I will need your war experience to take this house with little loss of men. You were once a mighty foe with the cunning of war, now I wish for you to stand with me," Edward boasts to him. "As you command my lord," William relays.

Alex wakes, his body no longer hurts and his strength has returned. He looks towards the back of the cave. Elizabeth sits naked on a skin washing her body. The look of her skin brings out his love, her hair flows down her back. He can just see the roundness of her breast as her hands wash her body. He slips from his bed easies up to her and kisses her neck. "My lord," startled she says. She tries to turn and face him but he wraps his arms around her, sliding his hands to her breast taking her mounds in his hands, nibbles her neck and breaths in the scent of her hair. "Alex you should be resting." "I have rested long enough," replying with a lust filled tongue. He turns her towards him passionately kissing her lips. The strength of his hands caresses her skin. She feels a new feeling in the passion of the wolf as he takes her nipple into his mouth. He forcefully but with the gentles touch lays her down. Her body burns for him as he enters her body and the new strength in his veins bring passion to her better than before. Darius walks to the mouth of the cave her passion echoes inside the cave and with the sound he goes back the way he came. "Darius how is Alex this morning," Jayel asks. "He is welled I believe he may be back to full strength," he replies with a smile looks back towards the cave adding, "maybe even better than before!" "Then I will speak to him this morning." He goes to walk off and he grabs his arm implying, "I would give them a little more time!" Jayel looks at his face and what he is relaying sets in, "Oh I see what you are saying." A smile finds his face. He turns and sits back down. Elizabeth breathes in short gasps as he comes close, she grips his sides as he brings passion to her. "Oh, oh God! My lord," her passion rings out. Alex releases his passion for her and he falls upon her chest sweat covers their bodies as the morning together has taken its toll. They both breathe hard recovering from their passions. He raises his face and looks into her eyes stating, "I thought I would never see you again and you were lost to me." "No, my love. I will always be with you and if you should find your death I will follow." He kisses her chest and looks down at what is wrapped around his neck. "Did Overlain put this on me?" "No. my love Darius did after he cast the spell." "The spell I told him that we would find another way." Elizabeth looks deeply in his eyes saying, "He did not do this on his own, I forced him into it, my lord you were wounded in battle and I feared for you and I could not bear to live without you, he cast the spell to please me." "My lady but what now lays in me?" "Alex whatever is in you is a part of you. I fear nothing that comes from you." "The beast is wild at heart! I have seen the savage work of it." He rolls off her sits up and faces away from her. She glides her hands around his waist whispers in his ear, "I do not believe it, the wolf becomes the character of the person it lives in, and you are a noble man, so will it be." She kisses his lips, he smiles, and they roll back to the covers. Time passes. They come from the cave as night begins to cover the light. "My lord I am glad to see you up and about," Lucas says to him. "My lord," Overlain says. "Elizabeth, I wonder if you would not mind waiting for me? I have something I need to discuss with the men," Alex requests then kisses her hand and she goes back towards the cave. "Overlain do you still have the book to release us when it is time?" "No, my lord. The book is lost to us now, but I hold the secret to releasing you." Alex finds comfort in knowing he could be released but Overlain quickly reminds, "There are many more evils inside its pages." "Then we must retrieve it and place it in your care," Alex suggests. "My lord I did not do this to offend you or disobey you." "I know she told me I was in death's grasp." "You owe a great deal to her she took some of the pain from you and kept you alive until Darius brought what I needed," Overlain states. Alex looks over towards her tent, he can see the outline of her body cast on the side of it saying, "She has my heart and my life. I can offer her no more." "Kronus I am glad to see you up and about," Alex turns and says. "Thank you, my lord. I will say the same for you." "Alex what do you intend to do? By now the army marches for the noble home of Johnson. He will be no match for them," Jonas relays. "First we must learn this power we now possess, or we will be of no use to them," Alex says then turns to Overlain asking, "Overlain how do we make the change?" "You have to channel all your energy towards it," he explains to them. "Come my brother let's take this out of the camp. The people here have already seen enough." Alex calls the best guards he has ordering, "Watch over her until I return make sure no harm should come to her!" "As you command my lord," the honored guardsman says. They surround the tent with him stepping inside. "My lady I must leave the camp for a short while but I will return." "I will be right here waiting for you." She kisses his face he takes a moment to look into her eyes then turns and goes with his faithful. They walk from the camp the moon shines her light on the water. The night creatures sing their songs as they come together. Overlain waves his staff over a pile of wood and it burst into flame. They sit facing one another. "What do we do now," James asks from out of the silence. "Just focus, think of the wolf and let it come out," Overlain suggests. They sit and nothing happens. "Overlain," Alex reaching for the key to it asks. "You must think of something else," Overlain suggests. A soldier comes running up from the path they followed with blood covering his hands informing, "My lord they attacked us from the darkness!" Alex feels a burning inside of him. He starts to run for the camp and with every step he becomes the wolf, and his faithful follow suit, their hearts pound as they swiftly make it back to the camp. Their eyes peer but find the sight of nothing. Overlain gallops up on a horse asking to them in their new wolf forms, "How did I do my lord?" The pack turns and looks at one another their passion burns less and they take the form of themselves. "You might want to put these on before all of you make it back to camp," Overlain implies throwing them cloaks to cover up with. They walk back into the camp with the power that rests in them is found. Alex slips into the tent saying, "My lady." She stands and walks over to him inquiring, "Where did you lose your clothes?" "That is a long story." They turn and make it back to their cave. "My lady, we will head for the Johnson castle tomorrow and help a fellow country man defend his home." "Alex, I need you to send a rider with this," Elizabeth requests. "What is it?" "It is a letter to my father informing him of what has transpired here. If we should fail in our task. How long before they strike out to against other countries?" "I will see to it Elizabeth." He takes the letter from her hands then quickly sends a rider to bring it to him. "Put this in no one else hands but his then, look for us in the north that is where we should be." "As you wish my lord," he relays taking the letter from his hand mounts a horse and rides for the coast. He walks back inside the cave. She opens his cloak asking, "So are you going to tell me how you lost your clothes?" "We found the power that rests in us and when I transformed back. I was naked before God and men." She steps back from him. "I wish to see this. Will you show me?" "No, my lady. What if the beast were to turn? I could not live with myself," he walks by her to gathering clothing to place upon him. "Alex, I need you to show it to me so I can prove to you I am not afraid." "Please do not ask this of me Elizabeth." "I just want you to know I will love you the same so do not be ashamed of what you are. Alex if you did attack me and take me from this world know that I would not have done it any other way for each moment I had with you was more than if I hadn't," she relays with her blue eyes burning into him. Alex stands to his feet. He lets out a slight moan as his body starts to change, she backs off fear strikes at her heart as his legs become more wolves like, his ears grow, his mouth stretches, his claws form, and he stands before her the wolf. He slowly turns and looks at her. She lets her eyes taken in that which stands before her, as she stands gazing upon him, her heart pounds in her chest. The love for him conquerors her fears, her hands reach for him and touch his fur, soft to her touch, she comes closer as she runs her hands over him. She looks him in the face, his teeth long, his eyes of a beast and she wraps her arms around him embracing him in that form. Alex slowly returns to normal and she holds onto his naked body she slowly looks in his eyes relaying, "See my love I can hold on no matter what you can become." They take a long look in each other's eyes. Elizabeth lets her cloths fall to the floor and they make love into the night.

At the peak of the sun thunder of horse's feet fill the air as the army of York rides out to conquer another noble man. The army slowly marches in their ranks. Edward and his minions follow from the rear. "Lord Edward, we should be there before the day is out." "Just keep them moving forward with enough strength to fight when we get there," Edward suggests. "Edward my lord what if we were to trick them say we ride under a flag of truce, me,you and our brothers of the wolf go inside and discuss this like civil men once we are inside we can take them by surprise that should save many men," William tells him. "That is why I have you with me Sir William, your father was a great man and you serve him well," Edward reveals letting a smile find his face.

"Is everything packed and ready?" "Yes, my lord." "Then with all speed we ride," Alex announces and his faithful with him ride off towards a friend in need. Elizabeth rides proudly beside him with her warrior skills proven to the men that she rides among. They travel hard and fast, covering as much earth as they can, until the horses need rest. "Drink some of this." Alex hands her some water. She drinks it down, her tongue parched from the ride. They sit beside a small creek. "Overlain take her sword and bless it," Alex requests throwing it to him. "My lady you sure you can handle that weapon, Alex questions. "Well I don't know my lord maybe you should teach me." Jayel throws them two wooden swords and the men gather eager to see. "Watch out my lord she is full of surprises," Darius relays. Alex looks over his shoulder and smiles informing, "I plan to go easy on our lady." Elizabeth finds no humor in his remark saying, "Shall we?" They hold up their swords and begin to play. "No, my lady. Do not hold the sword like that, hold the sword like this." Alex walks up to her and she kicks dirt into his eyes, she moves and knocks him from his feet holding the wooden sword to his neck. "Is that how I should hold it my love?" "Suddenly I find myself very foolish," Alex says lying on the ground "What is wrong my lord? The men of this land do not teach its women to fight?" Alex sits up and men begin to laugh. "Here help me up," Alex asks. She sticks the sword in the ground and reaches for his hand, he flips her and she lands on her ass. Alex spins around and holds the wooden sword to her neck. "You can fight and handle a sword but the one thing that I can teach you is to never let your guard down!" She taps him on the waist and a sharp metal object sending coldness on his skin. "I don't my lord!" Alex smiles proud that such a beauty can hold her own in battle and says, "You surprise me every day!" "Come on the show is over we must move on," James suggests. "My lady you have proven yourself once again," Overlain says as he hands her back her sword. Alex helps her onto her horse and mounts his. Darius rides by saying, "I bloody told you Alex." They move on across the vast lands through the forest heading for what will lay ahead.

"William did you send word to her father?" "Yes. I did my lord. We should find him in good favor with us," William relays. They watch as the soldiers form the line in front of his castle. "Come William let us ride out and speak with him." Edward and his faithful ride out under a white flag. The noble Johnson comes from his gates to speak with them. "York you will leave my land you cannot have the whole bloody world," Johnson says. "My lord Johnson, I really don't want to watch a massacre let us go inside and talk of a solution to what lies before us." Johnson thinks for a moment then says, "Come in and we will see if we can negotiate something." They follow him down into the castle. They walk into the great hall of his home." Please gentlemen leave your weapons here," a general in Johnson's army requests. Edward with his minions takes off their swords and lay them down. Johnson and his closest do the same they walk into the room together. They sit down at a big table and his servants treat them with respect. "Lord Johnson I would really like to gain your support with my house. All the other nobles of the south support my flag or have suffered my wrath," Edward relays. "What do you offer if I fly your flag with mine?" "I will give you this land and two other houses when I have the crown placed upon my head or I can burn this house to the ground and give this land to another noble," Edward warns requesting, "search your feelings well if you stand against me you will stand alone." Edward's words reach his ears with a bitter coldness. "It is true my fellow noble, you know my face. We tried to stand against his army and failed now my father's house stands with him," William says. "Why should I fear you and your army," Johnson boldly inquires. "Titus can you show him why he should fear us," Edward requests. Titus stands from the table and he begins to change. The noble man's eyes behold what is in front of him, his heart pounds, his breath draws short. "What demon is this," he yells. Titus leaps from where he stands; knocks him to the ground, his claws wrap around his neck his face inches from the teeth that wish to taste of his flesh. The spit drools from his mouth. Edward walks up beside him and places his hand on the wolf's shoulder asking, "What say you my noble man? Do you support me or shall I have my friend get his meal?" "Yes, yes, I will support your claim to the throne," Johnson fear filled announces. Titus releases him from his grip. Johnson's soldiers stand horrified by what they see. He transforms back to his human self. Edward takes an apple from the table bites it and chews on what he has in his mouth passes him still lying on the floor. Edward sits down on his throne, turns and looks at him his eyes take the color of the wolf informing, "a very wise choice my noble friend." Johnson with no way to understand what he just seen bows his head to him saying, "Thank you my lord what is your command?" Edward laughs and it rings off the walls of the castle as his soldiers slowly begin to enter the city and its people know a noble house has fallen. The night grows long. Alex and his men come closer. "Tell me Sir Johnson is their people who live on the outskirts of the castle?" "Yes, my lord, there is many farms stretched out over the land." "Then send out a call to arms and have your men ready to march in the morning. We ride out to confront Sir Richard and bring an end to this long war," Edward proclaims before informing, "We shall use this castle as the base camp and you will stay to defend it. Do you have a problem with that?" "As you command my new king," Johnson says. "Come with me my brothers we were deprived of a meal," Edward states before turning to request, "Tyrolean make sure our noble stays inside the castle while we are out." "Yes, my lord." He turns and looks at the men his eyes are the color of the wolfs, "Shall weee.. His voice becomes a growl as he turns into the wolf and his minions follow him out into the night, they strike out to feeding upon the people who call the castle home.

"Lord Alex I have made it to the castle and it has fallen to York. His flag now flies above Johnson's." "Damn it we are too late," Alex states. "My lord it fell without a fight I see no signs of a struggle around it." Alex thinks for a moment then turns ordering, "Darius I place her in your watch." "Where are you going," Elizabeth asks. "I will go and sneak into the city and talk with Sir Johnson." "My lord what if you are captured," Elizabeth asks. Alex climbs on his horse with a smile he replies, "Then come and rescue me my lady!" He turns his horse ordering, "Lucien come with me." They ride off into the night the others make a small camp.

The pack slips up on a farmhouse the ones who call it home have no warning of what will soon be upon them. They slip up to its walls and to the door, letting the passion of the kill burn inside of them. Beasts leap in through the walls the door flies off its hinges. The people inside scream as they begin to eat of their flesh. The pack kills everything in sight leaving nothing with life in its body. "Alex how will we get through the gate," Lucien asks as they slip around the walls of the castle. "Not through the gate but over the wall." Alex lets some of the wolf's strength find him and he leaps onto the wall. Lucien seeing it does the same. They slip around the castle and find the window to his room. Alex looks inside Johnson sits with the look of a beaten man, still trying to grasp what his eyes beheld. Alex taps on the window. He walks over and opens it for him, Alex holds his finger to his mouth and they climb inside. "My lord," Alex says in a greeting he holds the candle closer to his face inquiring, "Alex what are you doing here, I though your house supported him." "My lord, my father's house stands divided his sons find themselves foes to one another. I come to offer help against them" Alex replies. "How can a human man stand up against what they become," Johnson quickly answers. "We have found the secret to them." "Then what will you need of me?" "I have a small band of soldiers we ride to help Sir Richard. He is the last of the nobles who will stand in his way to the throne like it or not we are allies against a common foe," Alex suggests." "I can have my army ready to take them on when they return," Johnson states. "No, my lord, just play out this path. We will take them by surprise in the moment of battle." "Alex you certain you know how to defeat him?" "I give you my word the word of my noble name. I will see you on the battlefield," Alex replies with a proud voice. Johnson holds out his hand and a promise is made with the shake of it. Alex and Lucien slip back out of the room and with the speed of the wolf they leave the castle. Johnson looks out of the window. "Are you planning on going somewhere," Tyrolean asks him as he slips into the room. "No, my lord. I was just enjoying the night air," Johnson relays. Tyrolean turns and leaves the room ordering to a soldier, "Post a guard outside of his window." The soldier points and another goes out and stands on the ledge. The pack travels fast to the castle moving in wolf form, they transform back to themselves in returning to the castle their lust for blood filled as the mangled bodies of a family lay inside of their home another deed unpunished.

James hears the feet of the horses returning seeing them he asks, "Alex did you achieve what you were after?" "Yes. I reached the noble and he will attack from out of the ranks." "So where do we head now," Jonas asked. "Gather the men we will cover more ground tonight then set up camp rest then ride for Richard and his army." Alex climbs from his horse with his feet on the ground he asks, "Where is Elizabeth?" "She is down by the big oak waiting for you." Alex moves over the ground until he sees Elizabeth. Reaching her he informs, "My lady there will be no need of a rescue." She stands and kisses his cheek with him asking, "Did you miss me?" "Always," she replies softly. "Darius thank you for watching over her brother." "I still hold my word my lord. I will guard her with my life." He pats Alex the shoulder and leaves them to themselves. "Where are we going now?" "We ride for Richard so we can join forces with him, we will have surprise on our side. Edward York will not expect it," Alex informs her. He takes her hand and leads her to her horse. The men climb on and they ride putting distance between them and their foes. Their ride is long and they rest for the night.

The sun rises as any other day and Edward's army gather in front of the conquered castle. "My lord the men stand ready for the journey ahead," Titus relays. Johnson rides up with more men. "I told you to stay with the castle," Edward reminds. "My lord and soon to be king, I swore an oath to you and I will honor it on the battlefield." "Loyalty like that is hard to come by," Edward assures with a smirk with Johnson proudly adding, "These are the best soldiers I have." "Will they live and die at my command," Edward asks. "They will serve you as they have served me," Johnson relays. "You there come here," Edward points saying. The soldier rides up to him. "Kill your noble and prove your worth to me," Edward requests with a coldness sitting on his horse and his men gather round. "You have your orders and I have told you what must be done," Johnson states to him. The soldier pulls out his sword knowing that he has been told what will happen on the field of battle. He trusts his sword into his heart, and his noble falls from his horse and hit's the ground with a thumping blow. "I guess I can take your word for it," Edward says to the dead noble; kicks his horse and they ride for their long journey. The soldiers ride off from him lying dead on the ground with one's heart heavy in honoring his noble's last words. "William you were right when you told me we could take the castle with no loss of men," Edward smiles with pride in his face. "My lord, do you think we will be able to reach them by the full moon," William inquires. "That is my intent." "Your spies have reported his army is vast and he will be a mighty foe. Even with the wolf on our side the task will not be easy," William says. "That is why we will make more of our brothers." "My lord they will not be able to control the beast that lives within them they are liable to kill our soldiers as well." Edward looks at him with no expression on his face, "But they will kill his too." William turns to Tyrolean asking, "Tyrolean is there any way to control the beast they will become?" "No. You wear the only thing that keeps you in the mind of the beast." "Relax William I am sure you will think of something before we get there," Edward relays to him. "My lord we could go and call upon the mostly dead to fight for us," Tyrolean says." "That maybe a thought my sorcerous friend," Edward suggests they ride towards their destination.

"Sir, a rider just brought this to the castle," Elizabeth's father opens the letter. "What does it say my lord," a servant asks. He reads the letter written by William. "It brings news that my daughter is dead, killed by the soldiers of Sir Richard the lion heart, it requests my help," he answers. A father's love fills his heart along with a father's anger. "Gather the men we sail to give him our support!" The servant leaves and goes to gather his men.

"Alex did you sleep well last night?" "Yes, my lady, always when you are with me." He brushes her hair from her face. She loves the feel of his hand on her skin. "Come on we need to get up and get moving," Alex suggests. Alex goes outside of his tent the men are gathering their things. "Have we received word of where Richard could be," Alex asks Darius. "No, my lord our rider has not returned." "Then we must leave Essex and go into the land of Mercia. He should be traveling from out of North Umbria. We should be able to catch him in Mercia we will join with him there," Alex suggests. "I will tell the men we will pull out within the hour." Alex and his faithful leave for Mercia hoping to catch Richard before he would engage York and his minions. Edward and his army march across the land savoring the battle ahead.

My lord the ships are ready and loaded the army awaits your orders." Elizabeth's father puts his sword in his sheath saying, "Come we sail for their land!" They turn and walk out of his castle and they move towards the water. The navy of his country waits for him to board. He rides his horse onto the ship. "My lord, my lord," he hears from out of the ranks waiting to board he turns to see a man riding for the ship. A soldier stops him before he can get to her father. "Sir! Please! I bring a letter from your daughter!" "That is impossible she is dead," he answers from his horse. "No! my lord she lives and sent me here with this." The soldier tries to take it from his hand. He pulls it back from his grasp informing, "My lord I was instructed to put it in your hands!" He dismounts his horse and walks down the ramp he places it in his hands. He unrolls the paper, stands and reads what is written. "My lord do we still go to their land," the captain asks. He looks out at the water his brow carries the feeling inside of him and with an angered tone he answers, "Yes and not what we set out for. Prepare to set sail!" The soldiers raise the ramps the messenger rides on the boat with them. The wave's crash on the bow of the boat as the wind gives them the speed they need. Elizabeth's father turns towards the messenger and asks, "Boy what is your name?" "Kevin my lord. I am a faithful servant in the house of Lancaster." "The letter tells me strange things if they were not told to me in my daughters writing. I would not believe it." "I have seen the beast she speaks of with my own eyes my lord." "Tell me how she is not in the care of William." "William is in league with York and he has this beast in him, my lady is with his brother Alex." "Alex his younger brother how did this come to be," confused he asks. "I cannot say my lord but she is to marry him." Her father turns and looks out over the waters, the ocean breeze blows his hair in the wind and the smell of salt fills his nose, but in his mind, brings a father's worries.

"We have traveled far my lord the horses will need to be rested," James requests to Alex. "Very well we can camp on the river tonight." They unpack their things. The men build the fires and put up the tents. "Here Elizabeth," Alex says handing her a meal while she sits warming her hands by the fire. "Thank you, Alex." They sit and enjoy each other's company. Overlain walk up to them. "Evening my lady, Alex." "Overlain come and share the fire," Elizabeth requests. He takes a seat beside them. "I have not seen you today what has kept you," Alex asks. "I have spent my time searching for something." "Did you find what you were after?" "Yes, I did." He pulls something from the pocket of his cloak. Alex reaches for it, "It is not for you my lord but for the lady in waiting." He hands it to her. "What is it," she asks. "It is part of the crystal you held in your hand. I give this to you as a wedding gift it will serve as an unbreakable bond between you too." She holds it up the firelight shines upon it and it carries a certain glow. "Well put it on," Alex suggests to her. She connects the chain around her neck at it finds rest between her breasts carried over her heart. "You didn't get me anything father," Alex says with a wink of an eye. "Father, you haven't called me that since I saw you in the church it is for you as well," Overlain suggests. "For me too," Alex inquires in a joking manner. Overlain looks towards the fire relaying, "Sure, it will remind you of the life in her eyes every time it sparkles!" Alex laughs to his statement then asks, "Overlain do you think Richard will accept us as we are?" "Who knows what will be in his heart but he will have no choice when he sees the army that stands before him," Overlain states then asks of Alex, "What will you do when the war is over?" "I will go out and do what we intended to do before you called me back," Alex informs looking at her then returns back to the fire adding, "I have no lust for the throne or the title of a noble man. My wife will be all I will ever need or want." She leans in and kisses his cheek saying, "My lord I will go and freshen up in the tent, I will await you." He stands and helps her to her feet. She places her hand upon Overlain's shoulder saying, "Overlain thank you for this gift. I will wear it always." "Thank you, my lady. I was hoping you would like it and keep it with you always." She turns and walks back to the tent. Alex and he sit and talk with one another. "Overlain I find myself where you once stood. I do not know if I could kill my brother." "You must my lord, I found weakness once and I do not intend to make that mistake again. We must be strong for it is hard to convince yourself that the world would be better without someone you love." "Do you love your brother," Alex questions. Overlain watches the flames dance in the wind replying, "Yes still to this day, but I see him for what he is, the power he beholds has made him drunk with it. What of you did you find any kindness in your brother that night in the cave," Overlain asks. Alex picks up a stick and begins to draw in the sand between his feet informing, "No I don't believe I did, all I could see was the lust in his eyes for her." Alex throws the stick into the fire. He stands to his feet stating, "If I had to choose between the two of them. I would save her. God forgive me for what I know in my heart." He turns to walk towards the camp. "Alex, if your brother truly loved you. He would not have put his pride before you. Carry that with you always because it will save you in the end." Alex walks from the fire and heads into the tent. "Overlain share a drink with me," James says as he sits down by the fire. "You know I do not drink wine." James looks at him smiles and informs, "You do tonight." Overlain takes the cup from his hand and they drink of the bottle with the wine filling him James says, "Overlain I am sorry for the way I treated you in the beginning. I see now you are a good man. You saved young Alex and in that I am grateful." "Tell me James can you kill William if you have too," Overlain asks before sipping his drink. "William was always drunk with power his father knew that. Alex should have been born first," James looks up to the sky and answers, "Yes Overlain, I can kill him. I pray to our father that I find him first and relieve Alex from the burden of it." Overlain and James finish off their bottle enjoying the company of each. The men rest for the day ahead, Alex and Elizabeth hold each other in the night keeping each other warm from the coolness in the air. A rider comes into the camp his horse covered in sweat from a hard ride across a plentiful earth. "My lord the rider returns," Enos informs sticking his head into the tent. Edward steps from his tent. The man walks up to him and he asks, "What news do you have?" "Richard moves into Mercia to seek you out," the rider informs. "Then we shall see if we can appease him. How far away if he?" "I cannot be certain when I traveled to a town. I spoke with soldiers going to join him they boasted that every man who wished to be as a free men was going to join him." "Tell the men we move," Edward turns commanding Titus. The army restarts their march for the battle that will be ahead.

"My lord the wind is in our favor we should touch their shores faster than expected. What are you going to do when we get there? Will we go seek out Elizabeth or take the fight to York," a commander asks. "We will seek out my daughter. Then we will stand with who she is with," Elizabeth's father sternly informs. The sun loses its hold on the land and the curtain of night covers the sky. The moon light shines on the water of the ocean her father watches it dance on the face of it, carrying him forward. His heart cares not for his duty as a King of a land but as a father's love for a child.

"Are these the men I requested," Edward asks gazing on them behind the bars. "Yes, my lord. Criminals and outcasts each noble had to offer." Rexstin informs walking with him. They stand just out of the light of the fire. Edward and his minions stand with him. William walks up to him suggesting, "My lord if you are to mark them it should be somewhere no one can see or the plan will not pay off as well as you hope." The men are forced into a line as Edward transforms to the wolf. The horrified men try to flee their chains but each in turn are marked creating more wolfs in the ranks of his soldiers; mindless beast to be driven against those who oppose him. Edward and his army march north into Mercia. Richard marches his army towards the south, Alex and his soldiers ride north towards them. Lord Sand when arrived will ride from the coast east to find her. The battle written in the pages of time lay ahead. Edward's soldiers marked from him heal from the wounds placed upon them. A three days pass bringing the conflict closer.

"My lord a rider returned. He has found Richard resting at the river ahead," Jonas relays to Alex. "Tell him to take point and lead us too him!" The rider changes horses and begins to lead them to who they seek. "My lord we have found him in time," Jayel says as they move or the land. "Now all we need to do is convince him of what will lay ahead," Alex states knowing the task will not be easy. They move across the land through a forest and to the river then see the smoke from the fires as they get close to his camp. "Lord Richard more riders approach!" Richard stands to his feet and looks out towards them. "Halt who goes there," guards rush out demanding. Alex reaches into his bag taking out the flag with the emblem of his family then shows it to him informing, "I am Alex Lancaster these are my men and we wish to give support to Sir Richard against a common enemy" "Come with me. I will take you to him," a soldier says then turns his horse and they ride for a big tent in the center of the camp. "Sir Richard the house of Lancaster rides here to speak with you," the soldier announces handing

him the flag. "Alex or William," Sir Richards requests. "Alex Sir Richard."
"Where is your father?" "He rests eternally from the hands of York," Alex
informs. "I am saddened for you. I had the up most respect for your father
even though we stood apart on many things." "Sir Richard these are not the
times to remember a time pasted, but for working together in the common
interest of this great land." Alex dismounts his horse walks before him
and kneels at his feet swearing, "Richard I pledge my loyalty to your flag,
I have no noble claim to the throne of this land. I am but a common man
fighting for freedom against an army lead by an unholy man, if he gains
control of the throne dark times will cover this land." Richard finds truth
in his words then says, "Stand to your feet Lancaster and welcome! Come
inside and get out of the heat." Alex walks back and helps Elizabeth from
her horse. "Darius set up camp where they tell us too. We will meet you
there when I am done." Darius rides through the camp following a soldier.
"Darius," a voice yells from all the men gathered. He turns to see who has
called him. He looks and sees a foe from days past. "So, you have come to
support Richard," he asks with a smarten voice. "I have come to support
my lord Lancaster and nothing else," Darius relays. "Like it or not we are
thrust to fight a common enemy," he suggests Darius unsure of him waits
for the next move. He walks to his horse extends his hand saying, "I have
certainly had enough of fighting against you. I am glad to have you with us!"
Darius shakes his hand and catches back up with the soldiers of a common
flag. "James, keep your eyes and ears open we are among friends and foes,"
Darius suggests quietly making it back to them. Alex with Elisabeth walk
into the tent. They sit at a table his servants place food and drink before
them. "Miss Sand for once the rumors are true you are a beauty for the eyes
to hold." "Thank you, Sir Richard." "Was she not given to your brother,"
Richard questions. "That Sir Richard is a long story and for another time.
You must know what you face in this army that comes to conquer you!" "I
have heard the rumors across the land and I can find no truth in it they are
but lies to strike fear in the eyes of their enemies," Richard declares. "My
lord, do not turn a deaf ear to what you have heard, all are not lies," Alex
implores. Richard looks out from his chair gazing out the opening of the
tent then turns back asking, "What do you know?" "Have you heard of the
sorcerous Tyrolean?" "Yes, his name has reached my ears." "Sir Richard
please will you send a servant to my tent and have them bring the one called

Overlain to this tent." Richard sends out a servant Alex goes on, "Tyrolean has cast a spell upon Edward and his closet, they can become beast before men, with this, he has gained an advantage no human army can conquer," Richard shows his disbelief but Alex continues informing, "I have seen this with my own eyes my father castle was burned to ruins because he would not listen to the words of Overlain." "What kind of beast can they become," Richard requests with Alex replying, "Wolves bigger than men." "Young Alex I feel you have been in the sun to long. I cannot believe what you tell me these things should not be heard by a Christian man." "I know it is hard to believe but you must take my word." "Sir, who you have requested is here," a servant informs with Overlain walking into the tent. He bows his head to him asking, "My Lords you sent for me?" "Overlain I was just explaining to him the beast that lives in them but it falls on deaf ears," Alex informs. "Sir Richard he speaks the truth my brother has unbalanced this world and it must be set right." Richards grows impatient informing, "Alex you and your men are welcome to share the battlefield with me but I will hear no more of this." "As you wish Sir Richard," Alex relays they stand bow their heads and leave his tent. They walk back to where it is they will find rest. "He is a fool Overlain," Alex says entering their tent. "My love a thinking men only truly believe what their eyes can see," Elizabeth relays Alex smiles kisses her face saying, "Thank you my lady you have given me an idea." He turns to Overlain requesting, "Overlain I have need of you this night." Alex relays to him what he has planned then sends him to get what he will need. "Darius I see they have treated us well," Alex informs looking at the commendations around them. "So, far my lord," Darius answers. "Go and gather the men in our circle. We have someone to convince this night," Alex orders. Darius does as he is asked with his plan revealed; the men wait. Alex and Elizabeth spend the rest of the day in the company of their circle.

"My lord the man has returned from the sea," Titus states as he comes in through the front of the tent the man walks in behind him. "Did you deliver the letter to him," he bows to a knee informing, "Yes I did my lord!" "And," Edward asks. "He rallied his troops to set sail for here." "Well done now go and rest from your travels." The soldier leaves to tent. "I see your little lie has paid off," Edward suggests to William. "Then we must send a rider to meet with him," William informs. Edward turns to a commander of the army, "Send a soldier to greet him when he lands." The commander does as he requested. "We must not let him know that I left her in the cave with my brother all but dead." "Yes, I would agree." William goes to walk out of the tent. "William what if we use bringing him here to our advantage," Edward suggests with a devilish grin. "Meaning what my lord?" "Well it seems to me we could take the moment to kill him while he is here. I mean it is better to do it now than to sail to his land where he could have the advantage over us." "I think we could arrange something my lord," William relays smiling and lets the flap of the tent close with his departure.

"Did you find what you will need," Alex asks Overlain with his return. "Yes, it rested in the forest just put these herbs in with their meal and it should knock them out long enough to take him from the tent." Alex looks at the beauty of his life saying with a smile, "Elizabeth I have need of you." "What do you ask of me?" "Place this in with the meal to his most trusted when you bring them their food." "How will I get them to eat what I bring they will certainly have their own cook to feed them?" Alex smiles at her informing, "I think the beauty of you will accomplish that." He kisses the back of her hand. She turns and takes her handmaid with her to help accomplish the deed. "Lucas, James, when you see that the herbs have taken affect you must grab Sir Richard from his tent and bring him to the spot we picked today." They bow their heads and leave his stead. "Darius we will need a diversion do you think you can provide one," Alex turns to him asking with his reply," "I am sure something will come to mind." Darius smiles and walks out of his tent. Elizabeth walks towards the soldiers the sun sets in the back ground the crystal around her neck sparkles as she walks along as with her eyes, her full round cleavage shows as is her handmaid's as well. "What is this," the captain of the personal guards asks. "It is just a little something for Sir Richards finest," her handmaid says letting a well-placed smile show upon her. "I am quite sure it has been a long time since a woman has cooked for you fine gentlemen," Elizabeth relays. "Your wives must really be missing such well-made men in their beds," her handmaid adds. She begins to fill their plates and they eat it down with hunger in the eyes. Elizabeth with her start to gather the plates to leave when one inquires, "Where are you ladies off too?" Another pulls Elizabeth's arm with her informing, "I must get back to my tent before I am missed!" "No stay awhile let me show you what a real man can do," he boasts pulling her into his lap, tries to taste of her lips as the men begin to laugh. He leans in waiting for her soft lips to press against his. Finding a sharp point of a dagger to his throat Elizabeth asks, "Do you really want a kiss this bad?" He releases her arm. She holds the point to his throat it slightly digs into his flesh as she pulls away informing, "Come on Carissa. I think we are done here." She pulls the blade from his neck and starts to back off. A soldier unseen cuts off their retreat informing, "I don't think we are finished!" "What are you men doing get back to your posts now," Sir Richard says stepping from the mouth of the tent. The men release them and snap back to their posts he turns to them, "What are you ladies doing here? You best go back to the tents of your men." "Yes, my lord it was but a small miss understanding," Carissa suggests then takes Elizabeth's hand and they make their way back to the tent. "Did you have any problem," Alex asks with their return. "Only a small one my lord but it was nothing that I could not handle," Elizabeth answers. He leans in and kisses her cheek suggesting, "I have found that there is not much you cannot handle." They wait till time slips forward. "Alex the men grow tried," James relays. "Darius whatever you are going to do now would be the time," Alex relays. Darius walks to the tent of the one who called out to him earlier. He sits in front of a tent drinking wine and talking of battle. "Darius welcome have a drink," he requests as he walks up to him. Darius takes the cup from his hand and downs the liquid filling the cup. "It has been so long since the days of old," the man deep into the wine proclaims adding, "Glorious days were they not?" Darius begins to laugh with them he puts his hand on the well-made man's shoulder saying, "You know old friend I have not forgotten the arrow you placed into me!" He punches him in the face and knocks him for his seat. The men grab him as their lord regains his feet. "Release him at once I can handle my own," the man declares. The soldiers of the camp see a conflict starting and turn their attention to it. "Well come on old friend you will find it hard to stick me when I am facing you" Darius boasts pulling out his sword throwing it to the ground reminding, "We are allies in words spoken to Richard." The man takes his sword out and does the honorable thing. The dust flies from the ground as the sword hits then they begin to circle around one another. James and Lucien sneak into the tent bound and gage Richard place him on a horse and take him from the camp. Darius and his foe now friend fight with all they have. Darius knowing, he could easily defeat him rolls with the punches. They roll off on another and lay on their backs. "You have fought well like the days of old," Darius tells him. "Yes, we did," the well-made man declares with a hardy laugh. They begin to laugh and they stand to their feet. "You were right old friend it was bad of me to shot you in the shoulder when your back was to me I had that coming," the man suggests. They walk over back to the tent he hands him a jug and he takes one in his hand "To victory and death to the York's rise to power." The crowd begins to chant victory and they swallow the jugs down. "It was good to see you again old friend and I will stand by you on a field of battle," Darius informs patting him on the shoulder then leaves them to their boasts. Richard rides on the back of a horse. His heart pounds in his chest not knowing what will lie ahead. James helps him from his horse and sits him on the ground. The men stand around a fire. Overlain stands in the center. Alex walks up and pulls the hood from his head. Releases his bounds and pulls the gage from his mouth with it removed he demands, "What the hell is this! You ride into my camp under a flag of truce and deceive me!" "No, my lord I still hold my loyalty to you," Alex informs. "Then why have you brought me here in this way?" "I need to show you something and in the camp it would have caused a battle to begin and I need you to see what will lie ahead." Alex backs off the light of the fire barely shows them standing with him yelling, "This is madding what is this thing you wish to show me?" Their eyes begin to change, it is the last thing he can see before they stand in full darkness; his ears hear the sound of their bodies popping and the growl of the wolf. Fully transformed they step back into the light of the fire. Richard's heart beats faster his mind screams to the sight as Alex and his faithful stand before him as the wolf. "What in all of hell is this?" He begins to stand losing his footing falling back terrified of what his eyes behold. Alex leaps and grabs him by the neck lifting him until his feet barely touch the ground. Then he releases him and the wolf stands before him. Alex begins to take back the form of his human self. Richard's eyes behold it all. Alex stands before him breathing hard from the change asking, "My lord do you know believe what your eyes have seen?" The other still in wolf form draw closer in. "Yes, yes I must," he shudders to say. He reaches out with his hand and touches his face, his hand shaking as it touches his skin requesting, "What kind of devil is in you?" "Not a devil Sir Richard it is just a spell cast upon them. The wolf is only evil if the man who becomes it is," Overlain stresses. "Where did you get that charm my eyes have never seen its match,"

Richard asks looking at it resting around Alex's neck. "The medallion gives us control of the beast without them the wolf would be wild like its nature," Alex informs. "My lord. My brother has placed this same spell on York and his minions and they go out to devour this land." "Why would any man bare such a burden", Richards asks of Alex. Alex dresses as do the men replying, "I was wounded in battle and it was a fatal blow it was the only way for her to save me, some of my men bore the mark of the beast and would soon become it any ways. I tell you Sir Richard if the beast marks you and you live when the full moon raises it will consume you," Alex implores. They mount their hoses and Alex hands him back his sword stressing, "I beg your forgiveness for bringing you here in such a manner but I could think of no other way to convince you I spoke the truth." They ride back for the camp. Richard rides in silence. His mind still tries to grip what he has been showed. They journey a short distance when Richard pulls on his reins finale speaking, "My god in heaven what if he has made more of this kind?" His eyes fill with the horror in his mind. "Fear not Sir Richard Overlain can give us the weapons we will need to drive back this army," Alex rides to his side proclaiming. Richard sits for a moment then kicks his horse and they begin to move. "Sir Richard is gone," a servant yells as he looks inside of the tent. The men begin to scramble searching the camp for him. A commander walks up he sees the soldier dead in their sleep. "Someone has drugged them commander," a soldier with him suggests. "You there was any one around them today," he inquires of an older man resting nearby. "Just the lady in waiting brought here with Lancaster," the old man suggests. The commander turns and rushes to the tent. He steps in and pulls her out demanding, "Where has Lancaster taken Sir Richard? Speak now or I will gut you here for all to see." "My lord I know not where they are," Elizabeth explains. Richard with them return and Alex sees what is going on rushing away from them Richard yells, "No wait Alex!" Alex rides in swift and strong with using the speed of his horse and the strength of the wolf. He places his father's sword to his head angered informing, "I swear to you if you do not unhand her you will find me a most unpleasant kind of man!" His soldiers move to surround him. Sir Richard rides up ordering, "Release her!" The commander releases her and Alex places himself between them. "My lord we thought they took you," the commander relays with Alex glaring to him. "No I found the men asleep and I rode off with them to discuss the days ahead," Sir Richard informs. The commander puts up his sword and walks away from them. "Commander I believe you owe the lady something," Richard suggests. He turns back to them and bows his head imploring, "My lady, forgive me." He turns and walks through the soldiers. Richard rides closer requesting, "Forgive him Miss Elizabeth. He is not the most pleasant of a man but his skill on the battlefield few can match." Elizabeth nodes her head he turns to Alex requesting, "Sir Alex will you come to my tent in the morning and bring Overlain with you? We have much to discuss." "As you wish my lord," Alex answers bowing his head. Richard rides back for his tent. Alex walks her back to their tent and the men go their way. James and Lucien stand guard out in front as they slip inside. Alex walks up to the table and places his sword upon it. He stands with his back to her informing, "It almost got away from me." He looks down at the ground. "It would be understandable my lord," Elizabeth relays. "No, you don't understand," turning to her he says with his eyes filled with tears. He grabs her by her shoulders and pulls her to his face declaring, "I would have killed them all if one hair of your head would be hurt!" She looks in his eyes and she can see the wolf begin to come out the rage inside of him builds. Cooling his desires, she asks softly, "My lord stay here with me it is ok." She wipes a tear from his cheek her touch draws down his emotions. He hugs her holding on to her with all the love in his heart informing, "I just would lose it all if something would happen to you." "Come my lover let me wash this day from you." She backs up undoing her top. Her beasts slowly come into view she takes his hand and softly places it on her breast saying, "Come my husband to be, bring the passion of the wolf to me." Alex blows out the candle lighting the tent. He kisses her with passion and they fall to the floor as they grow their love for one another into the night. "Do you ever wish you could trade places with him," Lucien turns to James asking. Her cries of passion come from the tent as they stand their guard. "Every time I can see her beauty," James tells him they smile at one another holding a dream that will never happen.

Alex wakes. The sun warms the ground. Alex goes to the tent of Sir Richard and he takes Overlain with him. Entering he greets, "My lord?" "Come in Sir Lancaster," welcoming Richard says. Alex and Overlain walk into the tent. He stands from the table and offers them a seat. The servants place a meal in front of them and they take their seats at his table. "Alex I am still taken in by what I saw last night," Richard declares. "I know my lord it is wondrous to the eyes." "How you must struggle to keep the beast at bay." The charm I wear does help in such matters," Alex replies. "What power it must have to hold down such a thing what would happen if it was to fall from your neck," Overlain looks up from his meal with Alex answering, "Then the animal side of what I become would rule. I would have no control over what it would do." Richard looks out of the flap on the tent then turns back implying, "Then I pray it never leaves your neck!" "Sir Richard, we have ways to fight against this beast that comes and away to remove the spell cast upon them," Overlain states to share a light of hope. "What weapon would stand against them," Richard sits down asking. "We need all the silver we can lay our hands on, it should be forged into spear heads, arrow tips, we can sparkle the dust of the silver onto the swords already forged, Overlain can bless the silver with a spell and it will be deadly to them," Alex states. "Is that all we can do," Richard still taken in by the power of it asks. "No, my lord you have me and my faithful," Alex assures. Richard takes their words to heart, stands from his table claps his hand and a soldier comes in with him ordering, "Go out over the land and gather all the silver that can be found and bring it into the camp!" The soldier goes out of the tent never to question the words of his lord. Alex stands from the table and bows his head to him, "My lord me and my men shall set out to help." Alex walks out of the tent. "Overlain please remain here with me until they return I have questions," Richard requests with Overlain's reply, "As you wish Sir Richard." Overlain retakes his chair. Richard now seated across from him then asks, "What does the York and his followers wear to keep in their beasts?" "I cannot answer what they are forged from or the cup he used to cast the spell," Overlain says adding, "The ones Alex and his men wear were forged from the nails that hung him to the cross." "Does night have to fall for them to become what they are," Richard requests. "No, my Lord they can change at wills. Only the full moon will have a sway over them." Richard stands walks to the front of the tent looks out the mouth of it implying, "So during the full moon they will become the beast." "That is what I am saying my lord." "What happens is someone was bitten by them and lived?" "They will become the wolf when the full moon stands high but they will be weaker than the original and would have no control over the animal they become." Richard walks out of the tent and stares out towards the landscape. Overlain moves with him. "York could spread this curse from shore to shore," Richard suggests. "Yes, my lord, the only hope we have is to defeat him, cast the spell upon him and release this curse he would spill upon men." "God be with us in the dark days ahead," Richard asks in a prayer liked manner.

The white gulls fly against the back ground of the sky, as the ships make port. Sir Sand is the first to ride off the ship and his most faithful follow closely. "Sir Sand, Sir York sent me too lead you to him. I am sorrowful for the loss of your daughter," a servant in the York army informs, greeting their arrival. Sand rides closer to him thrusting his dagger into his heart. The man grabs his chest in pain slowly falls from his horse. The dagger rests in his chest with Sand informing, "You can give him that when you see him in hell!" Sand with those around him set out for the land ahead. Soldiers pour off the ships and follow in his path. Sand and his army ride swift until they come to a town with seeing a man walking the road Sand asks, "My good man what do you know of Sir Richard and where I might find him?" "Rumor is he rides out of Mercia. Lord York rides to meet him this is to be the last fight for the crown of this land" he answers. "What happen to the noble of this land?" "He fell in battle to Sir York, he is master of this land and the crown I am afraid." "We shall see," Sand boasts then brings his horse into motion departing from him. His passion of being a father guides his search and those who follow with him.

"My lord the men are ready to move," Connor tells Edward surrounded by his generals. "What of our rider has he returned," Edward asks. "No, my lord he may be on his way back," Connor suggests. "Keep me posted," Edward requests before returning to look over a map of the land in front of him. Seeing the place upon the map he desires, he informs, "We will travel to the valley of the moon and wait him on the west side. The valley we must cross to the west will help cover the rear flake," he turns and looks at William saying, "Order the men to start moving." "As you command my lord," William replies with honor.

The soldiers roam from home to home gathering what silver they can find. Many peasants scream at them for their loss. "I do not like having to take things from these people Alex. Some have saved a life time for this," Darius informs holding up the silver in a bag. "I know brother but they would not understand if we told them what it will be meant for. It would simply make it worst. To these people here, the things we can become are just whispers of fairytales." They ride on in search of another farm or home. The men travel the land retrieving sliver where they find it dusk falls over the face of their world and Alex returns. "Darius take what we have to Overlain I go to see Elizabeth," Alex requests passing by the first tents of the army. Alex turns and rides across the camp. Darius climbs from his horse sticks his head inside of the tent, "Here Overlain this is all we could find." He puts the bag on the ground and he picks it up. "There is not much to work with," Overlain states. "I know but maybe others will find more," Darius says letting the flap close on the tent. He pulls on the reins of his horse and it follows him back to his tent. "Where are you Elizabeth," Alex asks as he sticks his head inside the tent. "Alex love," she jumps up saying with eyes filled with joy. She kisses his lips with him asking, "I was wondering if you might take a walk with me under the stars tonight?" "I could think of nothing that would please me more," she joyfully replies. He grabs a bag and puts what they will need in it. He reaches out and takes her hand requesting, "Come my lady, shall we." They walk from the tent and into the forest. She has no fear when she is near Alex, his new found senses guide their way. "So, tell me my loving man where are you taking me?" "You will see James told me he saw it when he rode into the forest." They travel a little more and she sees where they are heading. The moon's light shines on the fall as its water spills out over the rocks. With its breathtaking sight she informs, "Oh Alex it is beautiful." They let their clothes hit the ground slowly journey into the water and they sit on a rock as the water spills over them. They hold on to one another. Alex lathers her hair running his fingers across her scalp she relaxes and lets her passion build. She leans her head forward and lets the water do its work in taking the soap from her hair then stands and turns to him, her beast fully show in the light of the moon, proudly showing her excitement. The moon shines off her milky white skin with him taking a moment to behold her body, then reaches out with the softest touch running his hands over her hips up across her stomach and up between her breasts then gently pulls her lips to his. Their tongues dance, his hands roam her body. He slides his fingers into her and she pants with pleasure, their hearts beat faster, their passion burns as they dance to the same music. Their bodies fill with desire and their love spills out of them as they climax together. "My man, my lover, I love you more with each breathe in my body," she caringly informs. They hold on to one another as the water spills off their bodies. Richard sticks his head into their tent but he cannot see them. Seeing Kronus he asks, "Where is Lancaster?" "I believe Elizabeth and he had found a place to be alone," James over hearing his question answers. "He will return in time," Kronus assures adding, "When he arrives I will see to it he comes to your tent." "I remember the feeling of being in love," Richard states with a smile adding, "I will see him when they return." Richard turns and walks from their camp. The blacksmiths of the land, melt the silver and make the weapons to bring down their enemies with Overlain blessing the silver as it is passed before him. Alex and her walk hand in hand back towards the camp she leans against his shoulder to keep him close as their horses follow the pull of their reins. "My lord Sir Richard came looking for you," James informs. He walks her into the tent. "My lady I will return shortly." He kisses the back of her hand and goes outside of the tent requesting, "James please keep an eye on my lady." Alex walks through the camp and to his tent. "You need to speak with me my lord?" "Yes, I have received word that York's army marches for us they move north towards this place," Richard informs pointing to a place upon the map on the table. Alex leans over saying, "Yes I know where it is. The locals call it the valley of the moon." "Will it give him a tactical advantage," Richard questions. "Only in that it would make it harder to flank them from the rear." "Then at first light we will set out to engage him," Richard informs. Overlain comes into the tent seeing him Alex asks, "How many weapons do we have?" "Not many I am afraid, enough for three hundred arrow heads and twenty spears heads and there was only enough silver dust to bless a very few swords." "It will not be enough to face them all," Richard stressed to the information stated. "My lord we only need the silver weapons to kill the beasts after they have been beaten it will be man to man and we should prevail," Alex says to steady his mind. "How do you think we should play this out," Richard asks to him. "If you and your men stand ready to face his army he will not think we are as they. Edward will only expect to face mortal men. We will use the element of surprise to run through his ranks." "I would rather have you by my side Alex," Richard states finding favor in him. "I will leave Overlain and Lucien with you my lord to protect you in the battle ahead. They will give their lives to protect you," Alex boasts for them adding, "Remember he will not unleash the beast within him until the night falls." Richard shakes his hand in their agreement. Alex bows his head and turns to walk away when Richards asks of him, "What will you do when the battle is over?" "What I had intended to do when I took Elizabeth and left my father's castle. I will go out and live a simple life. I care not for the rule over a land or the power of the throne." "Would you consider staying" Richard request adding, "I need men with your courage to help hold the land." "My lord if we survive in the dark days ahead I may consider it," Alex informs then looks up towards the stars then back at him. "I might ask you why you seek the throne? My father once told me the throne room was a prison." "Yes, I know what he meant, but I feel I could lead this country into better times after all people need someone to guide them." Alex pats him on the back then leaves for his tent. Overlain turns to go his way with Richard asking of him, "Overlain do you think it wise for her to be here with us? I could have an armed party escort her home." "She must stay with him, if they were to capture her they would have the one thing that his heart desires and then control over him," Overlain informs. "Can we win the day," Richard asks. Overlain takes a moment then in his wisdom answers, "Good wins out in the end my lord, but it is always darkest before the light. We must keep faith." Overlain goes his way and Richard goes back into the tent with the weight for a ruler on his brow.

Sir Sand rides across an unknown land stopping where he can to rest, gathering information from homes he passes seeking Richard, riding with the worry of a father's weight in his heart. Three days pass before him. The mighty battle that lay ahead rests with the men of the land each traveling with pride in their heart, feeling the pull of it in their bones. Each side boasts of glorious passed victories and dream of their enemies driven before them.

"Sir the men leave now to join them," William walks in Edwards mist saying. "I like the plan of sending loyal soldiers from us marked by my hand into their mist they will be as sheep to the slaughter with wolves' among them," Edward says looking out at the men dressed in the colors of Sir Richard adding "I could not have made a better choice than putting my blood into your veins." William fills with pride to his compliment smiling as the men ride out of the camp to perform their Judas act. "The others marked can be driven into them with the guidance of Tyrolean. We will send the degenerates to take their first blow," William adds.

The thundering sound of horses pounds the ground as her father drives his men and their horses. A soldier closet to him rides up beside him informing, "My lord I know you seek your daughter but we must rest these animals and the men or when we reach them we will not have the strength in man or beast to engage anyone!" He rides harder and fast but the sweat from his horse covers its body seeing this, his words sets into his ears. Sir Sand begins to slow down his horse coming to a stop peering at the landscape before him with a heavy heart he states, "Very well we will rest them and leave as soon as we can." "My lord Elizabeth will be fine," a commander suggests. "I find no comfort in your words," Sand relays climbing from his horse. Takes its reins and walks to the lake those around him leave him to his silence.

The night grows long. Alex stiffs the air, "What is it Alex," Elizabeth asks with his departure from their bed. Alex looks from out of the tent informing, "We have stragglers riding in wait here and I see if I know them." The men ride up to Richard's tent his soldiers ride up with them. "Sir Richard these men ride in for the battle," a soldier informs. Richard walks from the tent. Alex walks in among them hearing some of what they reveal to Sir Richard inquiring, "You say you have seen York's army within a short ride?" "Yes, my lord their camp lay just this side of the valley," one of them points out saying. "How did you men find us?" "We rode under cover with the Army with are garments hidden. Our noble's house fell in battle and we swore an allegiance to York from the fear that no one could stand against him," the soldier climbs from his horse kneels on the ground before him saying, "We are here to serve this flag." Alex breathes in the air and a scent fills his nostrils. Richards turns to him asking, "Alex do you know these men?" He walks among them getting a better look then informs, "I have never seen their faces but if they come to fight against a common foe then we should welcome them." "Arise and welcome," Richard says to the man kneeling before him. With their names given to him they ride off with Richard's soldiers and they take them where they can rest. With his turning towards the tent Alex request, "My lord I need to speak with you in private." Richard holds the flap to his tent open and Alex steps inside informing, "My lord York has sent those men to betray us they have the smell of the beast upon them." "You mean he has marked them," Richard asks. "That is what I am saying the moon will be full tomorrow night and they will become mindless animals in our mist." "Why would you welcome them here," Richard questioning his action asks. "If we would have tried to take them a moment ago one could have escaped. We still hold the secret of what we are that will turn the tide in the battle ahead," Alex suggests. "What should we do with them?" "Just leave them to me. I will take care of it," Alex says then goes from the tent walks back to his camp to his faithful. "James, Darius gather the men we have something to do." The men gather and head to where the soldiers of York rest. Making it to them Alex says, "Hello at the camp might we join you?" "Come ahead and welcome," a soldier answers then walks over to him extending his hand. Reaching the fire another says, "Sir Alex we heard you were dead." "No just lies and wishful thinking," Alex remarks bringing a laugh to those surrounding him. "But your flag backs York with your brother," another relays. "Yes, like many wars before this one my family finds itself on different sides." The men talk of days past as they gain the trust of them. The night carries on as they eat of a meal and drink with one another with many words spoken a soldier says, "Sir Alex me and my men have ridden far we will need our rest for tomorrow will weigh heavy on everyone." "Just one more thing before you retire tonight," Alex leans over to him informing, "I know why you are here and what your purpose here is to be!" James and the other hiding from view pull their swords charging into the men. All but one finds their deaths quickly he rushes jumping on a horse fleeing from them, "My lord he is escaping," Kronus yells. He rides fast Alex rushes for a horse before he can pursue he falls from his horse from an arrow fired into him. Out of the darkness he hears, "Did you miss me my love?" Alex turns and she holds her bow proudly with a shot made. "Yes, my love always," greeting her with a smile then turns saying, "Lucas their heads must be removed or they could come back to haunt us." Alex puts his sword inside of his sheath turns to walk off and pauses requesting, "Take their clothes I have an idea." Lucas and the men begin to remove the heads from their bodies burning them in the flames before them. "You surprise me yet again my lady," Alex informs walking with her holding onto his arm. "I went looking for you because you had not returned. I just happened to find you." "Well whatever the case would be you saved me a long ride into the night." They slip back into their tent and rest for the night.

Elizabeth's father looks over the map seeing a captain come into his presence he asks, "Are the men finding rest?" "Yes, and the horses are recovering we should be able to ride out as the sun rises." "Good we will leave at first light we should be able to be at this valley of the moon by night fall."

The clouds move across the sky as the sun lights the world. "Pick out the same amount of men and have them dress in their colors I want York to think they are still among us," Alex reveals to Darius. The soldiers form the line. Richard rides in the middle of the men that have come to fight against a common foe for their hopes lie with him, as the side to win the day and to who will hold the crown of the land they all call home. The birds fly against the skyline going where men cannot, waiting for the feast ahead. Richard looks left and then to his right seeing his countrymen from all parts standing proudly with him. The wars that had ravished a land for more than a hundred years will come to an end in the horizon before him. He prays as he rides that God will be on his side. They ride from the forest that covers the land and in their sights the landscape opens before them. The army that stands against them waits across the way, seeing them Richard says, "Well Alex this day is upon us." Richard says as they stop. "Overlain, Lucien you must stay with Sir Richard and guard him with your life. Wait to release the beast until I set the charge we will catch them off guard," Alex orders. Alex and his faithful slide face shields down to keep their identities unknown. "My lady you will find it safer to remain behind the army," Sir Richard suggests. She sits on her horse with her face covered answering, "I will keep my place with my future husband." "As you wish," He replies then turns and rides down the ranks stopping at a general ordering, "Commander, get the infantry prepared to fight. Archers take your places!" Richard rides out in front of the men who support him seeing the fear in their faces he speaks, "Men that follow me today, I know you grow tired of the many battles we have fought with one another and the many battlefields we have shared together. Noble and common we all have fears but it is what you would do with the fear that burns in your breasts. We shall win this day and put these wars behind us then we will come together in a common interest for this great country we all call home! Stand strong and be brave, you will see many strange things in this day, keep God in your hearts and if the cries of battle grow quiet and you find yourself in a place strange to you relax you are in heaven with no more worries!" His horse walks up and down in front of them. The men focus upon him. "I will say that the gray fights for us and that it sounds strange but by the nights end you will understand." He pulls his sword from out of his sheath declaring, "Death to the York army life for this land!" The men scream out what he has said as they send their chants across the landscape. "My lord. do you tremble at the army before us," William asks with a smart tone on his tongue? "Come William ride out with me to see if we can talk him out of this battle." Edward, William and Duncan with his personal guard fly the flag of peace and ride out into the field that separates them. "Sir Richard they await us," his commander says. "Darius stay with her until I return." Alex joins them as they ride out to see them. He covers his sword keeping the rose hide from his brother. "Sir Richard it is a nice day for it," Edward cocky says with his arrival. "Sir York I do not tremble before your army." "Sir Richard we could spare the men today if you simply renounce your claim to the throne." "I will not renounce my right to claim the crown of this land. You save your men and announce me king," Richard suggests. "I will not give up the right to the throne Sir Richard." "The crown of this land should be worn by someone who will prosper this land not lead it into darkness," Richard proclaims. "The crown of this land should be worn by who can take it and hold it!" "Then so be it," Richard declares pulling his reins to depart from them. They each ride for their army. The ranks split as they ride back into the line with Sir Richard ordering, "Send up the flag." The general raises the flag signaling the foot soldier to prepare. "My lord they will just keep us busy until the night then they will ride out in full force," Alex suggests. "Yes, I know but many men will lose their lives long before darkness sets in." A horn makes it sound which rings out over the land. The men stand silent for a moment of time then with a mighty battle cry they charge for one another. The men lash out with their swords engaging in battles. "Archers move up to hold this position," Richard commands. "James, Darius, Lucas you are with me," Alex says before riding out on his horse to join the battle in the field. Elizabeth rides out finding her place with the archers. "Darius stay with her," Alex commands driving his horse. Darius pulls the reins on his horse and finds his place with her. The swords clash and men cry out as many find their way to Abraham's bosom. Alex leaps from his horse. James and the men follow his motion. James rushes among them his arm is fast and his strength unmatched cutting into many. James kicks one in the head, his axe strikes out cutting the men before him. Sir Richards's army wins the first wave of the day they scream out in victory as they stand in the field.

"My lord the mercenaries still lay in wait," Titus reminds. "Good then send a word to them to ride in from the west when the moon sets high and they hear the sounds of the beasts." "Mercenaries my lord," William puzzled inquires. "Why yes William I sent word to them a week before you came into my company. I have an iron clad deal with them." "Very wise my brother." "I should think. Richard has enemies in other lands I think it best to gather against him." "Send out the reserves!" Alex walks out in front of the men draws a line in the sand. A commander looks out over the field blurting, "Insolent bastard!" The horn sounds and many men stand up before them seeing their numbers James suggests, "Alex my lord, do you think it wise to provoke them?" "Scared my very large brother?" James laughs as the men prepare for them. The horses charge and they stand their ground. The swords clang. James drives a spear into a horse knocking its rider to the ground with one mighty swing he ends all of his worries. "Pull back," Alex commands. The men gather their horses and ride back towards their army getting in the range of the Archers their arrows find their marks. Alex jumps from his horse and finds her. "I think you pissed them off my lord,' Darius relays with a smile. The chasing army turns their horses to get back from their range. "Shall we, Darius turns to her asking with a smile finding her face they spring up from their cover taking their aim as the men stop a distance from them. "Why do we stop here," a soldier asks his commander. "We stop here to hold this line it is well out of range of their arrows." The soldier hears the wind and their arrows find their mark he falls from his horse with arrows sticking out of his head. "Where were the two of you aiming, Alex asks to them. "The right eye," she swiftly answers with Darius replying, "The left!" "I am glad you two are with me!" The battle rages on and the day grows long neither army can advance against the other. The sun grows heavy and sinks behind the earth with seeing it slowly disappearing Alex commands "Pull back and get closer to the men." They get back to the front of the lines. "You held them Alex," Richard says proudly. "Yes, but the battle will be when the sun sets." "James have the men take their places in the front of the ranks let them see their colors." The men find their ways to the front. "My lord I can see them among their ranks," Titus says looking through a spyglass. "My lord I have the explosive tips ready for the charge," Tyrolean informs holding spear tips in his hand. "I see you found a use in this battle." "I live to serve my lord," Tyrolean again informs. "Take these to the horsemen have the archers place them on the ends of arrows they can fire them from the backs of horses," William suggests. "Tell them to wait for the signal," Edward commands. "Come William the night falls fast and we set out to end this hundred year's war!" They ride out in the center of his ranks. The soldiers wait for the light to fade. "Men gather around," Alex commands. The men form around him. "When the moon begins to rise you will see many strange things, men that become beast. Shoot them with the arrows with silver tips and place them well!" "What did you tell us," A soldier close asks. "Beasts what kind of beasts," He adds. "You will see men transform into wolves before you." The men hold his words with no weight. "I know it is hard for you to believe but the rumors you hear of York and his minions are true and those who ride with me share in this same power and when you see us transform. I will need you to all scream in terror but hold in your hearts we fight with you." "What is the reason for this," another soldier asks. "The men who wore these colors were sent here to strike out from within our ranks. We must let York still think they serve their purpose." Richard rides in looks to Alex asking, "Are they ready? The night sets in!" "Yes, my lord I have prepared them the best I can." Elizabeth rides over to him. "My lady I want you to stay with Richard and guard his back. I do not need you here," Alex requests of her. Richard looks at her, "Come my lady I welcome those skilled eyes" "My lord should I go with her," Darius asks. "She can handle herself I need you here with me." The men light the fires against the night. The stars shine and the moon sets high. Alex and the men feel the pull of the moon. "Tell them it is time," Alex turns to a commander revealing and his faithful remove their mask. The soldiers form a line and the soldier covered in their cloths disappear behind them and the men begin to scream. "My lord it has begun," Titus says hearing their screams with the change coming upon him. "Signal the mercenaries," Edward orders before his speech is replaced with growls. The men send the signal and the mercenaries begin their charge coming from their west. Edward and the pack stand before the army fully changed then begin their charge. Edward with being the Alfa the mindless beast driven by pure hunger follows his path. "My lord what is this," a soldier says in a prayer like manner turning and seeing Alex and his faithful standing in the form of the beast. Richard hearing his cries orders to them, "Look forward and stand fast the wolves are with us, the gray beasts are soldiers of ours!" Alex and his brothers hide behind the men waiting for the charge to reach them. "Hold," Richard yells as they hear the sound charging for them. "Hold! Hold the fear inside and stand your ground," Richard's words ring out. The soldier's hearts beat faster as the unknown charge for them. "My lord riders attack from our right flank," his commander yells. The Horsemen leave their position to ride out to face the charge from their flank. The men's eyes finally behold what comes for them as the beast strikes fear inside their hearts. Titus leaps for the meal he sees before him, and the men part. Alex and his faithful leap out to face them. The wolves circle like dogs growling and pawing the ground the dust rises as they engage one another. "Fire the silver tipped arrows into the beasts," Richard commands. The archer's fire their arrows finding many of the mindless beasts killing them in their steps. Jayland charging behind them leaps for those in front of him a skilled archer fires an arrow striking him through the ear piercing his brain and death finds him. Others strike out at William and Edward but they pull from the fight. The men who killed their noble strike out inside of the York ranks. "My lord a common soldier screams with seeing Contour in wolf form knocking Sir Richard from his horse. He falls to the ground turns over and sees the jaws before him his eyes grow wild and the fear of a man sets in as the wolf moves in for the kill. Contour leaps in the air and at the moment of striking he falls dead upon his chest. Elizabeth holds her bow in her hands her well placed arrow sticks out of his head as he regains his human form. Richard rolls him off and stands to his feet. "Send in more of our army we have them in our grasps," York's commander says. William bites the arrow from his shoulder pulling out the thing that burns in his skin. He looks out from cover watching as the wolves meet their end. Alex, James, Darius with Lushien stands with the soldiers as they drive silver spears into the mindless animals created by Edward. The landscape explodes in the back ground and men scream into the night. "My lord they send more rides, they have us," a general with Sir Richard says. says. Elizabeth's father rides up to the field, his eyes hold the battle of the day. With a closet to Sir Sand peering quickly over the field he informs, "Look Sir Richard's flag!" "Men we ride to them," Sir Sand states pulling his sword from it sheath then points it out in front of him to lead the charge. The horses run with speed in their legs covering the ground quickly. William leaps out from the bushes knocking some from their saddles striking the ones closet with his claws their blood splatters the ground. Lucas charges out and attacks him leaping unto his back. "My lord what in the fires of hell is that," one of Sand's finest recovering his feet asks. "I don't know but it has taken the other from us!" Sand regains his horse and follows those charging into the men engaged in battle. The battle wages. Sir Richard with his forces gains the advantage of the day. Alex and his faithful stand with the men as a few still engage one another. One of sands soldiers seeing the beast charges in striking at James cutting the medallion from his neck and his beast becomes wild. James driven by hunger slashes out toward the men and strikes fear into their hearts. Alex leaps snatching it from the ground landing on his back and places it around his neck. James regains control of the beast. Alex and his faithful back way from the men, and seek solitude into the forest. Elizabeth stands upon the field. The ground burns in the night and she sees her father on his horse. "Father, she yells. Her voice covers the air and in all the battle noise her words find a father's ear. "Elizabeth," Sand yells in return riding for her, jumps from his horse and a father's arms wrap her with the ringing sound of retreat crying out. The York army pulls back. "Yeah, victory, victory, the men begin to chant. Edward and his army retreat into the valley of the moon. Alex and his brother search over the land letting their nose lead them to find their fallen brother. Alex and the pack stand looking at Lucas with his head removed from his body from the battle with William. The sorrowful cries of the brother's ring out, their howls echo over the landscape.

The bodies lay on the field now to be set in all time as battle in the valley of the moon. The birds of the air feast upon them with their bodies broken, heads lay open as the sight of the battle fills a soldier's mind. Overlain having ridden out at first light goes to find Alex and the men. "My lord the beast came out of me I couldn't control the hunger," James says sorrowfully. "I know my brother but all is well. I replaced it back upon your skin nothing happened just rest easy!" They hear the sound of a horse as Overlain rides up. Making it to them he throws them some cloaks saying, "Here my lord you and the men can cover up with these." They dress and walk behind him on the horse. "We have got to find something that will cover us when we wake. I no longer wish to see you naked my lord," Darius suggests. Alex and the men laugh making light of the battle in the night. They walk over the horizon. The soldiers seeing their return begin to chant, "Lancaster,

Lancaster," Alex pauses for a moment standing for all to see with his name echoing into the valley. Alex walks down to them they bow their heads in respect as he makes his way back to his tent. "Elizabeth," Alex calls entering the tent. Not finding her he dresses and walks back out of the tent with haste in his steps. "Have you seen Elizabeth," Alex starts to ask moving through the men. "She is in my tent," a voice replies from behind. Alex turns to see her father. "My lord Sand, it good to see you again," Alex bows his head saying. Sand walks by and enters the tent. Alex pauses and walks in behind him. "You have been staying with my daughter?" "Yes, my lord I have been with her." Sand sits down out the table then asks, "What do you intend to do with my daughter?" Alex searches deep into his heart answering, "I love her and I intend to marry her and to love her all of my days, if you will but grant me the hand of her." Sand stands walks up to him and looks him in the face. "Elizabeth told me she loves you but her right is to marry a noble." Alex heart begins to sink with her Father saying, "I will say one thing to you." Alex looks at him with respect to the honored man before him. Sand strikes him on the face with the back of his hand saying, "That was for taking her into your bed without the commitment of marriage first." Alex takes the slap in strife saying, "Yes my lord it was wrong of me, but from the moment she looked upon me she had my heart I never meant to dishonor your family." Sand places his hands on his shoulders suggesting, "As far as a noble man I could think none better welcome my son." Sand takes him out of the tent his arm rests on his shoulder saying, "Bring me the wine we have much to celebrate for I welcome a son!" The men in the camp cheer and Elizabeth runs to him leaping into his arms. "My lady I was worried about you," Alex kisses her lips her father rejoices as he walks by. The men shout in glee for the great day ahead and a battle won.

Chapter Six

A New Alpha Rises

William having caught a horse feeding in the forest rides back to the valley having been too weak to return in wolf form. "Sir William," a commander says to greet him then informs, "Lord Edward is in here!" He climbs from the horse still sore from the battle and walks inside. Edward lies upon the ground his body slowly heals from the arrows placed into it. "Has the others returned?" "No, my lord, Jayland, Contour will never return they lay dead on the field of battle!" Edward's rage swells a servant washing his wounds sits close he grasps the bucket of water flinging it across the tent ordering, "Leave us now!" "But my lord your wounds," the young maiden suggests. "My wounds will tend to themselves!" The servants leave the tent. "You told me your brother was dead, but he lives and with the same power we hold," Edward relays. "My lord I do not how he survived the last I saw him he was all but dead." "No matter we must return to the castle. I will find more soldiers to regain the numbers!" "But how my lord the medallions that they wore are in the hands of them or lost for all time they just be mindless beast," William reminds. "Tyrolean," Edward yells. He comes inside of the tent. "You told me there was no way he could cast the spell without the book and yet he did!" "My lord he must hold another book," but with his words Tyrolean lets a grin find his face. "What is there to grin about we were defeated in battle!" "It seems to me my lord they will need the book I hold to remove the spell, so we have what they want. Alex and his followers will have to seek us out. The battle was lost but we shall win this war," Tyrolean says. "We must return to the castle and make our stand there," Edward commands. The York army makes their way for their castle. Edward makes the ride home in the rack pulled by a horse. The ride home is not as glorious as his travel there.

Overlain looks out at the dead men in the field. Alex with James walks to his side. "Alex the bodies must be burned and their heads removed or they will return from the dead and feed upon the people of this land." "I will see to it my lord," James says then walks towards the field. "Alex before you leave I have something I wish to give you," Overlain informs taking something from his cloak. With it in his hand, "This is also part of the crystal Elizabeth held in her hands to keep you here it will always remind you of the bond between you." Alex places it around his neck it finds rest with the medallion. "Thank you Overlain I will keep it with me always." Overlain pats him on the back and they turn and walk back to the camp. A soldier lying close to them marked from the beast sees what the men are doing. His body bleeds but he finds the strength to leave the field fleeing into the forest with the sound of James's axe echoing in the valley. Alex walks into Sir Richard's tent saying, "My lord." "Alex victory is ours Edward and his army returns towards their castle." Richard proudly informs. "Yes, my lord for this day but Edward and his army will return once he has licked his wounds. We will have to follow them there and finish this war once and for all." "But not today for today let us enjoy it!" Alex toasts and drinks from the glass before him.

"My daughter, I fear I have let you down," Sand relays siting in her tent. "No, my father you have not" Elizabeth proudly answers. "Then why would you run with him and disappear into the night?" He walks over, brushes her hair from her face, looks upon her with a father's love, "All you needed to do was send word. The union I made for you was important to both our countries but your happiness would have meant more!" "Father I love him and I do not mean to break my father's heart but if it meant I would live a peasant's life with him then it would be all I would ever need." Sand pulls her close and hugs her. The small child that used to fill his eyes is now replaced with a woman. Alex walks up stands outside of the tent requesting, "My lord could I speak with you?" They walk out of the tent she walks holding on to his arm. "Alex where have you been most of this day I have missed you," Elizabeth inquires. "I am sorry Elizabeth that things steal me from your beauty when I am finished with your father I will return." She leans in to kiss him. Alex softly kisses her cheek and then the back of her hand his gesture gains favor in her father's eyes. Elizabeth returns to her tent as they walk away. "My lord, I would ask you if you would take her home until this war has ended and Richard sits on the throne," Alex requests as they walk. "She will not want to go back with me," Sir Sand states. "I know she is a stubborn woman with a strong heart but yours must be stronger. I will send word when this war is behind me. Then you can bring her back so that we may be married in front of God and you." "Tell me Alex the reason for it? I mean if I am to make her return with me and suffer her wrath. I would like to know why you would send her away." Alex stops and looks in his eyes, "You have seen the beast inside of me. I must end this war, remove the spell from me so that I can be normal again," Alex lets a horror show on his face adding, "Sir if something was to happen to her by my hands. I would die inside and nothing but a shell of a man would I be." Sand reaches out and holds the medallion in his hand resting around Alex's neck, "So it is true this gives you power over the beast." "Yes, my lord and if it should fall from me I would be as a savage animal." "I will have her return with me." "Thank you," Alex says. Together they roam through the camp with Sand taking this time to get to know the man he will call his son. They find their way back to his tent. "Elizabeth," Alex calls. She comes out of the tent. Her father sees the light shine in her eyes and the warm she has for him. "Alex, everyone has stolen your time from me this day stay here with me," Elizabeth requests with Lord Sand walking away to leave them to their moments of time. She takes his hand and leads him away informing, "I missed your warmth against me last night." "I am sorry my lady but with the men seeing the beast that rest in us. I thought it best to sleep away from this camp." "It is okay my lover I will have you beside me this night." Alex stops and turns to her, "About that my love I cannot share a rest with you tonight to honor your father we must save it for our day of marriage." "If you think I am going to go without you in my bed until we are married then you and my father have another thing coming," Elizabeth quickly relays. "My lady please we must respect his wishes as a father." She pulls back from him. "I also need you to return with your father to your homeland because I fear for your safety." The tears begin to fill her eyes. She turns and runs back to her tent with Alex calling out to her, "My lady! Elizabeth!" She doesn't look back in her steps to her tent, rushes inside closing the flap behind her. "Is there a problem my lord," Jayel asks. "No, she is just upset because I told her I wanted her to return with her father until this war would be over. I fear for her well-being." "She has proven herself capable of battle," Jayel reminds. "Yes, her fighting spirit I do not doubt but what if they were to capture her there would be no lengths to what I would do to have her back even if it meant turning on Sir Richard himself," Alex suggests looking down to the ground. Jayel pats him on the back saying, "You make a wise choice my lord she will see things your way." "Alex we have everything prepared if you wish to send our fallen brother from this place to the next," James walks over informing. "Very well James, I will be there in a moment."

"Elizabeth my I enter," her father asks. "Yes, father come inside." Elizabeth sits in the middle of her tent with her eyes redden from the tears streaming down her face. "What upsets you this night?" "Oh, it is just Alex he says he will not stay with me this night and that I must return with you home until this war is over. He thinks I would ever leave his side," Elizabeth states. "Baby we must all do what is right before the eyes of God," Sand suggests. "Don't give me that father! I was married to this man the moment I laid my eyes upon him! If that is not joined in the eyes of God then I do not know what is." Her father shakes his head up and down then replies, "My daughter you must do what he asks of you and return with me," her face becomes red she starts to speak but waits for his words, "If you are to take him as your husband then you must do your part and do as he asks." "There is but one way I will leave with you." "What would it be my daughter just ask and I shall make it happened," Sand proudly relays. "I know you have a vision of how your daughter's wedding day should happen but it doesn't matter to me I would have him as my husband this night." He pulls her to her feet wipes the tears from her face places a father's kiss upon her cheek then turns and walks out of the tent.

Alex stands before the men gathered around Lucas's body placed over the wood wrapped in his warrior attire. "Our brother gave his life so others would live, I will not disgrace his death with tears from my eyes he was a soldier in my father's house but most of all a brother to me!" Alex turns and lights the fire then backs off as it engulfs his fallen friend. The soldiers and his brothers of the wolf watch until it burns into the night; returning his body to its former form and sending his sprit to the river of sticks. Sand returns to her tent walks inside and she lies on her place of rest. "Elizabeth you awake?" "Yes, I am just laying here father." "Will you rise to your feet. I have something to show you." She wipes her tears and stands to her feet. "Close your eyes sweet princess." She closes her eyes, he places something on her head saying, "You could not get married without the proper attire." She looks in the mirror placed inside her tent a veil covers her face, he places a dress upon her table. "Keep in well spirits tonight. I will give you away tomorrow." Elizabeth leaps into his arms and hugs him like days of old, "Thank you father but how did you get this dress?" "It was your mother's. I have never told you but I carry it with me always, besides you, it is the only thing that remains of her." She looks and sees the love found in his eyes. "Father I will wear it with honor!" He kisses her cheek and turns and leaves her tent walks until he finds Alex. "Alex, come and walk with me." Alex readily takes his side and they walk. "She agreed to leave with me, and she is not mad with you it's just she will have to be without you for a while," Sand relays. "I wish there was another way but, I cannot run the risk of my brother getting his hands on her it would surely be the death of her." "She knows your reason son." "How did you get her to leave with you," Alex inquires with his answer, "I will answer you with a question of my own. Do you have something to get married in?" "The only cloths I have are what I have on surely nothing to marry with." "Then we shall have to render that for tomorrow you will marry her," Sand informs. Alex walks a little farther before the words finally set into his ears, then the joyous feelings roam through his body, "Married tomorrow?" Sand smiles and slaps him on the back, "Yes Alex my son, married!" "I must go to her sorry, sorry my lord," Alex suggests stumbling over a log but regains his footing then hurries away. "What is wrong with him Sir," Darius asks in seeing his clumsiness. "I just told him he was to be married in the morning. I guess it shocked him." "My brother's wedding day is tomorrow! I must go and tell the men," Darius leaves him and begins to spread the news. Alex runs to the tent and finds her handmaid guarding the flap. "Elizabeth," Alex calls out. "I am sorry my lord but you cannot enter." Alex asks as she steps into his path. "What do you mean I cannot enter? Elizabeth." "Alex Lancaster this is my wedding night and you may not see me," she yells from the tent. "But my lady I just." "Just nothing, you can see me in the morning as I walk to you," Elizabeth informs running her hand from out of the flap with her wrist bent. He kisses her hand the fragrance from her skin feels his nose like a favorite drug it numbs his senses saying, "I love you my lady." "I love you too," she answers pulling her hand back and he turns to walk off with a reminder, "Go back with my father indeed." Alex stops in his tracks, "My lady." Her hand maid steps to him suggesting, "Trust me my lord it is best to let it go. Now don't you have people who would celebrate this night with you?" Alex turns and walks away drifting through the camp. Seeing him slinking, "Where have you been my lord it is time to celebrate," Darien suggests. With his faithful pulling him into a tent they sit him down at a table. The music begins to fill the air. "Just a little reminder of what you can have no more," Kronus says to him with women of every color dancing their way to him. Their bodies flow smoothly and the men around them whistle and howl. They drink of the night and celebrate the bonds between them. Alex and Darius his closet sit by the fire the other haven found their partners for the night. "Darius you think he will be okay when morning comes," Alex asks with doing his best to keep his head straight. They look over at Overlain passed out from the wine. "You know for someone drinks not much he caught up tonight," Darius suggests slurring his speech. They laugh at one another their speech clouded by the wine in their bellies. "She is a fine woman and a prize to hold above all others, but are you sure she is the one? I mean the dark headed girl who danced for you maybe she could be the one." "Darius my brother if I had a thousand woman such as her they, they, it would not begin to match the warmth I feel in her arms, her eyes are like the sun burning inside of my heart, her skin is like the freshness of cool water flowing over my skin, her kiss touches me in a place I cannot name," Alex informs before the wine in his belly catches up with him and he falls backwards from the log. "Her kiss touches you in places you cannot name," Darius asks with a chuckle. He turns and his legs drape over the log. "Rest here tonight my brother and I was just teasing I know she is the one for you," Darius remarks before standing up and begins to walk away, he turns up the bottle of wine in his hands, as it hits his lips he falls backward unto the ground where he will rest for the night.

The morning sun comes quickly with James and Kronus standing over him. "My lord, you must wake up," Kronus requests. Alex doesn't move. James kicks his leg but still he slumbers. "Let me have the bucket of water over there," James requests. "He will not be happy!" "Yes, but as soon as he remembers why he must be up! He will be." James dumps the water over his head. "What the hell! Who did that," Alex demands wiping the water from his face? James throws down the bucket, "Sorry my lord but I could not wake you and today is the day." Alex quickly snaps back to this day saying, "Good lord I will marry this morning." Alex goes to walk away. "My lord if I may I think it wise that you wash this morning," Kronus suggests. Alex smells his clothing, "I see your point." Alex walks towards the creek with the two big men trapped in his head beating on his brain.

"My lady I cannot believe this day has come at last," her handmaid tells her with preparing her attire. They laugh as school girls with their hearts filled with joy.

Edward sits upon his throne beaten and bitter. "Tyrolean is there no other way to control the beast their numbers out match ours?" "No, my lord the medallions are the only way," Tyrolean answers. "Then we must retrieve them from their grasps!" William walks through the doors, "My lord the men have dug the trenches and the provisions are within the gates." "Has any word come of them moving on us," Edward asks of William. "No, my lord, if they have moved at all, it is not within our rides vision." "My lord, we must take all the silver and make as many weapons as we can," Tyrolean suggests. "Go and do what we must!" "How about the mercenaries," William asks. "They returned the payment I gave to them saying, "men cannot stand against Gods," Edward informs with dismay upon their names then asks, "How do you think we should handle this?" "They will attack before the next cycle of the full moon to keep the odds even so there will be no need in making more soldiers into wolfs. I feel we should attack them from behind when they are focused on the castle they will think we would keep all the men inside these walls," William answers. "No, we should ride out and meet their challenge," Edward demands letting his ego speak for him. "We must wear down their men then ride out to finish them off. We should not give up every advantage we have" Edward rises from his seat informing with a stern tone, "It may be the wrong choice but I still rule here and let us not forget who gave you the gift you indulge yourself in." William bows his head with asking, "My lord what may I ask is the rule of a pack?" "That the strongest should lead," Edward replies to a smile coming over William's face letting the change begin. Edward being well rested transforms as well. The beasts circle each other in the throne room. A servant comes in and screams at the sight, the soldiers rush to see. William and Edward begin to ripe and tear at one another, mighty howls are given, each stands their ground but William finds the upper hand then bites and rips the head from off his body. "My lord," Titus screams as he changes into the wolf. The battle is short and he finds himself under the paw of William. Titus turns back into his human form in a sign for mercy. William growls and looks in his eyes then returns to his human form. "Who rules this house," William asks of Titus being Edward's strongest. The Loyal houses of Lancaster that had fallen to York, rush in behind the soldiers. In seeing the men Titus informs with a bowed head, "You do my lord!" William stands naked and looks at the men they turn and go back to their posts. "Get this thing from out of my throne room," William orders walking over to pull something from his bag. "When you have gotten rid of his body you will host this up on the pole!" Titus bows his head and takes the flag from his hands, uses it to cover his naked body and walks out of the room. With time moving forward and Tyrolean returning to see the new flag hosted he busts into the throne room demanding, "What have you done with the master of this house?" "Before you say another word, I found something that belonged to you," William relays picking up something by his side. He holds the glass object in his hands. Tyrolean steps back. "So, it is true, your life essence is in here and just a slip of my fingers and that would turn out bad for you would it not?" William gets up from the throne. Walks down towards him suggesting, "Relax my sorceress friend me and you have much in common," he pours wine into a couple of glasses relying, "It seems we find ourselves in the same place. Our brothers of birth come here to kill us." Tyrolean takes the glass from his hand. "You see my dear brother thought of me as a saint but he never knew the moment I would have gotten the crown a dagger through his heart I would have placed. Family is the worst thing to keep in the throne room." William hands him the object Tyrolean most desires saying, "Take it I do not need men loyal to me by fear, but with trust in their hearts, your lord would have had all of us ride out to our deaths. I have better ways of dealing with my enemies." Tyrolean drinks from the glass then requests, "Tell me my lord why ride with him as you did?" "My father was an honorable man but he never learned that sometimes it is easier to gain the trust of someone who is your foe and strike out when they least expect it," William replies then sips his drink adding, "but for the most part he killed my father does a son not have the right to revenge?" "I find you as wise as the owl and as slipper as the ell," Tyrolean boasts. They bump their glass and drink a toast to a new found union. "Now down to business, is there any way to remove the spell from them so we would have this power alone," William requests. "We would need the cup that they drank the blood of the wolf from. Then we would fill it with a virgin lamb simply cast the removal spell and it would be done." "Is it the same with us?" "Yes, my lord," Tyrolean answers. "Then bring me this cup so that I may see it myself." Tyrolean leaves the room going to retrieve what he requested. William begins to discuss things with his commanders.

"Alex you had better hurry up or you will be late for the wedding," Darius yells as he washes in the creek. Alex scrubs himself and gets out of the creek. He looks down at the rags he was wearing drapes a cloak over his body, then walks back to the camp. "Darien, do you have something I could wear for the wedding," Alex asks as he passes him. "No, my lord I do not." Alex walks through the camp and finds nothing he seeks. "Alex, I believe Sir Richard took care of it," Overlain relays as he passes him. Alex runs back to his tent. He looks down on the table. The clothing is silky to his touch almost a king's attire. The cloak made to hang from his neck bears the flag of his father. He places it on and leaves his tent, walks through the camp and up too Sir Richard's requesting, "My lord may I speak with you this morning?" "Yes, Alex come in and welcome," Richard answers. "I would ask how you got this cloak of my father's." "In this long war each noble's house has fought against the other. Your father and I were no different. We faced off on the field of battle and I won the day. Your father was an honorable man something most nobles lack he gave it to me as a fallen foe and now I return it to you a brother in arms," Richard informs bowing his head to him. "My lord in the days we have been among you I see my father's face in yours. I could think of no other better for the crown of this land." "Might I give you some advice" Sir Richard suggests. "I always welcome advice from men wiser than I." "Take her and hold her with everything you are, for the days you can share with the ones you love, are the most important to men. We are here but a short while so hold her each day." He walks over and places his hands on his shoulder smiling at the man before him. "I will do as you say my lord. I will love her with all my being until the life leaves my body." Sir Richard pats him on the shoulders and Alex turns and leaves the tent

Elizabeth stands in her mother's dress her face covered by the white veil, her father stands outside of the tent waiting, she moves out the front, takes his arm, she looks down the long path to him, the men form a line down each side of her walk, Richard sits upon his horse the music fills the air as they walk towards him. Alex stands by the one who will join them under the eyes of God. Darius stands beside him his other faithful brothers stand behind him. Alex watches as the dress flows with the wind her beauty covered by the fabric over her face, but the color of her eyes still burn through, at this moment his love knows no bounds. What seems like minutes to him is only but moments to those gathered. Sand places her beside him. "Who gives her to this man," the priest asks. "I, Sir Leon Sand, her father, give her to Sir Alex Lancaster to wed from this day until the day death will separate them." They turn and face the priest her father then steps back and finds his place in line. Alex lifts her veil and just like the times before her beauty stills his breath. "I Elizabeth Sand, take you Alex Lancaster for my husband to love and hold through sickness and heath even after my death I shall await you on the shores of the river Jordan," Elizabeth proudly vowels. "I Alex Lancaster take you Elizabeth Sand to be my wife in sickness and in health with the love without end until death do we part and I too shall await you on the shores of the river Jordan." The priest blesses them with their lips finding each other's the kiss means more than any before this moment. The crowd yells out and the doves find the sky. "This day will be yours for all time," Overlain walks up and says too them. The music changes and the celebration of their union sets the atmosphere. Sand walks over to Richard as the youth spin around and the men make themselves merry. The crowd parts as they share a dance to set with them for all time. Elizabeth smiles, her eyes glisten with love in her heart, her beauty stills the air from his lungs and his heart beats faster and within this moment Alex finds out how happy one person can truly be. "Sir Sand, please take a sit at the table with me," Richard offers. "Thank you," Sand says in sitting down with him. "I wanted to tell you thanks for helping in the battle you and yours turned the tide." "I did what a father would do and as ruler. How long would it be before the land he has conquered would not be enough and I would find him upon my shores? I sent her here so that I would have a say in what would happen with this land, for one will in time effect the other." "York and I are the only ones left with a claim to the throne. All others have fallen in battle or do not have enough support to hold the crown" Richard relays looking out of the crowd. Seeing the love Alex and Elizabeth has found, "As a father I am glad for you this day. I never got to be blessed with a daughter and this war has taken my sons from me. You have an allied in this world Sir Sand with all the respect a ruler can have!" They raise their glasses and salute the day.

"My lord the thing you requested," Tyrolean relays walking up to the throne placing the cup into his hand. The pack walks into the throne room. "William I would speak with you," Devilian says. "What is own your mind?" "You have killed our brother in the wolf and my ruler!" "This is true, but I ask you one question. What is the difference in killing him one on one or in the field of battle, your noble fell to me in the old ways and the strongest survived," William declares before raises from the throne asking, "Do you challenge me for the rite to lead?" Devilian knowing Edward his better pulls back bowing his head answering, "No my lord." "Good then now that this is behind us. You are a warlord none can match will you serve my flag," William asks "I will serve you as I did he." "Then I double your lands as with all of my brothers." He walks back to the throne soldiers bring in boxes filled with gold. "Take as much as your pockets can hold. Edward should have never used it to pay for a man when all he needed was the wolves with him." All his brothers of the wolf reach their hands into the gold. "This I hold in my hands is the only thing that could take away the power we have," William informs turning their attention back to him. Throwing it upon the throne room floor the cup shatters into many splitters, "My bothers we will live forever and we can rule over men for all times!" William's won over minions begin to chant his name. The soldiers move about the day, digging hidden holes for men to sneak up on their enemies, preparing for the battle that will lie ahead. "Tyrolean you spoke of dead soldiers rising?" "Yes, my lord. The mostly dead." "The mostly dead," William confused asks. "Yes, my lord. This band of men rode out to turn the tide for many royal men in a time long past, but a wizard cast a spell trapping them between this world and the next but a wizard his equal cast a spell that they could be released with the cross of fandom." "Then raise as many as you can to fight with in our ranks!" "There is a price to be paid my lord I will need bodies that the warriors will inhabit I will need forty soldiers from your ranks," Tyrolean informs. William lets a smile find his face replying, "I can think of better people to lose then a trained soldier. Take Eric and Derrick the twins and go out into the villages to round up the peasants." "As you command my lord," Tyrolean bows his head saying. Tyrolean leaves the castle taking soldiers and the twins with him. The twins travel in their forms as the wolf not caring if the common man should see them. From house to house they roam pulling men from their families placing chains upon them. With their numbers gathered they proceed to the resting place of the mostly dead.

A new day dawns with the celebration behind them. Alex takes her hand requesting, "My lady I will not have you here tomorrow will you take a ride with me?" "Yes, my husband I will ride with you this day." The men hold their horses they climb on and ride for the forest. Their pace is slow just talking as they leave. "This is by far the greatest day of my life Elizabeth. I cannot see another to ever match it," Alex proudly boasts. "My lord there will be many days in your life when you will achieve greatness," Elizabeth answers with pride in her husband. "That might be true my lady but I will hold this day as the greatest in my life." She reaches out to hold his hand. They talk of the day as they ride on. The forest is vast the wild flowers bloom the birds sing their songs of the forest. The sun rays light the forest floor, the breeze blows her hair in the wind the fragrance fills his nose. "Where are you leading me my love?" "Wait and you will see." They ride a little farther and a valley known only to a few comes into view. The flowers of every color fill the bottom of the valley song birds fly and eat of the day. "My Lord in heaven Alex! This is right out of a fairytale the beauty of it is breathtaking," Elizabeth relays with the full view of the valley. Alex takes her down into the valley, climbs from his horse, helps her down and places a blanket upon the ground. She sits and he brings out the food then pours the wine into the glasses. "Alex this is the most beautiful sight my eyes have held," she says as she looks over the valley adding, "There is so much hidden beauty in this land that I now consider my home." "Yes, my lady but to me it doesn't even come close to you." He leans in places his lips upon hers and their tongues dance with their lips parting she asks, "Are you thinking you can get lucky with the wine and the view?" "No, my lady I could just be with you this day." "Alex Lancaster, you mean to tell me you don't want this," She asks reaching up to release her dress with her soft mounds coming into his view. "Well since you put it that way," Alex says throwing his glass and kisses her fully laying her back against the blanket. Her breath becomes short as they pull off their clothes to lay naked under the sun and God. The medallion rests in the valley of her breasts it fills cool against her skin while her body burns of passion. He moves between her hips as she can feel him slip in and out of her, her passionate cries echo over the plain, he stares into her eyes, looking into her soul, her passion over flows as she grips his butt, he pushes in far and she can feel his release, her finale wave hits with his. "My husband I could have you like this for the rest of my life," she pants adding, "The way I feel when you take me! I cannot describe it!" "I love you with each breath of my body and the feeling of you is intoxicating to me," Alex replies in return. They hold on to one another until his passion rises they make love through the day again and again until their bodies are spent. They dress and she lies against him sitting in silence to remember the day. Alex plays with her hair as he takes in the time shared. "My lady you know the only reason I would want you to leave my side is your safety. I know what would lie in my brother's heart." "I know my love I should have not left you in such away. I was just sad, I would not have you beside me," Elizabeth answers. "This war is all but over just one finale battle lay ahead, then you can return and I will have you with me always." She turns and looks into his eyes saying, "I will miss you every day that we are apart know that my heart will be heavy." "As will mine but it is the only way. I cannot fight his army with my worries with you." She kisses his lips and slides back down his body looks out at the beauty of the valley and asks, "Tell me Alex can you go through with it can you kill your brother?" Alex's eyes become distant answering, "I could not answer that until I have him before me. My mind tells me the world will be better without him, but with the power taken from him, he would just be another man and mortal men could deal with him" "What if the spell cannot be removed you know what it would come too." Alex leans down and kisses the top of her head replying, "Yes my lady I know in my heart." She turns around and unties the crystal from his neck. She leans to her knees and looks at it. "Alright you have seen it long enough I told Overlain I would keep it with me always." Elizabeth replies with a smile, "Oh you want this do you?" She stands to her feet and twirls it around her finger encouraging, "Well come and get it, you big bad wolf!" He begins to stand and she runs through the plain, he chases her like they were children of a time past, she runs around the base of a tree. "Give that to me!" "No, my lover you must catch me to get it!" He runs to her side of the tree, she fakes him. Alex falls to the ground. Laughing she runs from the tree into the flowers blooming in the valley. Alex smiles and uses the speed of the wolf to catch her grasping her in his arms. She slides it into her bosom. They fall to the ground and his hands roam her body, "I told you if you wanted it to get it!" Alex uses his mouth to undo her dress kisses his way down her cleavage savoring her mounds. He looks at her with the crystal in his teeth her hands find it and replace it on his neck. They laugh and roll in the valley. The dusk sets in and they return with a day like no other. "My lord did you two enjoy the day," Overlain asks as they ride into the camp "Yes my very wise friend we did," Alex halfheartedly answers still lost with her in the day. They ride for their tent as if they were the only two people in the world and go inside. They hold onto one another the bitter coldness of the night can find no rest with them. In the same night Tyrolean and those with him find their way to the resting place of the mostly dead. "Place them into the valley and put archers over them on the rock shelving surrounding this place, make sure they do not stand on the whiten stone that is the territory of the mostly dead at the moment of the blue mist tell them to place their arrows into them and if one should be standing on the whiten stone then the mostly dead will consume them," Tyrolean states as a warning. "As you command lord Tyrolean," a commander replied. The soldiers drive the men into the valley; Tyrolean stands upon the high stone in the center drives his staff into it. With the archers in place he begins to cast his spell his eyes begin to glow the crystal upon the end of his staff releases the power resting in it. A great wind blows over the men and the blue mist rises from the ground. The horrified men begin to scream as the mostly dead hide within the mist. The archers place their arrows well and the mostly dead consume their bodies. The fallen warriors of a lost time stand where a common man once stood. The leader rises from the ground making great speed towards Tyrolean grasping his sword he demanding," Who dares wake us from our slumber?" Tyrolean uses his magic and freezes him in his motion. "I am Tyrolean sorcerer in my time." "It was someone of your kind that placed us into this realm," the warrior informs adding, "send us back we will not fight for men of your kind." "My great warrior I come with a promise that if you help defend the castle of my lord then you will be released from the prison that holds you, and catch the fairy-man to the next world." "That is not possible without the cross and it has been lost to time," the warrior reveals. Tyrolean waves his hand to the men they walk out to them and uncover the cross. "It was lost in time but I now possess it. Now will you fight for us?" The warrior turns to his men then turns back to Tyrolean with a smile for his answer. With Tyrolean's task complete, they return to the castle. "My lord all the silver that could be found is being forged into weapons," Enos informs" "Devilian did you put the explosive substance Tyrolean created into the slings resting upon the walls," "Yes my lord on all side of the castle." With Tyrolean's entry into the throne room William asks, "Did you convince the mostly dead to join us in battle?" "Yes, my lord as you commanded." "Everything is proceeding just like I planned, Now my brother come and get what you desire," William boasts to those around him. The night grows long.

The sun rises and its glow brightens another day her father sits upon his horse waiting for them to say a goodbye. "My lady it is but a short while I will see you soon," Ales relays reaching into his pocket pulling out the medallion once worn by a fallen brother requesting, "Take this with you it may come in handy for you." Elizabeth takes it from his hand replying, "I will return it at the moment your arms hold me." He kisses her cheek then he places her on her horse. She pulls the reins on the horse and Darius rides up to her. "He will travel back with you," Alex informs. She looks at Darius saying, "Come father the sooner we leave the sooner I can return." "Alex she will be waiting on you," Sir Sand suggests with a smile adding, "I am proud to call you son." Her father pulls his reins, he watches as they ride away, with the last moment of sight she stops and waves to him then disappears over the land. "Darius do you still hold your vowel?" "As before my lady. I will give my life so my brother could have you with him." "Darius I find you a pleasing man why haven't you found someone to share your life with," Elizabeth asks riding for the shores. "I cannot answer my lady. I guess I have never come across the feeling the two of you share." Her handmaids giggle and laugh in the background. "Why do they giggle for my lady," Darius asks turning back to them. "Carissa finds favor on you." Darius face becomes red. "What is it Darius," Elizabeth asks laughing. "Nothing my lady," Darius answers before picking up the pace of his horse. Elizabeth slows her pace until her maids catch up. "Do you think he likes me my lady," Carissa asks. "By the way his face turned red. I would say he feels something for you." "Tell me my lady what is it like," Carissa inquires with the girls in the back ground giggling. "What do you mean?" She looks at the question written in her face saying, "Oh that well it is kind of hard to explain, it hurts but you get pleasure from it." A common soldier turns back to look at them with Elizabeth suggesting, "Eyes up front soldier." He quickly turns back. "How do you begin it," Carissa curiously inquires. Elizabeth looks at her saying, "Trust me when I tell you, it will come to you when the moment arrives." The girls riding with her continue to giggle to all the questions on her lips. They ride for home.

With many days passing, the day dawns with Alex already up to meet the day, with most of the distance to the castle covered. He makes his way to Sir Richard's tent. "My lord, you sent for me this morning?" "Yes, Sir Lancaster, what are we to expect from our foe?" "Expect the unexpected for my brother is well schooled in the art of war. He will have something laid out for when we arrive," Alex states with the highest pride in his father's teaching. They discuss battle plans as the men pack up. The days move on and they set out for the castle. Elizabeth and her father get closer to the shores. The hands of time move on. "Sir Richard we should rest for the night, York's castle is only a half days ride from here," Alex suggests. "That sounds good to me the men will be well rested for the battle ahead," Sir Richard informs and his army finds their rest. The same moment in time Elizabeth watches the shore going farther from her view. "Father please tell me that all will be okay I worry for him," Elizabeth asks in hoping a father's voice would bring her comfort. Sand pulls her close wraps his arms around her and kisses the top of her head comforting, "He will be fine my daughter these days will pass with time you will have him to hold soon enough." His words find no comfort with her as the wind brings the cold from the sea watching the moon shimmer on the face of the waters, the smell of the ocean fill their noses with the sound of the waves bouncing off the base of the ship.

"My lord all the preparations are complete," Tyrolean informs. "Good now we will just have to wait for Sir Richard and my brother to arrive, William informs then turns to his brothers ordering, "Titus take Devilian and Enos and set out for their camp do not try to engage them fully just find the ones on the out skirts for your meal." "As you command my lord, Titus and Devilian reply. The pack leaves the castle to handle their task. Fallen nobles to the flag of York talk with themselves inside their ranks. "My lord we should pledge our strength with Sir Richard. William's own brother serves his flag," a general to the noble implores. "Yes, at the moment of battle. We will make are intentions known, go and make sure we are part of the men sent out to hide and wait," the noble suggests. The nobles most trusted heads off to make sure they are part of those chosen to hide with in the darkness. "My lord would it not be better to serve this house," a counsel man to him asks. "I only pledge my loyalties because of the beast inside of them. If sir Richard men possess this power that will even the odds, we will support him, if not, when this war is over there will be nothing for my noble name. William will lash out and devour us all," the noble insures. Alex and the army rest in the night as the wolf pack slips up to the camp and hide in the night waiting. A soldier walks his guard, Kronus hides in the tree watching as he walks savoring the taste to come. The soldier turns back for the other direction, he leaps taking his life without a sound another walks beside a tree to relief himself. Devilian strikes out from the darkness splattering his blood over the ground. Their scent flows downwind with Alex raising his head with alarm. "My Lord," James says slipping to the front of his tent. "Yes, I smell it too," Alex answers coming from inside of the tent. Alex sniffs the air saying, "They are close sound the alarm." James begins to blow his horn. "Look sharp men they are among us," Alex yells. Soldiers rush from their rest standing fast. Alex with James lets their wolves come out and run into the darkness. The pack sees them coming and scatters into the night. They walk back to the camp then pick up their cloaks to cover their bodies. "Alex," Jonas calls to get his attention. Alex walks over and sees their bodies with one still finding life in him. "Do what must be done Jonas," Alex suggests. "I will free him my lord," Jonas answers. Alex turns to walk away as his sword is released freeing him from the curse flowing in his veins. "What was it? Sir Lancaster," Sir Richard asks rushing out with his sword drawn. "It was soldiers of York sent here to disturb our rest. My guess is they were to take as many as they could." Richard looks out towards the darkness, "Are they gone?" "For the moment. We will stand guard for the rest of the night." Alex walks away and with every step the wolf comes out he runs into the darkness. The night moves on with Alex trades out standing watch with his faithful, each finds a little rest until the morning sun.

Darius stands on the deck of the ship watching as the sun gets higher in the sky, "My lady you are up early" "Yes I found I have no reason to stay in bed with Alex not here to hold me." She looks out over the water asking, "Where do you think they are now?" "With any luck my lady they have

reached his castle and soon the dark days of the land will be behind us."
Carissa walks up behind them. "My lady your morning meal will be ready
shortly." Darius looks upon her a smile finds his face. "Why don't you keep
Darius busy this morning. I will tend to myself," Elizabeth suggest before
walking away leaving them to share a moment. "She is a great friend to you
my lady." "Yes, all the days of our lives she has never looked down on me even
though I am a servant bound to her," Carissa informs. Darius looks back
towards the sea she stands close and he places his arm around her shoulder.

William walks out to the balcony to stand with Devilian standing his
guard. William sees the first horse come over the hill, it pauses and then
the army behind him comes into sight. "Did the men find their hidden
spots," William asks. "Yes, my lord. They left before we returned," Devilian
replies. Tyrolean walks out with them seeing the army before them he
relays, "It looks like this day will be the day to end all things." William lets
a stern look come over him saying, "At the end of this day, my brother will
be no more." "Kill Alex and we will kill the heart. Kill Richard and we will
kill the head," Tyrolean replies to assure their victory. "And what of your
brother Tyrolean," William asks with a reply, "He has been a thorn in my
side long enough." "May the brothers of this house stand and their house
fall to the ashes of time," William proclaims. Alex rides to the top of the
hill. He looks over the walls into the yard a new flag comes into view. "My
lord it bares your father's flag," Jonas says. "It could mean only one thing my
brother rules the house." He turns his horse and rides back into the ranks.
"Sir Richard, I think we should attack the castle from the forest side it will
give us cover from their Archers," a commander suggests looking at the lay
out of the castle. The ground around the horses begins to move and soldiers
appear from their secret places. "Protect Sir Richard," the commander yells.
The soldiers rush to engulf him on all sides. "Wait, wait," the noble screams
with an announcement, "We support Sir Richard!" He drops his sword to
the ground and falls to his knees. Alex rides over, "Then why would you ride
so long with him?" "We had no choice the beasts run through my house
conquering it! Lancaster I supported your father's house in the past, now I
will support Sir Richard!" Richard rides over requesting, "Alex let him
speak. We have all stood against each other in times past." Alex listens to
what the noble speaks informing, "Then you will be the first wave to attack
the castle! I will not trust you behind me, my brother is cunning!" "As you

command my lord," the noble answers with Alex quickly turning to ride away. "I should have known his house would turn, he hasn't got the stomach to do what must be done," William states watching the soldiers he sent for a purpose join their ranks. "Tell the men to stand ready they will be on us soon," Titus orders standing with William. The day moves on and the battle begins. "Sir Richard we cannot get close to the gates and their Archers have killed many," a soldier rides up to say. "My lord may I make a suggestion," the turned noble asks." Alex looks at Sir Richard. "By all means," Alex suggests. "When we took Sir Lancaster's castle. I found myself in the same place," the noble reveals with Alex looking over at him, "I am sorry Alex but it was war!" "Do what you must to get to the gates," Richard commands. "Alex will you come with me," the noble asks. Alex turns his horse and rides in a different direction. "He will find forgiveness for you in time just get the army into the gates," Sir Richard suggests. He rides off. His men gather the body shields, taking them down to the front of the lines, ties them together, using the horses to pull their weight. The shields do their job as archers fire from the cover striking the men from the walls as the horses move swiftly at the base of them. With a covered shield in place the noble yells from the gate, "Bring down the battering ram!" The dusk begins to fall as the mighty log is rolled down to the gates. "Alex he has proven is worth, he has kept his word he fights for Richard," James relays to remove Alex's anger for him. "William they have reached the gates," Devilian reports. "Fire the substances created by Tyrolean down at the gates," William orders. The soldiers sling down the barrels and they exploded in the men. Overlain seeing the power unleashed rides over to Alex as they watch the flames begin to consume the men informing, "My brother has given them this power." "What substance does he use to cause great fire to engulf them?" Overlain rides off with no answer given, his horse finds full speed. He rides down toward the gates. The crystal on the end of his staff burns with the fire of the sun blinding the men on the wall ordering, "Back pull back to the lines!" The men retreat with the castle surviving the first wave of attack. Alex and James ride down to the edge of the forest to study the castle farther Overlain rides over to them. "You ride well for an old man," James suggests. "Overlain what would you need to achieve this consuming fire," Alex asks. "They will have taken anything that I would need into the castle." "We only need one barrel," Alex informs looking down at the gates. "I will do my best to find them my lord,"

159

Overlain informs before riding off with a few soldiers. Alex looks and sees the noble hunched over on his horse. The flames of the fire have marked his body. Alex gallops down and helps him from his horse, "Easy we will get you to the healer." "It's too late the fire has consumed me," his states with his breath becoming short Alex holds his hand, "Forgive me Lancaster I only done what was best for my people, I will send your love to your father." The life leaves his body and his hand losses its grip. Alex drapes him over his shoulder and takes him back to the camp. He slowly lays his broken body onto the ground informing, "We will bury him right, he was a soldier of Sir Richard!" Alex turns back to the castle ordering, "Tell the men to pull back from their walls." Sir Richard rides up, "They have us stumped and if we keeping attacking the castle we are going to lose all men your brother has sealed the castle well." "Overlain has set out to give us the advantage, tell the men to hold their ground we will open the gates when he returns." The men rest just outside the reach of their arrows the night has set in. "Overlain did you find enough of what you needed?" Alex asks with his return. "Maybe enough to fill one barrel," Overlain answers. "It will be enough all we need to do is open the gates." "How are we to get it to the gate it is too heavy to move swiftly," Sir Richard inquires. "Just leave that to us," Alex answers with a grin. Overlain prepares the substance places a pine-soaked rope into it as a wick seeing Alex asks, "What is the rope for?" "It takes fire to create the great fire just get it to the gate the fire already burning will do the rest." "I think we can handle that," Alex suggests. "My lord you just make sure it does not cross with fire before you get it there," Overlain reminds. Alex and his faithful roll it down towards the gate then let the wolf inside emerge using the strength of the beasts they fling it to the gate. "Look out a soldier yells seeing the barrel in flight. The men in hidden faithful to William rush from their places striking out at ranks. The swords clash screams of death ring out into the night, the barrel finds its way and a great explosion rings out. Alex in wolf form waves the men on with the walls surrounding the castle lying open. "The walls are breached," a look-out yells just before a soldier's arrow finds its mark. The foot soldiers waiting inside the castle run to the gates and meet the charging men. Alex and his faithful run past with one purpose in mind to bring an end to the conflict of men. "My lord the castle is fallen we must retreat, Tyrolean declares. "We have not lost the castle yet," Duncan declares and lets the change come over him he lashes out of the halls and into the streets. Damien follows with him. "Lord William you must not be as foolish as them we must withdraw," Tyrolean implores grasping his arm. They slip out of the throne room sneaking through the halls Devilian, Titus, Enos and Rexstin follow with them. The mostly dead cover their path with being personal guards to William killing everything within their path. Damien hit's the city with in the castle, with the speed of the wolf. He slashes out at the men biting, ripping their flesh from their bones, with the strength of his claws. James in wolf form leaps in front of him. With a challenge made they circle one another with their teeth shown. The mighty growls of the beasts scream out. The dust flies as they leap to each other. Meeting in their leap they begin to claw and biting at each other's bodies, spilling the blood over everything they touch. Duncan waits in the shadows. James with his back turned engaged with Damien, Duncan leashes out from behind sinking his teeth into his neck. Jonas running in knocks him from his back, and with one head removing bite, he ends Duncan's life. His lifeless body hit's the dirt. He turns and faces off with Damien, bitten and wounded from the fight with James and no match for Jonas he swiftly finds his end. Jonas howls into the night sky over his fallen prey. "I cannot believe we will leave the castle it is over they have beaten us," Titus says. "Worry not my brother we will have another day all is proceeding as I have planned," William states. "What do you mean it is all in your plan," Titus turns and asks. "My brother you act like we should be in the throne room tonight but did it ever cross your mind that we will live longer than any of them will be alive" William answers. They slip out to the back of the castle. Alex and the wolves with him, wait. "Come William we must flee before they catch us," Tyrolean suggests. "Wait I smell," Devilian states before Alex leaps in and knocks him from his feet taking William down also. Others with William begin to transform. William regains his feet saying, "Now brother you seem to have me at a disadvantage." William's voice becomes that of the wolves as he begins to transform. Titus leaps in and knocks Alex away from his brother. Jayel leaps for Tyrolean and his drives him back with his magic then pulls a silver dagger from his cloak and drives it into his heart. Jayel finds honor in his death. The warriors of the mostly dead quickly move in to engage in the battle. Tyrolean slips into the forest casts a spell to cover his tracks. Titus and Kronus fight with each other slashing and biting. Their fight carries them into the forest. Devilian and William circle Alex trying to attack him from both sides, striking out, biting at his legs, slashes and clawing at his body. Alex fights well standing his ground but they have the advantage. Overlain finds them fighting with sending the magic from his staff he drives them away. He turns and sees soldiers fighting with ghostly sprits and with words from his mouth burning into their souls he drives them away. Alex regains himself and runs after them as they flee into the night. "Jayel," Overlain says as he climbs from his horse. He rolls over his body. He finds a familiar dagger resting deep in his heart. Jonas slips through the city, helping the men kill those who still fight, leashes out striking at the men. The remaining York army falls and Sir Richard's army stands victorious. A soldier with but little life pulls an arrow from his quiver finds the strength to rest it upon the string of his bow fires it into the heart of Jonas with his back turned and the silver punches his chest a mighty howl is given as he falls to his knees. A soldier close by runs in and holds onto his paw that slowly transforms back to his human form. The soldier pulls at the arrow but it will not move. Jonas releases his last breath at him. He reaches down and closes his eyes. "Sir Richard, their flag has fallen! The land and the crown are yours," a commander proudly informs him. Richard rides into the castle the men give a mighty salute of victory for their new King. "We will not celebrate this day men, many brothers of the sword have found their death," Richard informs looking around at the bodies broken over the land. He turns his head and looks at his commander suggesting, "This is the price I paid to rule this land!" Richard turns his horse riding off to seek solitude with the weight of the day resting heavy in his heart

Night turns to day and Alex returns coming up empty with the search of his brother. "You did not find him my lord," Overlain asks with his return. "No, I lost their scent down by the river. I searched everywhere." "My lord James and Jonas have passed on." Alex looks around seeing the soldiers dragging the dead towards their final resting place and for an instance he can see his fallen brothers waving their last goodbye as they fade into but a memory. "Yes, we have lost many brothers this night" Alex dunks inside of his tent dresses and comes back out, "Has Kronus returned?" "No, my lord he ran off after one of the wolves. I was hoping he was with you," Overlain relays. Alex takes the reins of his horse climbs in the saddle. Darien with Overlain follows in his steps. "Sir Lancaster, Sir Richard requests to see you this morning," a commander relays in seeing their departure. "Tell my lord I will see him when I return, we have a brother to find." Alex kicks his horse and they gallop out of the camp. They ride until they find the spot from the night before. "The tracks lead this way," Darien informs. They form a line each checking the ground for the path they might have went. "My lord the tracks lead down into the valley," Darien remarks. Alex lets the air flow into his nose to let the scent lead the way. They across a stream climb the hill on the other side down into a small mountain range.

"My Lord the men are requesting to have a great feast tonight to honor are fallen soldiers," one of Richards closet relays. "Did you find Lancaster this morning," "Yes my lord, a commander said he rode out in search of one of his own. He said he would see you when he returned." "Then see to it the men get what they wish send out hunters to kill some meat and we will serve it in the castle." "As you wish my lord," He says then opens the flap of the tent and hurries on his way.

The crowd gathers as a great celebration is planned. Elizabeth rides beside her Father sitting proud in his saddle as they ride up to the castle gates. "Father, even though I am glad to see the castle, it is not like days of old." "What do you mean Elizabeth?" "It is just not home to me anymore. My place is with he who is my husband," Elizabeth sadly reveals. "Well I am glad to have you home for one last time," her father remarks. With seeing her face long, he suggests, "I was wondering if Alex would expect a noble granting in my house." "I don't know father I can discuss this with him when I have him with me," Elizabeth informs with a happiness she could have the two men who mean the most to her under a single roof. "I feel confident he will say yes if you ask in the correct manner," Sand suggests knowing the beauty of her. A smile finds her face and it warms his heart. The crowd surrounds them with greetings and well wishes. Darius comes up and helps her from her horse. They walk into his castle. The men of government quickly tell him of what has been done since his departure. Her father walks off to handle the affairs left undone. "Darius come with me and I will show you where you can stay, until you return me to Alex." They walk down the hall with Elizabeth showing him pictures hanging on the walls. "This is a portrait of my mother. I was but a little girl when it was painted." Darius admires her beauty captured in time, "You look very much like her your beauty honors her!" They walk on until they reach a door. "Here we

are, you can call this home for now. Carissa will tend to your every need."
Darius pushes open the door. Carissa stands by the bed placing new sheets
upon it she smiles to him. "My lady you do not wonder very far without
telling me. I am sworn to guard you until your return." Darius reminds. "I
will not wonder off without informing you first. I know the duties you are
sworn too!" Elizabeth closes the door to his room, walks to the room beside
his and into the place she slept as a child. Elizabeth looks around her room
what was once a place of comfort reminds her of but a child. She looks in
a mirror and a woman is standing where a child once stood. She sits down
upon her bed picks the crystal up from her neck the tears flow slowly with
her heart longing for her husband.

"They fought here my lord." "I think I can see him," Alex stresses looking
down into a small gulley. A human arm lays out just noticeable to the human
eye. He leaps from his horse, removes his clothing, lets the transformation
come over him. The speed of the wolf along with its strength, he brings his
broken body back to where the horses stand. Alex places his body on the
ground and steps back. The others cover his body as Alex takes his human
form. He dresses and walks over to him. "My lord from what it looks like the
others joined their brother and it was just too much for him to overcome."
"Yes, but he took one of them with him. It was not his arm I saw from above,
but that of Rexstin, one of Williams minions. Damn it, I tracked them all of
the night, if only I knew I could have done something," Alex says feeling the
loss of another brother. "Rest easy my lord, the wars are over and Richard
can restore order to the land and no more of our brothers need die in an
endless war. Their lives paid the way for better days," Overlain suggests.
"Overlain is there any way we can track my brother?" "No, my lord they have
slipped through us this time." "One thing is for sure my brother will not rest
until he sits upon the throne." They place him over the horse and with heavy
hearts they ride for the camp. The day grows long and they return to the
camp. "Take him and place him with our other fallen brothers, we will lay
them to rest before the sun sets," Alex says stepping off his horse. Overlain
with Darien take his body and lay it with his fallen brothers. Woman of
the camp wash them and dress them in their armor for the warrior's rest
that awaits them. "My lord you sent for me this morning," Alex asks coming
into the tent. "Come in Alex, sit you must be parched from your journey."
The servants place a cup in his hand and fill it with drink. "Alex this will

mark the end to this destructive war for the crown. We have lost much in the years that will lay behind us," Richard relays. "Yes, my lord. I pray that you will bring order back to the land and protect its people both noble and common!" "I will wear the crown with a heavy heart so many had to die for it to rest upon my head." "That is why you will rule wisely my lord! You have the people at heart," Alex proudly informs. "Alex before you send for her I would ask that you accompany me back to the English castle it takes three quarters of the nobles to crown me King." "You have enough without me my lord," Alex answers longing to hold his wife. "I know Alex Lancaster, but you would do me proud to have your name on the paper that sets it to law. Besides I cannot help but think your brother will attack before the crown is placed upon my head!" Alex stands to his feet, "My lord and King it will be an honor but my I ask one request?" "Ask my young noble." "Have word sent to my wife, she can return by a couple of months end to stand with me." He shakes his hand and walks out of the tent a spy placed in their ranks slips away from the back of the tent with his ears filled with what he needs. He sends a loyal soldier with word for William and he regains his place in with the men. The bodies of his faithful are in a circle, each resting on a plank of wood; their uniforms shine from the torch light of the camp. The music fills the air with a sadden song sung by men left here by their brothers. Alex walks out with the torch in his hands, removes the medallions from around their necks. He steps back from them, "Too my faithful brothers, I could have searched and never found better men then you. Your lives were given to this land we all call home. I would ask the father in heaven that your names would be remembered in the hands of time!" The men give a great salute as he drops the flame to the wood, lighting them each in turn. The fire engulfs their bodies returning them to the ground that they were formed from. William retreats to a place selected by him but Enos and Rexstin never return from the siege of the castle. William waits for the days ahead.

A KING RETURNS

A CYCLE OF THE MOON PASSES, WORDS SPREAD quickly throughout the land a rider is sent to and fro, requesting that all nobles send someone to speak in the new government to be formed. The army of a new King marches their way to the main castle of the land. All the nobles that remain come to give their salutes and respects to the crown and to the man who will wear it.

William sits without his brothers in his new castle forgotten in time his brothers having been sent across the land to mark men as they walk. William awaits their return surrounded my men from over the land not loyal to Richard. "My lord William we cannot just sit here his army rides for the castle and the crown and Sand's daughter returns to him at the Sherman port," Titus reminds. "We do not have enough numbers to stand against his army he will unite the nobles and its people," a non-supporter of Richard proclaims. William stands from his chair slams his fist upon the table his eye take on the form of the wolf then change back, "This is not about standing up to King Richards numbers, if we remove my brother and his last reminding faithful then we will be the only ones to possess this power of the wolf and no army could stand up to us then." "Then what is your plan my lord," a noble still faithful to him asks." William goes to answer but Tyrolean returns with his brothers, "Tyrolean welcome back did you carry out what I requested," William asks with his entry. "Yes, my lord we spent a moon's cycle marking all in our paths." A noble man rises from his seat saying, "My God in heaven they will devour this land." William turns to those gathered revealing, "You see my loyal nobles when the full moon raises the beast in men will come out. King Richard will have to divide his numbers to hunt and destroy those we have created weakening his numbers around the castle." "So, we will attack him with force inside the new castle," another noble asks. William gives no reply. "What of your brother, he possesses your power he could run through them with ease." "I find truth in your statement," William relays then lets a devilish grin run over his face, "My brother will have things to worry his mind!" William and his men talk of the plans to come. "You see Tyrolean I have taken to heart what you said we will remove the heart of this army." "And what of the head," Tyrolean asks in return. "You and those gathered here knows a head cannot live without the heart."

Sir Richard rides up to the castle, his soldiers follow close. "Sir Richard the castle will finally have a master after all these many years," one of his closet states seeing the castle before them. Richard sits out looking upon it. The wilderness engulfs its walls its shell is old and worn down. Richard kicks his horse then rides into it. Spider webs and the marking of night creatures show in the great hall. Richard walks through wiping time from his path. The servants begin to take care of the tasks in front of them wiping, sweeping to bring it back to life. Richard looks inside the throne room then walks before the throne. Richard closes his eyes to see it in its former glory a servant comes in breaking his day dream. "My lord the master bedroom is a mess." Richard answers with a smile, "I guess I can sleep out in the surrounding of the castle." Richard leaves the throne room and finds his generals inside the great hall, making it too them he requests, "Commander take this table from out of here and place it in the gardens tonight we will all celebrate and the nobles who remain will sit at it to give their opinions on what we should do next."

"Father I do not think you will have to return with me you do have a kingdom to run." "All is second nature to me. I will see my daughter returned to her place in this world," Sand informs riding onto the ship with her. "Darius do you intend to marry her or just lust after her for all time," Sand asks with a joking voice. "I, I, I", Darius tries to answer. "What is wrong my warrior friend has some one removed your tongue?" Sand asks laughing. "Oh, father must you tease him so?" Carissa rides up beside him, "Do not worry with him we can discuss this tonight!" Darius's mind fills with lustful thoughts. The nights with her before come fresh to his mind.

The torch fires burn around the castle. Men and women work around the great castle restoring it back to its former self. The soldiers of an army find peace in its surroundings, they rest from bitter days. Richard and the nobles sit around the table. The stars shine bright in the new sky of night. Alex and Overlain sit by one another, Richard at the head his most trusted by his side as is with each of the nobles of the land. Richard rises and holds his cup in front of him, "Noble men of this great land, we come together this night to usher in a new era in time. Though we have all laid claim to the throne of this land it is I who will rule, but in my heart I know that any noble man here could do well where I sit. Let us put the times of the past behind us and bring unity and pride to the people of this land. Too my nobles, my governors, the knights of my court, I salute you!!" The men all stand and drink of their cups. The servants bring the crown of the land. The men become silent as they take in the beauty of it. The flames bring it to sparkle, the jewels place in it glisten for their eyes to behold. Many Kings before him have let it set upon their brows. "Sir Richard if you do not mind," Alex suggests looking over towards a red carpet placed upon the ground a priest waits for him. Sir Richard stands from the table walks up the carpet to the priest, then kneels before him. "Sir Richard the lion heart may god give you the wisdom to watch over this country, may he give you the knowledge to judge the people of the land with truth and justice in your heart! Amen." Alex places the crown upon his head saying, "Arise King Richard!" He stands to his feet the nobles pull their swords from their sheaths point them towards him then turn them to their faces saluting a king in their mists. Richard does the same and salutes them all. They wait until he is seated and then rejoin him. "Now that the pleasantries are over what will be the first order of business," King Richard asks to those joining him. The nobles begin to shout their demands. Alex hearing the same things from times past stands to his feet, and slams the table, a growl escapes him, the men become silent. "Men of this table noble by birth but what does it mean to be noble? Is it a title placed upon us by men or does it come from God above?" Alex walks around the table the men follow him with their eyes. "For what it is to me to be noble is the simplest of things, knowing when you have to give for the good of the people, knowing we will have to pull together to bring the land back to unity, the wars fought for the throne are over," Alex looks over the table, "King Richard rules the land and we must do are parts to serve him. My father once told me that to sit on the throne was to make discussions that would not set well with everyone and sometimes go against the nature of the heart, to give up things so that others would be happy." He looks toward Richard, "It is not with lust for power or the pleasure of ruling he places the crown upon his head, but a calling! Serve him well." Alex turns and grabs his cup holds it towards him saluting, "Long life to King Richard!" He swallows his drink and walks from the table leaving the men to figure it out, Overlain gets up to follow, "Wait up Alex," Overlain requests. Alex waits in his steps. "You would have made a great ruler Alexander Lancaster," Overlain suggests patting him on the back. "No, my wise friend. I hold no lust for the prison that will become the crown," Alex looks out over the horizon informing, "A simple man's life is all I need. Elizabeth and the children she will bare me." "That is what makes a great ruler, to fight the temptation of the power." "Richard will do well ruling this great land. I have sent for my wife she returns as we speak, I will wait here for Darius to bring her to me then we will set out to find my brother and release him from this spell or see him dead at my feet." "Where do you think he will run too?" "There will be signs in the land," Alex suggests putting his arm around Overlain places the charms from his fallen brothers in his hands, "I long to end this spell and become normal again without any fear of the beast inside," Alex relays. "My lord you have gotten a king for this land why not remove it now before she returns, let the King worry of the days ahead," Overlain asks. "No. I must finish this for my brother will never stop I cannot leave England to his lusts!"

The days move through time many days have come and gone. Elizabeth rides off of the ship at first light of a new day, her personal guards and her father ride with her. "Darius how long will it take to get to the castle from here," Elizabeth asks as her horse's hooves touches the shore. "Two days journey my lady. I figured we would ride until we reach the valley of rivers then we will set out at first light in the morning." "Do you think William is dead?" "I cannot say but I think he would not dare attack us with the numbers surrounding you," Darius states.

Alex wakes with a smile knowing she will be with him soon, his heart beats wild for the woman he loves. "My lord the king wishes to see you this morning," a servant girl says entering his room. "Tell him I will be with him shortly." She walks out of the room going to Richard to relay his message. Alex finishes with his morning preparations then goes to the great room. "You needed to see me this morning?" "Yes, my young noble. I have use of you this day, I would ask if you will ride out to the village of the north and see to it the people who live there know that a king has been place upon the throne. They have not sent a representative to this castle." "My lord I was going to ride out and meet my wife in the valley of rivers. If I should be detained. I will have to wait another day to see her there are men in government better suited for this task." "I would tend to agree with you, if it had not been for this parchment I received late in the night. A noble traveling from that direction heard strange howls in the night and that could mean only one thing," King Richard stresses. "I will see to it, King Richard," Alex turns to walk out, "Alex rest easy she will be here within the next few days." "I wonder if you would send out a rider to guide them back. I worry for her safe return," Alex requests. "I can do that for you," Richard answers then asks, "Is there any news of your brother?" "No, my lord. I have seen no sign or even a whisper of where he could be." "He could have fled these parts," Richard suggests. "No, my lord. He is here somewhere; I know it in my heart." He turns and walks out of the room, with his departure Richard calls, "Squire!" A young man barely twenty runs into the room. "I have use of you his day," Richard informs the young man. "What do you command of me my lord?" "Ride out towards the valley of rivers and bring back Lord Lancaster's bride, he awaits her." "Yes, King Richard I will leave at once!" Daniel runs to the stables takes the finest horse the stable has to offer, brings food and water, and sets out for the land ahead. Alex rides with soldiers from King Richard's army his brothers of the wolf tend to tasks of their own. Alex sets out knowing his journey will consume the day time moves forward. Alex and the men ride up to the village with no one in sight. The village having the setting of a tomb. "Go and check the stables, see if any horses are there," Alex commands. A few soldiers leave the ranks to search the stables. The others slowly ride into the village with Alex. Alex gets off his horse and opens a door. He pulls back when he sees the rotting decay of the body inside. He walks up and checks to see what could have killed him. He moves his shirt and finds his heart eaten out. "There is two more over in the stables my lord," the soldiers rushing back inform. Alex pulls his sword, "Look lively men they may still be here." They walk through the village finding people dead with each door they pass. Alex opens a door and walks inside he turns and looks in each room, he begins to walk out when he hears the faint cry of a child. He pauses to let his senses lead his way then reenters a room. Alex ducks down and looks under a bed, a small girl is curled up. "What is your name girl?" The child draws back farther. "Come out from under there so I can see you. Come on I am not going to hurt you child." She pauses for a moment then asks, "How am I to know you are not like them, they were men too until." Alex can see the horror in her eyes, "I am just man now come out so I can take you to the new castle." The little girl slowly crawls out from under the bed. Her little body dirty from her stay underneath the bed. Picking her up Alex inquires, "What is your name?" "Lisa." "Lisa I am Sir Lancaster noble to the house of King Richard and you are safe." He takes her hand and they walk out into the street the other soldiers walk up. "It is the same everywhere my lord." Alex holds up his hand, "We will discuss it later." He walks over to his horse places the girl into the saddle he swings his body up into the saddle behind her. "Where are we going now my lord?" "We must return and tell King Richard what has happened here and take her to a safe place then we can return to deal with the dead come on the light will leave us soon and I do not want to run into anything while this child is with me." He kicks his horse and the little girl holds on tight to his arms. The horse finds a steady pace and they ride for the castle.

"My lord William everyone is in place for the night," Eric informs. "Good tell the men to make sure they do not harm her and to leave one alive to deliver a message to my brother." "Why do we not just transform and take her my lord," Titus asks. "Because my dear brother we must stay downwind from them she has a wolf traveling with her our scent will lose us the element of surprise," William relays holding the looking glass to his eye watching them ride for the valley. He turns his horse to make his way to meet his men. "We should be at the valley within the hour my lady," Darius says. "Good and when you take me to Alex you can spend more time with her," Elizabeth suggests looking back to Carissa then turns back forward adding, "I know she is a servant in my father's house sworn to me by birth, but I have always seen her as a sister. She is quite taken with you." "My lady I do care for her in that I have no doubt, but I have little experience

with matters of the heart. I have spent my life a soldier, it is all I know."
"Just keep doing what you have been doing and you will do fine," Elizabeth
suggests. They journey on and they reach the valley. Elizabeth looks down
a Cliffside, "That would be quite a drop!" "Yes, I could take someone a
good day to climb up it but at the base is a magnificent water fall where
the three rivers merge its beauty is untold," Darius informs. "Then this is
a place Alex and I must return to, Elizabeth relays then asks, "How much
father before we reach the castle?" "A rider could make it in a half day if he
was not loaded down and did not care much for the animal. We will pitch
camp here then leave out early in the morning." "I wish I could hold him
tonight I miss him to no end." "Relax my lady I will see to it you rest in his
arms tomorrow night."

Alex returns to the castle with the little girl asleep from the journey. He
carefully carries her into the castle, slips her into a servants arms, "Just put
her down in my bed tonight in the morning we will figure what to do with
her." Alex walks down the hall and into the throne room, "My lord I have
news from the village." "If you will excuse me we will pick up on this later,"
Richard requests to those gathered with him. The men of government leave
the table and close the door behind them. "My lord the village was ravished
from the looks of it, wolves killed them all," Alex states. "So, your brother
still roams the land." "It seems that way but I do not know the reason for
killing all the villagers." "For whatever the reason I am going to have to
send patrol parties to make the people feel save." Alex pauses for a moment
then suggests, "That may be what he intended for you to weaken the army
by spreading them over the land." "What choice do I have I cannot let him
simply kill my people," Richard implores. "I know King Richard that is why
I have decided to take my brothers and Overlain to seek out my brother
and put an end to this curse we all live with now." "Alex your lady returns,
I cannot ask you to set out for such a task." "My lord she will be safe within
these walls. He will not risk a head on battle, he does not have the numbers
for it." "I sent a rider to guide their way back they should be here by dusk
tomorrow." "Thank my lord I cannot wait until tomorrow's sun. Oh, I
brought a little girl back she was the only one still alive, I will need for you to
decide what must be done with her." "I could think of a purpose for her now
my young noble." "What would that be my lord?" "She could help soften the
blow of when you tell Elizabeth you will leave her again, it would give her

someone to look after until you could return." Alex bows his head saying, "You are a very wise man my lord." Richard smiles to his compliment. Alex leaves his stead going to seek out Overlain. He wonders through the castle until he finds him, "Overlain can I speak with you?" "Why yes Alex you know my door is always open for you." Alex walks into his room and sits at the table relaying, "I miss the long talks we had before I knew this face." "Speak what troubles you this night?" "My brother is spreading this curse throughout the land. I know I must put an end to this." Alex sips from the glass on the table with it resting back on the table, "we will set out in two days." "My lord your wife will have the wrath of the Titians when you tell her you must leave her again." "I know but when she sees the horrors in the little girl's eyes she will see I must do this." "A little girl," Overlain inquires confused. "Yes, I found her in the village. She was the only one alive I will leave her in the care of Elizabeth. I leave so that no other child should bare the scares she now carries." "Then my God be with us in the task we both share," Overlain requests adding, "I should have ended my brother all those years ago if I had this curse would not be on the face of the land." "My brother has become drunk with the power of the wolf. I know in my heart he will never drink from the cup." "Yes it is a hard thing to see the people we love for who they are, even as a child he lusted for the power of the throne," Overlain states. They talk more of the days passed.

Elizabeth and those traveling with her find rest from their journey. "The stars are bright tonight," Carissa says to Darius and Elizabeth finding warmth around the fire with her. Darius looks up to the sky, "Yes we will have good weather tonight." He pauses for a moment, the scent of the men enters his nostrils, quickly rising to his feet, pulling the sword from its sheath yelling, "Men stand to your feet!" The soldiers of William come from the darkness. "Run my lady find a place to hide!" His sword clangs with the men around him. Swiftly Darius draws blood from two they hit the ground dead in front of him. He backs away and the darkness engulfs him. The next sight seen to the men is the wolf leaping from the darkness; he lashes out striking the men with his razor claws, killing them with the mighty jaws of his mouth. "We have him busy send the men for her," a commander instructs to those around him. The young man sent to retrieve them, rides up and sees the conflict. He pulls his sword and rides for the battle. "Elizabeth," Sand yells as two soldiers pull her by the arms dragging her towards the darkness. Sand cuts them off declaring, "Take your hands off her now!" The men begin to move around him with a swing of his sword they engage in battle. "Father," Elizabeth yells as Devilian in wolf form slips up from behind him. Her father wipes his sword around and drives it into him it finds his body but not a death blow. Devilian howls into the night with the pain of it. The warriors of the mostly dead surround him and thrust their swords into him. "No," Elizabeth seeing him falling yells, rushing out to help grabbing a sword from a dead soldier as she runs by him. Titus leaps and knocks her from her feet hitting the dirt her head strikes a stone knocking her out. Darius leaps beside her and the men and the wolf surround him. William rides up on his horse the mostly dead warrior's lust for the battle ahead as their ghostly forms drift over the ground surrounding Lord William, "Stand down and I will spare you." Darius digs his paws into the dirt giving out a mighty growl striking out at the men and the wolves leap for him knocking him closer to the cliff. The men of the mostly dead drive their blades into him driving him over the cliff, his body strikes the rocky side until he finds a grip on a tree growing from its side catching his fall just before striking the bottom. "Grab her, and put her on a horse," William commands. "My lord this one rode in to join the battle," a soldier throws him in the dirt in front of his horse. "What is your name boy?" "Daniel from the house of our King Richard the lion heart," the young man answers with pride. "Well Daniel, I will send you back with a message for my brother. Tell him to come alone and bring the cup he drank from or he will never see her again!" He pulls back on his reins of the horse then turns back over his shoulder, "Devilian, send the boy back with a mark. Boy you tell him to meet me at the castle in the valley where we played when we were kids." Devilian lashes out and marks him with his claw. They gather themselves and join him on the ride. Elizabeth rides tied to the saddle her father lays dead in the mist of the men. Daniel reaches for his back and feels the blood run down his skin. He gathers a horse and rides for the castle. As he passes he grabs the reins of another horse, pulling it behind him, he kicks the horse running it for all it's worth traveling fast and hard on the landscape before him. Elizabeth wakes from her slumber, "What is this release me now!" "Sorry my lady in waiting I cannot grant your request," William answers. "I am no longer a woman in waiting. I now bear your same last name." "He married you? So, at last he fulfilled his betrayal of me," William suggests. "Alex never betrayed you. I love him. We could not help what we felt for one another." William gives a weak smile. "How can you do this to your flesh and blood," she asks him. "How could he take you into his bed?" "I will not be used to hold over his head so kill me now or if I get the chance I will kill you," Elizabeth assures him. "Oh, so eager to die? Just rest easy my sister. I will not kill you I have a special purpose for you." They ride on into the night crossing many streams laid out over the landscape. The coolness of the night sets in the moon lights the world for them to see. "See that Elizabeth? She will be full tomorrow night and the land will be feasted upon in the days ahead!" Titus still in form moves closer to her. "Do you think you can get this animal father from me," Elizabeth asks. William turns to Titus, "Easy my brother for my sister must be in good health when my brother arrives." They come to the top of the hill and look over at the castle. "This castle belonged to a noble that has long passed in time," William informs. They ride down and his men open the gates. "Take her to the dungeon and get the men ready my brother will be here by days end." The soldiers begin to make preparations. Titus takes her to the dungeon puts her in the cell and wraps the chain around her wrist. "Enjoy your stay," the guard requests. Titus and he walk out of the cell with Titus suggesting, "Keep a careful eye on her she is a cunning foe!" Elizabeth pulls at the chain testing their strength then her thoughts linger to Alex and what he will do when the word of her capture reaches his ears. Darius hangs unto a branch clinging in human form, waiting until his body is strong enough to gather the power of the wolf. With every fiber of his being he holds on to the branch waiting. With the day drawing closer his body changes and he climbs with the speed of the wolf. He does not bother with the men lying dead at the top he only gives a small glance towards her fallen father then he sees her broken body. Carissa lies dead on the ground before him. Moving to her he picks up her hand; his wolf hand engulfs hers. He gives a meaningful howl into the air then lets his nose lead him towards their path and the vowel he made to a brother.

Daniel runs the horse dragging the other behind him. The animal's sweat covers its body it begins to slow its pace, he draws out his dagger and stabs it in the meat of its thigh causing the horse to regain its speed. The horse runs, runs, until no strength can be found in its body, its legs give out and it comes crashing to the ground. Daniel with a heavy heart takes out his knife and finishes off the animal. He removes the saddle and places it upon the other horse and rides for the castle the night moves fast and the morning is but a heartbeat away when the castle's torches come into his view. "A rider is coming," the guard yells from the wall at the front gate. Daniel rides into the castle with the gate barley to the ground. "Where is Lord Lancaster," Daniel asks a soldier. "He is asleep," the soldier replies. "Then we must wake him his wife has been taken," Daniel reveals struggling to get off the horse with his body beaten and battered from the nights events. The soldiers wake Alex and the King they gather in the great hall of the throne room. "Young man what is your name," Alex asks. "Daniel lord Lancaster," he answers with Alex pulling his shirt down to see the marks from the wolf. "Speak," Alex implores. "My lord your brother has her, Darius fought well but I saw him fall over the cliff in the valley of rivers." Daniel hands him a parchment with writing upon it. Alex unrolls it and reads the writing, "Alex if you have this in your hands you should know by now I have her, and I await your arrival, but come alone and bring the cup used in the spell placed upon you, or leave her to the fate of me. Remember the castle we rode for as kids. I will be waiting" Alex slings the writing to the floor he begins to walk out with King Richard requesting, "Alex what does it say?" "My brother has her now I go to retrieve her." "Wait and we will come with you!" "No, he said to come alone this is for me." King Richards rises from his throne relaying, "You are doing just what he wants of you it is a trap!" Alex does not listen to the words of his new King. He turns and hands the young man a medallion instructing, "You will need this to never leave your skin!" Daniel takes it from his hand Alex moves to the doors of the great hall. Overlain stands in the hall listening to the acts of the throne room he quickly walks back to his room and waits for Alex. "Overlain," Alex calls as he enters the room. "Yes, my lord?" "Where is the cup?" "It is here but if you give it to him you will have no way to remove the curse upon you!" Alex looks at him in the face, "Do I look like I care whether I can remove it or not? It will be better to be cursed for all time then to live without her! My only concern is to free my wife!" "I cannot give you the cup of Christ the power of it is too great," Overlain pleads. Alex lets the wolf come out and his face begins to change he grabs him by the throat. Overlain lays the cup in his hand and his face returns to normal. Alex looks at him for a moment then leaves the room becoming the wolf with every step, transformed he rushes from the castle. Overlain gathers his staff rushes from the walls of the castle gathers his horse as he passes the guard posted by the gate he slings a crystal to him instructing, "Put this in the hand of King Richard it will guide his path." Overlain casts the cloak spell and becomes invisible to the eyes of man then follows the path of Alex. "Run with the speed of the wolf star, run with haste in your heart," Overlain requests to his horse. The horse runs over the landscape. The soldier rushes in and places the crystal into his hands, "Overlain told me to give this to you my lord." "What will you do my lord" a commander asks. "Bring me my armor and ready my horse. I owe him for the throne I now sit on," Richard states. Alex covers the ground quickly the people of the land see the wolf in the new day as he runs for his beloved Elizabeth. Overlain's horse gallops trying to keep strive, but the horse is unable to keep pace with him. The people of the land can only see the dust from the horse hooves when he passes; they grab their children and cross themselves to what they think is unholy. "Come star, you are losing speed," Overlain proclaims then reaches into his clothing to pull out a crystal. Overlain places it on the horse's neck the energy from it drains into star bringing strength and speed back to its legs.

Richard with his chosen few prepares to leave. "Keep the castle sealed until I return," he commands. "My lord I must go with you," Darien says. "No, you must stay with the castle. I leave you in command if this is just a trap to lead us away. I will need you here with the power in you to protect the people!" Richard kicks his horse with the crystal resting in his hand and they ride for the castle but time is not with them. Alex runs all through the day. He reaches the front of the castle he stands on the outskirts letting his wolf's eyes get a peek into what will lay ahead. He slips, waits, then leaps into the men slashing and ripping them into pieces. A mighty howl rings out, "My lord your brother is here," Titus suggests. "Quickly bring her into the throne room," William orders. Tyrolean runs from the room making haste he reaches her and brings her towards the throne room. Alex leaps and climbs the wall the archers fire their silver arrows into him but none give a fatal blow. Alex leaps into the room his claws make a tick tacking sound as he walks over the floor. He reaches up and painlessly removes the arrows from his body. "Well brother it seems you made good time," William says to stir the anger in his brother. Alex lets out a mighty growl, his jaws stretch. "Careful brother you might kill me but she will be dead before we are finished!" Alex whirls around and Tyrolean holds a blade to her throat. "Change back or watch her die!" "No Alex! You must stay as you are," Elizabeth screams. Tyrolean pushes the blade to her neck a little harder. Alex begins to let himself change moments go by and he stands before them naked. "Here Alex, cover yourself with this," William suggests throwing him a cloak. "Now give me the cup I asked for!" Alex throws him the cup requesting, "Now let her go please brother!" "I have plans for her," William reveals walking over to rip the medallion from his neck. "That was for just in case you try to transform." "What makes you so sure I want and come for you," Alex inquires. "Because brother I know you," William states adding, "You will not risk killing someone to get to me remember you won't let your beast run wild as it was meant to be." "What do you intend to do with her?" William leans into his ear saying, "I promise you dear brother I will not harm a hair on her head!" He waves his arm and the guards take them to the dungeon and seal them into a room. A window sits high too high to see from, its only purpose to let the cries of doom men escape. Overlain slips into the city still unseen by man. He walks down the castle's halls lurking his way towards the dungeon. "Alex my love," she says as she embraces him. "Elizabeth how good it feels to taste your lips." He places his lips upon hers their tongues entwine breaking their kiss he informs, "My lady we need to figure a way to get out of here. The moon will be full and I will have no way to control this beast within me!" "Fear not my love I still have this," she reaches in the soft cleavage of her breasts and pulls the medallion he placed in her care. "Thank God in heaven you still have one!" He holds her tight trying not to let the nightmare that played in his mind take hold. She looks deeply into his eyes suggesting, "Alex it would not matter whether or not I would have had this. I could not believe any part of you could ever hurt me! Love would have tamed the beast!" He holds her tighter. "Did your father make it?" "No, he gave his life protecting me." The tears fill her eyes with Alex comforting, "It will all be okay. I am here for you now." The door makes a creaking sound as it opens. "What a touching scene," William says with a smarten tone entering the room. "Brother you will let her go," Alex demands. William walks around the cell. The guards pull her from him, they struggle to hold unto one another but they pull her away. "Chain her over there," William orders but with her struggles sees a flicker of it shine, "Wait!" He walks over and reaches in her cleavage pulls up the medallion. "Well that would have just ruined my plans," William suggests with a smile. "Brother please let her go!" "I told you I would not harm a hair on her head," he gives a faint smile adding, "The two of you claim to have a love for the ages well I say we will put that to the test!" "If something happens to her dear brother there is no place on earth you will be safe from me for I would ride into hell itself to find you," Alex proclaims. "In that I would have no doubt. That is why the men will be waiting above you and outside the door, when you have eaten of her flesh they will kill you. I just wanted you to cross over the river of sticks with the weight of killing her in your heart!" He turns to walk out of the cell with Alex saying, "If I have to sell my soul to the fairy-man, I will be waiting on you when you get there brother!" "Oh, there is one more thing," William says as Tyrolean brings in the cup. The soldiers place it upon a stone a big man with a hammer walks into the room. With a mighty swing of his hammer, the cup breaks into pieces. "Noooo," Alex yells. "You see brother there will be no cure for either of us." William holds his hands out declaring, "To think you actually thought I could give up being a God in this world!" The door closes behind him, as the men leave the room. Alex bangs on the door. The sound of his fisting beating upon it echoes through the hall. Overlain slips in silence with them his brother notices the flame on a torch move when he slips by. "My lord, do you think it wise to keep him alive better we kill him now!" "Relax he will be dead by morning" Tyrolean whirls around says a spell and Overlain stands revealed to all. "Seize him," The soldiers place their hands upon him before he can say a word Tyrolean covers his mouth to keep him from using magic to escape saying, "Welcome by brother! You forgot the flames of the torch would pull towards you." Overlain can say nothing as the men drag him away with Tyrolean ordering, "Take him to my room!" They do as they are told and Tyrolean casts a spell, and imprisons him there behind a wall of magic. Tyrolean stands with the wall of magic between them holding Overlain's staff in his hands. "I see you replaced the one you lost to me all those years ago." "Brother how can you take the gift we were both given and use it to bring destruction to this world it was given to us to heal not hurt." "You see brother that is what separates us from one another. Why have all this power if not to rule this world," Tyrolean states. "We are of a different kind you and I, it is for men to rule this world," Overlain implores. "And a man shall rule with me guiding his way!" "No when you have fulfilled your use William will strike out and destroy you." "Not likely my brother there is still the silver curse. You would not think I would cast a spell without the power to control it." "I implore you Tyrolean my brother let me lose, and free Alex and her before it is too late!" "For me in the path I have walked it is too late, you cannot save me Overlain." "Then my brother is truly lost." Tyrolean walks away. Overlain knows in is heart his brother will never be as he once was. The thought of what will come weighs heavy on his heart. Richard and the small army ride with speed as the moon grows high. Darius covers the land with the speed of the wolf letting his nose led the way. "I hope dear lord this will work," Overlain says in a pray like manner pulling a crystal stone hidden on is body. He flings it towards the wall holding him prisoner a bright light glows and it takes the spell into it. Overlain slips down the hall. "Elizabeth I want you to know I love you with all my being," Alex says with the passion in him standing against the wall, then looks up towards the window with moon's light shining in, "My love it's starting." Elizabeth stands, watching the wolf begin to come out, his fingers grow long his body pops as the growls escape his body. Alex fights to keep the wolf at bay but the moon holds her sway. Darius runs up to the castle bouncing through the soldiers letting the scent of her pull him to her. "Oh Alex," Elizabeth cries as he stands before her in full wolf form. Alex trapped inside with no control over the beast just the hunger driving its desires. He begins to move for her. "Alex, Alex it's me," she screams before the beast. "Oh, brother it is nice to let the beast run free," William says with his last words as the change comes over him. Alex moves to her his jaws inches from her face the drool dips down her neck into her cleavage. He grabs her and picks her up in the air, her feet dangle then in a moment her scent flows in his nose. With the sent familiar to him the beast goes to draw down. Darius seeing in from the door leaps in to protect her and Alex in his animal lust leaps for him. Darius living out a vowel finds himself in a fight with his brother. "No, No Alex stop," she pleads as the tears run down her face. The wolves slam each other against the wall and it caves in and they spill out into the street. Overlain slips his staff from where his brother placed it. With it in his grasps, "Reveal to me what you have hidden." The cross used to hold the mostly dead appears before him, along with the thing most dear to his brother's heart. Overlain takes what he has found with him, then slips through the castle towards the cell. He looks in the cell Elizabeth sits chained to the wall her tears and sighs come from her body. "My lady," Overlain says coming to release her. "Overlain you must do something they are killing each other," Elizabeth pleads. Overlain uses his magic and releases her from her chain. "My lady," Overlain yells as she runs out of the wall. She stands in the street screaming for them to stop. Suddenly the horn of Richard blows as the soldiers begin to lay siege upon the castle. The wolves circle each other within the conflict Darius's medallion is knocked from his body and they fight as two wild animals ripping and tearing at each other. Each gives deep wounds to the other. Alex being the first gains the advantage slinging him away he slams through a shed where they store the weapons, a silver sword finds its mark. Alex paws the ground as the dust springs up giving a victorious howl into the night. He sees the men riding in and takes a mighty leap fleeing into the woods running wild into the night. Elizabeth runs for the shed she finds him turning back to his human form. "Darius," Elizabeth says grasping his hand. "My lady," Darius answers with weakness in his breath, "I fulfilled my vowel now I find my way into the next and join with her." His body goes limp. Darius finds himself standing upon a lost shore waiting on the fairy-man a smile finds his face as he sees Carissa waiting on the boat for him. Overlain sees Tyrolean riding out of the castle he calls his horse. Overlain mounts his horse to pursue his brother seeing the mostly dead killing the soldiers of King Richard's he holds the cross in front of him casting the spell to release them to the next world then makes haste for his brother. The warriors of the mostly dead let joy fill them as they hear the words and are released. Elizabeth stands in the street. Men fight all around her she flees back into the cell looking for a weapon. Titus waits in the hall, she goes through the door, turns, and Titus is there. He grabs her and bites her in the neck she gives out a gasp and kicks her feet until her body grows leap. Titus savors her flavor in his mouth then lays her upon the ground. The crystal around her neck begins to glow her sprit joins with it trapped between here and the next life. Titus flees the castle to meet William with a plan fulfilled. Overlain rides with speed, coming through the cannon he slows his pace. Tyrolean leaps out with his staff in his hands striking him from his horse. He walks over towards him, reaches down to roll him over and Overlain knocks him from his feet. They back off one another to face each other. "Come brother let us embrace for a finale time," Tyrolean suggests. "So be it," Overlain replies whipping his staff over his head pointing it at him. The power inside shoots from the crystal resting in his staff their power meets in front of them, pushing against one other. The magic entangles, sparks fly, a mighty explosion takes them both from their feet. Tyrolean casts a spell. Overlain counters it as they battle with the words spoken from their tongues. Tyrolean casts a spell the dust flies up from the ground engulfing Overlain he leaps and drives his sword into his body. "This time I will make sure you are dead dear brother." Tyrolean pulls his sword from his body whips it over his head preparing to make the finale blow "You forgot something brother," Overlain states as he strikes down with his sword. Overlain pulls the thing that holds his life force it comes into view too late for him to stop the sword smashes it resting in his hands. Tyrolean stands straight on his feet the sword falls to the ground the blood of his brother dips from its edges. "You left me no choice my brother," Overlain says as his body falls to the dirt. Overlain with his life draining from him, rolls to his side and grabs his staff and casts a spell to merge with the crystal cradled in it.

Chapter Eight

A Love Lost in Time

ALEX WAKES IN THE WOODS A DEAD goat lays beside him. A feast for the wolf in the night. "Elizabeth," Alex says in his horror, wiping the blood from his face, regains his feet, runs into the woods, his feet strike the ground with haste but feels no pain from the forest floor, as the stickers and sticks pound his feet. Alex runs up to a farm house pulls some clothing from the line to cover his body and takes a horse from inside the barn. The owner comes out screaming as he rides for the castle. Alex kicks the horse, smacks it on the ass, keeping the speed in its legs. With his return he can see the smoke rising from the castle, he gallops in from the gate. "Lord Lancaster," a soldier yells as he passes the gates. Alex leaps from his horse, "Where is Mrs. Elizabeth my wife?" The soldier does not answer. He grabs him by his throat, "I asked you where the hell is she," the wolf tries to slip out but Alex holds it back grasping the soldier. "My lord I," the soldier answers not letting the truth sip from his lips. "Alex," he turns to see Richard standing in the street of the castle. He runs over to him. "Where is she?" "Alex she, she's dead," Richard mournfully states. "No, she cannot be!" Alex runs for the opening inside the wall, "Alex wait," Richard implores. He runs inside sees her body laid out on the floor of the cell screaming, "No, No! I couldn't have!" The horror strikes his eyes, he kneels down beside her, lifts the covering from her body he glances down upon the bite, "I couldn't have, no! You said love would have tamed the beast," Alex cries then picks her up to hold her tight against his neck. The tears pour from his body he rocks her back and forth, her lifeless body just hangs in his arms. Time moves on and he holds her. "My lord you will have to let her go," a soldier says trying to gather her body. Alex snaps back to the day, "Where is Overlain? Maybe there is something he can do." "No one can find his body all that was found was his staff it was found with Tyrolean's dead body." Alex slowly places her to the ground he kisses her lips and pulls the crystal from her neck, walks out of the wall as they gather her body. His head looks to the ground, sorrow fills his heart, the medallion lost by his brother shines in the dirt he pulls it from the dust and walks to the shed. Darius's body lies in the shed the silver sword stuck through his heart. Alex kneels down beside him. A soldier steps in behind him. "What happened to him who done this?" "You did in wolf form, the two of you spilled out of the wall you got the upper hand," the soldier mournfully informs. The thought of his death weights heavy upon his heart knowing it was by his hands. "My brother may you cross the river of sticks with honor. You keep your vowel to me, you honor me even in your death," Alex says before placing a small kiss upon his forehead. Alex reaches over and takes a silver dagger from the shelf then places it on his neck, and begins to slice the skin. The silver burns his skin as he cuts a groove around his neck. The soldier with him begins to plead, "My lord! What are you doing?" He tries to stop him but Alex slings him out of the door demanding, "Leave me be!" Alex makes the circle around his neck lays the chain inside of it then the folds his skin, slowly his skin begins to cover the medallion. "King Richard you must stop him," the soldier pleads as Richard walks up. Richard walks into the shed. Alex kneels on the floor the blood slowly sips down his body like the tears from his eyes revealing, "I will never be without it again this beast in me must never be allowed to run wild again this thing in me killed her and my brother whose only job was to protect her. I wished he had killed me in the fight." Alex stands to his feet and walks off down the street, guilt and sorrow follows his steps. "Why did he cut himself like that my lord," The soldier asks of King Richard coming from the shed. "He placed the medallion inside of his skin so it could never be removed." King Richard walks off back down the street. "My lord we captured this one alive," a commander says as he throws him to his feet demanding, "Tell our King what you told me!" The soldier says nothing at first. The commander sticks his finger inside the arrow hole in his shoulder. "Arhhh," the man cries out before revealing, "He has turned many men into the beast he has inside of him, and turned them lose across the land, they will feast upon the people!" Richard turns and looks out of the landscape saying, "My God in heaven they will kill people for all time." Richard looks down at him kneeling on the ground, "He is a soldier of a fallen army treat him as such." The commander takes him from the ground then slings him to the soldiers gathered. They place him on a horse, tie his hands around his back and place the rope around his neck. A priest stands by his side and says the finale blessing. A man strikes the horse the horse runs pulling him from the saddle and is left to swing in the wind. Alex finds a spot by a stream; the tears keep streaming down his face. The soldiers of the army gather the dead. The day moves forward.

William with his followers meets in a cave chosen by him. William seeing Titus arrive asks, "Did he kill her?" "No, my lord another showed up to protect her!" "Then she still lives," William suggests. "No, my lord I tasted of her flesh!" "Then he will be without her for all time," William says with pleasure adding, "let him find a way to exist now. The heart of King Richard's army is dead." A plan played out sets well in his heart. "Did you see Tyrolean along the way," William asks adding, "He should have been here by now." "No, my lord. He fled last night when Richard and his army rode in and laid siege upon the castle." "We will gather our numbers let our new wolf's ware them down and attack at the right time!" "What of Tyrolean," Titus asks. "If he doesn't come here, then we must believe him dead and the secret of how to release men from the spell died with him!" "Titus go and use your senses of the wolf to find our brothers who have not returned and bring back the medallions placed upon their bodies." "But my lord we have no way to make a person into our image," "Yes I know but if we attacked at the full moon it would give us brothers for the night." Titus leaves in search of his brothers. William rests inside the cave with his numbers gathering with him. The day grows long and many men are laid to rest. "My lord we have them prepared if you want to say a few words over them," a servant informs King Richard. Alex walks back to the castle he passes by everyone and walks into the throne room. Richard stands in the throne room preparing to leave to say the words. "King Richard I would speak with you." "Speak Alex of Lancaster." "My lord I would request that this castle be granted to me, in the name of King Richard, and their bodies to be laid in tombs in the bowels of this castle so that I will have them with me for all time." "I will grant your request and honor their names for all time." Alex bows his head to him and walks from the room. The King orders their bodies taken inside the castle. The soldiers build their tombs as Alex requested with time slipping across the land. Alex dressed in the clothing of a noble, his Family crest shows on the back of his cloak, as he speaks over them. Elizabeth rests in her dress of blue and white her hair still shines of gold the jewels of a queen surround her neck. Darius's armor glistens in the light with a soldier's attire covering him. "My lady, my love for you shall never die inside my heart. I will carry you with me for all the years. I will walk this world. My brother you will forever honor me with your life and your death and when its time. I hope I can find the courage in your veins to live out a vowel." The music fills the castle, tears roll down his face as they place the stone coverings over their bodies, Alex walks back up into the castle. Richard waits for him in the great hall of the castle. "Noble Lancaster, I know this may not be the time, but I must speak with you." "What do you need to say King Richard?" "Your brother has sent out many wolves among the sheep of the land if they are not stop they will consume its people, Richard relays with Alex looking distant, "Are you hearing me my young lord?" Alex takes a deep breath answering, "Yes King Richard I hear what is on your lips. I will take three days to mourn by beloved wife then I will set out over the land to stop this madness my brother has set upon it." Richard places his hand upon his shoulder, "I must return to the castle my place is in the throne room so I will let the people know a King still stands for them." "I understand my King." "I wish sometimes my young lord I was not placed where I sit if not then I could stay and mourn with a son." Alex finds comfort resting with his words and requests, "I will need you upon your return to select the finest and bravest soldiers to come with me upon my quest. The task will be a job for few not many." "Alex for what it is worth my heart extends to you over the loss of her. I too laid my bride to rest it will leave its mark upon you forever." Richard walks out of the hall gathers most of his soldiers leaving a few with Alex. He turns sitting on his horse to give one more look at the castle with one of his finest suggesting, "He will never be the same my lord." "Yes, I know," Richard truthfully answers. "Do you think he will return to the castle?" "Yes, with all my heart I believe it so. He knows what it is to be noble." Richard kicks his horse and the men follow him back towards the throne room of the land that calls him King.

Alex sits on a worn-out throne, the cob webs linger about the ceiling, a few soldiers make repairs to the walls and the castle. Alex sits in silence. The happy memories of two brothers playing inside the castle are but a distant memory to him. "God did she make the wrong choice in saving me, if she had not placed this curse inside of me. She would have been in her homeland." Alex grows angry and slings the helmet from his head it strikes the wall with a mighty thud, it falls to the floor knocking Overlain's staff leaning up against the wall down to the floor. Alex hangs his head to his anger walks over and picks it up. The touch of his hand brings life into it and the crystal placed at the top of the staff begins to glow, the light blinds him at first, he turns his head and closes his eyes, the brightness dims his eyes slowly open. A figure stands before him glowing light outlines his body. "I was wondering how long it would take you to touch the staff!" "Overlain," Alex says with joy rushes to place his hands on his shoulder but passes through his image. "I am not truly here, Overlain reveals." "Then how do you stand before me?" "I am in sprit, a dream if you will." "But how?" "When I faced my brother in the finale battle he ended me and I him, I cast the essences spell, placing my life force inside the crystal with the last breath I had in me." "I killed Elizabeth Overlain how am I to live with this forever," Alex says as the tears find hid face again. "You did not kill her! She was alive when I set her free. She watched the two of you fight in the street." Alex feels the weight lift from his soul asking, "Then who could have killed her?" "That I cannot answer that my lord," Overlain says but asks, did she have the crystal I gave to her around her neck?" "Yes, I pulled it from her after I found her dead." "Then she will be able to answer it for you!" Alex fills a charge run through him, the excitement shows upon his lips asking, "What do you mean I can ask her?" "The crystal I placed upon her neck kept her sprit here in this place." "You trying to tell me she is trapped between the here and the afterlife," Alex suggests. "In a manner of speaking," Overlain answers. "Overlain, why would you do that she will have no finale rest?" "Because I could not bear the thought if you had to live without her," Overlain reveals then states, "She can be brought back to you again." Alex feels the warmth of her arms embrace him inside his soul asking, "How, how can I hold her again?" "You must find someone who is in the last moments of their life place the crystal I give you with hers inside the cup. Elizabeth's holds her soul and yours holds the power of the spell when they have mixed inside the cup pour it into the body and her sprit will live where there was once another." Alex answers with a heavy heart, "Overlain I have no way to remove this curse or release her. My brother destroyed the cup I drank from." "The cup of Christ can never be destroyed not by the hands of mankind anyways." "I saw the hammer bust it to pieces," Alex stresses. "The cup you saw broken was not the cup of Christ just a simple cup." "Then you sent me out without it?" Overlain sits down beside him and reveals, "Yes Alex I did. The cup of Christ is more valuable than one life. I knew in my heart he would try to destroy it and when he found he could not it would have been lost for all time." Alex fills a little betrayed in his heart listening to his words. "If you would have not let love blind you then you would have known that he was never going to let her go in the first place." Alex looks down out the floor saying, "I know it in my heart. I should have done something different. I should have kept her here with me maybe, I would still have her." A tear rolls off his nose and strikes the ground at his feet. "Get the crystal you took from her hold it in your hand along with the one around your neck lay down and sleep young noble and you will see her again." Alex rushes over to the throne inside the room, opens a pocket in the arm of the throne, pulls out the crystal grabs the staff and takes them to his room. He lies on the bed he closes his eyes but sleep cannot find him. Alex opens them and he sees a hand wave over his eyes with a soft voice saying, "Sleep me young noble, sleep." The words of Overlain sip into his mind his eyes grow heavy and slumber finds him. In an instant he feels a hand on his shoulder his skin longs for the touch of it. Alex springs up in the bed with Elizabeth staring back at him. The tears begin to stream down his face. She reaches for his face with her hand the tear turns to light as it touches her finger. "Elizabeth is that you?" She places a kiss upon his lips, "Does it feel like me my love?" Alex grabs her and holds her tight, "Okay love you can let me lose now." "Where are we?" "I don't know, but it does not matter I am here with you." "What happened did I do this? "No, my love. I told you in the last words we spoke I could not believe anything of you could hurt me, I was right love did tame the beast," proudly she answers. "Then how did you die?" The tears fill his eyes at the mention of her death. "It is okay my love," Elizabeth says reaching for him, "All I can tell you is I went back into the castle turned the corner and a beast was there that is all I can tell you the next thing I remember is waking up here." Alex gets the look of wild anger in his eyes informing, "When I take them I will have the one who did this to you!" "You can think on that when you return to your world, but for now do not let it ruin the time we have together," Elizabeth softly requests. Her fingers trace his neck her tips run over the ring in his flesh asking, "What is this?" "I placed the medallion under my skin it will never leave my neck again!" "Oh, Alex you should learn to trust in yourself I cannot believe anything of you could be evil!" Alex pulls her close tastes her lips, "I hope and pray with this animal in me you will be proven right." Elizabeth pulls back from him and stands to her feet reaches under her hair on the back of her neck. Her dress slowly falls to the floor with her nipples reflecting the feeling she has inside of her. She pushes back on his chest and climbs on top, her lips find his neck she nibbles on his ear suggesting, "Let me take you away from all the death you have endured, let me fill your heart with love for all the days ahead." Her hands pull the shirt from his chest, her hands slowly glide their way down his belly with her touch intoxicating him. The same fragrance that has brought him so much joy fills his senses. She pulls off the rest of his attire and looks at him lying naked before her. Elizabeth kisses his nipples while her hand feels him grow to her touch then places him inside of her. The feeling of her warmth runs over his body the wetness she holds for him brings passion to him grinding her body upon his. Alex's hands reach for her breast softly caressing them as he stares into her eyes. Her pace quickens their breath becomes short his passion explodes inside of her body. Elizabeth falls upon his chest holding onto his hand. The feeling of him inside her relaxes his mind, his eyes close. "I love you Alex! We will find the way to be with each other in your world I promise, sleep, put the bad dreams behind you now!" She kisses his lips and fades into the air back into her crystal. Alex dreams through the night of every touch, every taste of her lips, resting peaceful until the morning sun.

"Lord William a spy has come with word from the battle," a soldier comes into the cave informing. "Speak tell me what you know," William says. "My lord King Richard rides back for the castle your brother sits mourning her." "You see Devilian I told you he would be removed from the board. Now it is only Richard we must bring down." William turns to the spy, "You have done well, ride back to Richard and keep me posted." The soldier rides out, passes the dead bodies lying about having been feasted upon by William and the band of brothers he keeps. "William when are we to attack the castle? The longer we wait the more hold he will have over the country," Devilian stresses. "I thought we might leave here for a while and let a few of the full moons ware down their defenses." "Where would we go?" William walks to the mouth of the cave saying, "It seems to me there is a throne in France that has become vacant. I think we should find allies in other countries." A servant walks up to William and hands him a parchment. William reads the words upon it then turns to Devilian with a smile saying, "I will send you into Scotland with the notion that if they will support my claim. I will consider them free men." "As you command my lord," Devilian answers. With the task in front of him Devilian leaves the cave taking with him a band of soldiers. "Eric, take your brother and find me a ship to call my own. We set sail for France in three days." Derrick grabs a chest filled with gold and they depart. Titus returns to the cave carrying the medallions in his grasp. "My lord I could not find Enos's body." "Then his medallion will be lost for all time," William replies taking the medallions from him.

Alex wakes to the light shining in from the top of the castle, awoken with the love filling his heart from the world of dreams. He sits up in his bed reaches for the staff of Overlain. The light shines and he stands before him. "Overlain tell me where you placed the cup." "I placed it with the book of spells in the caves north of the castle." "I know you explained this to me yesterday but all I could hear was how I could see her again so explain to me again. How I can release this land from the curse that is me." "You must put the blood of a virgin lamb into the cup mix it with the water blessed by a man of God and speak the words I have marked in the book then drink from the cup and you will be released from the beast inside." "Tell me again how I can release her from the place that holds her." "You must place the crystals into the cup wait for them to dissolve then pour it into the body of someone who is dying at the moment their sprit will leave the body then hers can fill it and she will be of flesh and blood again." "So, someone must die for her to live again," Alex states. "That is true my lord a price must be paid by the living." "How long do we have?" "Like you she will live forever unless the crystal is lost or broken in time." "Thank you Overlain," Alex says before standing to his feet to place his clothes on. "What are you going to do my lord?" "I will set out to cure this land of this curse then I will set out to stop my brother from the evil that has become him!" Alex informs then walks out of the room. Overlain fades back into the crystal. Alex walks out into the courtyard of old. In seeing the pride back in his steps, a commander says in a greeting, "My lord it is good to see you up and moving in the world." Alex smiles then informs, "I place this castle into your care, when I return I will expect it to be a place to call home," Alex reaches into his bag, "Take this gold to hire people and to help buy what is needed for my castle." "Where do you go my lord?" "I set out for King Richard's castle then out over the land to release the beasts that live inside of men." "I would rather ride into battle with you my lord," the aging general informs. Alex gives a smile and places his hand upon his shoulder informing, "I know you would but I have need of you here to bring some order and work to the people given for me to govern. I place you in my stead, I can think of no one better suited for the task." "As you wish my lord," the aging general says with pride. Alex turns and walks back into the castle gathers his things. The staff of Overlain, his father's sword, places their crystals around his neck. A flag of his father lies in the bottom of his bag Alex pulls it out and traces the crest with his finger then walks from the room and into the old part of the castle. A cross sits inside a room meant for prayer, he kneels before it. "God in heaven I pray now before you that you give me the strength to conquer my enemies and enemies to the throne of this land. My brother has become an enemy to me. I pray I can treat him as such!" Alex crosses his heart, stands and walks from the place he will call home. A servant brings his horse to him. Alex puts his foot into the saddle and mounts the horse. Sitting with pride he looks at his surrounding saying, "Bring this place to a former glory, I shall return in time. If word comes to you it must bear this seal or treat it as invalid," Alex says holding the flag of his family adding, "Host this high so all the people will know a Lancaster watches over them." The servant takes it from his hands and carries it over to the aged general, "I will stand in your place my lord may God stand with you." Alex kicks the horse and it gallops out of the castle.

King Richard rides over the top of the hill. The horns begin to make their sound as the King returns. "King Richard the castle looks like we left it." "Yes, and it is pleasing to my eyes," King Richard replies. They continue the ride for the castle. The servants meet them as the gate lowers. "My lord where is Lord Lancaster," Darien readily asks. "Join me in the throne room. I will tell you all you wish to know." Richard walks from his horse. Darien walks behind him they enter the castle and walk into the throne room. Richard sits on throne given to him by the people of the land. "My lord is he dead," Darien asks. "No but we paid a price. Overlain is dead, "and what of Darius and Elizabeth?" "They both lost their lives in the battle." Darien lets his head hang low to the news but asks, "Then where is Alex?" "I left him at the castle it is to be his home. He will govern for the crown there." "Is he going to return?" "Yes, he will come here. He just needed time to gather himself he took her loss with the heaviest of hearts." "I must go to him he will need someone to pull him through," Darien relays. "If you honor his name and the man you must stay. Lancaster will return he will need this time to set it right in his mind." Darien's heart wants to be with his brother but to his request he stands his place. "He gave me a request before I left him but I will leave it to your hands." Darien lifts his eyes from the floor. "He requested that I hand pick a few soldiers to ride with him. He will go and seek his brother." "Thank you my lord I will see to it," Darien replies then turns and walks out of the room with a task before him.

Time moves forward as Alex rides for the castle. William sets sail for France to lay the lies upon men's ears. Devilian slips through the country towards Scotland bringing false hope to a foreign land. The morning sun shines in the back of Alex as he rides over the hill. He comes into the view of the soldiers on the walls. The horns sound the coming of a rider. His horse gallops on into the castle. "Welcome back Lord Lancaster," a soldier tells him as he dismounts his horse. "Where is the king?" "He should be taking his morning meal." "Where is Darien?" "He has been taking his rest in your old room my lord." "Announce my return to our lord and king and tell him I will see him later in the morning." Alex walks into the castle passing through it until he reaches the room he once laid his head. He knocks upon the wooden door. He waits. "Yes," Darien asks. "Are you going to make me stand in the hall or open the door?" The door flies open, "Alex!" Darien reaches for his hand, Alex clasp his, "I was worried about you my lord" "What have you been doing since my leave," Alex inquires. "I took on the task of putting the special group of soldiers you requested my lord," Darien informs. "Have you found who we will need?" "Yes, I have and all are sworn to the cause." "Good! Gather the men and tell them we ride before the midday sun," Alex requests taking his leave. As he opens the door Darien asks, "What happened to Elizabeth and Darius?" Alex with a slight cold told suggests, "We need not bring things of the past to the future, they gave their lives in this damn war." Alex walks from the room letting the door close behind him. The loss of them walks with his every step. Alex walks through the castle until he stands in front of the doors to the throne room. He lays his hand upon them and pushes them open. Richard watches the doors part. "Alex! I was not expecting you this soon, but it is pleasing to see you again." "Thank you my lord but let us get to the business at hand. I will take the men and set out to destroy this curse magic has set out over the land." "What of your brother?" "I think we should find as many marked men across the land, before the full moon or it will spread like the plague across the country side. William will find his end in due time." "Then I empower you to seek out and find the beast men keep hidden in them, cure them or destroy them where you find them" Richard states. "Thank you my lord and might God guide you to carry out all the duties placed on you when you placed the crown upon your head." Alex turns to walk out of the throne room Richards words hold him in his place, "Before you leave my noble I have something for you." Richard claps his hands and servants bring it to him. "I give this to you to mark your noble house." Alex un-wraps the gift his eyes behold the new flag of his name, a red rose held in the mouth of a gray wolf with the sign of Richard underneath. Richard walks to him informing, "What was wrongfully taken from you I now replace, fly it with the honor with the courage you have in your veins." "Thank you my lord I will." Alex rolls up the flag and leaves the room he heads out to meet with Darien and his new chosen men. Making it to him Alex asks, "Darien is the men gathered?" "Yes, my lord they wait you in the army room." Alex walks towards the door and Darien follows behind him. He opens the door and twenty are waiting for him. "My lord we stand with you to the death if need be" one of them proudly informs with his entry. Alex walks around the table Daniel sits at one end "He is too young to know how a woman feels around him," Alex suggests into Darien ear. "No younger than you and I the first time we rode into battle with your father." Alex shakes his head then stands before them. "Men we ride out to set things right across this land if we cannot remove the curse upon those we encounter then we must destroy them as if we were stopping a plague on the people. Alex reaches in his pocket, "I have six medallions left if one of you should be bitten then one can be yours, if not and we cannot cure you then you must suffer the fate before you." "We knew the risk when we signed on for this," the men boast. "Then it is decided." Alex puts his hand out requesting, "Then join me in my quest my band of wolf hunters!" The men give out a whoosh and they leave out the door. Alex hands Darien the flag he attaches it to a staff, his colors flow in the wind as the men begin to ride out for the country side. "Where do we head to first my lord," Darien asks. "We ride for the caves to the north we have something to retrieve." The horses with the men fade into the sun as they ride over the hill.

William and his loyal soldiers board a ship and it sets sail for a foreign land. He plots his path for the throne, the lust in his heart builds for the power to rule.

"My lord the mouth of the cave is just over the hill," Darien informs. "Be careful when we reach the cave be sure to trend lightly if I knew Overlain he will have rigged the cave against anyone but me retrieving what we seek," Alex warns. They ride over the hill and start down into the valley, the mouth of the cave lays covered. Alex steps from his horse then removes the trees covering the cave. "Light a torch if you please," Alex requests. A soldier strikes the stones together and the torch begins to burn. "Daniel, Darien the two of you come with me," Alex says adding, "Half of you cover the rear. The rest of you wait here until we return." "As you command my lord," the wolf hunters reply. Alex takes the torch and walks into the mouth of the cave "Where would he have hidden it," Daniel asks. "I cannot say but it will not be easy to find." They walk deeper into the cave, bats and other creatures that call it home run from the light. Alex, Daniel with Darien reaches to where the cave splits into three different directions. "Which way do we go Alex?" Alex stands for a moment then removes the crystal from his neck holds it to each entrance. The left tunnel brings light to the crystal, its green color reflects off the cave walls. "This way," Alex suggests. They walk down the path until it opens into a great room. The cup sits in the middle in full view of their eyes. "There it is my lord," says Daniel as he goes to walk by and grasp it. Alex grabs him and pulls him back relaying, "Do not be so eager to get it, it is not that simple." Alex looks at the room then pulls his sword from its sheath then jabs it into the sand of the floor, a great sound arises the sand begins to run out from under their feet. They jump back to the opening in which they came, the sand drains and a great gap appears before their eyes. Seeing it Alex suggests, "Looks like the wolf will have to retrieve it." Alex passes the torch to Daniel then steps into the darkness. The sounds of the change echo off the walls of the cave, his eyes light in the darkness as the light strikes them. He stands in the entrance looking at the distance. The strength of his legs carries him the stone in the center clasping the cup in the claw of his hand then leaps back for the opening. Alex regains his human form, dresses; they walk deeper into the cave. "What do we seek now my lord," Daniel asks. "We seek the book of spells." They search inside the halls of the cave the crystal leads them on their path, they step inside another great room. The crystal around his neck losses its light with Alex informing, "It is here somewhere." They search all around the room. "I do not see it my lord," Darien relays. Alex shines the light high over his head. Seeing it he informs, "There it is at the top of the ceiling." Darien changes into the wolf and climbs the wall of the cave knocks it from its rest and Alex catches it as it drops. Darien leaps back to the floor changes and they walk out of the cave. "Did you find what you were after my lord," a soldier asks with their return. "Why yes I did," Alex answers before gathering branches and leaves. With the pile placed in front of Alex he requests, "Give me the torch." Darien hands it too him. "What you doing my lord," Daniel asks. "I will ensure that no curse will ever plague man from this book again." Alex sets the blaze upon the ground takes the book in his hands pulls the marked pages from its contents then drops it inside the flames of the fire. With the flames growing stronger colored smoke begins to fill the air. The flames change colors as they watch it burn, great leaps of power and sparks leap into the sky, ghosts with Demons held in the pages of the book fly out and around their stay. The men become restless, "Come my lord let us leave this place!" "Go ahead I will watch it until it turns to ashes!" The men find courage and stand their ground. The flames settle down and the book is no more. Alex walks over and moves the ashes with his shoe. "Come we must find where a wolf would hide." Alex mounts his horse and kicks the animal it runs from the fire and the men follow. They ride for a village at the base of a foot hill. "We will find shelter from the night's air in the village below, we must search well for anyone marked from the beast," Alex instructs. They let the flag of his house unroll then slowly make their way down into the village. The sun sets in the landscape behind them. "I have room enough for you and your men my lord," an inn owner says as they ride up. "Put the horses in the stable," Alex requests then walks inside of the door and sits down at the table. "Inn keep," Alex calls to him. "Yes, my lord?" "Has anyone made their way into town with a bite mark or maybe scratched by an animal?" "No my lord, not that I am aware of," he wipes off the other tables, "I keep to myself the best I can." The inn keeps daughter comes in the room and sets a glass of wine in front of him. The other soldiers come into the place. "Then can you tell me who speaks on behalf of the village," Alex inquires. "Mr. Hills is the one who handles that." "Then I was wondering if you would be so kind as to ask him to join us. Tell him Lord Lancaster needs to speak with him." The inn keep sends out his daughter to take care of the task asked of him. "Did you see any horses rode recently," Alex turns to Darien asking. "No, my lord there was nothing that stood out," Darien replies. Hills walks into the room the girl closes the door behind them she walks out of the room tending to the task for the day. "You needed to speak with me?" "Yes, I do. I ride under the flag of King Richard I would like you to call the people of the town to a meeting." "For what purpose," Hills requests. "I cannot say at this time but it is the up most importance." "I can have them assembled by morning." "Make a list of the people who call this village home and deliver it to my commander," Alex requests pointing to Darien. Mr. Hills walks to the doorway and Alex walks up the stairs to the room waiting on him. Darien follows behind him. "Darien place guards outside of the village see to it no one leaves." "As you command," he answers. Darien leaves the room and sends soldier out to do as he was asked. Alex uncovers the staff places his hands upon it the light glows in the room, the inn-keep walks by the room, it shines under the door into the hallway. "What is that light Papa," she asks passing the doorway. "I do not know Child but it is best to just mind our business!" They hurry past and head back down the stairs. "Overlain I did as you asked I destroyed the book of spells." "You will also have to seek out and destroy its sister the one my brother held, Overlain requests then asks, "Did you also recover the cup?" Alex unrolls it from his pack. "Yes, I did." "Guard it well, for without it you cannot free yourself," Overlain warns. "I will guard it with my life if need be!" A knock comes upon the door. Overlain takes his place back into the crystal. "Coming," Alex informs before opening the door. "Dinner will be served shortly my lord," the inn keeps daughter informs. "Thank you, young maiden. I will be down shortly." The girl bows her head and walks back down the stairs. Alex sits in the dining room others join him in the feast, soldiers and the people of the town. He finds himself relaxed and the scent of a wolf catches his nose, he looks around the room but cannot place its origin. "Lord Lancaster, what is the meeting in the morning about," a town's person asks. "I cannot say you will hear what it is for in the wake of a new day." "Did King Richard say anything about how he will help the village? It has been ravished with these long wars." "That is for the men of government to decide. My duties fall under a different task. You must send someone to the castle to represent the people of this village." The conversion of the room carries on with the night moving forward. They finish their meals but Alex cannot determine who the wolf could be.

William watches the stars as the boat sails for its destination, the men lay about the boat sleeping under the stars. Devilian draws closer to the border of Scotland the world turns in time. Alex lays awake in his bed puts the crystals tightly in his hand. His eyes grow heavy and slumber falls upon him, he can feel her hand slip across his chest. "Evening love I have missed you all this day." Alex looks into the eyes that trap his soul saying, "I long to have you stand with me every day even though I can hold you in this place." "A moment of your touch upon my skin is worth the longing to see you each day," Elizabeth states. "Kiss me and let me feel your lips upon mine," Alex requests. He rests into the night his soul is at peace with her laying there beside him. The night moves into the dawn of a new day. Alex raises his head as Darien knocks upon the door. "Yes, I will be down in a moment." Alex kisses the crystal and places it back around his neck, dresses and walks down the stairs and out into the street. The people gather waiting for him to see them. Alex stands before them, "I guess by now you should have heard the rumors and tall tales seeping out over the land." The people make small talk among themselves, "I will tell you there is truth in some of the things you have heard. I stand here now before you offering a way to remove the curse that has been thrust upon you." "What curse do you speak of," one of them asks. "The curse of the wolf, it can be passed to you either by a scratch or bitten by it." The village people become uneasy when the soldiers that ride with him surround them. "Has anyone in the township been bitten and survived?" "There is no one here that has been marked in anyway," a man stands up and says. Alex begins to walk down through the people letting his nose lead him to what he is after. The people pull back as he passes over them he turns his head, "You" "Me," the younger man asks surprised. "Yes, come here before me." He does not move and the soldiers place their hands upon him and move him in front of Alex. "What is your name?" "Kevin." Alex begins to move the shirt off his shoulders. "The rest of you my go I have who I am after." "That is Kevin he has lived here all his life," a friend says to defend him. The people gathered begin to let their anger be known, the sound of their swords leaving their sheaths brings silence over the crowd. "I tell you now I intend him no harm," Alex announces then turns to him saying, "Kevin inform the people now how you have been bitten." Kevin looks down at the ground. "It was a month ago. I was coming back to town from a trip into the forest, I was attacked but it healed fast, I knew nothing of it until the light of the last full moon, the next morning I awoke in the forest with the strangest dreams placed in my head, I was as naked as the day I was born. I told no one of this for fear I would be cast out as having the devil in me." The people sit with disbelief upon their faces. "Relax young man. I can send the nightmare way. I have need of a virgin lamb to be sacrificed to save this man who will bring me one." "I have two in my stable," a longtime friend of Kevin says. "I will help you get it," Daniel being of his age suggests. They walk away from the crowd so they can retrieve what is needed. "My lord I do not know what I did in the night, I have dreams and visions that bring fear into my eyes," Kevin reveals. The description brings the night of Alex's flight fresh to him. Daniel and his friend bring him the lamb. "Where is the priest of this village?" "I hold that title, Sir Lancaster," an older man informs. "I have need of blessed water." The older man reaches under his clothing and brings out water in a sealed bottle. The people gather as he pours the water into the cup. Alex reaches in his sheath and pulls out a dagger he drives it into the heart of the lamb. The blood drips inside the cup, Alex makes small circles as with the cup in his hand as Darien speaks the words of the spell, then offers it too him, "Drink and release yourself from what has been placed upon you." Kevin's hands terrible as he places the cup in his hands. The cup touches his lips and the fluid touches his tongue. He stands before them grabs his chest and his body falls to the ground it shifts and spams for all to see. Cries of pain escape him as the wolf begins to leave his body. "What is this you have given him something that will kill him," he friend rushes to him saying. "No just wait!" "Stop it you are killing him!" Alex pulls his sword and places it to his throat suggesting, "He will be fine let the beast come out of him!" They look in horror as they behold a wolf of vapor escape his body. He lays there in silence. His breath becomes normal and he lifts his head. "It is gone," Alex informs stretching out his hand to help him from the ground. "Go and live in peace," Alex says then turns and walks from the people. "Come our work is finished here," Alex suggests passing Darien. The men gather their things and leave the village behind them riding out over the landscape in search of the next village ahead. Daniel rides up beside him. "My Lord why have you not had me drank from the cup?" "The same reason I have not drunk from it you will need the strength of the wolf to finish this fight." Daniel makes a motion with his head in approval. "Make no mistake young Daniel, if you lose the medallion around your neck it will take over you as well and I would do what I must." Daniel gets a long face. Alex pulls up on his reins the men stop and listen. "Men I tell you now no one here is over the people or me. If this beast in me should escape then I would expect any one of you to do what you have sworn to do!" He looks upon their faces and finds the truth in their eyes they ride on over the land.

Devilian enters the outskirts of Scotland. He rides with his face hidden. "When will we reach our destination," a soldier asks. "We will ride into the next town to meet the person to bring us to the clan leaders."

William rides the ship as it sails for the shores of France. "My lord we should be at the shores by night fall," the captain informs him. "Good I grow tired of being captive to the sea." The longing to let the beast run wild has seeped into his soul the hunger builds inside of him. Titus walks up as he looks out over the ocean asking," My lord for what purpose do we travel to this land?" "My brother, do you not enjoy the thought of a new landscape," William asks as a reply. Titus stands firm. "Very well, we travel to take a meeting with Sir Warrick he held no regard for Sand or his family. When we see him. I will pledge if he will help me in my quest for the throne I will in turn provide the soldiers he will need to seize the throne of this land then France and England shall have an alliance to one another." Titus with the information given finds faith in his brother once again. The days move forward and each finds their places in time, Alex rides in and out of the townships of the land curing or killing the ones marked from the beast. Devilian meets with the a few Clans of Scotland.

A group of men sit around a fire, a rider rides up to them reporting, "Commander, Alex Lancaster rides out over the land killing or curing our brothers of the wolf." A man stands quickly to his feet, "We must ride out and see if we can stop him before Lord William returns." He and the men with him finding comfort in the mark placed upon them gather their things and they ride out to seek them. Alex and his men find themselves riding into a town. "My lord it is just a few more days before the full moon," Daniel relays. "Yes, my very young friend. I feel the pull of the moon upon me too," Alex says then kicks his horse and they ride into the town. The flag waves in the wind as they reach the street of the town. "Go and find us a place to stay," Alex tells Daniel. Alex and Darien walk down the street the soldiers place their horses in the stables. "Alex when do you plan to return to the castle. We should report to King Richard and find out what has arisen," Darien suggests. "I intend to return to the castle shortly. We have cured many these past weeks but God only knows how many people still bear the mark." "I think it will be a time for someone to attack King Richard," Darien suggests. "I would agree. My brother's intentions are to keep King Richard's army divide so he can conquer the throne that is why I left Lushien with Lucien to Guard him. The more time he has to deal with the cries of wolf. The less time he can spend uniting the people." They search into the night but no one has the mark they rest from a long journey.

William with his men reaches the shores of their destination and finds their rest in a village. Titus travels on to find Warrick. William creeps from his stay with his lust for blood driving his passions. The medallion hangs around his neck he no longer wants to miss the trill of the hunt. The beast and he now serve the same purpose. He slips into the night waiting for the time to let his beast feed. He wonders about the streets looking, waiting, a young woman walks down her street. William stalks her letting his hunger grow, releases his clothing to let the transformation begin. No longer does the change bring pain but a joyous bliss to his being. The wolf slips in the darkness. She walks along the road knowing in her eyes lays the door to her home; suddenly the feeling of fright seeps into her soul. The cold shiver and feeling of flight quickly rush upon her. A sound catches her ear her pace quickens she pauses at the door hurrying to unlock it. William leaps from the darkness striking at her the blood splatters her door. A slight scream escapes her lips as he feasts upon her body. A soldier hears the scream and rides up to see, he just catches his body as he flees into the night. "My god in heaven what was that," his mind screams. He rushes from his horse, the sickness seeps into the pit of his stomach as he takes in the damage down. William runs back to his clothing and returns to normal with the blood still covering his face. He cleans it with the water in a barrel he passes then hurries back to stay. He rests for the night.

With the morning Titus knocks upon his door. "Come in," William answers. "My lord I found someone who can take you to Warrick," Titus informs entering the room. They gather their things and set out for his castle, they journey over the land, passing towns along the way, some of his soldier's ride with him others have stayed to guard his ship. Reaching a town Titus goes into a place then returns with a man. "You can take me to Warrick," William asks seeing the man before him. "Yes, I can lead you to his castle." William flings a bag of gold to him. The man gathers his horse and they follow behind him riding most of the morning. "How much farther," William asks to the man he follows. "His castle lays in the next valley," he answers. They ride until they reach its gates. "What is your purpose here," a guard requests? "I wish to speak with Sir Warrick," William informs then turns to those riding with him waves his hand and they place a chest full of gold at his feet. "This is for Warrick if he will hear my words." The soldiers stand guard as he leaves. With his return he replies, "Lord Warrick will see you and he bids you welcome to his castle." Warrick waits upon his throne. The servants bring them in, "Welcome to my castle." "Lord Warrick I am William Lancaster I bring you an offering and news of your Kings death and now this land sits without a King." "Then the nobles of this land shall put in their claims to take his place now why would a noble from England care about the throne of this land," Warrick asks. "Lord Warrick if this land finds itself in the same wars that has gone on in my country then your land will suffer. I suggest a union between you and I." "What will you request of me?" "I need soldiers who have not felt the strains of war. Their lust for new battles will give me an edge and when we have driven Richard from the throne we will turn the forces on the nobles of this land and I will stand with you a King in your claim to the throne of France." "How do you know we can drive him from the throne?" "I will show you the power hidden in me," William says then backs away from him and he lets the change begin. "What witchery is this," Warrick says as he falls back to his throne. Titus walks over to him saying, "Fear not my lord it is still him he has control of the beast." Warrick walks over and touches the wolf William lets a grin come across his face then changes back before him. William places a cloak upon him then informs, "Lord Warrick, imagine if I told you I could give your soldiers within your ranks the power resting in me. Then no army of this land could stand up to you." Warrick walks over to William and extends his hand. They shake and a word is given to set the bond between them.

Alex rides for King Richard's castle. The men follow with him. "We will camp by the river tonight and reach the castle tomorrow," Alex suggests. They stop and place their tents by the river. The men of a different allegiance follow their path waiting for the darkness to fall. "My lord I smell something in the air," Darien walks over to inform. "Yes, I smell them too, just act like they are not there, we will have them tonight." They finish their night's meal and take their rest. Alex and Darien slip out from the rest to let the wolf come out then wait for the men to strike. The night grows late and the scent becomes stronger, they rush in, but find the men ready for them. Alex with Darien leaps from the darkness taking their way of flight from them. Their sword clash and the wolf hunters of Alex cut them down. Alex holds one alive in his teeth. The men lay their hands upon him. Alex returns to normal places a cloak over his body then asks, "How many of these little bands did my brother send out?" The soldier holds his tongue. Darien still in the form of the wolf steps behind him, his claws dig into his shoulder. Cries of pain proceed from his lips before informing, "There are twelve bands of us!" Darien eases off on his hold. "How many men," Alex requests. "There are fifty or more men with the wolf in them." Alex grabs his father's sword steps in front of him saying, "I offer you away to remove the beast from you then we can release you or I will put you to death." "To live without the power of the beast I chose death." "So be it," Alex remarks then drives his father's sword into his heart, his body falls dead to the ground. "Remove their heads and burn their bodies into the night," Alex orders. A soldier who waits with their horses slips up behind them he watches them burn their bodies, he slips away heading to find others of his kind. "He says there was fifty like us," Darien stresses. Alex looks out over the landscape saying, "My brother will murder many come the full moon." "We have cured many in the last month my lord," Daniel relays. "Yes, but those were the ones not chosen to bear the curse. His soldiers will wait to feast upon the land and how many will survive and become like them?" Alex walks back to his tent he goes inside and slips the crystals in his hand. In his heart he knows the dark days ahead. The men burn the soldiers of William. Alex slips into slumber where she will hold him in the night. The prison that holds his beloved is the only place he can find true rest from the struggles before him.

The day begins new. Devilian meets with the members of the clans not loyal to the governing body of Scotland. Douglas, Kenedy and MacDuff all come with their men to a meeting held in secret. "Members of the clans of Scotland, thank you for coming, and I hope we can find a joining of forces suited for both are future interests." "What do you offer if we ride with you." Kenedy inquires. "Lord William offers an iron clad deal that will free Scotland, from the hands of England, "Devilian assures then continues to speak, "By now the word has spread to your ears, Richard now sits on the throne of England, I come in the name of Lancaster who still holds claim to the throne. Devilian walks among them, "If you should find it in your best interest to support our cause. We would find favor in you and pledge forces in your quest against the clan who rules you. Lest you not forget Richard has never found favor with Scotland." Douglas stands to his feet, "I have learned that Alex Lancaster now rides with Richard and he has always kept his word to my clan." "Alex has been twisted by the King himself. He is no longer the noble man you once knew; his very own father removed his name from the house of Lancaster." Kenedy stands to his feet revealing, "I have heard strange stories of beast that roam your land." Devilian sits down at the table his eyes show a small sign of the beast saying, "What you have heard of is true." The clan's members mumble about themselves then Kenedy asks, "How can this be?" "Williams brother turned to sorcery and gained a power over normal men then attacked his father's castle in the name of Richard. William with my former Lord York had to achieve the same power to balance things among the people, his brother betrayed him with his wife to be, when her father struck out he turned to the beast and feasted upon his flesh, he holds with Richard and if we do not unite, Richard will send Alex to spill his hatred of Scotland upon you." "How are we to defeat a man who can change into a beast at will," Douglas questions. "Lord William suggests you can seek out the best among you to be granted this gift, then your clans could rule Scotland with an iron hand," Devilian suggests to them spilling William's lies. The men with their lust for power become drunk with the idea of what this could hold for them and strike a deal with a former foe.

The days move over the land. William receives word from Devilian of the numbers pledged by the Scot's, Warrick the king maker gathers his followers. Warrick being a great leader of men is given the gift of the wolf along with his closet soldier Blain. Two members of the clans are given this gift also James Douglas, Henry MacDuff also join the brothers of the wolf. Alex and his soldiers ride out over the land many are cured three of the men and a young maiden join his ride across the land joining the cause for their feelings of guilt in the things they did when the wolf had control over them.

Alex returns from a quest over the land. "King Richard I bring news from over the land," Alex informs standing before him. "What have you heard young noble." "It is rumored that William stretched out his hand and is now gathering soldiers from Scotland and he sails from France with Warrick the warlord." "Yes, these things have fallen upon my ears as well. We are making preparations to meet this army as we speak." Richard waves the people from the throne room they stand alone. "Do you think your brother has made more in his image?" "It was told to me that the cup used by Tyrolean was destroyed by my brother he can only turn men into beast at the sight of the full moon. I hold the only cup that could make men into the thing that I am." "Alex what if the words spoken to you were lies," Richard suggests. The memory of the man clasped in his jaws resurfaces in Alex's mind with an answer, "Trust me my lord the words are truthful." "But what if he infects his whole army with this curse?" "There are only so many charms that can control the beasts that live within men they would just be mindless beasts," Alex informs. "Alex I do not think your brother would care. I think he would rather see the beasts consume this land than to have me sit upon the throne." Alex listens to his words and they rest upon his soul gripping him. "Alex have you given thought that maybe we should have more with your gift to meet their armies?" Alex walks over and gazes out the window saying, "Yes, my lord. I have given much thought upon this but I do not wish to place this burden upon anyone." Richard steps from his throne places his hand upon his shoulder. "Have you given thought as to what will happen if there are too many and he gains control of the throne?" Alex turns to him saying, "Terror strikes into my heart at the thought of it." "Then you will have to decide what fear is greater," Richard pauses for a moment, "I will not order you to do this. You have been a loyal noble to me and your burden is great." Alex places his hand on his shoulder relaying, "I will give much thought to it my lord. Now who will be sent out to meet the Scott's?" "I will ride out to face them with Lushien and Lucien my guards you placed in my trust. They have experience in battling with people of your kind I will need them." "The brothers will serve you well my lord their courage knows no bounds and what of me?" "I will send you and your men with half the army out to face your brother in the hopes you can end this before civil war engulfs the land!" "I will do my best to stop this invasion upon the land," Alex takes his leave as his generals enter the room. Alex slips to his bed grips the crystals in his hand, finds slumber, the feel of her touch blesses his skin. "Hello my love! Did you have a long day," Elizabeth asks? Alex kisses her lips her scent sets his heart to a better place, "Yes my lady but what must I do?" "Do about what my love?" "Surely my brother has made more men into beast, now I am faced with the discussion to make more to counter his efforts, but I do not wish to burden a person with this thing in me!" Elizabeth places her soft hand on his face her touch is so warming to him. "Alex if he has made more of the things men fear, than you have no choice. You still hold the cup they can be cured after the battle ahead." "Maybe you are right, but now I just want the taste of you on my tongue." Alex pushes her higher slips under her dress savors the taste that is her. Their passion flows into the night. Finished their bodies lay beside one another sweating from their nights loving. Alex plays with her hair as her head lies on his chest, "I will choice the best I can to become like me, Alex informs adding, "my God in heaven forgive the things men do." Elizabeth looks up to his face, "I believe it too be the best thing you can do." Alex pulls her up to taste her lips then embraces her.

The day comes fast. William sails for the coast of home, ships sail on both sides of him to carry war back to the shores of his home. Devilian gathers the army in the north. They set out to cut the land into slices. Alex calls two men and a woman to his stay those who have served him well in his band of the wolf hunters. They enter his stay. "I have thought long and hard about this but I can see no other way to stop my brother's assault for the throne." "We would stand and fight by your side and King Richard until we have no breath left in us," Nora states proudly. Alex opens a box takes out the medallions given to him by Overlain then grabs the cup from his cabinet "I offer the power of the wolf to stand against those who would send this country into hell on earth." The men stand ready to accept but Nora draws back saying, "I do not want this curse upon me again my lord. The men who stand here with me do not know the hunger of the beast." "Nora we fought with you and slain many beasts on the quest with Alex. We have seen its power," Steven answers. "Yes, but you have not had it control your mind," Nora looks over her shoulder stressing, "My lord when you found me covered with blood from the people the beast in me killed. I wanted you to kill me but when you cured me of it. I then dedicated my life to you and the stopping of this plague that moves over the land. I do not desire to have it in me again." Alex walks over to her places his hand on her shoulder informing, "That is why I chose you Nora. ou have no lust for the wolf and will use it to defeat our enemies and not for any other purpose." Steven with Max finds a seat at the table with the words she spoke lying heavy in their hearts. The choice is not easy but they accept what must be done. Alex cuts his skin and the blood fills the cup, the symbol burns bright on the side of the cup with the spell still upon it, each in turn takes it into their bodies. The medallions hang from their necks as the symbol shows on their heads then vanish with a glimmer. "Hold onto the charms around your neck with dear life for without them you will be a savage beast when it is released." The new pack leaves his stay and Daniel comes to his door. "Young Daniel what can I do for you this day" Alex asks. My Lord why have you not made me as you are? I already have the beast in me. Would I not be better served as you and others are?" "My young friend I would suggest to that you drink of the cup and free yourself from this thing placed upon you." Alex looks into the face before him. They day moves on each find their place in the hands of time.

The new army pledged to William moves from the north into England. Scottish blood boils for the wars shared over time. The ships of William rest on the shore a war cry is heard over the land as their feet strike the sands of the beach. "Set out men of war and make your voices heard down through the ages," William yells then places his foot in his saddle, pulls himself onto the horse then rides out with Warrick set high by his side. The beast in him waits to be released at the first sight of the full moon. Richard with all the men rides out from the castle. "Fight well my King," Alex says. "Yes, may victory find us both in the days ahead. If things should go bad we will retreat to the castle and make a stand here," King Richard reminds. "Have faith my king, we will win the day! Darien, Lushien, Lucien, guard him well let no harm befall him." "We will give are lives to save his!" "I would expect no less my brothers." Alex bows his head then turns his horse; the army begins to split with each taking men with them. "I think it may be as fate that we should meet them in the valley of the rivers," Daniel suggests riding beside him. "Yes, young Daniel it would be a fitting end," Alex remarks. Steven, Max and Nora also stay close to his side. "The moon will be full by weeks ending my lord," Max reminds. "That is why we must not let my brother escape from the valley. If we engage him with no moon to hold her sway it will give us the advantage." "Commander," Alex calls he rides up fast saying, "Sir Alex?" "I want you to take one hundred of the best men we have to offer and ride fast and hard for the valley then keep yourself hidden until you hear the sound of Daniel's horn. This will catch my brother off guard, kill enough goats to wear the skins upon your skin this will confuse my brother's senses, he will not be able to smell your scent when he passes." "As you command my lord," the commander answers, "Care not for the animals you ride, just be sure you get there!" "We will make it there before they can arrive my lord," he informs. The commander blows his horn. His trusted men pick up the pace and ride out from the others with speed in their hearts. "My lord you do not think he will push hard to beat us to the valley," Nora asks. "My brother has no reason to hurry. He doesn't know spies have told us he would be arriving and he cannot afford to lose his animals, you forget he must reach the castle with strength enough to wage war upon it." The men ride into the night hurrying to reach the valley. William and his army ride slowly over the country side to keep his army rested for the battle ahead. "William how do you intend to take the castle," Warrick asks. "I have not given it much thought, William answers adding, "I thought that was the job of a warlord such as you!" Warrick grins and gives out a hardy laugh. "How tall are the walls surrounding the castle," Warrick inquires. "Say about fifteen twenty feet in places." "We will need to stop along our journey to cut a few trees," Warrick suggests planning the siege in his head. "We will find everything we will need when we reach the valley of the rivers." "They must be tall enough to build ladders to breach the walls. There is but a few who could make the leap," Warrick states. "It only takes one to lower the gate," Titus reminds. "Yes, but knowing my brother and Richard, the gate will be almost impossible to get too. We would lose many men trying to lower it," William answers then asks with sarcasm, "unless you would like to try it yourself?" Titus gives no reply as they ride on. "Devilian and the Scotts should be a half day behind us," William informs. "Yes they will not be expecting an attack from the rear. We will be the decoy for them, if we can keep them engaged until weeks end, then the wild beast should finish them off and the throne of this country will be yours," Warrick boasts before saying, "Which I am hoping when the spoils of war are tallied the French will not be forgotten." "I would not dream of it," William assures but informs, "Now the Scotts on the other hand will have to be disposed of when they have served their purpose. I never did like anything that could come from Scotland." Warrick laughs again as they ride for the valley. The night moves quickly. The first light of a new day dawns, the men sent to hide find their place. They dig their trenches and place marksmen well hidden. The day moves into dusk. Alex and the army ride to the mouth of the valley in the distance they can see the dust rise from the movement of the coming army. "They should reach the other side within the hour we must prepare," Alex remarks kicking his horse. The others follow with speed into the valley. The lines are formed, shields are placed upon the ground, long spears laid out in front, archers find their places and Alex sits out in front of the rest in waiting for a brother to arrive. Richard and his army ride far to find the right ground for them to make their stand upon. The soldiers waiting the battle ahead, prepare their minds. Richard sits upon his horse with the crown of the land resting proudly upon his head, like the sands of time he waits for the dawn."

"Commander, take half the men and flank their rear wait until the battle has begun and turn his army with their back to the valley," Alex instructs. "Will you be able to hold them until we can reach their flank," the commander questions. "We will do are part, make haste I will meet you in the middle," Alex assures. The commander rides taking soldiers with him they slip through the forest. The commander holds his hand in the air as William and his men move passed them hiding in the lush vegetation of the forest the skins hang from their bodies blood from the animals bathed on their skin. William rides over the hill the men hidden go unnoticed to him and finds Alex directly in his path. "My lord we are betrayed they know we are coming," Warrick stresses seeing him waiting. "It seems that way but either way if we are to conqueror this land he will have to fall," William reminds. Alex sits with the patience of a statue waiting for the land before him to be crossed by his brother. His eyes stay focused as his brother's army pours out into the view of the men. Alex holds his hand up telling the men to stand fast. He kicks his horse and rides out alone seeing his motion William suggests, "It seems he has something to say." "Do you want me to ride out with you," Titus asks. "No. This conversation will be between me and my brother!" William kicks his horse and sets out to meet him. The ride is short the air grows thin as they can reach out and touch one another. "Have you no love for King and country? You would thrust us back into civil war for the power of the throne." "It is my right to rule brother," William proclaims. "William, do not ever speak to me as your brother again, that all came to pass when you took her from me," Alex answers with the rage for him burning. "I took her from you? It seems to me she was mine to begin with, it was your lust that stole her from me!" "Can you not know she loved me and I her? You have had many women over the years William. She meant nothing to you, but for me she was everything," Alex replies. The horses make their sound as they keep their eyes upon one another, "You put a woman before your flesh and blood how far you have fallen Alex and for a whore no less." Alex pulls the reins of his horse to move closer to his brother with his anger reaching its peak, "William Lancaster by the order of the King, I command you to take your army and swear allegiance to Richard or die here today!" "I will not swear allegiance to him the throne is mine," William states. "Then I will strike out against you and this army you bring to the shores of this country. I will have you in chains or dead at my feet this day. William you will pay for taking her from me." "I told you Alex I would not harm a hair on her head. I didn't kill her." "Your plan your men. When we part from this place William. I will do my best to kill you on this field of battle," Alex informs with hate in his voice to William's reply, "So be it brother after this day there will be only one Noble named Lancaster." The brothers depart from one another and each ride back for their men. "The bastard thinks I should worry with the small army in front of me! Today we take them tomorrow Richard," William proclaims making it back to his men. The army of William begins to form their ranks. "Men none of the men we face today should leave this field of battle! We must not fail in the task ahead," Alex proclaims holding up his shield with removing his sword from its sheath declaring, "Earn the right to hold these for King Richard!" The soldiers give out a great cry. The sound of their voices echoes across the sky. The men hold tight as the emotions build inside of them. Alex holds his sword high in the air, the soldier beside him lets the flag unroll on its staff. "Take them! Take them now," Alex yells. The riders and foot soldier race out into the land, William and his men rush out to meet them, shields splitter, swords clash, men's screams fill the night air as many begin to find their deaths. The army with Alex holds their ground but the numbers of William's begins to rule out. Alex and the men remaining find themselves surrounded. "Now Daniel, sound your horn and signal the men," Alex says as he begins to let the change come over him. The horn sounds and the men rush from their hiding to engage them. Daniel turns and Alex stands in wolf form. "It's a trap William," Warrick yells as Nora Steven and Max in wolf form leap into the men. The men run in from their flank the soldier pin them with the valley to their backs. William lets the change come over him. The men ride in and the battle begins again. Titus being in wolf form tares through the soldiers, blood splatters the field. The brothers Eric and Derrick slash out at the soldiers preparing to fire upon William. Titus holds a soldier inside his mighty jaws and Alex slips up behind him. Titus turns and gives a mighty growl as they face one another. Alex howls and they engage in battle, their claws strike, blood pours from their bodies their teeth sink into one another. Titus gains the advantage holds Alex on the ground his jaws stretch for the finale bite. "No! my lord, a soldier in his band of wolf hunters screams." Alex remembers the bite that ended his love and put her in the place she calls home. The anger swells inside his strength fueled by rage gives him the power to turn the tide. He knocks him from his back paws, and sinks his teeth into the back of his neck. Titus's head begins to separate from his body and his torso hit's the ground with a sounding thud. Titus's body takes its human form as Alex howls in victory above him. The victory empowers the men and they reach deep into their souls the finale push needed to drive them back. "Warrick give up this day and drop your weapons now," a commander to Alex stresses. Nora leaps behind him in a show of force. Warrick looks around him and his men. They find themselves surrounded with the other wolves moving towards them his sword hit's the ground and the dust rises as it strikes the earth. William fights valiantly sending many men over the cliff and to their deaths. Alex leaps in front standing between him and his men. Nora, Steven, and Max rush to stand with their noble, their teeth show, the drool drips from their lips. William stands with his back against the cliff with wolves stopping his every direction of flight. Alex transforms back to his human self, "William surrender and change back to your human form!" The wolves draw nearer their claws dig into the dirt ready to strike. William looks at his brother. Alex transforms back to the wolf his claws make a popping sound as he is fixing to strike. William becomes calm and begins to change back Alex with seeing him to his human form changes as well. "It seems you have me at a disadvantage Alex." "Give it up William!" "I guess you pulled one over on me Alex, you didn't give me the correct cup." "So it seems William, and I will use it to take this power from you." Alex walks towards him, "Wrong answer brother!" William leaps from the cliff his body disappears into the darkness of night. He strikes the stone sides and it bounces him around until he hit's the waters of the river, the current washes him away carrying him the path of the waters. "Damn it," Alex says as he walks to the cliffs edge. Max in wolf form climbs down the rocky edge. "Come Nora let's find who is still among us," Alex suggests walking from the edge. Steven follows behind them. "What are you to do with me and the remaining men," Warrick asks with Alex in front of him. "That is not a question I can answer. It will fall to King Richard." "Commander," Alex yells. The commander rides in through the men, "Yes my lord?" Alex looks down at the medallion around Warrick's neck. Max leaps back up from over the cliff with his search turning up nothing. "Keep him in the silver chains he has been marked by my brother. Keep a watchful eye upon these men there is no telling who will turn with the rise of the moon tomorrow night. Make your way back to the castle." Alex looks around at the bodies lying dead upon the ground, "Burn their bodies to ash we do not know who could have been marked by my brother." Lord Lancaster the twins have escaped our capture they have fled into the wilderness," A soldier returning informs." Alex looks to the wilderness saying, "We must let them go, their animal lusts will led us to them in time for now we must go." "Where are you going my lord," the commander asks. "I must go and stand with Richard." Alex transforms his wolf pack joins him in his flight rushing to Richard hoping to get there by the dawn letting their sense of smell lead their path.

Richard sits high upon his horse, the men wait in the line, the birds of the air fly in the morning sun. The puffy white clouds begin to float in the sky, a soldier looks up and when his eyes meet the landscape the army comes into full view. "Stand your ground men, defended our home and the land that is mother to us all," King Richard proclaims. "I see they knew we were coming Devilian," Kenedy relays. "By the looks of it, it sure seems that way." Devilian pulls up on his reins the movement of the men come to a stop. "Get the men ready." The commanders get the army set. Richard rides off with Darien, Lushien and Lucien by his side other follow out to protect their King. Darien flies a white flag under the seal of Richard. "Devilian they look like they wish to talk," Douglas says. "Then we will ride out to meet them." Devilian rides out. Douglas with MacDuff and soldiers of the army follow his steps. "Douglas you have no business in this civil war of ours or have the Scots declared war upon this nation" King Richard says. "I am not here at the command of the counsel we stand apart," Douglas replies. "Devilian you will withdraw the troops from this land. This is a command from your King and not a request," Richard informs. "King, not mine I serve William Lancaster. The true King of this land," Devilian disrespectfully replies. "You will be treated as a traitor to this land now withdraw the men and I will pardon you this country has seen enough war in these long years, many men have died so this land could have a King, now let these men go home and love their wives and their children," King Richard implores. "I cannot do that, unless you place the crown upon William Lancaster's head and declare him King," Devilian says with arrogance upon his lips. Richard gives no reply turns his horse and the men ride away, returning to their armies. "Men I tried as the ruler of this land to find a peaceful solution. I am sorry but I will have you to stand and fight one more time against an enemy of the crown, stand strong, stand tall, rein victorious upon this field of battle," King Richard requests sitting on his horse in front of his loyal men. The men give out their war cries. In a moment in time silence takes hold over the land each searching for the strength in him. Bravery rises to the surface in each, a mighty cry rings out of the silence and the soldier rush out for the battle ahead. "Archers," Kenedy yells from his horse. The arrows leave the strings of their bows. The charging men throw their shields in front of their bodies, many find the mark in their shields but some strike the charging men. "Riders strike out," Richard commands as he welds his sword to lead the charge. The men rush out with him. The foot soldiers of the Scot's rush out to engage in the battle. Swords clang, bones break, men cry out over the land. The first wave is defeated and the men ring out a cry of victory but it is silenced when more of the army comes to full view. "Devilian has convinced the Gintore to fight under William's flag," a general proclaims, sitting proudly beside his King. "Sir William paid their weight in gold to buy their allegiances," King Richard suggests stating, "for gold is all they carry in their lusts." "They have us my lord," a soldier says seeing the wild men charge over the land. Richard swings his horse, "I think it is the time to reveal your selves." Darien Lushien with Lucien change in the wolf. "Reform the line," King Richard commands as the wolves stand with him. The men move back into their ranks. "Charge for them men win this day, no retreat, no surrender," Richard cries out. Their horses gallop, the men run for the Gintore. The clan of warriors who hold no fear, their hearts beat fast, fear begins to fill their souls, but pride in the charging of Richard keeps their feet moving, rushing to the Gintore, suddenly the men begin to part. Alex, Nora, Steven, Max and Daniel holding their form of the wolf, rush out from the charging army and meet the battle driven soldiers head on. Their razor-sharp claws cut through the men; the soldiers who have been known to hold no fear, suddenly it strikes them inside their very essence, as their eyes behold the power of the wolf. Alex and those sworn to him turn the tide. Devilian lets his wolf out and begins to strike out over the men. Daniel leaps in front of them protecting those less equal. Devilian rushes to strike out at him their battle begins. Daniel gives as good as he gets, but the battle wisdom of Devilian begins to take its toll upon him. He lashes out for the finale blow but Alex knocks him off of the young wolf. Alex with burning fury stands between Daniel and Devilian. Devilian turns to retreat but the soldiers cut off his path. Alex slowly begins to move for him. The men pull back on their arrows, the silver tips shimmer in the light of the sun. Devilian holds down his head and begins to take his human form then drops to his knees in surrender. The Scott's retreats back for their homeland. The remaining Gintore run from the beast that strikes fear into their hearts. Richard pulls his sword from a soldier's body holds it above his head. The blood from the soldier dips down towards his hand a great victory shout rings out for the world to hear. "Devilian stand to your feet," Alex in human form requests adding, "I hear by place you under arrest to the charge of treason." Alex slaps the silver made cuffs around his wrists, it burns his skin, "Just encase you decide to use the power in you." "How can you go against your family like this," Devilian asks. Alex pulls down on his cuffs they dig into his skin, "My family died in what was the war of roses, take him away." The soldiers' place him on a horse. The sliver tipped spears rest in the hands of the ones guarding him. Alex walks up to Richard. "We should kill him now," a commander suggests. "No! He must stand trial for the charge of treason. The people of England must know that the law rules the land," King Richard relays. The commander rides off and finds his place by Devilian then they take him towards the castle. "My Lord we must start back the moon will be full tonight. I think it best if we cover a lot of ground before the night," Alex remarks. "Did you capture your brother?" "No, my lord. He dove over the cliff rather than face the charges," Alex informs. "Did you find his body?" "No King Richard. We searched but could not find him." "Do you think he survived?" "I cannot believe the fall would have killed him, but it would have weakened him deeply. Worry not my King he has no more pack to run with now. We have stayed off his last chance at the throne. He will be a lone wolf now," Alex informs adding, "Come my lord we ride for home." The King begins to ride for home. Alex with his pack rides along with their King. "Thank you Alex you saved me from my fate," Daniel says. Alex pats him on his back. "It was the least I could do for a brother!" Daniel feels joy seep into his soul knowing his noble has declared him a brother. "Come on we have much to do." The soldiers begin to burn the bodies into the day as the King and those riding with him make their way towards the castle. William finds himself lying on the banks of the river with the sun baking his naked body. One of his loyal soldiers who had escaped the clutches of King Richard's men finds him. "My lord," he says climbing from his horse pulls a cloak from his bag then covers his body. He pulls him from the sand and places him over his shoulder then lays him over the back of the horse and sets out for the hills. He searches until a cave comes into view, removes him from the horse and places him inside the cave. He rides out hoping to find the others. "Vincent," he calls to a rider on a horse. The rider gallops to him. "I have him, he is in the third cave on the left, go and watch over him I will find the others." Vincent rides for the cave and the soldier rides out to find the ones who are left loyal to his noble. The soldiers find their way back to the castle. Richard sits upon his throne. The elected council sit in judgment of the men. "Warrick this court holds no rule over you. We have sent word to the government of your land. They will decide what must be done with you," the council member informs. The guards pull him from the room. "Devilian of York. The charge before you are treason. How do you plead?" "Treason how can it be treason. I never swore allegiance to this King," Devilian informs. "That has no weight in this court. A King has been declared and unified under the nobles of the land," the council swiftly informs. The court proceeds through the day. "Has the council reached a verdict," King Richard asks from the throne. "We have my lord!" Devilian stands in the center of the room, people from the surrounding villages fill the room to hear the verdict. "Guilty, guilty, guilty," each of the council members arise and state. "Devilian you have been found guilty of the charges," King Richard informs. "Then what will be my sentence Richard the lion-heart," Devilian rudely inquires." "You can willing have this spell removed from you and if you chose to do so. I will pardon you of your crimes or if you refuse the sentence will be death," King Richard informs. "To live without the wolf is death," Devilian replies. "Then you will be taken from this place and a silver stake will be driven into your heart and your head will be removed from your body!" The soldiers take him from the room, their swords of silver shine in their hands. They take him to the center of the castle. Devilian finds himself chained to a pole. A soldier drives the silver stake into his heart. The axe makes its sound moving through the air and his head leaves his body. "May God have mercy on your soul, may he find the forgiveness for you that man could not," the priest asks in prayer as the soldiers remove his body. "Burn his body and scatter his ashes to the wind." Alex tells Darien then turns and walks away.

A cycle of the moon has come and gone the soldiers marked by the beast show their true form confided to the dungeon of King Richard's castle. Each in turn drinks from the cup and are released to live out their lives throughout the land there no signs of a brother. Only whispers and rumors. Alex walks back into the great room. "King Richard I must speak with you and the counsel." "Come my young noble speak," King Richard says with the council members regaining their seats. "I have heard rumors of my brother trying to regain his forces." "Yes, this counsel has been discussing what must be done or civil war will ring out over the land once again," King Richards remarks. "I think I can capture my brother or put a stop to him." "How do you plan to achieve this," Richard asks "By now the word has spread over the land of the cup that can remove the wolf from resting inside a person. William knows the only way to remove the curse is to drink from one of the cups Overlain and Tyrolean used to cast their spells. He will need the cup to regain his pack. I think we can catch him coming for the cup." "Explain that a little deeper," the council requests. "I have come up with a plan to have someone steal the cup and offer it as a token of faith to him." "That is a great risk. If he should gain control of it he will have the power to make more in his image and the country side is overrun with the notion of where the wolf may lurk. The village people have become to refer to them as werewolves," the council informs. "I know it is a great risk but I can see no other way to bring him out of hiding." "Alex if you will remove yourself the council and I will talk among yourselves and decide," King Richard requests. The counsel converses among themselves. Alex stands in the hall waiting for their decision. The door opens and a servant informs, "They wish to see you now my Lord." Alex walks before them. "Alex of Lancaster you may put your plan in play, but this counsel gives its warning if the cup would be lost then there will be no cure for the curse placed upon men or women. We cannot allow beasts to feed upon the people so take care of the cup, should be lost the wolves will be hunted and destroyed." Alex bows his head and leaves the room, walks through the castle and into the dungeon. Warrick sits chained to the wall. The door makes a squeaking sound as they open it for him, "Warrick the king maker," Alex suggests entering the room. "I fear my king making days will be over. When I return to my home," Warrick replies. Alex reaches inside of his cloak. With it revealed he asks, "Do you know what this is?" "No, I have never laid eyes upon it.' "This was the cup of Christ," Alex states. "If you say so but what has it to do with me?" "It will remove the power in you." Warrick looks at the cup with Alex saying, "I have two things to offer you," Alex moves before him kneels down informing, "All I ask is the place I might find my brother." "What do you offer," Warrick asks. "I offer you freedom if you drink from the cup or death from my sword. I cannot let you go with the wolf in your veins." Warrick looks at the sword in his sheath replying, "I can only tell you the names of places he has mention. I know not the land." "Tell me the names and gain your freedom." "He told of a gathering place called the valley of the half moon, does that ring a bell?" "Yes, it does," Alex informs standing to his feet. Alex pours the blood into the cup along with the water, swirls it around inside the cup speaks the words then hands it to him informing, "Drink and you will be free to return to your country, but I warn you here and now if you return to this land. I will hunt you down, reach in and pull the life from you!" Warrick drinks from the cup. Alex stands back as Warrick feels the pain as the wolf struggles to stay inside. The vapor in ghost form rises from his body a howl is given as it fades into nothing. Seeing the beast released Alex opens the door and instructs the soldiers, "Take twelve men and put him on a ship then watch it sail away with him on its deck or bring me his head in a basket." Warrick picks his head up from the ground saying, "Thank you Alex of Lancaster I will be in your debt!" Alex walks out of the cell. He walks through the castle. Alex stops by and pays the little girl a visit, then walks into his room, he closes the door behind him grasps the staff and calls Overlain before him. "Overlain is there any way I could track the cup if it were to be lost" "Yes if you place it over the end my staff and speak the word seek, it will mark it in a way unseen to man if it should be lost you must hold the staff in front of you and repeat the word. The closer you become the brighter the light will be," Overlain informs then asks, "Why would you ask the cup rests with you." "Because I intend to draw my brother out of hiding with the promise of the cup," Alex reveals "This is a bold move if the cup is not returned you will not be able to release yourself from this spell." "If we can track the cup to where it rests than my worries are less." "My Lord it will not be as easy as I made it sound if you are not close enough to the cup the light will not be bright enough for your eyes to see, it could take a life time to find it." "It will be a risk I will have to take my brother must be brought to justice." "Do you even know where to seek him," Overlain inquires. "He may be in the valley of the half-moon along the western coast." "Alex it is for you to decide but what of the men who are loyal to you? If the cup is lost you will not only seal your fate but theirs as well." "Yes, I know and I will offer them the choice of being released or join me in the hunt." "You are wise Alex and a great leader of men," Overlain informs. "Thank you Overlain I am glad I can still seek you when I need too." "I will always be here." Overlain vanishes back to the crystal. Alex places the cup upon the end of the staff. Alex reaches into a box, pulls the crystals from its hiding place lies on the bed gripping them in his hand. With his slumber, "My lady I have missed you much this day." Her arms wrap around his waist, "I am here for you now just rest in my arms." Alex turns around brushes the hair back from her face gazes deeply into her eyes, he informs, "My lady, I love you more than anything I have ever known in this world," he kisses her lips, "I need to have your advice."

She runs her fingers through his hair. "What is it Alex?" "I plan to draw out William with the cup but I fear it could be lost for all time and I could be cursed to live forever with this beast in me. And you will remain in this place forever." "Alex if it would stop your brother and take the curse from the land than it would be worth it." "Elizabeth it is not only you and I worry for. The council have stated that if the cup is lost the people who have the beast in them will be put to death whether it was willfully received or they survived an attack." Elizabeth runs her fingers through his hair suggesting, "Why don't you release yourself from the magic that flows in your veins with those sworn to you?" "I cannot my lady. If I lose the power of the wolf there would be nothing to stand in the way of his quest for the throne. I have to remove it from him then I can return to normal," Alex kisses her again, "besides I would grow old and leave you in this prison that you live in now." Alex holds her tight to his body saying, "Losing you was bad enough but the thought of you not being with me when I cross the river of sticks is too much to bear." "Relax my love just rest in the arms of your love, hold me through this night and in the morning do what you must," Elizabeth requests. They embrace, kiss and fondle each other into the night. Alex falls asleep beside her. Elizabeth gently runs her fingers through his hair letting the love in her heart behold the man that lies beside her.

"I am almost back to full strength," William tells a commander. "But my lord you are the only one of your kind. Richard keeps a pack with him we cannot stand against them," the commander implores. William grows angry slaps the man to the ground proclaiming, "We will regain our numbers and set out for the throne of this land!" The commander finds fear in his heart looking around at the bodies lying dead. The young maidens, children that have been feasted upon by him to regain his strength, regaining his feet he replies, "As you command my lord. I will set out to gather our troops"

Dawn shines its face over the land and with the awakening of Alex she fades back into the crystal. Alex stands to his feet grabs the staff speaks the word given to him removes the cup from the staff, dresses and walks from the room, down the hall and into the battle room of King Richard's castle where his pack await him. "Morning my lord," Darien greets. Alex sits down in his chosen place. The men sit around the great table Nora stands against the wall. "I called you here this day to tell you I have decided to use the cup to call out my brother." "Alex if the cup should be lost we will stay the way we are, I wish to have my children watch me grow old," Steven informs. "That is why I bring this before you. You can be cured this day or take the risk with me," Max stands to his feet, "Alex my lord I have been with you all this time but I care not for this to stay with me forever. I would take this from me." "And you my long-time brother," Alex asks of Darien. "You will need someone to help with the power of the wolf. I will take the risk" Alex turns to the youngest among them, "Daniel what do you say?" "I hold no lust for the wolf in me but I will take the risk with you. Nora you have not voiced your say." "My lord I have been cured of the beast once then I chose to have it replaced in me. I will not leave you to fight Sir William alone," Nora answers. "My lord what of Lushien and Lucien they are not gathered with us." "I meet with them before I came here this morning. I told them they had served me well in their duties as guards to the King. I asked if they wished to remove the beast from them and their answer was they would remove the spell the day I drank from the cup," Alex relays then asks, "Are there any more questions," with none asked Alex says, "Then it is settled." Those who wish drink from the cup the wolf flees from their bodies. "Bring in Eldon," Alex requests. They open the door and the one chosen for the mission sits down at the table. "You are to guard this with your life." Alex lets the cup fall into his hands. "I swore to you when you found me and removed the nightmare from me, I would be indebted to you. I will not fail you my lord," Eldon relays. "We will lay the trap for him in the village of Rustle it is just south of the half –moon valley. We will wait until he arrives and end this!" Alex with his loyal subjects covers every detail of the plan. They leave the room each with their task ahead. Alex stands on the wall watching Eldon ride out over the hill. "My lord I did not ask this in front of the men but why not send him off with a fake cup," Darien questions. "I thought of that but my brother is wise he will surly test the cup once it is in his hands. It has to be the real thing or this will not pay off," Alex informs. "I sure hope this works my brother," Darien says as he places his hand on his back.

Time passes and Eldon finds himself near the coast Eldon sees riders baring the symbol of William. He rides over to them. "Are you from the ranks of Lord William Lancaster?" "Yes, and who are you?" "I am a run away from the dungeons of King Richard," Eldon informs "So you want to be a soldier in this army?" "No, I am not a fighting man. I have other talents." "What good would you be if your sword arm is no good," the soldier requests bring a chuckle to those with him. "Tell Sir William I want women and a castle to call my own when he gains the throne," Eldon relays. The statement made brings a bigger laugh from the soldiers with one requesting, "Why would you think he would grant you that?" "Because I have something he would trade a kingdom for stolen from his own brother's protection." "You talk in riddles he has the ramblings of a mad man," one soldier tells the others. "Just tell him what I said and if I were you I would ride to him now! His brother will surely set out for what I hold. I will await him in the village of Rustle." Eldon turns his horse and rides for the town. Their commander rides up asking, "Who was that?" "A mad man claiming he wants William to give him a castle for what he holds in his keep," one of the soldiers informs. "Did he say what it was," the commander asks. "No but he said he stole it from his brother's keep and that we should hurry because he would surly set out to retrieve it." "I want you to ride for Lord William with all speed," the commander instructs a soldier turning to the others ordering, "The rest of you come with me!" "He speaks words of a con man," the soldier suggests. "Ride out this moment and tell him what he said. We will go and keep an eye on this man now ride as you are commanded!" The soldier shakes his head in disbelief but rides for William. They ride for the village covering the ground quickly. "You go and find the man that told you this," the commander instructs entering the village. "Yes commander." The soldier roams the town. The soldier looks inside the inn and finds him eating at a table. He makes haste until he finds his commander, "Sir he is inside the inn." The commander kicks his horse and rides up to the inn, the soldier runs up behind him, "He is there my lord." The commander climbs from his horse walks inside the room and sits down at the table with Eldon. "Who are you," Eldon quickly asks. "A commander in the ranks of William Lancaster," the commander informs then reaches out and pours his glass full suggesting, "I am told you have something of value to trade." Eldon eats of the food, swallows then informs, "Yes I do I have something of great value." "How can I trust you and where is this thing you hold," the commander requests. "It is in safe keeping for now," Eldon quickly informs from fear of his safety. The commander moves fast and holds the dagger to his throat, "What is it you have? Speak or I will silence you here and now!" "No, no my lord, do not kill me! It is a cup!" The commander releases his grip with Eldon continuing, "I saw what it can do in the dungeons where they had many men! I have seen the wolf be released from them." "How did you come by it?" "I was supposed to hang for treason! I stood with Devilian against King Richard in the battle of the morning sun. I picked the lock, escaped the prison. Sir Lancaster was not in the castle the night I ran from there. I took it hoping to find comfort in the ranks of Sir William's army, please I have many talents but I am not a fighting man!" Eldon falls from the table and kneels before him "Get up from there," the commander suggests. Eldon takes his place back at the table. "If what you tell me is true then many a man will kneel at your feet!" The commander stays with him, the rider gallops into the camp. He jumps from his horse, William just feasting from a girl, lets his human form take over. "What is it," William demands. A sick feeling finds the pit of his stomach as he views the bodies. "Speak now!" "There was a rider who said he had something of value he stole from your brother, something he would seek him out for. He wishes to find safe haven here in the ranks," the soldier informs. "Did he say what it was?" "No, my lord, but a commander waits with him in Rustle." William dresses quickly and rides for the village his trusted ride with him. Alex and the soldiers move the people quietly out of the village his soldiers take the place of the workman in the town. William rides up as the mid-day begins to settle. He sees the commander's horse in front of the inn. He lets his senses breath in the air of the town. "Are you sure we needed to hide in these horse droppings," Darien asks Alex hiding with him in the stables. "Yes brother, it will hide our scent the others want set him off." Darien puts his hand over his nose. William smells nothing in then climbs from his horse. With his entry the commander bows saying, "My lord." "Is this the one who has something for me?" Eldon quickly kneels before him saying, "Yes my lord. I have something of great value!" "Then stop wasting time on the floor and go and get it!" Eldon gets up from his knees with William instructing, "Go with him!" "As you command my lord," a soldier quickly answers. They walk into the stable, he takes the cup from where he has it hidden, turns, "Let me see that," the soldier orders. Eldon slowly places it into his hands. He looks it over then hands it back to him. They walk back into the inn. William sits at the table drinking from a cup. They walk in and set back with him. Eldon places the cup in front of him. "How am I to know this is the real cup?" "The cup does what I said it can do. I give you my word!" William smiles at him saying, "You say you wish to find a place in my army?" Before Eldon can answer William slings a dagger into his body which strikes his shoulder deeply. Eldon falls out of his chair William walks over to him pulls the dagger from his flesh, slices his wrist and lets the blood flow from him into the cup mumbles the words given to him by Tyrolean, "For your sake I hope it is real" William pours the blood down his throat. "We will wait to see if the wound heals quickly is it does then I have what is needed to rebuild my pack," William informs his commander. "But my lord without the medallions they will become wild animals with no way to control them!" "Relax I still have four of the medallions and others search the land for more." William gives a smile as he holds the cup in his hand. "What of him my lord?" "If he heals then he will be of no service to me as the wolf. I need men of battle to serve me on the field." The day passes with Eldon in the mist of William with seeing the wound healing quickly William walks back to the street. The soldiers carry Eldon to a horse. "It seems the cup you brought to me is as you said it was," William informs seated upon his horse. The commander walks up to his side he starts to strike out at Eldon, "Wait I think I could use someone of his nature after all." The men begin to slowly ride out from the inn. Alex, Darien and the others transform waiting in the shadows of the dark. William rides in front of the stables the men follow closely behind him. The earth moves as men climb from the holes dug to hide the men, rush out from the town, surrounding them. Alex and Darien leap from the stables. Nora with Daniel leaps in from the way they came. The men pull their swords and the town becomes a battle field. William strikes out with the cup in his hand. He rides upon the horse until the wolf is released then jumps from it back. Alex gives chase running with all the speed. Alex catches his brother with a cliff and the sea to his back, brothers by birth, but born to the wolf in different ways now face off. William looks out over the edge then back at Alex. William lets a grin move across the face of the wolf and with a mighty thrust the cup flies from his hand. Alex leaps to try to catch it but it finds its way to the sea. Alex begins to climb down the face of the cliff, but hears the cries of Nora as she has engaged William stopping his flight. Alex quickly turns from his path scales the wall of the cliff quickly runs for his brother knocking him from his feet, before the finale bite to kill her can be delivered. The battle begins their mighty teeth bite into one another, their blood flows from their bodies, dirt flies into the air, growls and howls echo over the land until Alex finds himself on top of his brother his teeth sunk into his neck. William begins to change back to his human form. "Brother you cannot kill me. I would surrender to the king!" William cries out as the teeth ripe his flesh. Darien and Daniel find them. Nora in human form laying battered and bruised cries to him, "My lord please do not change the nature of what you are by killing him! Do not take the path of your brother!" Alex tastes the flesh of his brother his teeth sink ever so deeper. Darien takes his human form informs, "My lord we have him! He must be brought before the King and counsel no one is above the law" Alex drops him to the ground places his paw upon his chest William lays bleeding looking up at his brother. Alex gives a howl for the victory of the night then begins to let his human take over as more men arrive by horse. "We are victorious my lord we got them all," the commander gladly informs. Alex looks out at the sea the sound of the ocean fills his ears informing, "Not totally!" William laughs at the words he speaks they slap the silver cuffs around him. The burning begins upon his wrists." Alex moves towards him. "No, my lord! He will pay for what he has done," Darien stresses as he grabs his arm. "Where is the cup my lord," Daniel asks walking up to them. "He threw it into the sea. I could have saved it but I heard the cries of Nora fighting with William!" Darien looks as they place Nora on a plank pulled by horses revealing, "You made the right choice Alex you saved Nora and we have William. Now maybe this country can move forward." "Yes, but in doing so I have imprisoned us with the beast until the cup can be found." "Alex have faith what was lost can be found again it will just take time," Darien suggests. The soldiers gather. Alex and the men make their way back to the castle. William rides in the center, his hands bound, soldiers ride on either side with silver arrows aimed at his head. Alex rides with heaviness in his heart. "Alex as soon as we have placed William in the custody of the counsel. We can strike out for the cup," Daniel suggests. "Are you forgetting about all the wolves my brother has set out over the world. We still have to find them and with no way to cure them they will have to be put to death," Alex stresses. "My lord these were found with William's horse," Darien reveals handing Alex the medallions worn by William's pack. "Yes, but we are not God! So how do we judge the just from the unjust," Alex questions. They ride over the country taking the path back to the castle.

Chapter Nine

THE FATES OF BROTHERS

WILLIAM STANDS IN FRONT OF THE COUNCIL. King Richard sits upon the throne. Alex finds his place along the front row of seats. Other nobles are seated around the room. "William Lancaster you are charged with being a traitor to the crown and the throne of England. This counsel also charges you with the murder of its people being in the form of the beast or in cursing men with the beast. How will you plead," the council asks? William laughs as he finishes his words. "Traitor, I am a rightful noble of this land and I have claims to the throne!" "Richard was ratified by the nobles of the land, he is the rightful ruler in this house," the council insures. Alex sits looking to his brother and sees the lust for power his brother has found. The memories of two brothers playing in the field leaves his mind and the madness that is his brother sets in. The council lays out their case against William as the trail moves forward and Time slips from the land. William is brought from his cell. He stands before the people, counsel and King of the land. "Has the counsel reached a verdict," King Richard asks seated upon the throne. "It has my lord." "What does the counsel say?" Each one stands and faces William declaring, "Guilty!" "William Lancaster you have been found guilty by the peers of this great land," King Richard states. William tries to transform to the wolf but the silver placed around his skin keeps the wolf in check angered he declares, "You have put this charge upon my head and in it you have sealed your doom! I will lash out with the power in me and devour each in turn!" William tries to find the strength to unleash his fury but his efforts go unrewarded. The King stands from his throne, "William you will be taken from here and you shall be put to the sword until death finds you, then your head shall be removed from your body!" Alex stands and walks before the people gathered. "My lord I would ask for my brother's life to be placed in my hands!" "Trying to save your brother's fate how touching," William smugly says as he passes by him. "Sir Lancaster this council cannot have your brother running free his lust for the throne and the power in him is too great," a councilman states as a fact. "Death is too easy for my brother. I have a fate worst then death for him," Alex informs. "What do you propose Sir Lancaster," King Richard asks. Alex turns and faces his brother informing, "I purpose imprisonment for all time!" Alex walks up to his brother where he can only hear, "I shall leave you as you left her, me and the others cursed with the beast." Alex turns from William announcing, "If you grant this to me I will pledge to rid the land of this curse and my loyalty to you King Richard as long as I have life in my body." The King sits down in the throne. The counsel men talk among themselves. A counsel walks from the table and whispers in Richard's ear. "Very well Sir Lancaster your brother I will leave to you," King Richard informs. The King leaves the throne and the people begin to leave the trial. Alex's loyal men seize William and take him from the room. Alex stands in the center of the room until he finds himself alone. The day moves forward the night falls and many days come on go. William sits inside his cell he watches as his tomb is built before his very eyes. A stone casket is formed in the shape of a cross words of warning are carved into the stone that will seal it from the world.

A sailor of a ship pulls the nets in from the waters as the fish pour onto the deck the cup makes a thud as it spills out with them. "What is that," the captain asks him. "It is just a cup that found its way to the sea captain," he answers before trying to return it to the sea. "Stop bring that to me," the captain requests. The sailor places the cup into his hand with the captain suggesting, "No sense in throwing away something that has use." The cup finds itself placed in the cabinet of the galley. The ship moves across the seas for many days until the ship is swallowed up by the sea. The cup sets out across the waters until it washes up upon a foreign shore, finding itself in the hands of a peasant man fishing from the shores. He takes it home and places it on his shelf. His sickly little girl lies in her bed near death. "Papa I am thirty please bring me some water," her weakly lips asked. Her father being a poor man washes the cup he has found, not knowing the reason he lets her drink from it. He places it to her lips, the water flows into her body and he sets it beside her bed, kisses her forehead and runs his fingers through her hair she drifts off the sleep. Her Father sits with the heaviness of losing a child as he slowly runs his finger through her hair.

The morning sun comes and his daughter springs from her bed as she has been made new with the cup. Her father holds her tight weeping and sends praises to heaven. He drinks from the cup and it brings more life to him. He being a man of faith, takes it with his daughter to the church. He shows his daughter and explains the cup and what power rests in it. The church takes it from him and it is placed into their care.

Alex walks into the cell his brother sits on the floor the chains lay around his body. "So, you have come to place me into my prison?" Alex sits down on the bench informing, "Yes William I have come for you this day." William stands to his feet saying, "This would be a fitting end for me, placed in a prison by a brother who betrayed me." "I loved her brother with everything that I am. Why could you not have just given her to me?" "She was mine as was the throne of this land. We lead the strongest house until you spilt it," William anger relays. "I am sorry we found ourselves on different sides of history William, but you must pay for your crimes." "And will you pay for your crime Alex of Lancaster," William asks with hatred seeping from him. "The same way you will in a prison of living without her and with this beast living in me for all time." Alex walks over to his brother hugs his neck. William gives back no affection. Alex waves the men in. They seize him and take him before the tomb. They force him inside the stone prison. He transforms to the wolf trying to lash out at the people around him. Nora, Steven, Max and Darien pull the chains tight to force him into the casket. Silver spikes are placed over his arms and feet then driven into his flesh. Alex walks over to him, he looks down at his brother, placing his father's sword over his body then drives it into his chest just to the side of his heart. William growls and howls then begins to transform back to his human form declaring, "I will have my revenge upon you brother. I swear this upon the wolf!" The lid is placed over him. The silence of the stone quiets his hatful speech. "Alex you sure this is the way for your brother," Darien asks with seeing the stress of it in Alex's face. "Yes, death would have been the easy way out for him! Let him die many of life times to pay for the life times he stole." Alex turns and walks from the room. Darien and the men place him deep into the earth. Stone tablets are placed into his tomb, each with a warning for anyone who might find it. The earth is shaken loose by the men it falls and seals the room for all time. Alex walks before the king. "My lord," Alex says as he kneels before him. "Alex we find ourselves victorious with all the nobles now pulling in the same direction, I thought this day would never come when I could say that there is peace throughout the land," King Richard relays. "Yes, King Richard it is a great day, and will be remembered for all time," Alex suggests still kneeling before him. "May the land never return to the wars that ravished this country," King Richard says. "My Lord you gave me my brother's life now I would ask in my duties to you what would be your command." King Richard stands from the throne walks by Alex kneeling. Alex stands and turns to him as he gazes out the pictured glass of the throne room. "When you took the cup to capture William it is lost to us and with a cure for those inflected gone and it is with a heavy heart I must order you to strike out and kill those with the beast resting in them." "My lord some of the people inflected are not wicked and it is not by their hand it was placed upon them" Alex implores. Richard turns to him placing his hands on his shoulders saying, "Do you not think I know this Alex, but like a plague moving across the land you have to destroy the ones it infects or it will consume all the people," King Richard relays the turns back to the window saying," You once said to sit on the throne was to make decisions that sometimes go against the values of a man, but must be made, today I find myself in such a task." "I well serve in my duties my Lord," Alex heavy hearted answers. Alex turns to walk away, "Alex I would ask one more thing of you," Alex stands in his steps with Richard requesting, "In the days and years ahead my young noble. I pray you will remember me as a man who stood with you in battle and not the King who has sent you to destroy the beasts in a person." "My Lord you will always be my King and Brother, but I would ask if you would assembly men to com the lands in search of the cup so that I may one day become a healer again and not a destroyer of men." "I will send men out to find the cup," King Richard answers. "I will leave Lushien and Lucien to guard you my King they will be in service to you until death finds you." The King bows his head to Alex and he leaves the room. In the days ahead Alex sets out with Nora, Daniel, Max and his loyal hunters of the wolf. They ride over the land and with each full moon they find and destroy many werewolves in hiding. Some are glad to be released but others are drunk with the power of the beast. The book once held by Tyrolean is lost to the world many of the medallions also became lost to the knowledge of men. The years passed by. Alex sits in his bed each night loving his wife inside her prison, searching with the staff in every place he finds himself until he returns to the castle.

Alex walks into the throne room. Richard sits, age has found his face and time has taken almost everything from him, "My lord," Alex says as he kneels to him. "Alex! It has been many years," King Richard says through a weak voice. "Yes, my lord, time has slipped from us." "Not from you, your face looks the same to me as it always did." "Yes, my lord another curse of the wolf, everyone around me dies and I will have to see them laid to rest." "Tell me of your journeys for the throne room became my prison and this castle my tomb." "We rode far my King curing the land of the beasts. My task was not easy to me. I lost many loyal friends in my duties." Richard tries to stand from the throne Alex stands to his feet and helps him revealing, "I lost Darien." "How did it happen," Richard asks as Alex stands with him gazing out of the pictured glass. A sorrowful look takes over Alex, a tear runs from his eye as he informs," "Years ago we fought in a battle against a band of man who William had placed the beast in, my horse and I were knocked from a cliff and fell into the waters of the great river. The medallions I carried in my saddle were lost for all time so I no longer could save a person here and there. We found a young maiden with the beast in her she had devoured a town at the light of the full moon. We found her naked with blood covering her body as she cried out what had happened to her. I tried to put her to the sword my lord but Darien stood between us. "My lord she is but a young girl we cannot do this!" "My brother we cannot release her she will kill with the fullness of the moon." Richard coughs loudly and Alex turns to see the old man beside him continuing, "Darien drew his sword in what I thought was to defend her but he kneeled before me took the medallion from his neck and I gave him a soldiers death. The girl still lives to this day and I found great sorrow and pride in his last deed upon this earth." "Forgive me Alex I am but an old man," Richard says as he struggles to reach inside his robe with his hands trembling as age has taken its toll, "I have been waiting for your return to hand you this. I owe you a lot and in my finale days I hope this will repay you." King Richard hands him a parchment. Alex unrolls it and reads over the writing. "When did you get this my lord?" "About a year ago. I sent riders but no one could find you." "I am here now and thank you for this," Alex says looking upon his age. "Do I look so old to your eyes?" "No, my lord, not at all," Alex informs. "That is one of the things I loved about you Alex, the kindness of your words." Alex reaches for his hand and places a kiss upon it, "Thank you my King." Alex sits with him for a little while then finds his way to his room. He places his hands upon the staff and Overlain appears before him. "Overlain we have word on the cup!" "Where do they say it is?" "A church in France claims to have held it in the last few years," Alex relays. "Then you must set out to find it." "Not yet King Richard is sick and will not be among us much longer. I pledged my life to him and I will fulfill that vowel." "Just keep in mind that you must have it to release yourself and her," Overlain reminds. "Yes, I know Overlain, but what would you have me do? Leave him in his last hours." "No, my lord. I know you better than that, you have always been a man of your word that is the thing I admire you the most for," Overlain relays places his ghostly hand upon his shoulder then turns to vapor. Alex lies upon his bed grasps the crystal's in his hand, finds his slumber then feels her hand upon his face. "My husband," she kisses his lips saying. "Elizabeth how I have hated that you should be placed inside this prison all these years," Alex stresses. "Alex it is better to be here than to never have you to hold again. What troubles you this night?" "It is just sad I should have to see Richard old and broken." "All things will pass before you Alex." "Yes, my lady another prison placed on me with this curse to see everyone I love find their eternal rest with me left to walk the earth until the end of days." Elizabeth holds him tight suggesting, "Alex you look on the dark side of things what a gift you will have to see the world change around you." She kisses his lips another time then raises from the bed; her clothing falls to the floor, her naked body comes to rest upon his body. Alex's hands softly run up and down her back. While they make love into the night King Richard finds himself standing at the river of sticks waiting for the fairy man to bring him across. Many Kings warriors both friend and foe stand on the banks when the boat finds the shore, they hold out their hands and many give their salutes in saying, "Welcome brother."

Alex rises from his bed, dresses and walks to the throne room as he walks into the room his eyes behold a throne upon it sits an empty crown. "My lord the King died in the night his body just gave out," a servant informs. Alex looks at her as if her face is unknown. "Do you not recognize me my lord you brought me here so many years ago," she informs. Alex steps back then her face becomes known and hugs her neck saying, "What a beautiful woman you have become." They begin to talk when a noble comes into the room requesting, "Lancaster I would speak with you." Alex turns to the little girl he saved bows his head saying, "My lady I will see you again." She walks away and closes the doors behind her. Quickly the noble informs, "With the king dead many will lay claim to the throne of England." "What do you seek from me?" "I wish for your pledge to me and my house," the noble urgently requests." Alex turns and looks at the empty crown resting on the throne suggesting, "So it will all begin again? I will not pledge my name to anyone, when the king is buried I will take myself from this place in search of what I desire." "Please Alex of Lancaster the wars will begin again if a King is not named soon." Alex looks away knowing that time will always repeat it-self suggesting, "Then may the best house win, I will not serve any longer." Alex walks from the room. The day moves on as his body is made ready for its finale rest. Time moves forward and many come to the castle. Noble names from all across the lands come to lay him to rest and give their finale respects. Alex watches as his body is placed inside its tomb. The nobles gather inside the throne room after the funeral is done, "My noble house has claim to the throne," a noble of the land claims. Another noble stands proclaiming, "Hold on my house has a claim!" Many stand and lay claim to the throne the arguments begin. Alex grows tired of the fight for the throne and he turns to walk out. "Lord Lancaster you not going to lay a claim for the throne," a noble asked of him stopping Alex in his steps. The room becomes silent as the men wait to hear his words. "No, I will not lay claim for the throne! It sickens me that he is just laid to rest and a war has already begun. You do what you must with the crown of this land my loyalty died with him," Alex informs then walks out of the room and his men follow him out closing the door behind them; leaving the arguing men to their claims. "Where do we go my lord," Daniel inquires. Alex turns and looks to his loyal subjects, "We do not need to go anywhere. I release all of you from the vowel you gave me." "How could we do that my lord our task have not been finished," Nora standing with Daniel states. Alex seeing Lushien and Lucien with their duties complete standing with them says, "Then go and saddle your horses. We will leave before the sun sets." They each go their ways to gather what they will need for their quest that lies ahead. Alex removes his things from his room, places the staff in his hands, carrying the box he keeps for her crystal. Drapes a sword made especially for him by a black smith in a town he once cured of the wolf over his shoulder, takes a finale look inside the room, then close the door behind his departure. The girl he saved stands before him waiting in the hall. "Are you leaving for good my lord?" "Yes," Alex informs sorrowfully. "Then God be with you and thank you for bringing me to this house so many years ago." She hugs his neck then watches him leave down the hall. His pack sits in their saddles waiting for him. "I see everyone is here." "Until the quest for the cup is finished my Lord," they all salute. Alex climbs on his horse and they stretch out across the land. They ride with the staff leading the way. The days move by and many miles are covered under the steps of their horses. They find themselves at the shores of the ocean. "It seems we will need a ship my lord," Lushien suggests. "It seems that way old friend," Alex answers. Alex and those riding with him go into a town and find a ship to carry them to another shore. They stand on the deck watching as their home land becomes smaller to their eyes. "England will never be the same its nobles will bring wars back to the land," Lucien suggests reliving the wars in his mind. "Yes, Lucien but one day someone will rise from the ashes of war to lead the people back to better times!" Lucien walks into the ship, Alex remains to find peace looking upon the waters. "My lord, do you think we can find it and remove this curse upon us," Nora asks walking up beside him? "I do not know Nora, but it is the first news of the cup to reach my ears theses long years, Alex turns to her lifts her head. The young beauty before him sets in his eyes, "I should have never replaced this cures upon you my lady." "My lord I have much to repay for my time under the wolf's hunger. For every wolf we have taken from the world is a life we will have saved." Alex turns back to the sea places his arm around her with Nora relaying," "Besides my Lord who would be there to watch your back." Alex lets his mind walk back to the time when a silver spear was laid in the hands of a soldier created by William his back is turned and Nora leaped in to save him. "That is true my young maiden," Alex informs with a sense of pride. The wind drives the ship as the waves send it up and down. The scent of the ocean fills their nose; a new moon gives its light over the face of the waters. Time moves through the days. Alex and his men step off to a foreign land they pull their horse from the ship. The men and Nora mount their rides and Alex holds the staff in front of him. The light barley glows on the end of the staff. "We have a long ride in front of us," Alex suggests climbing on his horse and they strike out over the land. They ride until late in following the glow of the crystal finding their way into a village to find rest for the night. They stop in front of an inn. "I will go and see how many rooms they might have." "Good I will be happy to sleep in something that doesn't move." Lushien informs. Alex climbs from his horse asking with a smile, "What's wrong brother the sea not set well with you?" Alex walks into the inn silence fills the room with every step. Standing at the counter he inquires, "I would like to know how many rooms you might have." "We have no rooms for you Sir," the inn keep rudely informs. Alex looks around the room informing, "I have journeyed far with my men, are you sure you could not put us up for the night?" "These are strange times my good man people are eaten by the light of the full moon. We do not let strangers stay within our mists," the inn keep informs. "Maybe we could lead a hand and search for the one who could do this." "Who are you my good man?" "Alex of Lancaster once a loyal soldier to King Richard." The inn keeps demeanor changes with the mention of his name, bowing his head he relays, "Your reputation precedes you Sir Lancaster." The inn keeper reaches for a few keys then hands them to him. "Tell me sir, did a stranger come into town in the days of the full moon," Alex asks. "No one that could be found Sir Lancaster," he informs. "Then in the next days I will search for the people living with in the town and find the werewolf living among you." Alex takes his leave and walks back to his men. "We have a wolf somewhere in the reach of town. My worst fears have been realized this curse is now upon a foreign shore. Tomorrow morning send the men out to see if we can find the one who bares the curse." Alex requests to Lushien. "Yes, my lord." They climb from their horses and go into the inn. They rest until the morning sun shines in through the window. Alex hears a knock on his door requesting, "Come!" Daniel walks into the room informing, "My lord the men wait for you out front." "Tell them I will see them when I am finished dressing." "As you command my lord," Daniel answers then walks out of the room to the hall passing people inside the inn, goes through the door and waits with the men. Alex walks out of his door letting his senses lead the way for a moment a scent grabs his nose but the scent passes quickly. Passing the front counter, he asks of the inn keep,

"Are you sure no stranger stayed in the inn?" "Yes, Sir Lancaster no strangers were in town the last full moon." Alex turns and walks out the door. Making to those traveling with him he informs, "Lushien take some of the men south and look for signs. Lucien you go north with some of the men. The rest of you will go with me west. "My lord it is going to be impossible to cover all the land around the town. The wolf could have come from anywhere," Nora suggests. "That is true but we must try to seek it out." They search to the end of the day. With nothing shows itself and they return to the town. Alex walks back into the inn seeing his return the inn keeper asks, "Did you find anything Sir Lancaster?" "No, I found no sign of the wolf but the full moon is some weeks off." "Will you stay to find the wolf?" "No, I have other reasons for coming to your land," Alex informs with the inn keep imploring, "You cannot leave us to the mercy of the beast." The inn keeps daughter walks behind him filling the barrel with mead a scent finds his nose again. "I did not come to France to hunt wolfs, but I can instruct you on how to defend yourselves." Alex watches her leave the room. Then he turns and goes to the back of the inn and waits for her to come down the hall. She rounds the corner. He waits until she is upon him then pushes her into a room she gives a faint scream before the door closes. "Speak or I will end you here and now," Alex demands pulling the sword from it sheath. She begins to let the tears pour from her eyes informing, "My lord please! I was bitten some weeks back while riding back for home in the night." "At night, why would a young maiden as you be riding so late at night," Alex asks of her. "I snuck out to see my boyfriend, he is not in the same class as me, my father has forbidden me to see him, please, please do not tell him," she begs as the tears stream down her face. Her father hearing her faint screams comes into the room. "What are you doing with her," he demands in a father's voice. "I think you should close the door," Alex suggests. Her father closes the door behind him. "I have found the wolf that has devoured your town's people." "Who is this person we must destroy it," her father readily states. The words come from his mouth he sees the look upon his daughter's face seeing the terror grip her he inquires, "You do not mean it is my daughter do you?" "Father I was attacked by a beast some weeks ago, I did not know it was me until the last full moon when I woke in the forest with a body beside me, God has cursed me for my lustful heart," she mournfully suggests. Her father sits down on the bed she grips his leg to find comfort he reaches down and pulls her to his chest, "My god in heaven what must I do?" Alex reaches inside his cloak revealing, "I should kill her to protect the people," pulling his hand from his cloak, "But I have another way." "Please Sir Lancaster tell us and I will honor it," Her father pleads. Alex sits down across from them a medallion rests in his hand informing, "In the beginning of the wars there were twenty-four of theses but most have been lost to the winds. This one came back to me in the hands of a thief. Place this upon your neck and make sure it touches your skin it will give you control over the beast." She grasps it from his hands as if her life depends on it quickly placing it upon her neck. Alex stands walks over to her father still trying to grip what has happened. Alex puts his hand upon his shoulder suggesting, "You must leave this place it will not be long before people figure her out." Alex walks from the room informs the men they will be moving on walks back to his room gathers his things and leaves the inn. Sitting in their saddles Lucien asks, "My lord are we to leave the people here to the wolf?" "There will be no more problem here, beside I must find what we came here for." Daniel looks back towards the inn then turns to follow him as he rides out of the town. He holds the staff in his hand and it lights the way for them to travel. They ride out over the land passing many along the road they travel resting by night. Sometimes in the towns of the land, others on the landscape. "My lord who was the wolf in the first town we came too," Daniel asks of him resting around the fire. "It was the daughter of the inn keep." "Did you put her to the sword?" "No, I could not find it in my heart to destroy her. I gave her the medallion we found on the thief in the town of Villa to control the animal within her." "My lord we cannot leave wolves among the people," Lushien reminds. "And what are we but wolves. How do we know one of us did not create the beast that attacked her? We must regain the cup then we can cure anyone we come into contact with." "What for the people around her," Nora asks remembering her past. "God be with them if she ever removes the charm from her neck," Alex relays pouring out his drink in his hand and walks away from the fire disappearing into the cloak of night. Lushien looks back at the fire knowing the subject will be closed for discussion. Alex roams the darkness he pulls the crystals from his neck finds a log and sits down upon it his head finds rest on the stump of the fallen tree, slumber comes over him. The breeze blows over his face then the fragrance of her fill his senses. "My lady," he says reaching out and pulls her to him, "Oh Alex, I love it when you hold me like this!" "Like how Elizabeth," Alex asks lost in her eyes. "Like the first time you held me inside your arms and I felt the love within you." She looks up towards the stars while she leans back in his arms looking up towards the ceiling of her prison suggesting, "It has been so long since I have seen the night sky!" "Yes, I know my lady, it saddens me that you are held inside a prison." She smiles at him and kisses his lips then says, "Alex my love, I am here with you always. Time will not break the bond we have! I will love you each day you are in this world and into the next." They hold each other as the night goes on, the morning sun awakes him and he hears the sound of a horse. She turns to vapor to his eyes as the horse becomes clearer. "My lord there you are the men are ready to move on." Alex rubs his eyes then looks up saying, "Lushien I am sorry if you did not agree with the decision I made with the girl." "No, my lord, it is me who should be sorry, I should not question your judgment with such things for you are my noble," Lushien responses. Alex stands to his feet and walks along the side of his horse as they make their way back to camp walking along Alex informs, "Lushien you are one of my finest soldiers and not because of your skills as a warrior, but that you are not scared to voice your opinion and in the days ahead that is what I will expect you to do!" They make their way back to the camp. Alex takes the reins of his horse and climbs into the saddle, "Which way my lord," Lucien inquires. Alex pulls the staff from his saddle then slowly points it in each direction. The green light of the crystal lights their path. Alex kicks his horse and the men follow behind him. "My lord how much longer, do you think it will take to reach where we are going?" "I could not answer we will just have to follow the crystal until we reach it," Alex informs. "Will we have time to take in a town some of us wish to find the warmth of a woman," Lucien asks. "I am sure there will have to be a town along the ride." "The days have moved forward my lord and the full moon will be among us," Lucien informs. "Yes, and it will be best if we keep ourselves hidden during that time," Alex suggests. "Do you think we will ever find what we seek," Nora asks riding among the men. "I hope and pray every night Nora, if not we will cross the sands of time as we are." "Have you ever though what the world will look like in the days ahead," Daniel young and vigorous asks. "No, I am hoping not to have to find out!" "What of her? If you cannot find a body to release her too, will you still drink from the cup," Nora asks. Alex gives no answer.

They ride over the landscape. A few days go by and they find themselves riding into a town. The men find smiles when the woman of the town wave to them as they pass. "Come on Alex let's forget our task for just a little while and enjoy a drink," Lushien suggests. "You go and enjoy yourself." "Alex does that mean you will not have a drink with me," Lucien asks. Alex looks at the men then back to Lucien saying, "Well maybe just one." The pack lets laughter find them as they dismount their horses and walk into the pub. Nora and the men find laughter and what they seek drinking in the pub. Alex is lead to the back by a woman. She takes him to the tub. He undresses and climbs in the water, washing the road from his back. He finishes then dresses and heads back into the bar, the men who ride with him find comfort in the women of the pub. Alex sits down at the table a pretty girl sets a cup in front of him, her eyes meet his and she smiles asking, "Is there anything else I could do for you my lord?" Alex sees the meaning in her eyes replying, "You are a beautiful woman and most men would jump at the chance but I cannot for respect for my wife." Alex downs the drink turns to Lucien saying, "I will be waiting for all of you north from the town when you have had your fun come and find me." "Alex do not leave you should learn to have some fun." Alex pats him on the shoulder saying, "Do not worry for me my brother. I will be fine, have fun!" Alex leaves the pub and mounts his horse. The sounds of enjoyment leaves his ears as he rides away from the place. He journeys until he finds a place to rest. "I admire a faithful man," the girl says as she pours their drinks. "His wife is not in this world anymore but he still remains faithful to her," Lushien responds. "A love to last a lifetime what more could a woman ask for," she replies still to admire the man. Lucien holds his cup in front of them the others raise their cups with him, "To a love that will never die!" The soldiers with his pack and the woman sitting with them hold their glasses up and drink to the toast purposed. The night goes on and the men find the joy of the town with women in their beds. Alex finds rest in the arms of his love enjoying what time they can share with each other.

The morning sun shines and the men slip from the beds they shared in the night find their horses and ride from the town. Their heads hurt from the wine they drank in the night. "Does anyone else head feel like mine," Daniel asks to those among him. "Yes, my young friend, but that is part of the enjoyment," Lucien reveals laughing. They ride out until they find Alex cooking over the flame of the fire. "By the looks of it, you men will need food!" The men do their bests to dismount their horses and walk as straight as they can to find a seat by the fire. "Did you men find what you desired," Alex asks with a sense of humor." The men begin to discuss the events of the night, filling each other on the details shared in the night. With the men and Nora refreshed they mount their horses. Alex stretches out the staff, the crystal lights their path. They journey across the land until they find a monastery, the light burns brighter than in times past. "The light glows brighter my lord, "Daniel states marveled by the magic of it. "Yes, it will seem we will have to go in and talk with the priest." Alex turns and looks back at his men suggesting, "Some of you may want to talk more with the priest inside." The men look around, knowing the sins of the night. Alex climbs from his horse his feet bring dust from the ground saying, "Wait here, I will go and speak with the monks." Alex walks up to the doors. He uses the cross placed on the door to knock. Alex waits and the door begins to open. "Welcome to the house of God," a monk says with Alex walking through the doorway adding, "Your weapons are not welcome in the house of the lord, please remove them and place them by the doors." Alex removes his sword and places it in the corner behind the door. "What brings you here this night," the monk questions. "I come in search of a cup that might have been here." The monk gets a look upon his face asking, "Why would you seek a cup?" "Do not play games with me father. I know the cup was here at some point." The monk sends out the others in the room, they close the door behind them. "Why do you seek the cup of Christ, for it was not made for mortal men?" "I know the power it possesses, I have seen it with my own eyes," Alex states walking over to a statue of Christ hanging on the cross then kneels before it revealing, "The cup was used to create beast upon the earth now I need it to set things back into balance." "The cup was here but it was taken by the church in fear that men would destroy the church for it. People in the area have witnessed its power," the monk informs. "Can you tell me where they might have taken it?" "The rumor is three noble men were charged with hiding it from the hands of men. They were sworn to secrecy only they truly know where the cup will be placed." Alex stands to his feet and begins to walk out of the room. "Ask yourself do you seek the cup for personal gain or the good of men?" "A little of both I think," Alex confesses. "You do not have to leave here brave knight. You and your companions are most welcome to stay here as long as you desire." "Thank you father I will go and tell them of the offer." Alex walks back out of the church and to the men waiting for him saying, "Put the horses in the stables we will rest here for the night." Those with Alex place the horses in the stables then meet Alex at the door. "My son the female with you will have to go to the other side of the church. The nuns can see to her needs," a monk informs seeing Nora with them. Alex walks to her, "My lord I should stay with the men," Nora requests. "Nora the men who live here keep their desires hidden and your beauty could open their desires." "What am I to do with nuns," Nora asks adding, "I think I will rest in the forest." "I will go with her my lord to watch over her until your return," Daniel suggests. Alex smiles to him saying, "We will ride out at first light." Nora and Daniel turn to walk away with Lucien suggesting, "The two of have fun tonight." Nora quickly informs, "If he could be so lucky." Alex smirks as they walk from the door. The others place their weapons by the door and join the monks for dinner. They bow their heads as the food is blessed keep silent with the monks gathered around the room. "If you men are done eating. I can show you where you can rest," a monk informs. Alex and the men follow him down the hall, in turn, he shows each where they can lay their heads for rest. "Thank you father, we will be leaving by first light," Alex says with the monk closes the door as he leaves the room. Alex pulls the crystal his neck grasps them then slips into slumber. "Alex where are we this night," Elizabeth asks. "We are in a church in the out lands of France." "So, we are in a holy place?" "Yes, my love." "So, I guess we should save are loving making for another night," Elizabeth suggests curling up beside him, her hair splashes across his chest his arms wrap around her waist holding her with love in his heart. The door creeps open. Alex lost in the world of dreams does not sense it. He lays holding on to his love suddenly he is awakened by the sword thrust into his body. The monks fearing the men that seek the cup for power do the work of God in their minds. "Alex," Elizabeth screams as she fades to vapor and Alex returns to this world. His anger is fierce and the wolf begins to come out. The monk falls in horror, as the beast becomes clear to his eyes, Alex leaps over him and runs down the hall knocking down the others ready to strike at his men. A mighty howl fills the church as the monks begin to believe the devil is among them. Nora and Daniel break a moment shared in hearing the howl echo the land. They dress and rush back for the church.

Alex finds an older monk, reaches out with his hands the claws on the end of his finger strike fear into him wrapping around his neck. Alex picks him off the ground pulls him closer. His eyes behold the mouth of the beast and the teeth shining in the light praying, "God in heaven help me!" Alex places him down in his seat and walks over and closes the door as he turns his body becomes normal again and he stands before the monk naked as the first day he was born asking, "Why did you invite us into the church then try to kill us in our sleep?" Lushien and the others come into the door holding other monks to the point of a sword. Alex turns to them ordering, "Release them brothers, and go and saddle the horses we are leaving this place." Lushien with Lucien walks out of the room and gathers the men. Alex stays behind with the older monk waiting for his answer. "Because I cannot allow the cup to be brought out of its hiding place its power is too great." The priest places a cloak around him and slowly touches his skin trying to see if he is human. "Do you see now why I need the cup, York and his sorcerer brought this curse over the land, and now I will need it to release myself from this walking tomb. I serve Christ and the church. I only need it for that," Alex states then suggests, "Maybe we could strike a deal, I could bring the cup back to the church and leave it in your care then send those who wish to find forgiveness here to you." "I wish I could help you my son and with the burden you carry with you but the church has deemed the cup not to be in the hands of men no matter the reason," sadden the monk informs. "Father I will seek the cup until I have it, even if it places me an enemy to the church." Alex goes to walk out of the room. "Wait my son," the monk requests closing his eyes and says a prayer for him. He crosses his chest then opens his eyes saying, "Go in peace and may God be with you on your journey but beware all the churches will see you as their enemy." Alex goes back to his room, dresses, gathers his things and collects his sword by the door. The night breeze blows as he closes the door behind him. The light of the moon shows his way to the men he mounts his horse and the others follow him back down the path they were traveling. Nora and Daniel come rushing to them. Alex holds his hand up saying, "It is all over now you can put up your swords." Lucien turns to them inquiring, "What took you so long to get here were the two of you resting well?" Nora's face burns a red and Lushien smiles to the color. "Has the world gone mad? It has to be when you have to beware of holy men," a wolf hunter suggests. "Yes, it seems we will not find much help in finding the cup," Alex reveals. They journey down the road ahead silence fills the night as they make their way. They journey far until they find a place to rest by a stream, the running water is relaxing to their ears as its sound brings them to slumber.

Dawn breaks and the men gather their things. Alex stands in front of the men holding the staff to show them the path. They journey on. The days move through time and they ride over the land the moon has found them again. "You men find refuge in the village Lucien, Lushien, Daniel, Nora and I will hide in the forest our beast will be among this world tonight." "We will be here by first light of dawn my lord!" The men ride on for the village. The pack and Alex wait for the moon to hold its sway. The men make it to the village and the town's people are not willing to give them safe haven for the night. "Go away strangers are not welcome in the village this night. The moon will be full and the beast in men will show themselves!" The men look up and down the street of the town all the places are boarded up tight no one is along the streets. The men ride back for the camp as the men ride up to Alex. The moon begins to have her way over them. "Sorry my lord but no one would give us safe haven in the village," a soldier tells him. Alex and the pack slip back into the darkness in moments they walk out in full form of the wolf. A wolf hunter who finds favor on Nora tries to sit close to her as she stands in the form of the beast. Daniel with the drive of the wolf moves closer to him like a dog protecting a master he shows his teeth. A wolf hunter older and wiser walks over to him, "If I were you I would find another place to rest." The men lay around the flames of the fire the pack tolls around the camp. The moon shines bright and the coolness fills the air. A howl rings out over the landscape. A wolf hunter runs out of his tent declaring, "My lord a werewolf stalks the land!" The men gather their weapons against the beast they mount their horse and the wolves run out into the night. "Stay close men the beast will be out to fill his hunger," a commander in the wolf hunter declares. The hunters slowly ride out into the night their hearts beat fast with the feeling of eyes upon them. A scream echoes into the night. "In the village quickly," a wolf hunter informs. They ride with speed in their horses as people scream into the night. They ride into the village bold and brave, their weapons clinched tightly in their hands. "Look sharp men!" Their eyes search the area. "Look out," a hunter screams! The black beast leaps from its perched place upon the roof knocking the man from his saddle. The men ride in and strike at the beast. Its jaws open and close, its teeth sharp with growls mighty and fierce. With his mighty arms, he swings at the men their blood splatters the ground, suddenly Alex leaps into their mist. His teeth bared his claws sharp the beasts circle one another, the beast is fierce, but no match for the age of Alex. He bites until his head leaves his body, Daniel, and Nora leap to his side. They howl in one voice victorious in the night. The village men rush out from their homes declaring, "Strike out at the beast we must kill them!" They begin to sling their hoes and spears toward them. "No, not those for they are on our side" a hunter screams with Alex and his pack running from the place out into the night. The hunters look over the body of the wolf as it begins to show the person with the beast. "That is Bill he lives in the valley next," a village man informs. "Commander," a hunter calls out. The commander walks over, a faithful soldier lay bleeding on the ground marked deeply from the beast. He looks at the wound inflicted upon him then up at his commander requesting, "Send me to the next world commander, give me a warrior's death, I will not have the beast in me." The commander removes his sword from its sheath a fellow hunter reads from the bible letting the holy words fill his ears. The sound of the sword rings in the air a sure blow is given. The hunters look over towards the commander with him relaying, "I would expect any of you to do the same for me, we all gave a vowel remember." The commander places his sword back in its sheath and walks away from the men. In the night the village people burn the man's body to insure he will not return. The wolf hunters who ride with Alex do the same for a fallen brother.

Chapter Ten

A CURSE ACROSS TIME

THE SUN RISES AND ALEX WITH HIS pack ride for the village the men wait for them there. In the time that lay ahead, years become centuries, many faithful soldiers cross over the river of sticks, some by the beast they hunt others by the hands of time. Alex searches over the world for the cup but his search goes unanswered. In the time ahead the church strikes a deal with the pack, to be sent out, and destroy the beast that hide inside of men. Truth becomes legends, the book of spells stays lost in the place it was hidden. William stays locked in his tomb. The love of Alex stays imprisoned in the crystal given to her as a gift. Lushien and Lucien find their deaths standing against a pack formed to strike out at the men who wish to destroy them. In each of the battles across time werewolves were found some baring the color of gray, others black as the soul that created them. A new world came and many men traveled to the new land. Alex, Nora and Daniel also did travel to this new land of promise hunting the wolves created by them in their younger days. The Indians called them shape shifters, changing with the will inside their hearts. Many wolves found their death in the eyes of Alex until the days came when they could no longer hear the stories of old. Alex came to rest in the castle given to him by a King and upon its throne he sat with a heavy brow. Nora and Daniel found peace and love both in the beasts they are and each other. Kings came and went before him and nations rose and fell. He became a thing of legend, a whisper in the ears of children. In the centuries ahead Nora Daniel and he hide the beasts resting in them not staying in a place to long and his heart longed for his wife. Many women fell in love with him but his body and heart held true to his wife. Through the sands for time he kept the castle with her tomb in the bowls of its foundation with the slightest hope that she would stand with him flesh and bone not just a ghost to be held in dreams. The crystal does its best to return him to the cup but with every search he hands find emptiness. But that is another tale to be told.

Chapter Eleven

VOLUME TWO
(A NEW PACK IS BORN)

Printed in the United States
By Bookmasters